D1234289

RESTLESS HEART

T. William Phillips

iUniverse, Inc.
New York Bloomington

Restless Heart

This is a work of fiction. All of the characters, names, incidents,
organizations, and dialogue in this novel are either the products
of the author's imagination or are used fictitiously.

iUniverse books may be ordered through booksellers or by contacting:

iUniverse
1663 Liberty Drive
Bloomington, IN 47403
www.iuniverse.com
1-800-Authors (1-800-288-4677)

ISBN: 978-1-4502-3251-7 (pbk)
ISBN: 978-1-4502-3252-4 (cloth)
ISBN: 978-1-4502-3253-1 (ebk)

Library of Congress Control Number: 2010907689

Printed in the United States of America

iUniverse rev. date: 6/2/2010

To Cindy

BOOK I

Duty by Heart

I

MY RESTLESS HEART BEATS to a rhythm of its own. A rhythm that has been lost in time and nature and has become so deeply hidden that few ever hear it.

It took me eighteen years to finally hear the strange, offbeat drum in my chest. I could always feel it but was too ignorant and too deaf to listen to it. Aristocracy and expectation had created layer upon layer of fat that had muffled and softened the true beat of my heart.

My restless heart is a map with no end. It does not tell me where to go or how to get there, but it tells me when to move one foot forward and when to move the other foot in front of it. These steps are never rhythmic.

Training myself to break the rhythm was the hardest part. After living my life being taught to do all things to a rhythm, even if the rhythm was of my own creation, it takes great strength and discipline to un-train something that is not just taught but is ingrained in our minds from birth.

My restless heart began beating its inconsistent beat on December 21, 1820, when I forced my mother into labor one month before I was supposed to be born. I nearly killed her in the process, but she was a strong woman of strong German blood and recovered very quickly. My premature birth gave my mother an excuse to use such phrases as, "You were impatient coming into the world, and you're impatient to leave it," when I would do something dangerous and thoughtless, or she'd say, "Just because you were impatient coming into this world doesn't mean you are allowed to be impatient while you're in it."

I was no more restless as a child than most other children, and like all children do, I eventually grew up. I had to become mature and responsible. I had to go to school and learn manners and discipline. I lost my innocence and therefore lost the ability to listen to my heart, and for years I lived in an ignorant deafness.

It wasn't until the spring of 1838 that I began to hear the arrhythmic beat of my heart once again. As a child, I did not think about what my heart told me; I simply followed it blindly and without hesitation. As I was approaching the mature age of eighteen, I started to decipher the beats and ponder what they meant.

My friends were preparing to enter institutions of higher learning, and some of my more privileged friends had already begun apprenticeships at the businesses of their fathers, family friends, or distant connections made by family influence. I was being urged by my father to study at Harvard. I longed for a higher education, but not for the same reasons as my friends. Their families had made grandiose plans for them, and, like sheep, they were following these plans blindly and contentedly. They had grown accustomed to the luxuries and spoils, which their parents had provided for them, and their only goal was to be able to continue living in that fashion free of their parents. They would go on to their universities and receive great educations, and thus they would graduate to high-profile, high-paying jobs. Their jobs would not have them doing something they loved, for they did not even know what they loved. They loved what their parents and society told them to love, and what they loved was money, luxury, laziness, work, and conformity. I don't know how or why I started seeing these things in this light, but I knew I wanted something more. I did not want education; I wanted knowledge. I wanted to see the world and learn from experience as well as from books.

I longed to see Europe; after all, my mother, Lenora, came from the Mann family in Berlin, and my father, Rafael, came from the Quintero de Leon family in Spain; therefore, I decided to leave America to attend Oxford University in England. I wrote my father a three-page letter of why and how I had come to my decision. He read the letter and did not say a word about it for two days. Finally, he told me that he supported my decision and that I would leave for Oxford in the fall.

My leaving for Oxford was bittersweet, as I would come to learn is true of all partings, some more bitter or more sweet than others. In this case it was sweeter, for I was full of excitement for the unknown. I had never seen the world outside New York City except to go to the countryside a few times when I was younger, but I took comfort in the fact that for the first time in my life, I was following my heart, not simply because I listened to what it told me, but because I understood what it told me.

I arrived in London in September of 1838, after a long journey across the Atlantic Ocean, from which I learned that I do not get seasick, even after watching others lean over the ship's railing. I was met by my uncle, Friedrich Mann, whom I had never met before. He was not quiet and stone-faced, as I had imagined all Germans to be. In fact, he had kind, inviting blue eyes and a charming smile with which he greeted me. He shook my hand firmly, patted me on the back, and told me how pleased he was to finally meet his sister's son. He told me how much I looked like my mother, which I took as a great compliment, for I found his resemblance to my mother uncanny, and he was a handsome man. His cheekbones were high and sharp, resting symmetrically on either side of his gradual, pointed nose, and his long face ended upon a defined jaw line and a subtle chin.

We spent the night in London so he could show me around the city. I thought it was fantastic. I saw, of course, The Queen's House, where Britain's newest monarch, Queen Victoria, resided. However, what I found most interesting was the remains of The Palace of Westminster, which had been mostly destroyed by a fire in 1834. Friedrich told me that they had debated for two years what kind of design they would use to rebuild the House of Parliament. Neoclassical was the popular style of the time, but Britain associated it with America, revolution, and Republicanism. They finally decided in 1836 that they would go with a Gothic style. I thought it would be grand. Neoclassical and Elizabethan were boring to me. To me, Gothic was the height of man's architectural creativity and intellect.

The next day, we rode in a carriage to Oxford. I immediately fell in love with the city. I had never seen such buildings and structures except in paintings. I tried to contain my excitement as I thought about all that I would see over the next four years.

The carriage dropped us off in front of the building where Friedrich had reserved a flat for us on the River Thames, which in Oxford they called "The Isis". We met with the landlord, and I paid the rent for the first six months with the money my father had given me for room, board, and food.

My mother had written to Friedrich after the decision of my education had been made. She told him that his nephew had been accepted at Oxford and would be attending in the late fall. She told him that she thought it would be a great opportunity for us to get to know each other and that my father would pay for him to move to Oxford and live with me. Friedrich happily accepted the offer. I was a little uncomfortable and slightly irritated at first, for I was looking forward to the romantic solitude of living alone, and living with a man I had never met would be awkward. When I learned that my Uncle Friedrich was a master in the art of fencing, my mood changed completely as I thought of all that he could teach me.

Uncle Friedrich had owned a fencing school in Wiesbaden, which had been very successful and had brought him much money. An Italian fencing master had offered him a great deal for the school, and Friedrich had leaped at the opportunity to retire. He was at his peak and had no desire for his students to watch him slowly wither away. The Italian fencing master was young and passionate and would be a much better teacher to his students.

I began school shortly after my arrival in England, studying Physics and Philosophy at Oxford and participating in the Oxford Boat Club and the Oxford Union Society, which was a debate club. However, I received my real education from my uncle and many hours in Oxford's Bodleian Library. On my own, I studied history, literature, and politics. From my uncle, I learned Latin, the art of fencing, and gymnastics.

Uncle Friedrich had studied gymnastics under Friedrich Ludwig Jahn himself who was known as *Turnvater* Jahn, meaning 'Father of gymnastics'. Uncle Friedrich had served under Jahn in the Lutzow Free Corps, which was an army of Prussian volunteers who fought against Napoleon's army.

I progressed quickly in my physical training once I realized my natural athleticism. My body transformed accordingly to support the strength, agility, and endurance my daily activities required. The Oxford Boat Club added significant muscle mass to my shoulders and chest, while gymnastics strengthened and defined my abdomen, legs, and arms.

Fencing, however, was more of a strengthening of the mind. It sharpened my senses and reflexes, and it taught me to react quickly by knowing what my opponent would do before he did it. It was a true art with a great deal of science to it. It took me a good two years of daily practice before I could have a somewhat competitive fencing match against my uncle.

As a student at Oxford I was quite average. I performed well in class on assignments and exams, but my heart was never really in it. I seemed to excel much more in the subjects I studied on my own. Philosophy interested me greatly, but I grew restless in class while my teachers lectured and told me what I *had* to do and what I *had* to learn. However, I could spend eight hours at a time in the Bodleian Library reading from the massive collection of books the library had acquired, which included such treasures as Shakespeare's *First Folio, The Carte Manuscripts, Song of Roland, Codex Mendoza,* letters of the poet Percy Bysshe Shelley, one of the surviving complete copies of the *Gutenberg Bible,* and *Magna Carta,* which I was able to read after my uncle taught me Latin.

When school let out after my first year, my uncle and I left for

Spain for the summer. We lived in Madrid, but we spent a good amount of time in Seville and Barcelona. I was able to perfect my Spanish, which I had been taught from an early age, but my father had been the only person I knew who spoke it. Living in Spain allowed me to become truly fluent.

My plan had been simply to visit some of the great historic cities of Europe, but Uncle Friedrich insisted that I actually live in the cities. He said the only way to truly know a place is to live there. He said that one could not possibly learn anything about a place by simply visiting.

We spent the following summer living in Paris, where I had the great fortune of seeing the *Musée du Louvre, Chateau de Versailles, La Sainte-Chapelle, Notre-Dame de Paris, and Cathedrale Notre-Dame de Chartres,* which furthered my fascination with Gothic architecture.

We spent the next summer in Italy, where we lived in Rome and traveled to Milan, Venice, and Sicily. We saw the Coliseum, the Apostolic Palace, and the Sistine Chapel, which was magnificent down to the tiniest detail. We also saw the Pantheon and *Duomo di Milano.*

Along with seeing the historic sites, we were able to live our lives as did the locals. By the time we left each city, we knew it inside and out.

My uncle and I spent every Christmas in Berlin with my grandfather, Konrad, after whom I was named, and my grandmother, Rosalinde, whose eyes still glowed even in her old age. I saw where my mother got her dazzling, captivating eyes. My grandparents did not speak English, and that forced me to perfect my German, which I had also grown up learning.

My grandmother loved telling me the story of how my parents fell in love. She would tell me how my mother was a famous soprano in the opera and how her company would travel all over the world, until it finally brought her to New Orleans where she performed in one of the first shows at the Theatre d'Orleans before it burned down shortly after its opening. My father was there, and my grandmother said he fell in love with my mother the moment she sang her first beautiful note. After the show, he raced to find the nearest florist, bought a dozen roses, and waited outside the theater for three hours before my mother finally came out. He told her he had never heard a voice as angelic as hers. He gave her the flowers and begged her to sing a song just for him. My mother declined bashfully, for they were standing in the middle of the street. He pleaded, telling her how only her angelic voice could save his wretched soul. She was smitten by his charm and vulnerability, so she began to sing a song just for him right there in the middle of the street in New Orleans. As she sang, she drew him in, closer and closer, until by the last note of the song their lips were only an inch apart. They kissed a sweet, tender kiss and instantly fell in love. They married a few months later. After having much success in New Orleans in the restaurant business, my father promised my mother fortune in New York where he knew he would be even more successful. He was right, and he kept his promise. Then I was born.

It was a lovely story, but I felt that my grandmother had embellished it a bit. But she did tell it well and with great passion, and it did make for a lovely story.

II

I COMPLETED MY SCHOOLING at Oxford in the summer of 1842. I had no money to get home, for I had spent all that my father had given me on traveling and living all over Europe. Friedrich offered to pay my fare back to New York, but I wasn't quite ready to leave. I wanted to pay my own way by making the money myself.

I was able to find a job immediately upon my graduation by translating old texts from German, Spanish, and Latin to English. The job paid well, and in a few short months I had earned enough to pay my fare back to America and more.

As soon as I finished translating the texts I had promised to my employer, I collected my wages and booked passage to New York. I could not convince Uncle Friedrich to come back with me even after offering to pay his way. He was not interested in the West. He had been studying the cultures of the East recently and had grown very interested in traveling to Asia. He said that perhaps he would meet me on the Pacific side of America.

On the day before I was to leave England, I headed to the Bodleian Library to see it one last time.

I walked through the library exactly as I had the first time I had set foot inside. I stared in awe and spun in circles, as I walked aimlessly, gazing breathlessly upon the high walls covered in shelves filled with knowledge, art, and passion. I heard the whispers of the ghost authors reading their own words but all at the same time and too quietly for me to understand. It was eerie and intoxicating. It brought an excited fluttering to my stomach and an ecstatic smile to my face.

I allowed my initial excitement to subside and made my way down the row to my favorite book. I saw it sticking out from the shelf slightly. I must not have pushed it all the way in the last time I was there.

I stopped in front of the protruding book that was shelved at face level. I read the magical words as I ran my fingers down its spine — *Don Quixote*. I gently pulled the book out and held it lightly in my hands. I wiped away some imaginary dust and opened it to the title page, which read, *El ingenioso hidalgo don Quixote de la Mancha*.

I had looked at this particular copy of the masterpiece dozens of times in my four years at Oxford. I had only read it twice while I was there. However, I had read many other translations and copies throughout my life. Tobias Smollett's translation of *Don Quixote* was the first real book I had ever read. I had been eleven at the time when my father insisted. From then on, I had read it at least once a year. I have long lost count of how many times I have read it.

"Why am I not surprised to find you here, Master Konrad?"

The familiar voice made me jump. As the librarian had approached, I had been so entranced by the book that I hadn't heard his loud, hollow footsteps echo on the marble floor. I sighed in relief and shut the book. I smiled at my old friend and shook my head.

"How do you manage to sneak up on me every time I'm here, Mr. Jacobs?" I asked, as I slid the book back into place, making sure it was flush.

"We librarians take a vow of silence much like any priest, sir," he answered in his thick English accent. He walked over to me. "And startling young men such as yourself pleases an old man like me. Makes me feel... intimidating."

"I'm sure it's the most exciting part of your day."

He smiled and took down the copy of *Don Quixote* I had been admiring. He stared at it and smiled.

"For as long as my old mind can remember, you've been coming into this library and looking at *this* copy of *Don Quixote*. Why *this* copy? There must be a dozen different copies and translations here."

"You must know." I paused to allow Mr. Jacobs to answer his own question. He just smiled. I went into a passionate explanation of how Miguel de Cervantes had sold the rights to his book to a publisher who had printed four hundred copies and had sent them to the Americas in hopes of a better price. Most of the four-hundred first-edition copies were lost in a shipwreck near Havana. However, about seventy copies made it to Lima and from there were sent to Cuzco. The copy that Mr. Jacobs was holding was one of the last remaining first editions.

"Of course I know that, Master Konrad. I just wanted to see if you did," he said with a coughing laugh. I believed him though. He knew everything about every book in his library. After all, he had worked there almost every day for the last thirty years.

"I want you to have it," Mr. Jacobs said, holding the book out to me.

"I couldn't possibly . . ." I protested.

"It's a gift, Master Konrad. It would be rude not to accept a gift on the eve of your farewell voyage."

"With all due respect, Mr. Jacobs, doesn't it belong to the school?"

"It belongs to this library, and this is *my* library. This book is mine to give to whomever I please. Now take it — before I change my mind."

I took the book from him and held it to my chest. "I don't know how to thank you."

"You kept an old, lonely librarian company for the past four years. That's thanks enough."

"I'm going to miss you, Mr. Jacobs."

"And I you, Master Konrad. And I you."

We shook hands while he stared tenderly into my eyes. I felt sad to leave him. I had been the only student who ever really talked to him. I knew he was lonely and that this library was his life. I knew that he took great pleasure in sharing his life with me by recommending books and then discussing them with me after I had read them. I wondered who would talk to him now. Who would keep him company? But who was I kidding? Had I really become so arrogant to think that no one could replace me, that no one would strike up a friendship with Mr. Jacobs after me? Surely, there had been others before me and there would be others after me. But I had to believe that our relationship was special, otherwise, what would be the point of having one in the first place?

I walked out of the Bodleian Library with my new book at my side and made my way down a cobbled street in the middle of town. The hooves of horses *clop-clopped* by me as I stared at the familiar buildings, taking them in for the last time. I had walked these streets hundreds of times. I had become a part of them as they had of me. A strange sadness filled me and put a knot in my throat despite my excitement to leave.

I made my way to the Oxford Botanic Garden and walked slowly through the Walled Garden, as the fading rays of the sunset broke through the trees and cast a golden glow on the plant life below. There was a chill in the wind, and for a moment I wished I had brought my coat. That wish was quickly forgotten as was the cold biting through my clothes while I reminisced about the hands I had held and the lips I had kissed in this garden. The sun made its final descent as I came to the riverbank.

III

WHEN I ARRIVED BACK at my flat, Uncle Friedrich was ready to duel. He was practicing his counterattack on his weak foot with an épée, a sword that is a bit heavier than the foil which is typically used when practicing fencing. The heaviest is the saber. The saber was my favorite weapon, but it was also the weapon with which I was the least skilled.

When my uncle saw that I had returned, he stopped fencing the air and took a few deep breaths as he rested on his sword. He wiped the sweat from his brow and pushed back the wet hair that was stuck to his forehead.

Out of breath, he asked in German, "Are you ready for a duel, nephew?"

"You seem to be beaten by your shadow already," I returned in German.

He waved me off. "I'm just warming up. I only started five minutes before you walked in."

"Shall I warm up while you catch your breath, old man?"

Friedrich took an épée out of the glass case, which held his collection of swords, and tossed it to me. I caught it by the handle, pommel up, and spun it once around my thumb.

"An old man I am, and I need to warm up. You are young; you're always warmed up."

"I might pull a muscle. My muscles are cold from being outside," I protested.

Friedrich was growing impatient. "Do you warm your muscles before you lay with a woman? No. You'll be fine. Take your position."

"Yes, sir. I'll put on my equipment." I started to make my way to the protective gear.

"Damn your equipment. I'm not going to hurt you. Let's fight!"

"How will we keep score?" I asked, confused by Friedrich's eagerness.

"By the blood on our blouses, my boy!"

With a dramatic laugh, Friedrich attacked with an over-cut. Instinctively I defended myself. He came at me fast and hard and with a mischievous smile on his face. He was faster than I had ever seen him. Each stroke was swift and crisp and began and finished precisely where he meant it.

It took every bit of the skill I had acquired from my uncle's lessons to defend myself against him. I could barely keep up. What had come over him? Had he just been taking it easy on me over the years? On the day of my first lesson, he had warned me that when it came to dueling he would not hold back. I trusted that he had not. Maybe he had not reached his peak, as he believed he had many years earlier. Maybe by teaching me he had learned a few things himself. Maybe I was witnessing his absolute best at that very moment. He was in his prime; he was peaking, and I was a part of it.

At the perfect moment, I took a skillful step forward to stop his attack, which had quickly pushed me back the entire length of the room. Without hesitation, Friedrich raised his front foot to my chest and pushed me back to the wall.

I looked at my uncle in confusion, as he continued to grin that mischievous grin. I could not help but smile back.

Friedrich began walking backwards to the center of the room. I pushed myself off the wall and followed him.

"We are kicking now, huh?" I asked, still speaking German.

"Let's not be concerned with rules today. Let's make this duel a little less predictable than usual." He was speaking Latin now.

I shrugged and lunged forward to attack.

"Wait!" Friedrich yelled.

I quickly withdrew my stabbing motion. He did not flinch. I put the tip of my sword on the floor and leaned on it irritably.

"What is it now?"

"In Latin."

I repeated my question in Latin. With a quick sweep of his épée, Friedrich knocked my sword out from under my hand, sending it flying to the wall and causing me to stumble a step forward. He tossed his épée away as well.

"What are you doing?" I asked, beginning to grow impatient with his strange behavior.

Friedrich opened his sword case and took out two sabers. However, these were not the small sabers normally used to practice fencing. These were real briquets used for combat. I knew Friedrich had killed many men with his saber from the Napoleonic Wars. He tossed the other saber to me. We took off the scabbards and set them aside.

"Have you lost your mind in your old age?" I asked him, as we began to circle each other.

"I still have my wits about me, my friend. I'm just not listening to them!"

I knew he wanted to attack with the completion of what he thought was a clever statement, but I beat him to it before he finished his sentence. I attacked with an under-cut, which he hated for me to do since it left my torso more exposed for longer than any other attacking cut. Friedrich defended himself against my under-cut attack with expert technique and creativity. When an unexpected move was made, instead of quickly flipping through the pages of strategy in his mind, he threw out the book and created his own style. This skill certainly had taken many, many years to perfect. However, in order to perfect it, one must have a certain kind of mind, and I did not believe my mind worked that way.

As our duel progressed into the tenth minute of incessant clashing, I realized that I had only been on the attack four times (two of which were no more than three strokes). The rest of the time, I had been on the defensive. For a moment I lost confidence, but I quickly brought myself back up when I thought about how well I had defended myself.

With my newfound inspiration, I created an opportunity for a counterattack. My counter was executed perfectly and sent me on my longest attack yet. I saw the confidence in my uncle's eyes fade slightly. His mischievous smile shifted into a puckered opening in his lips to control his short, quick breaths as he analyzed my technique.

I kept my technique simple by using textbook cuts and stabs with a master-cut when the opportunity presented itself, but I used my moves in an experimental way that surprised me. Even better, it surprised my uncle.

After a long series of many cuts, I was able to force my uncle to expose his chest with a wrath-cut. I quickly thrust my blade at his open chest, but somehow he was able to displace my move. I mutated my thrust into a cut and landed the point of my blade on his right shoulder. I dragged my blade across his flesh for about an inch and a half and quickly pulled back to acknowledge my point. I had drawn blood — and first blood at that. That was a victory in itself.

Friedrich took no time to acknowledge his wound or my point. He quickly attacked. His attack was controlled, yet mad. Each move was deliberate, but there was some sort of chaos to it.

His attack progressed with the difficulty of the technique. It was something I had never seen before and combinations I had never imagined putting together. Then, suddenly, he broke into an unprecedented series of the five master cuts. He began with a wrath-cut, followed by a crooked-cut, which I barely defended. He followed that with a squinting-cut, to a horizontal-cut. The horizontal-cut caught me just below my left shoulder and was

15

quickly followed by a part-cut that sliced me across the side of my neck.

Friedrich pulled his sword back with a proud smile on his face as he observed my wounds — or rather — his points. The cut below my left shoulder was about two inches across and had barely broken the skin, showing very little blood. The cut on the side of my neck was about an inch across and was bleeding quite a bit. It was far away from the artery and not deep. I don't know why it bled so much.

Friedrich took out his handkerchief and handed it to me. I held it to my neck and winced as I put pressure on it.

"Two to one, my favor. Shall we continue?" Friedrich asked breathlessly.

"If I could lift my sword, I would gladly continue, but I'm afraid you have me beaten."

After pausing to address my wounds, I realized how tired my arms were as they throbbed at my sides. I could barely find the strength to hold the handkerchief to my neck.

"I'm glad you said that. I can't make another stroke." Friedrich looked at the clock. "I do not know what time we started, but we could not have dueled less than a quarter of a hour without stopping."

"It felt like an eternity," I complained.

"Let me look at your neck." Friedrich moved my hand away from my wound. "It's just a scratch, something to remember me by, to remind you how sloppy you will get when you tire. It will teach you to end your fights quickly."

"You did not win because I was sloppy. You bested me, Uncle. I've never seen you fight like that before."

"Likewise, my boy. I may have bested you in the end, but you bested me a few times in the middle. But most of all, you bested yourself. Congratulations, Konrad."

"Thank you, Uncle. And congratulations yourself."

Friedrich laughed and shook my hand firmly. He took my

saber, sheathing it along with his own saber, and then he walked back to the sword case and placed my saber inside. He started to put his saber in also, but stopped. He stared at it for a moment. He smiled, took it out of its scabbard, and walked over to me.

He stopped before me but did not look up from his saber. He studied every inch of it from pommel to tip.

"I've had this sword for thirty years. My father had it made special and gave it to me when I joined the Lutzow Free Corps to fight Napoleon's army. It is the greatest gift he has ever given me. You see the engraving here at the bottom of the blade? *Justicia Per Deus. Verum Per Animus. Officium Per Pectus pectoris.*"

"Justice by God. Truth by will. Duty by heart," I repeated.

"Yes, and do you understand what it means?"

"Yes, I think so. What does it mean to you?"

Friedrich chuckled. "To me, it means to leave justice in the hands of God. Do not let the injustices of the people around you irritate your mood and fill you with anger. It means that you will find truth in your life by your strength and determination to seek it. And, finally, it means that your duty to man and to yourself comes from what your heart tells you is right. No man can know another man's duty. Do you understand this?"

I nodded.

"Good. It is yours now."

Friedrich held the saber out to me. It was lying across his open palms, glistening in the candlelight. The Latin engraving flashed in my eyes.

"I can't. I couldn't possibly…" I did not know what to say.

"You can, and you will. It is a parting gift."

"But—"

"My father gave me this sword as a gift before I left on the greatest journey of my life. He promised that it would guide my way. Now, I give it to you as you embark upon your greatest journey. It will guide you as it has guided me."

I slowly took the sword from him and held it before my

face. I eyed it up and down in awe. It felt so light and so natural in my hands. It was a perfect sword. I had never seen such craftsmanship.

"Uncle, my journey is on a boat from Britain to America. It hardly calls for such a gift."

"So, you plan to go home to New York and get a job, do you? Work with all of those rich friends of yours, hmm? No, I think not. You will not sit still for long. There is great adventure in America, and I know that you will seek it. I am giving you this sword for a reason. It belongs with an adventurer. Those days are over for me, but yours are just beginning. I know you will not disappoint me."

I was struck dumb by his words, my mouth agape like a young boy who had just seen his first naked woman. I could not force any words to take form. I had not made plans upon returning home to New York and had no idea what I would do. As the day of my leaving approached, I felt that I had progressively been losing my mind while trying to figure out what in God's name I was going to do when I returned home.

My uncle's words had not made things more clear but only more confusing. He could see that he had made my mind race. He chuckled as he looked into my glazed eyes.

"Do not think so hard right now. You have a long boat ride ahead of you. For now, you must pack your things. We leave at sunup."

"Thank you for the sword, Uncle."

Friedrich smiled and bowed. I turned and went to my room to pack, all too aware of the fact that I had just received my final lesson from Uncle Friedrich.

IV

UNCLE FRIEDRICH AND I stood on the dock where my ship awaited me. The ship's crew was loading the last of the boxes of goods and supplies onto the boat, yelling and laughing at one another in good spirits as they did so.

My new sword hung at my waist, and I was gripping the handle nervously with my sweaty hands, as a cold, bitter breeze blew across the docks.

"All aboard!" one of the ship's men yelled from the deck. All of the supplies had been loaded. One of the men was beginning to untie the hawser that held the boat to the dock.

"Well, my friend, it looks like it is time for you to go home."

"Thank you for all you have taught me, Uncle. I'm forever indebted to you," I said sincerely. I felt a lump forming in my throat. How embarrassing.

"You owe me nothing. You have taught me as much if not more. I'm glad we had the opportunity to learn from one another." We stood there for a moment in silence. "You will write to me about your adventures, and come to visit me anytime you want."

"I will, Uncle."

"Good! Go on now, or your ship will leave without you."

Friedrich picked up my bag of belongings and handed it to me. We shook hands firmly and said nothing more. I boarded the ship with the rest of the passengers and gave one of the boat's men my papers. He nodded and gave them back to me.

I stood at the railing and waved to my uncle as the ship pulled away from the dock and headed out to sea. Friedrich waved and then stood there for a moment with a smile on his face. Finally, he turned and walked off the dock.

I watched him for a few moments and then turned away myself. The lump in my throat was causing my eyes to produce water. The last thing I wanted to do was cry in front of a bunch of rough sailors. It was a bitter parting.

I walked to the bow of the ship and watched as the ocean opened up into a blue abyss. I stared at the horizon and did not look back for what seemed like only moments. When I finally did look back, the Isle of Britain was gone. America awaited.

* * *

My voyage was long, but I made good use of it. I read a few books I had taken with me, including *Don Quixote* once again. I also befriended many of the crewmembers who were patient enough to teach me all I wanted to learn about sailing. I learned all the nautical terms and how to tie every type of knot imaginable. I learned how to work the sails and how to steer the ship. I even conquered my fear of heights by climbing up to the crow's nest. In return for these lessons in sailing, I would scrub the deck and keep the ship clean.

For a while I thought that the life of a sailor might be the life and the adventure I was seeking, but after four weeks of practically working as a sailor, I dismissed the idea. It was not the work that I disliked. There was not really anything I did not like about it. I guess I just grew tired of it. I was bored. I missed dry land. The ocean is vast, with nothing to see but water and sky. On land there are rivers, mountains, forests, and plains. Those were the things I longed to see and touch.

After six weeks at sea, I finally heard the comforting words, "Land, ho!" from the crow's nest. I was below deck reading the poetry of Lord Byron when I heard the faint call. I went up to the deck and saw all the passengers standing at the bow, staring ahead in quiet awe. Most of them were Irish and some were German, but almost all of them had never seen America.

I could not see what they were looking at, but from the looks on their faces, it seemed as if their hopes and dreams waited before them. I had seen America before, so I stood back and waited as they imagined what their new lives would be like in a world full of opportunity and riches.

The crowd began to disperse after a few moments, so I made my way to the bow to catch my first glimpse of home in four years. New York Harbor was in view. It was crowded with ships and full of life. Beyond the harbor, I could see smoke rising from the rooftops of homes and businesses.

It was not long before the ship was docking. I searched the crowded harbor for my parents but did not see them.

The ship was tied to the dock, the ramp was in place, and we began to unload. I said goodbye to the sailors who I had befriended and then made my way down the ramp. As I took my first step onto the dock, a man shoved me back into the line of immigrants with whom I had traveled. I told him that I was an American and had been attending school in England. I showed him my papers, and he told me there were schools in America.

"Yes, there are," I said, "but Europe is not in America, is it?"

The man looked at me strangely then chuckled. He held his hands in the air and gestured to the lines of immigrants waiting to be processed. There were hundreds.

"Look around you, boy! It is now!"

He handed me my papers, and I began making my way through the crowded harbor in search of my parents. It was a wild, busy, loud mess, and it took me a good ten minutes before I finally spotted them. They were looking around anxiously. They did not see me until I was right in front of them.

My mother cried out in excitement as she embraced me with the biggest hug I had ever been given. She kissed my cheeks and my forehead over and over. I pulled away, embarrassed, and told her that I was glad to see her. My father and I shook hands, and with a serious face he told me that he was glad to have me home again. Then he laughed and pulled me into his embrace. He patted my back hard.

My father took my bag, and my mother wrapped her arms around me as we walked to the carriage to go home.

21

V

My mother, my father, and I sat by the fire in the living room of our home, drinking the English tea I had brought back. I answered questions about my experiences abroad even though I had explained everything in my weekly letters — well, mostly everything. Growing tired of talking about myself, I began asking questions about what they had been doing and what had been going on in America, the answers to which I had already read in their letters over the last four years. We talked as if we had not kept in touch during my absence, but because of our constant correspondences, it was as if I had never been gone. But I loved hearing my mother talk. She could talk for hours about the trivial or the relevant, but mostly about the trivial. My father was never trivial. I admired that greatly about him.

"Now, why didn't you bring home a young woman to marry, Konrad?" my mother asked as she refilled our tea. The conversation quickly turned from tedious to uncomfortable for me.

"Well, Mother, there was no young woman to bring home," I said, as I hurriedly sipped my tea.

"What about that girl you met your first year at school? Katherine, I believe," she pressed.

"She wasn't right for me. I told you that."

"Well, what about Elizabeth? She was a lovely girl," my mother continued. Could she not sense my awkwardness?

"How do you know she's lovely? You never met her," I said with a chuckle.

"No, but I felt as if I had, the way you talked about her in your letters."

"Well, that was my second year, a long time ago."

There were a few moments of silence, and I thought my mother was done with the embarrassing questions. Her expression was thoughtful. I hoped she was thinking of a different subject to talk about. Suddenly, an excited expression came over her face.

"What about Mary?" she asked.

"We went our separate ways, Mother. That was my third year."

"Oh, no! I meant Sofia."

My father rested his cheek on his hand as he smirked at me with raised eyebrows. I smiled and shook my head.

"Sofia and I called it off in my third year."

"Well, then it must not be her of whom I'm thinking. No, I'm thinking of Annabelle. What about her?"

"She's from my third year as well, Mother," I said with a sigh.

"Well, isn't there anyone recently?" my mother asked, disappointed.

"No, ma'am."

"Why did you not court someone this last year?"

"I think he needed a break, darling," my father said, still smiling at my embarrassment.

"Konrad, you wrote to us about these beautiful young ladies as if you were deeply in love!" my mother said defensively, as if she was speaking for all women who fall victim to scheming men.

"I believed I did love all of them."

My mother sighed. "Well, I do not approve of that kind of behavior. You need to find a sweet, young lady, marry her, and have children. Your father did not run around chasing many women, did you, Rafael?"

"Of course not, Lenora. You're the only woman I've ever loved."

My mother smiled and shook her head. "I know you're lying, but I do love to hear you say it. Now, Konrad, speaking of lovely, young ladies—"

"Mother, please, can we talk about something else?" I pleaded.

"I'm sorry, dear. I'll stop," my mother said with a mischievous smile. "How would you like to go to the grand opening of the New York Philharmonic tonight? You remember your childhood piano teacher, Henry Timm, don't you?"

"Yes, of course I remember Mr. Timm," I stated.

"Well, he'll be helping Ureli Corelli Hill conduct the orchestra. We have great seats reserved in the balcony," my mother revealed excitedly.

"That sounds wonderful," I said. I loved the symphony.

"Great! Afterwards there is a party we will attend, and Miriam Monroe will be there. You remember her, don't you? The two of you were great friends when you were younger. Wouldn't you love to dance with her at the party?"

"We will see. But please do not try to set me up with anyone."

"Well, why not? What's wrong with a mother trying to make her son happy? Don't you want to get married?"

I shook my head in surrender and smiled. "You're shameless, Mother."

That night, we took a carriage to the New York Philharmonic, where we arrived to a great crowd of finely-dressed, upper-class citizens who were socializing as they made their way through the entrance of the grand building. My parents greeted a few people they knew, and we began making our way through the decorative hallways.

My parents stopped and talked to many people as we walked toward the stairs that led to the balconies. I was bombarded by the smiles, handshakes, and questions from my parents' friends whom I had not seen since before I had left for Oxford. They congratulated me on my graduation and my return home. I cannot count the number of times I was asked what I planned to do with my life.

By the time we were making our way up the stairs to the

balcony level, I was hot and short of breath. I felt on the verge of hyperventilating. No one should ask a youth who is at that important decision-making time in his life what his plans are. If he has not yet made a decision, it only causes him to worry. It is also quite embarrassing to say, "I don't know". If he has made a decision, it causes him to think too much about it and to wonder if he has made the right decision, and, well, he begins to worry. Nothing good can come of asking a young man what his plans are for the future. If any youth is confident and satisfied with what his plans are, then he is more lost than those who have no plans. The journey to self-discovery should be mountains and valleys with great rivers to be crossed, not a staircase. I was beginning to think that I should take that metaphor literally.

The very privileged and wealthy aristocrats stood in the hallway outside their private balconies in dignified conversation with one another, as they waited for the concert to begin. My parents mingled with a few of them, and I was happy when their acquaintances ignored me.

Just when I thought the worst of it was over, I heard my mother call out to Mrs. Monroe. Mrs. Monroe waved to my mother with a big smile on her face and began to walk over to us. My mother looked at me and smiled.

"Lenora, how are you? You look extravagant!" Mrs. Monroe complimented my mother.

"Why, thank you, Diana. You are absolutely gorgeous!" my mother replied.

"You're too kind," Mrs. Monroe responded. Then she looked at me and smiled as her eyes lit up. "Is this Konrad? My, how you have grown into such a handsome young man."

"Thank you, Mrs. Monroe," I said. "You are still as beautiful as I remember."

"You're so sweet."

"Where is Miriam?" my mother asked. Mrs. Monroe looked around.

"Yes, where is she? Ah, there she is. Oh, Miriam!"

Miriam was having a conversation with a man in a fancy officer's uniform. He looked to be in his thirties and wore a carefully-groomed mustache. She turned when she heard her mother's call, and her mother waved for her to come over to us. Miriam looked from her mother to me. Our eyes met for a moment, and then she turned to excuse herself from the officer. As she walked toward us, she did not look at me. She smiled to a few people she knew and stared at the ground without lowering her head. She looked much more mature than I remembered. She had grown into her chiseled facial bone structure, which had been overwhelming when she was younger. Her small button nose rested adorably between two rosy cheeks, which balled up into dollish beacons on the corners of her full lips when she smiled. Her golden hair hung in elegant curls just above her collarbone. She fit into her dress with a wonderfully curvy figure. The neckline on her dress was cut low and made her full breasts prominent. That was a feature I did not remember and the first I noticed. She glided toward me, and I could not take my eyes off of her.

She arrived in our presence with a confident sophistication that oozed independence.

"Hello, Mrs. Quintero de Leon. It is a pleasure to see you tonight," Miriam greeted my mother. Her voice was pleasant; that was also not part of my memories.

"And a pleasure to see you as well, Miriam. You remember my son, Konrad, don't you?" my mother asked shamelessly.

"Of course I do; we were childhood friends. How are you, Konrad?"

"I'm well — and yourself?" I asked.

Miriam remained silent and answered my question with an inviting smile.

"We'll leave you two to catch up," my mother said, and she and Mrs. Monroe walked away.

Miriam and I stood in silence for a moment. I felt awkward, but she seemed very confident standing before me in silence.

"Our parents want us to marry, you know," she finally said. What a statement to break the silence!

"I've gotten that impression," I agreed. "They're quite discreet, aren't they?"

Miriam chuckled slightly and looked around. "Well, what do you think of it?"

"Of what?" I asked.

"Of our parents wanting us to marry."

"Well, I'm sure they have the best intentions. I think you're a fine woman. You're beautiful! You've grown up since I last saw you." What was I saying?

"That happens over time. But you didn't answer my question."

"Oh… well… yes! I think you're a fine woman. Ah… I think you have great qualities. Um… What do you think?"

Miriam chuckled. "I think it's silly to even consider marriage for us. We haven't even spoken since we were children. I don't know anything about you except that you're afraid of heights."

"Actually, I'm not anymore."

"Well, there you go. I know nothing about you. Frankly, I don't ever want to marry — no offense."

"Of course not. I happen to feel the same way," I said, feeling a great weight fall from my chest. "Now, how do we break it to our parents?"

Miriam pressed her eyebrows together in thought. "We could run away."

"We could run away," I repeated. Not the worst idea, I supposed.

We stood there in silence once again. All the people in the hallway began making their way to their seats.

"Looks like the concert is starting. I'll see you afterward, and then we can plan our escape," Miriam said with a mischievous smile.

I smiled in happy confusion as she walked away. She was not at all what I had expected. I was very relieved.

I walked to the balcony and took a seat with my parents. Miriam sat with her parents in the balcony to my left and gave me one quick conspiratorial glance. The orchestra was in place on stage and ready to play. The theatre was silent. I could hear the echo of Ureli Corelli Hill's footsteps as he walked to his position before the orchestra. He took a bow to the audience and everyone clapped. The clapping ceased as soon as he turned to his orchestra and raised his baton. With one fluid motion from the conductor, the orchestra began the concert with Beethoven's *Symphony No. 5*. They played it magnificently.

I looked over at Miriam from time to time during the concert, but she never looked back at me. I tried to catch her stealing glances at me by looking at her through my peripheral, but she never did. Through the whole concert, she sat in the exact same position with the exact same posture and did not move a muscle. I had no desire to know this woman, yet she had my attention and she knew it. I knew she wanted to look at me, but she would not allow herself. She was playing with me and wanted to see how far she could drag me in. It was obvious that she had done this before, and I'd had it done to me before. I did not understand it. How does a woman make a man want her when he knows she is the last thing in the world he wants? Well, maybe she wasn't the last thing in world I wanted, but I was confused enough. I did not need a woman to complicate things. But I suppose that's what women do.

VI

AFTER THE SYMPHONY, MANY of the spectators and performers attended a party at a fancy hotel in Manhattan. A string quartet set the mood while the elite of New York City mingled. There was an abundance of fine wines and liquors, as well as a diverse selection of carefully-crafted *hors'd oeuvres*, which were carried around the room on silver platters by stone-faced waiters.

While they were mingling, I snuck away from my parents to avoid questions I did not want to answer and conversations in which I did not wish to engage. I was not feeling sociable in the least.

I walked around the room for a bit, observed the paintings on the walls, and watched the quartet in a hypnotic daze. I sampled each of the *hors'd oeuvres*. I could not get enough of the caviar, and the waiter eventually started to avoid me.

As I observed the people and took in the environment, I began to feel claustrophobic. I felt my heart racing, and my pulse was throbbing in my neck. I was short of breath and was growing hot as I had at the concert. Maybe I needed a drink to calm my nerves, so I had a glass of champagne and drank it quickly. It did not help. I needed something stronger. I had a glass of whiskey, and it did help a little. I poured myself another glass and went outside for some fresh air.

I took a deep breath of the crisp, cold air and exhaled slowly. I felt a little better. I took a big sip of whiskey and leaned against the wall.

"It's stuffy in there, isn't it?" said a voice out of nowhere. I turned to see Miriam Monroe leaning against the opposite wall of the entrance. I hadn't noticed her when I walked out in a desperate panic. She was nursing a glass of red wine.

"Yes, it is. I couldn't breathe," I said. She walked over to me and leaned against the wall.

"Me neither. These people bore me. Don't they bore you?"

"I guess... well, they don't really bore me. They just make me feel like I'm losing my mind."

"I don't feel like I'm losing my mind. I'm just bored. I've been attending this party with the same people my whole life. I understand how *you* would feel like you're losing your mind though."

"Do you?"

"Yes. You were just in Europe for four years traveling, learning, and experiencing, and then you come home to this. I would lose my mind, too, I believe."

"I suppose. Do you want to go for a walk?" I asked.

Miriam smiled as if she had been waiting for me to ask. "I would love to, but I have to get my coat."

We walked back inside and made our way to the coat rack, doing our best to avoid any eye contact with anyone so as to not get drawn into conversation.

"Konrad?" a familiar voice called.

"Damn," I said to Miriam under my breath.

I turned around to see Jonathan Shaw walking toward me. He was an old friend of mine with whom I had grown up. He had left for Harvard a year before I left for Oxford, and we had not been in touch since. There had been no falling out. One day I just stopped spending time with him and the other boys.

"Konrad Quintero de Leon! By God, it is you! I don't believe it!" Jonathan said excitedly. He was wearing a fine-tailored suit with the gold chain of a watch hanging from his pocket. His short, black hair was parted to the side, and he wore a thin mustache. His dark hawk eyes were as penetrating as I remembered, and his smile was as big as ever. He was always smiling. Except for the mustache, he was about the same. He had put on a little weight, however.

"Jonathan Shaw. It's been a long time, old friend," I said. He shook my hand and embraced me. He seemed a little drunk.

"It's been over five years! And it's just Jon now."

"Sure. How are you?" I asked.

"I'm well. I'm well."

"You look well. You don't seem to be starving," I said with a smile.

"Ah, my weight is deceiving. It's mostly muscle," he said proudly. Surely he was in denial. "But I am certainly not starving. My job requires me to spend half of my time doing business at the office and the other half dining at fine restaurants."

"Oh? That's nice. Where do you work?" I asked.

"I'm working for the New York Stock and Exchange Board over on Wall Street, directly under David Clarkson, the president. Surely, you've heard of him. Very smart man. He's here. I'll introduce you. You're certainly not the scrawny young man I remember," he said with a chuckle as he slapped my shoulder. He suddenly noticed Miriam. "My apologies, Miriam. How do you do? You look absolutely exquisite this evening."

"Thank you, Jon. But it's no longer evening. It's nearly ten o'clock," Miriam corrected him.

"Is it?" Jon took out his gold pocket watch, holding it out awkwardly to make sure I got a good look at it. "You're right. I seem to have lost track of time. Doesn't the night just fly by when you're having a good time?"

I would not know, I thought, and I'm sure Miriam was thinking the same thing.

"Konrad, have you seen the rest of the boys? Michael, Andrew, George, and Edward. They're all here. They've probably already gone downstairs for brandy and cigars. Why don't you join us?"

"Well, I was just—" I started to protest, but Jonathan put his hand on my back and led me away. I looked back at Miriam with an expression that begged salvation.

31

"Please, excuse us, Miriam," Jonathan said. "It was lovely seeing you."

"Goodnight, gentlemen," Miriam said with a mocking grin that only I saw. I rolled my eyes and let Jonathan lead me away.

Jonathan and I walked down a stairwell and entered a smoke-filled room where a group of about twelve young men were drinking brandy and smoking cigars. It was a typical picture of the upper-class elite, and I immediately felt nauseous.

I instantly recognized Michael, Andrew, George, and Edward who Jonathan had mentioned, as well as a couple of other young men I had grown up with and a few who had merely been acquaintances. The rest I did not know.

The gentlemen looked up at Jonathan and I as we entered the room. They were in the middle of having a good, throaty laugh.

"I hope you're not laughing at me, gentlemen!" Jonathan said, walking in as if he owned the room.

"We were laughing at you earlier, but now that you're here, it will be no fun to have a laugh at your expense," Andrew teased after a big puff from his cigar.

"You're a son of a bitch, Andrew," Jonathan jested. "I brought some fresh meat, gentlemen. Don't you recognize him?"

"Well I'll be damned! It's Konrad Quintero de Leon!" George said excitedly. He stood up and shook my hand.

Michael, Andrew, Edward, and Robert all jumped up excitedly to greet me with a handshake and kind words. They all looked the same. Michael was still stretching to stand five and a half feet tall. Andrew was still tall and lanky. Edward still had the smooth, pretty face of a teenager. George was still big-boned and stocky but had developed more of a belly, and Robert was still big-nosed and big-eared with thick, curly hair.

They were all dressed exactly alike and wore their hair short, parted, and matted down. Jonathan was the only one who wore a mustache. I imagined he believed it was a sign of his leadership in this exclusive group of young, rich professionals, and it seemed as if the rest of the men viewed it the same way.

I was introduced to the few gentlemen I did not know and was reacquainted with my old friends. We all sat down, and Jonathan poured me a brandy and gave me a cigar. They went back to their conversation and seemed to forget I was even there. I was not offended in the least. I was relieved, in fact. The last thing I wanted to do was sit there and be bombarded by questions about school, what I was doing, and what my plans were. I just sat back and enjoyed my cigar and brandy. I listened to their discussions about politics, money, art, and other things they thought they knew everything about. I was quickly bored by the conversation and tuned it out. I soon had another brandy and became lost in my thoughts. I snapped out of my daze a few moments later to realize that I had finished my brandy rather quickly, so I poured myself another and finished my cigar.

As the brandy started to take effect, while I observed these old friends of mine who I no longer knew, I noticed that my mood had shifted from bored and uninterested to angry and cynical. The more I listened to these men talk and pretend to be passionate about things they really had no feelings toward one way or the other, and the more I observed their pompous mannerisms and behavior, the more my mind raged. Who are these people? Their existence is pointless, these aristocratic pawns, these stereotypical representatives of a bankrupt society! These abolitionists who are so blind they cannot see that *they* are the slaves bound by the chains of business and government! How can I allow myself to sit here amongst them and inhale their empty words? Their words are no more than a regurgitation of the poisoned milk sucked from the breast of ignorance! Damn them all!

I took a deep breath and tried to calm my angry thoughts. I'd had too much to drink. Why should I allow my mood to become depressed by the way these people lived their lives? Why should their ignorance bother me? Was it because I saw myself in them? Was it because I saw them living the life that had been planned out for me? I knew that if I stayed in New York I would end up just like these men whom I once loved and now despised. No, I did not despise them. I felt sorry for them. It was not their fault. I was not like them, and I knew I could never be. I felt the restlessness in my heart again, beating faster and faster. I had to do something — something drastic. I had to sever all ties to this lifestyle, for if I stayed here I would surely die. I did not belong here. I could feel my heart telling me that. But what should I do? What *must* I do? I tried to listen to my heart for an answer, but my concentration was broken by the sound of my name.

"Konrad?" Jonathan called once again.

"Yes?" I answered, trying to bring myself out of my thoughts.

"Are you all right?"

"Yes, I'm fine. I was just… I'm a little dizzy, I guess."

"Aren't we all?" Andrew said with a throaty laugh. The others joined in.

"At least we know the brandy is good!" Edward said.

"Konrad, have you any plans for what you will do now that you've returned from Oxford?" Jonathan asked.

I hesitated for a moment. "Um… no, I haven't any plans."

"Any ideas?" George asked.

"No. No ideas," I said honestly.

"Well, haven't you mastered a trade or anything over the last four years?" Andrew asked curiously.

"No, I don't believe I have."

"Well, why the devil not?"

"I'd much rather spend a lifetime learning a little bit about many things than a lifetime learning everything about just one thing," I said.

The men were silent in their confusion.

"Interesting," Jonathan finally said. He quickly changed the subject. "Have you read Emerson?"

"Who?" I asked.

"Ralph Waldo Emerson, of course. Surely you've heard of him!" Jonathan said smugly.

"Oh, yes, I've read *Nature, Self-reliance,* and his Phi Beta Kappa address."

"What do you think of him, Konrad?" Michael asked curiously.

I did not feel like getting into a discussion about Emerson. I tried to think of something clever to say, but instead I just shrugged, shook my head, and said, "I think he has some good ideas. He's very enlightened."

"Yes, quite," Jonathan agreed. "You know, while I was at Harvard, I was in the Phi Beta Kappa Society when he gave his speech to us about five years ago. That was the first I had ever heard of him, and I have followed his work ever since. Have you read *The Dial*?"

I felt short of breath and lightheaded. I needed fresh air.

"I apologize, gentlemen," I said. "Would you excuse me for a moment?"

"Sure," Jonathan said in confusion.

I stood and walked up the stairs to the main lobby of the hotel where the party was still going on. It seemed as if there were more people than there had been when I left to go downstairs. I could hardly breathe, and my heart was racing. I needed air. I needed a walk. I needed to get out of this suffocating place!

As I pushed my way toward the door, I could feel the confused, disgusted stares of the aristocratic society around me. I heard their whispers of disapproval. Blast you, philistines! I wash my hands of you and this life!

I knew that it was all in my head. I just needed some air to clear my mind. What was wrong with me? I went outside and sucked the air in deeply. I could breathe again. I left the hotel and began walking the streets with no place to go. I lost track of time and distance, and by the time I was becoming sober, I did not know if I had walked for minutes or hours. My legs were tired, so I must have been walking for a long time.

I tried to decipher what my heart was trying to tell me. I knew I must leave, but where would I go? What would I do? What would I tell my parents? A great journey lay before me, but where did it end? What path would lead me to the man I was meant to be? No! Too many questions. What answers did I expect? What would I gain from the answers? Nothing. I realized that there was only one answer to all of my questions, and it was the same for each one: What does it matter?

The answer in the form of a question was freeing. I needed no goal, no destination, because the truth was that my journey would never end. Therefore, I asked myself, where did I want to go? The first place that came to mind was New Orleans. Why not New Orleans? That's where my parents had met, and they spoke very fondly of it. I had an uncle who lived there whom I had never met. It was a historic and prospering city with many opportunities. Maybe I should start there and see where it would lead.

A wave of relief chilled my body, and I began to like the idea of going to New Orleans more and more. I had no plans, but it was all coming together somehow. I couldn't help but smile as I stared at the full moon resting amongst the stars in the cold, midnight sky. Tomorrow, I would tell my parents my decision.

VII

By the time I got home, the sun was rising. I had not realized how long I had wandered the streets. When I walked into the house, my parents were waiting for me. My mother told me how worried she had been and asked why I had left the party and had stayed out all night. I told her I'd needed to go for a walk and had lost track of time. I told them I was going to bed and began walking to my room, but I stopped at the entrance of the hallway. I needed to tell my parents my decision, and I had to do it now.

"Actually, there is something I wish to speak to you both about," I said, as I turned to once again face my parents. I walked back into the living room and stood before them, as they looked up at me curiously from where they sat.

"What is it, son?" my father asked, while placing his newspaper on the table next to his chair.

"Did you get into trouble last night, Konrad? What happened?" my mother worried.

"Nothing, Mother. Please, just let me speak."

My mother and father looked at each other and sat back in their chairs, growing more curious every second that I hesitated. How do I tell them? What words do I use? In what manner do I speak? Should I sound confident or apologetic? Should I be firm or undecided? I decided that it was best to just say it and let it sound as it sounds.

"I have made a decision — not to stay in New York. I do not feel that my place is here," I finally said. It felt good to say it out loud.

My father straightened his posture and tilted his head slightly to the side, as he looked at me with inquisitive eyes.

"And where *is* your place, may I ask?" There was a dash of disappointment and anger in my father's voice.

"I do not know, sir, but for now I wish to go to New Orleans and see Uncle Raul. From there I would like to go out West and see the country. America is expanding, and much is happening on the frontier. I wish to see it before it is gone." I spoke with confidence and compassion, for I knew that no parents want to see their child leave — whether they support them or not. I tried my best to show that I was sad to have to leave but that it was something I must do.

My parents were silent as they looked at me, then at each other, and then back to me. My father leaned back in his chair and stared hard into my eyes. I knew he was looking to see if this was merely a whim or a genuine, thought-out plan. It was neither, but I stood firm and confident before him.

"Konrad, the frontier is dangerous! You can't just—" my mother began, but my father held up his hand respectfully to silence her.

"What will you do for work?" my father asked.

"I will find work here and there. I was thinking of working as a fisherman in New Orleans. I learned much about ships and the sea on my journey home from England. I participated with the crew on many fishing endeavors," I explained.

"A fisherman? I have paid for you to go to the best university in the world, and you want to be a fisherman?" my father asked incredulously. I was prepared for this statement.

"Only for now, Father. I'm not blowing off my education or saying I'll never put it to use, but right now my heart yearns for adventure. I want to explore and see the world. If I don't do this now, then when? If I stay here, I don't believe I will find happiness. You do want me to be happy, don't you?" I asked. It was a manipulative question, and I had not wanted to resort to this level.

"Of course we do, son!" my mother answered. "But why can't you find it here?"

"Because there is no adventure here, Mother!" I said in frustration.

"So, you're going to run around the wild frontier in search of happiness?" my father asked.

"I'm not searching for happiness! Happiness is in the searching! Why is this so hard for you to understand? I'm not asking for your permission. I'm asking for your blessing, and if I don't have it, then... well... I'm very sorry." I turned to leave the room.

"Konrad, stop right there," my father said without raising his voice. I stopped and turned to face him. "Please forgive us for questioning your intentions, but we are your parents. If you're going to set off to do something as big as this, we have to ask questions. You've presented us with a desire — but no plans — and for a parent that is worrisome."

"How does one plan an adventure?" I asked.

"One doesn't. We are not trying to stop you—"

"We're *not?*" my mother interrupted. My father flashed her a quick look and turned back to me.

"We're just making sure you've made your decision for the right reasons," my father said.

"I'm sorry. I just felt like I was being attacked."

"You *were* being attacked. And when somebody attacks you and questions your motives and beliefs, you stand firm. You don't lose your temper and run away."

"Yes, sir," I said.

My father nodded and leaned back in his chair. He sat silent for a moment. "I hope you will stay for Christmas and wait until the New Year to leave," he said.

"Of course, Father. Thank you."

"Rafael!" my mother exclaimed, looking at my father with anger and surprise.

"We'll talk later, darling," my father said. "Go get some sleep, son. I will write to your Uncle Raul today and tell him you are coming."

"Thank you, Father. Thank you, Mother." I quickly left the room before anything else could be said.

I lay on my bed, full of excitement. I could not sleep. I was not tired. I just lay there in my room, smiling like a giddy child as I thought about the adventure that awaited me.

* * *

Over the next couple of weeks, I planned my trip to New Orleans. I would go to Pittsburgh by way of horse, where I would then take a steamboat down the Ohio River for about twelve-hundred miles until it joined the Mississippi River near Cairo, Illinois. I would then continue riding the steamboat all the way to New Orleans, which would be another thousand miles or so.

I spent many long hours at the stores in the city browsing for the supplies I would need. Being as excited as I was, I wanted to buy everything I saw whether I needed it or not. I would spend hours talking to the storekeepers about this and that, from the most trivial of things to the most essential. However, I was able to control my excitement and only buy what I needed, which was minimal. I knew that I did not want to have everything I might need at my fingertips. I wanted to be tried and tested. I wanted to have to make do with what I had and improvise for the things I did not.

I bought a pair of leather riding boots that would last me a lifetime and a good hat to keep the sun off my face. I bought two pairs of wool trousers, one brown and one black. They were cheap, comfortable, and would be good for travel. I could not travel in the clothes I had. They were stiff and impractical, for they were only for show. I bought a light jacket for daily wear and a good coat for the cold. I also bought three white shirts. My clothes were simple and downplayed, for I did not want to look like a rich Yankee from the city while I was exploring the frontier.

On the day before Christmas Eve, I went to the city stables to secure a horse for my trip. It was the last thing on my meager list of necessary supplies. However, the horse was only needed to get me to Pittsburgh where I would sell it. That being the case, I bought the cheapest horse the stableman had, which was an old, honey-colored mare. The stableman said that she was not too old to travel but was certainly too old to get a man any further than Pittsburgh. He said that this would probably be her last journey and that I would most likely not get a very good price when I tried to sell her. That was fine with me. I paid the man and told him I would be back to get her at dawn on the first of the New Year.

After I secured my horse, I began making my way home through the city. I smiled as I took in the buildings and the people on the streets, reminiscing, just as I had when I was preparing to leave Oxford to return home. I came upon a café, which I used to frequent before I had left for Oxford. I would spend hours drinking coffee and reading books at this little gem. I decided to go in for old-time's sake.

I went inside, hoping to sit at what used to be my usual table, but I found it occupied by an elderly gentleman reading a newspaper. I sat down at the next table and ordered a coffee and a biscuit. As I waited, I noticed Miriam Monroe sitting at the back of the café with a few young women. She had already noticed me, and she smiled and waved. I smiled back. I saw her excusing herself from her friends. She stood up and began walking over to me. She arrived just as the waitress brought my coffee and biscuit. She asked Miriam if she would like anything, but she declined.

"What brings you here this morning?" I asked Miriam.

"Tea and pastries," she said.

I took a sip of my coffee and broke my biscuit in half. Miriam was staring at me strangely. I took a bite of my biscuit as I waited for her to say something that would match her expression.

"I also heard some gossip about you," she said finally.

"Oh, yeah? And what did you hear?"

"I heard that you're leaving New York again," she said. "You're headed to New Orleans — if I heard correctly."

"You heard right. I'm leaving on the first day of the New Year," I told her.

Miriam smiled and said, "I know we talked about running away, but weren't we supposed to run away together?"

"I never said you weren't invited."

"But you never invited me, did you? I had to hear about it through the grapevine," Miriam said, faking a look of disappointment.

"Well, I'm sorry. Would you like to run away to New Orleans with me?" I asked just to humor her.

"Yes, indeed I would."

I laughed as I chewed my biscuit, but while taking a sip of coffee to wash it down, I noticed that Miriam was not laughing. She was looking at me with an expression of seriousness and determination.

"You're joking," I said.

Her face did not change; she *was* serious.

"You couldn't possibly go with me!"

"And why not?" she asked. "I won't be a burden. It's just a short ride to Pittsburgh, and then we take a steamboat all the way there, right? How could I possibly get in the way?"

"Well, I'm not just going to stay in New Orleans," I said. "I'll be traveling. I'll be out West and on the frontier." I almost added that the frontier was no place for a woman, but Miriam did not seem to be the kind of woman who would take kindly to such talk.

"I'm not asking to explore the frontier with you. I have no desire to do any such thing. I just need a change. I'm tired of this city and these people. I'm not asking to see the world; I'm just asking to see something different. I can't spend the rest of my life here, Konrad. I'm tired of having my whole life planned out for me. I know you feel the same, and that's why you're leaving. It would be hypocritical of you to only think of yourself. All I'm asking is that you take me to New Orleans."

I sighed as I thought about what she'd said. I felt sorry for her. Men could choose to live out planned lives and become boring, pompous shells of themselves while they enjoyed luxuries and laziness. Women, on the other hand, were stuck waiting on men. They really had no choice but to marry the pompous shells. Miriam was the most independent American woman I had ever met, and that type of life would surely kill her as it would me. How could I live with that?

"What will you tell your parents?" I asked her.

"Nothing. It's not really running away if I tell my parents, now is it?"

"I'll be held responsible," I said. "They'll say I kidnapped you, or some such nonsense."

"My parents probably won't even notice," she said bitterly.

"I highly doubt that."

"You don't know them, Konrad. My father has always wished I was a boy and has never paid an ounce of attention to me because of that fact. My mother just wants to marry me off as quickly as possible and be done with it. Whether I get married or run away to New Orleans, it will all be the same to them."

I thought about it for a moment. If she wanted to come along, what right did I have to stop her? Besides, the companionship of a beautiful woman was not the worst thing in the world.

"I'll tell you what; I'm going to pick up my horse at the stables at dawn on the first of January. If you're there and ready to go to Pittsburgh, what can I say? It's your right to travel where you will, and it is my duty as a gentlemen not to allow a lady to travel alone. I will be obligated to escort you to Pittsburgh and on to New Orleans. How does that sound?"

Miriam laughed excitedly, stood up, and kissed me on the cheek. "It sounds perfect, Konrad! Thank you!"

43

"You're quite welcome. Just don't act too excited. You don't want anyone to suspect anything."

"Of course. I won't. I have to go back to my ladies. Thank you again! A million times, thank you!"

Miriam went back over to her friends. I smiled and shook my head. I knew that having a woman with me would complicate things, but the complication of a beautiful woman was usually worth it.

* * *

The next week passed more slowly than any week in my whole life. I spent every minute of the day imagining the great adventure on which I was about to embark. I tried to envision sights I had never seen before, such as the Gulf of Mexico, the Great Plains, the Rocky Mountains, the desert, and, most of all, the Pacific Ocean. The Pacific Ocean was not where my journey would end, but it represented the westernmost point that I could go before I had to decide what to do next.

After Christmas, my mother grew more affectionate each day as the New Year grew near. I had everything that would be needed for my journey, and I spent all of my time at home with my parents. I pretended to be sad to leave them, and in part, I was, but I had never been more eager and excited in my life.

On New Year's Eve, I stayed up with them all night long. We sat by the fire, talking about all sorts of things, everything except for my leaving, which was only hours away. I had packed my belongings the week before to avoid putting my mother through the misery of seeing me pack the day before I was to leave.

As dawn approached on January 1ˢᵗ, 1843, I brought my bag from my room and began saying my goodbyes to my parents. It was a very tough goodbye. It was not like when I had left for Oxford. Then, I was leaving with a specific time to return. Also, I was leaving to receive an education while still under the support of my parents. This was a different kind of goodbye. I was cutting the umbilical cord and heading off on my own. I would have to support myself and make decisions on my own. There was great risk involved, with no guarantee of return, and if I did return, I would not be the same person I was now. I would not be that innocent little boy they raised. I would be my own man. I would be a product of my self-discovery through growth from my experiences.

I imagine that our goodbye was quite typical for a goodbye of its scale. I saw my mother at her weakest and my father at his strongest. There were tears, hugs, and handshakes, and words of encouragement and caution. My father gave me his gold pocket watch as a parting gift. He'd had it for as long as I could remember. I remembered always wanting to play with it as a child. It meant a lot when he gave it to me.

I waved my final farewell as I walked out the door and into the cold, crisp wind that blew in the dawn. I wanted to remember my parents standing in the doorway, waving goodbye, with my mother crying and my father swallowing the lump in his throat. *You've done all you could by me,* I thought, as I savored the sight of them for a moment longer. *You should trust that as parents you have done well and take comfort in that. I am your son, and everything good in me is from you.* I should have said it out loud, but I think they knew.

With that last image of them in my head, I turned and began walking down the street toward the stables. I felt my heart rise to my throat, and my eyes began to fill with tears. After spending the last week hiding my excitement and pretending to be sad in front of my parents, I now realized that I had been in denial. The tears overflowed my eyes and rolled down my cheeks. Nobody was around, so I let myself cry freely. I had never felt a greater mix of emotions. For now, the excitement had left me, and I began to realize how much I would miss my parents. I wanted to turn back and hug them one last time, but not just a simple goodbye hug; I wanted to hold them for five minutes each; I wanted to tell them how much I loved them, how much they meant to me, and how proud they should be that they had raised me so well and had made a good, honest man of me. But I did not turn around. I just cried and kept walking forward. It was the hardest thing I had ever done.

VIII

I ARRIVED AT THE stables just as the sun was beginning to rise and the cold air had dried my tears. The stableman was saddling my horse when I remembered that Miriam was supposed to meet me. I wondered if she would show. I told the stableman to go ahead and saddle another horse. As he saddled an Appaloosa mare, I loaded my belongings into the saddlebags. When the saddlebags were full, I tied the rest of my things to the saddle. Everything just barely fit.

Just as I was beginning to lose hope in Miriam, a carriage pulled up to the stables. The driver opened the door and helped Miriam out of the carriage. I walked over and took her suitcase. It was heavy.

"I almost left without you," I told her.

"Well, thank you for being so patient," she said.

"Arriving in a carriage isn't exactly sneaking away," I pointed out.

"The driver doesn't even know who I am. I was at a New Year's Eve party with my parents all night long. I snuck out when they were good and drunk, and I saw him parked outside. He took me to my house to get my bag and then here. I paid him well." Miriam looked into my eyes. "Have you been crying?"

"What? No!" I lied. "It's the wind. It's cold. It made my eyes water. I had to walk here, you know. I didn't have the luxury of arriving in a carriage."

"Fair enough," Miriam said. She then glanced down at the saber hanging at my waist. "Are you a pirate now?"

"It was a gift from my uncle," I told her.

We walked into the stables where I showed Miriam her horse. She looked at the other horses and noticed a gorgeous, young, black stallion she said she'd rather have. I explained that we only needed the horses to get to Pittsburgh and that we were on a budget. She finally settled for the Appaloosa I had already bought her. When I told her to unload her suitcase and put her things in the saddlebags, she said she would not. She did not want her fine dresses to touch the dirty horse and the dirty saddle. I was not liking the way things were starting. I was not in the mood to argue, so I told her she could just carry her suitcase on her lap all the way to Pittsburgh.

I climbed on my horse and adjusted myself in the saddle. A sudden wave of excitement came over me. I was really doing it. Sitting on the back of a horse, I had never felt more right in my life. The stableman helped Miriam onto her horse, which was a humorous scene to watch. He then sat her suitcase in her lap. She rested her arms on the suitcase, and the stableman put the reins in her hands. She adjusted herself, looked over at me, and smiled.

"There. All set. Shall we?" Miriam invited.

I chuckled and shook my head. "Let's go."

I gave my horse a nudge, and we rode out of the stables and into town. It took us a good hour to get out of the city and away from the buildings and houses before we finally reached the open countryside. We were on our way.

It did not take Miriam long to begin complaining about her discomfort on horseback and how the suitcase on her lap was causing her arms and legs to fall asleep. She also had great difficulty guiding her horse. It made for a slow first day, but by some miracle we were able to make it to Allentown a couple of hours after dark. I told Miriam that Allentown was where the Liberty Bell had been hidden when Philadelphia was preparing for the British to invade the city during the Revolutionary War. She was not interested in the least.

We stopped at the first inn we came to and rented two rooms for the night. Miriam did not say a single word once we stopped at the inn. She went straight to her room in an irritated fit and fell asleep instantly.

In the middle of the night, I snuck into Miriam's room, laid out one of her dresses, and took her suitcase. I walked to the stables where we had left our horses for the night and began unloading her suitcase and packing her belongings on the saddle. I stuffed everything I could into the saddlebags, tied the rest onto the saddle, and covered it with canvas. Then I threw away her bulky suitcase. I hoped she wouldn't be too angry with me.

I awoke the next morning to the alarm on my father's pocket watch and a great soreness in my legs and lower back. I did not want to get out of bed. I looked at the watch, and the hands read 3:30. I winced as I pushed myself out of bed. I dressed as quickly as my aching body would allow and went to knock on Miriam's door. There was no response, so I knocked harder.

"Go away!" a voice in pain demanded. I shook my head and opened the door. Miriam was lying on her stomach with her face buried in her pillow.

"Come on," I said. "We have to get a move on. Long day ahead of us." I started walking around the room to gather up her things, but then I remembered that I had already done so last night. "Come on," I repeated. "I'm hurting just as much as you are, but we have to get going."

"You have no idea how much pain I'm in!" she stated irritably.

"All right, well… it does no good to complain. Let's just ride out the pain," I suggested.

"Riding is what *caused* the pain."

After unsuccessfully begging me to stay at the hotel and sleep all day, Miriam finally agreed to get up. She came out of her room wearing the dress I had laid out for her the night before. She was so tired and in so much pain that she didn't even realize that her suitcase was missing until we arrived at the stables and thought she had forgotten it. I explained to her what I had done with her clothing. Thankfully, she was too tired to be angry. I helped her onto her horse and climbed onto mine, and by 4:15 we were riding out of town.

Miriam and I did not speak much that day. The soreness and tiredness never left us as the morning progressed into afternoon and then as the afternoon turned into evening. Miriam never thanked me for getting rid of her suitcase, but I could tell that her ride was much more comfortable despite being in pain from the day before. She had control of her horse now, so we moved much more quickly.

At dark, we stopped in the town of Newville. We got two rooms at an inn and immediately went to bed.

The next morning, the alarm on my father's pocket watch went off at 3:30 once again. I was still a little saddle sore, but I felt rested and ready to go. Miriam felt the same way, and by 4:00 we were riding out of town. As the day progressed, Miriam became talkative once again. She asked me what I thought New Orleans would be like, what going to school in England had been like, and where I had traveled in Europe. My experience with women had been that they liked to talk about themselves very much, but Miriam was not like that. She was very interested in me and my experiences. It was refreshing. When I asked her about herself, she gave brief answers and said there was not much to know. I asked her what she thought her parents were doing, and she said they probably had not even noticed that she was gone. I told her I did not believe that, and we spoke no more of it.

We arrived in Johnstown just after dark. We took our horses to the stables and headed to a hotel in the middle of town. Both of us were feeling much better, so instead of going straight to our rooms and to bed, we had a nice dinner at the hotel restaurant. We ate slowly, and each of us had a glass of red wine. After dinner, we each ordered another glass of wine and took them upstairs. We sat in her room and talked for about an hour before she said that the wine was making her tired and that she was ready for bed. She kissed me goodnight on the cheek and thanked me for letting her come with me. I told her I was glad she had come and went to my room.

I lay in bed for a while, thinking about how I felt concerning our situation. When two people spend all day together on a journey, they become bonded in a special way. Certainly, some form of love must bloom from a situation of this nature. We had not seen each other in years, yet here we were, traveling to New Orleans with no idea what adventures and tribulations lay before us. I felt as if I was witnessing the rebirth of a woman who had been in captivity all her life, and I was grateful to be a part of it.

I was not looking for love. In fact, I was trying to stay away from it — for now. But who can control such feelings? Already she was starting to complicate things. I hoped it would be worth it.

IX

WE ARRIVED IN PITTSBURGH at half past ten the next morning. It had only been a short ride from Johnstown, and we had ridden swiftly. In Pittsburgh, I bought Miriam a new suitcase before we rode to the stables to sell our horses. I did not get what I had paid for the horses, but I got what the stableman in New York said I should get. I was satisfied, but Miriam was not.

"Why can't we take them with us, Kon?" She had started calling me 'Kon' that day. "They've been so good to us! Let's keep them!" she begged, as we unloaded our saddles and packed our belongings in our luggage.

"First you were complaining about what filthy animals they are and how uncomfortable you were, and now you can't part with your horse?" I asked.

"That was before I got used to her. After the first couple of days, she was quite pleasant."

"Well, I'm sorry, but you're just going to have to say goodbye."

Miriam walked around to the front of her horse and petted her nose gently. "Goodbye, my dearest angel," she said in the playful voice adults use to talk to newborn babies. "I will never forget you!"

We took our bags and walked down to the docks of the Ohio River, where steamboats were arriving or waiting to leave. The docks were busy with travelers preparing to board and head west and with workers loading and unloading the steamboats. It was loud and chaotic, but it was an extraordinary sight.

Miriam and I bought our tickets for a steamer leaving at noon. It was only eleven o'clock, so we went and had a quick bite to eat at a nearby restaurant. By the time we returned to the docks, our boat was beginning to board. We stood in line for a few minutes and finally boarded. It was a surreal feeling. It was at the moment when I set foot on the steamboat that I truly realized what I was doing. I was really going through with it. It felt liberating. I could see that Miriam felt the same way as she began running around the boat, exploring every part of it like an excited child. I smiled as I watched her.

"Isn't it just fantastic, Kon? It's just wonderful! The boat, the country, the people! I love all of it!"

"It certainly is wonderful," I agreed.

"Oh! It certainly is!"

Shortly after we had boarded and settled in, the horn on the boat blew with ferocity. Startled, Miriam jumped into my arms. She immediately extricated herself and began laughing. The steamboat pulled away from the docks with a loud thumping and swooshing sound from the paddle wheel digging into the water. We were off and heading down the Ohio River.

The countryside was breathtaking, despite the skeletal state of the hills of deciduous trees, which had shed their colorful fall leaves to be covered by a thin, white blanket of powder from the most recent snow. This bareness of the hillsides made it very easy to see the actual terrain of the rolling hills. The Ohio River, itself, was even more breathtaking. Thomas Jefferson once wrote, "The Ohio is the most beautiful river on Earth. Its current gentle, its waters clear, and bosom smooth and unbroken by rocks and rapids, a single instance only excepted." I had not seen every river on Earth or very many at all, for that matter, but for the moment I had to agree with him. It was like nothing I had ever seen.

I spent the entire first day aboard the steamboat staring out at the new world around me. I took in the wonderful sights for the first time and savored them, for I would never see them for the first time again.

Meanwhile, Miriam explored the ship, watched the gamblers, and mingled with the passengers. She was great at socializing. She knew exactly how much to say about herself and how much to ask about the person with whom she was speaking. She always made the people she was talking to feel special. For most of the people who were groomed in the world in which she was raised, conversation was a science and an analysis of the ratio between what one says about themselves and what one asks about the person with whom they are speaking. I believe the ratio is one to three, but it has been a long time since I have abided by the rules of conversation. Miriam did abide by these rules, but in a genuine way, and it was contagious.

Night fell upon us, and Miriam and I stood at the back of the boat and stared into the clear, infinite sky. There were so many stars. As we stood there, Miriam drew close to me. I could see that she was cold, so I put my arm around her and drew her in closer. We stood there in the glorious magnificence of the moonlight.

Then, Miriam looked up at me and boldly asked, "Do you want to kiss me?" I looked at her and smiled. "This just seems like a moment where two people should kiss, don't you think?" She did not show a sign of doubt or awkwardness in her bold question.

"Yes, it certainly does," I said.

I leaned in and kissed her as the steamboat paddled down the river under the stars. It was a nice, gentle kiss with very little passion. It was not forced, but it was not natural either. I think we both realized at that moment that we were not lovers — merely friends. It was not disappointing in the least. The kiss was good and suited the moment. We enjoyed it while it lasted.

* * *

Time flew by on the steamboat, and before we knew it, we were leaving the Ohio River and heading down the Mississippi. We stopped in Cincinnati, Louisville, Memphis, and Vicksburg, among other cities, to pick up and drop off passengers. After a little over two weeks on the steamboat, we were only a few days away from New Orleans.

I smoked a cigar as we drifted along the borders of Eastern Arkansas and Northwestern Mississippi. It was chilly in the humid, Southern air, but I stayed outside on deck. I had spent very little time inside where the gambling and socializing took place. I was afraid I would miss something. As I came to the end of my cigar, I saw Miriam walking over to me. I had not seen her nearly all day. She was with a tall, handsome gentleman in a fine suit. "There you are, Kon," Miriam said. "I thought I'd find you here. I have someone I'd like you to meet." I tossed my cigar into the river and turned to face the two of them. "Konrad, this is Charles Devereux. Charles, this is Konrad Quintero de Leon."

"It's a pleasure to meet you," Charles said, extending his hand.

"The pleasure is mine," I returned.

We shook hands, and I instantly liked the man. He spoke with the accent of a Southern gentleman and had a very kind, honest face. He had chiseled facial features but with enough roundness to his face so that he did not look sinister. His hair was dark-brown, and his eyes were a silvery blue. He wore a mustache that suited his tall, aristocratic figure very well.

"Charles owns a whole slew of steamboats on the Mississippi, including this one," Miriam bragged on his behalf.

"Is that so," I asked, genuinely interested.

"I wouldn't say a *slew*, but I do own a fair amount I suppose," Charles modestly corrected. "My father got into the business very early and did most of the work getting it started. When he died and I took over, all I really had to do was manage the business."

"Well, I'm sure it's a very prosperous business. I read that there are as many as fifteen-hundred boats operating on the Mississippi," I said.

"Yes, that is about right. It's quite busy and a very good business to be in for the moment. You never know what's going to happen. Some genius could invent a new, faster, more powerful boat and put steamboats off the water," Charles said, though his manner was not cynical but only practical.

"Where do you have your office?" I asked.

"I work in New Orleans. It's the only place to live," Charles answered. "Miriam tells me that the two of you are on your way there for the first time."

"Yes, and we are quite excited to be getting there," I replied.

"As you should be. It's the greatest city in America. It has everything New York has without the stuffy, pompous attitude."

"Well, then, it sounds perfect," I said. "Were you doing business up North?"

"I do from time to time, but every now and then I just like to take a ride up and down the Mississippi, which is what I'm doing now. As much as I love New Orleans, it's nice to get away from it all every now and then, as it is with all cities I suppose."

Over the next few days, Miriam and I spent a lot of time with Charles. I liked the man. He was humble, honest, and blasé. He was quite rich, but it did not show in his attitude. I could tell that Miriam had grown very fond of him. She was always asking him questions, smiling, and batting her eyelashes at him as she hung on his every word. I was a bit jealous at first, but as I got to know Charles, I did not mind it so much. It also made me feel relieved. I even began to hope that a relationship would blossom between the two of them, for then I would be free to go off on any adventure that presented itself, knowing that Miriam was taken care of and that I would not have to worry about her.

On January 25, after three weeks on the Ohio and the Mississippi, there came a commotion from the front of the steamboat. I was standing at the stern watching the paddles push off the water, when the horn of the boat bellowed and cheers began to drown it out. The people standing around me rushed to the front of the boat. I looked around to see what was going on but could not catch a glimpse.

Miriam rushed out onto the back deck and waved me toward her. "Come look, Konrad! We've made it to New Orleans!"

I quickly followed her to the front of the boat. She pushed through the crowd of people to the front, and I followed her path feeling very rude. Charles was standing at the bow railing. He looked back at Miriam and me as we made our way toward him.

"Come on, darling! Hurry up, now! You don't want to miss it!" Charles said. He took Miriam's hand and pulled her in front of himself. He looked back at me and waved me on. "Come on, Konrad! You must see this!"

Charles put his hand on my back and pushed me up to the railing where he had been standing, allowing me to have a front-row seat for the amazing sight that was before me. Miriam and I stared in awe at the great City of New Orleans. The docks were filled with steamboats, and the people were busier than any I had ever seen. Smoke rose from the rooftops and dissipated into a fog that hung over the city from the sea. The Gulf air was sweeter than any sea air I had ever smelled.

"Isn't it wonderful?" Charles asked, smiling at our awed expressions. "It never ceases to amaze me."

"It's fantastic!" Miriam said excitedly.

Anxious butterflies fluttered around in my stomach as our steamboat docked. Everyone quickly began to disembark. I was in no hurry, however. I rested my arms against the railing and leaned forward, and with a grin from ear to ear, I took in the superlative sight.

X

WE STEPPED ONTO THE dock with our bags and began making our way through the chaos. People were running around in all directions, carrying supplies and luggage or leading horses and cows. Miriam and I were in an overwhelmed daze as we tried to take it all in while making our way through. Charles walked calmly and confidently, smiling at everyone he saw and patting them on the back as they passed, even if he did not know them. He looked over at Miriam and me and laughed at our confused expressions.

"Come on!" he yelled over the booming madness. "Just follow me! Stay close and keep your eyes open!"

We did as he said and followed his path through the crowds of workers and spectators. As we came to the landward end of the docks, I noticed a big crowd gathered in front of a long line of Africans who were bound by their hands and feet, nearly naked. One of the Africans was standing on a high platform, while a short, fat White man stood next to him calling out numbers. The men in the crowd called out numbers to the fat man as well. It took me a few moments to realize that they were auctioning off the Africans to be slaves. I never knew that this was how the slave trade worked. My excitement quickly faded into an uneasy feeling in the pit of my stomach. I looked down at the ground in shame, though I had done nothing. Maybe that was precisely why. When I looked back up at the Africans, one of them caught my stare. He looked tired and beaten. His eyes reflected his hopelessness, yet they had a glimmer of defiance still left in them. Our eyes remained locked for what seemed like an eternity, until one of the slave traders violently pushed him forward.

When I looked for them, Miriam and Charles had left the docks and had climbed the steps up to the mainland. I hurried to catch up with them, and we quickly moved toward town and away from the docks. A few minutes later, we were away from all the chaos. It seemed comparatively quiet now, though it was anything but. Charles stopped after we crossed the street and smiled at us.

"What did you think of that?" he asked. "Fun, huh?"

"It was quite overwhelming," Miriam said.

"Now, where are the two of you headed? I'll show you the way," Charles offered.

"I have it right here, I believe." I reached into my jacket pocket and pulled out the letter my Uncle Raul had sent in response to my father's letter informing him of my coming. I opened the letter and looked for the address. "Ah, here it is. He says he lives in the *Vieux Carre* on *Rue Bourbon.*"

"Ah, the French Quarter! Wonderful!" Charles said.

"You know it?" I asked.

"Of course! Everyone does! It's the center of the whole city!"

"Oh, really?" Miriam asked excitedly. "Is it grand?"

"Grand hardly describes it. Come — I'll show you," Charles offered.

We walked through Jackson Square, which reminded me of a place I had been before, but I could not place it. I asked Charles what he knew of it, and he said that the square had been modeled after the *Place des Vosges* in Paris. That was why I had recognized it. It was a beautiful square. We walked toward the Saint Louis Cathedral and on past it into the heart of the French Quarter. I loved the look of it. It felt very European, Spanish mostly, but it certainly had its own unique flavor. Charles stopped at Bourbon Street and held his arms up in the air as if he was presenting it to Miriam and me.

"This is your *Rue Bourbon,*" Charles said. "Did your uncle give you any more directions?"

I looked at his letter. "Yes, *Rue Bourbon* at *Rue St. Louis.* Does that sound right?"

"Yes, it's right this way," Charles said.

We began walking southwest down Bourbon Street. "He says he lives above a restaurant called 'Leon's'. Do you know the place?" I asked.

"Sure do," Charles said. "Not the best restaurant in town, but not bad."

A few blocks later we arrived at St. Louis Street. We looked at Leon's Restaurant and then up to the apartment above it. It looked quite nice actually. It was simple and had an iron balcony like most of the other buildings I had seen.

"Pretty good setup you have here," Charles said. "French Quarter . . . Bourbon Street . . . doesn't get much better than that."

"Thank you for showing us here," I said, extending my hand.

"It's no problem at all," Charles said, shaking my hand. His eyes shifted to Miriam as he released my hand. "This Saturday, a new opera is coming to town. They will be performing *Les Huguenots* at the Theatre d'Orleans. You really should come. Afterwards there will be a big party. It would be a great way to be introduced to the city. What do you say?"

"That sounds wonderful!" Miriam said.

I was skeptical. Events such as this opera were precisely what I had been trying to get away from by leaving New York. However, it was mostly the people and the general attitude in New York that I did not like, and Charles had said that New Orleans was different. I loved the symphony, the opera, and the theatre. I had seen *Les Huguenots* in Paris and had thoroughly enjoyed it.

"Yes, that sounds great," I said.

"Excellent," Charles said. "I will leave three tickets for you at the box office desk. The usher will show you to my balcony."

"Three seats?" I asked.

"One for your uncle as well," Charles explained. "It was a pleasure meeting you, Konrad — and Miriam." Miriam extended her hand. Charles took her hand, leaned forward, and kissed it gently, looking into her eyes all the while. He was smooth. "I'll be looking forward to seeing you Saturday night."

Charles turned and went his way. Miriam sighed as she watched him walk away. I chuckled. Miriam turned to me and rolled her eyes.

"Don't be coy; just say what you want to say," Miriam allowed.

"I have nothing to say, other than I'm glad you found a new friend," I said.

"He's you're friend, too, Konrad," Miriam pointed out.

"Somehow, I think he's a little friendlier to you," I commented with a teasing smile.

"Are you jealous, Kon?" Miriam asked.

"Of course not," I said. "It's pleasant to see you smitten."

"I'm not smitten," Miriam defended. "Just interested."

"Whatever you say, darling. Shall we?" I asked, indicating the stairway to my uncle's apartment.

"Yes, let's go meet this uncle of yours."

We walked up the stairs to the only door that led into the apartment. I knocked, and we waited for a few moments. There was no answer. I knocked again. We began to hear some movement inside the apartment. Then there was a loud thump, followed by a good amount of cursing.

"Who's there?" yelled the voice from inside the apartment.

"It's your nephew — Konrad," I said. "Rafael's son."

The door swung open swiftly, and Uncle Raul stood before us with a big smile on his tired, red face. His thin, light-brown hair was wild and sticking up like weeds. He stood there barefoot, wearing an open black, silk lounging robe, with black trousers, and a simple, loose, white blouse that resembled the style of the Eighteenth Century. He was slightly pudgy in the gut and had a round face with a scrunched nose. He did not look anything like my father, but he did look good for a man in his fifties. His hair had not yet gone gray, and his face had only a few wrinkles, mostly around his tired-looking eyes.

"My nephew! Konrad! You made it!" He quickly grabbed my hand and shook it with both of his. He then looked at Miriam. "Ah, the nephew comes bearing gifts!"

Miriam looked at me in confusion. "Excuse me?" she asked Raul.

"Uncle, this is Miriam. She came with me from New York," I quickly explained.

"Oh! My apologies, my lady," Raul said with a bow. "Konrad's father did not inform me that he was bringing his lover."

"We're not lovers either, Uncle. We're just friends. And since my father does not know she came with me, I think it best we keep it that way."

"Ah! A secret! Wonderful! Come in, please!" Raul stepped aside, swooped his hand down across his legs, and extended it to point inside the apartment. "Welcome to my humble home."

Miriam and I walked inside and looked around curiously. It was much bigger than I had expected. In fact, it was quite spacious. The carpet was a velvety red to match the curtains. The walls were a very dark, almost reddish-brown. Two bookshelves covered the eastern wall and were completely full. On the opposite side of the room was a very fine, black piano. There were many chairs, couches, and stools placed carefully around the living room.

"This is a lovely home you have!" Miriam complimented.

"Why, thank you, my dear," Raul said as he shut the door. "Shall I give you the tour?"

"Yes, please!" Miriam responded.

He opened the double doors in the middle of the western wall that led to his bedroom. The bed sat high from the ground with four bedposts decoratively carved that stretched high to support the canopy over the bed. The window to the right of the bed overlooked the French Quarter. To the left of the bed was a dresser with a fancy, gold-bordered mirror resting over it. We then followed him out of his room and back into the living room. He opened a sliding door against the north wall, which opened into a bathroom with a very fancy and very big bathtub.

He then showed us the other bedroom, where we put our bags. I took my saber off my hip and placed it on the bed. The room had two beds. Raul said that he and my father used to sleep in this room. When their father died, Raul had moved into his room since he was the oldest.

We walked back out into the living room. He opened the curtains next to the main entrance of the house to reveal a set of double doors with giant windows. He pulled open the doors and showed us the iron balcony that overlooked Bourbon Street, or as Raul liked to call it with an over-emphasized French accent, *Rue Bourbon.*

We went back inside, and Raul closed the balcony doors and shut the curtains. We all sat down in the living room.

"Would the two of you like a drink?" Raul asked. "Certainly you could use one after your long journey."

"Yes, please. Whiskey would be great," I said.

"And for the lady?"

"A whiskey sounds just fine," Miriam said.

Raul's eyes lit up. "A whiskey drinking lady! How delightful!"

Raul quickly walked over to the liquor cabinet with the tail of his silk robe floating behind him, where he took out three glasses and uncorked the whiskey. He looked down at the table next to the liquor cabinet where a thick layer of scattered pages nearly covered the top. He put down the bottle and quickly gathered up all the pages and stuffed them in a drawer. After pouring the drinks, Raul walked back over to Miriam and I, expertly carrying two of the drinks in one hand. He handed us our drinks, sat down, and raised his glass. "*Bienvenue vers la Nouvelle Orleans!*" Raul toasted. We touched glasses and drank.

"*Merci, mon ami,*" Miriam said.

"Ah! *Parlez-vous, Francais, madame?*" Raul asked excitedly.

"*Peu* — a little bit," Miriam replied. "When I was a little girl, I dreamed of living in Paris, so I begged my parents to let me take French lessons. I studied for about half a year and then stopped. I hardly remember any of it."

"Did you ever go to live in Paris?" Raul asked.

"No," Miriam admitted sadly. "I have never left New York until now."

"That is a shame. Everyone must live in Paris at some time, even if it's just for a little while. I lived there for a year, although that was a very long time ago. I think it was eight years ago, nine maybe — a long time ago. I'd love to go back. Konrad, do you speak French? I know you've spent some time in France and abroad."

"I picked up a little when I lived in Paris for a summer, but not enough to speak it," I said.

"Then I will teach you both French. It's the most beautiful language! I think I love it even more than my mother tongue!"

"That sounds wonderful!" Miriam said.

"Now, madam, I can't tell you how much I would enjoy having you live here, but I do know that ladies, such as yourself, need their privacy. I was thinking that Konrad and I could sleep in the spare bedroom and that you could have my room, but I still don't think that would be appropriate enough for you. Now, I do own another apartment just a few blocks from here, which I rent out to people. It's in *Vieux Carre*. It's quite lovely and just a little bit smaller than this. I would be more than happy to let you live there for no cost if you think that would be better for you."

"That's incredibly generous of you, sir. If it is anything like this place, then I'm sure I would love it," Miriam said graciously.

"Oh, it is. I will show it to you after we finish our drinks," Raul said.

"How did you come to live in such a place as this, Uncle?" I asked.

"Please, just call me Raul. I don't like the sound of 'Uncle' for some reason."

"Of course… Raul."

"To answer your question, I have lived in this place for as long as I've lived in America. Has your father never told you the story of how we came to be here?" Raul asked.

"No, I don't believe he has," I answered.

"Well, our father, your grandfather, was a very successful architect in Spain."

"I did know that," I interrupted. "When my father told me, I became very interested in architecture."

"Yes, well, your grandfather was very good at it, and he loved architecture very much. After the great fire of New Orleans in 1794, our father was commissioned to oversee the rebuilding of the city. This was back when New Orleans was part of the Spanish Empire. Our mother had died long ago from an awful fever, so my father brought Rafael and me with him to America when I was seven years old and your father was five. After all that was destroyed had been rebuilt, my father was offered a great deal to stay and continue building the city. We lived here in this apartment, which my father had built. Then, in 1809, our father grew gravely ill and passed away. Your father took it the hardest. I imagine that's why he never told you about it. Anyway, your father and I continued to live here. We had inherited a great sum when our father passed. A year later, we decided to invest some of it in a restaurant. We bought the space directly beneath us and turned it into Leon's. It was very successful, and we opened up three more restaurants in the city. All were very successful. Then your father met the beautiful opera singer, Lenora, and ran away with her to New York. I had never enjoyed the restaurant business and did not want to run everything alone, so I sold all of our restaurants. They've all since changed into different shops and hotels, all of them except the one right under us. Leon's has remained the same since it was opened, though it has lost the popularity it once had back in its prime. And because of all of that, I have not needed to work or sell this wonderful home in twenty-eight years. However, I do still work."

"What do you do?" I asked.

"I paint signs for stores and restaurants all over the city. It doesn't pay much, but I love to do it. It keeps me busy," Raul said. "I also enjoy doing more artistic paintings, but I don't try to sell those. They're just for me. I write poetry as well, but I don't try to publish it either."

"So, you are an artist! How wonderful!" Miriam said.

"Well, aren't we all?" Raul asked.

"Have you always been so artistic?" I asked.

"I believe so. I just didn't notice it until later in my life. I didn't start painting or writing until after your father left."

"What inspired you to start?" I asked.

Raul hesitated for a moment as he looked down at his glass. He smiled, looked up at me, and said, "Well, a woman of course."

We continued to talk as we finished our drinks. I liked Raul very much. He talked quite a bit and was nice to listen to. He had many stories, and he told them well and with much passion. He was very casual and talked very comfortably with us as if he had known us our whole lives.

We had one more drink before we headed over to the apartment where Raul had told Miriam she was welcome to live. It was not as big as Raul's apartment, but it was just as nice and just as finely decorated. Miriam loved it and said she would live there. I was happy about that. I liked Miriam very much, but the thought of living with her had been worrying me a little. This would be a much more comfortable situation.

Soon, we were all settled into our new living arrangements in a new city. I was very excited and so was Miriam. I had made it to New Orleans. I had completed the first part of my journey. Tomorrow, I would see what kind of work I could find.

XI

THE NEXT MORNING AT sunrise, I went down to the docks to see about a job as a fisherman. It was not nearly as hectic as it had been when I arrived in New Orleans the day before, but it was still quite busy. Steamboats were loading goods and passengers as they prepared to head north up the Mississippi. Most of the fishing boats were already heading out to the Gulf to begin their long day, while a few were still scrambling to load last-minute supplies. As I watched the boats head out to sea, I began to lose what little desire I had to be a fisherman. I still wanted to learn how to fish in the deep sea and experience what that life entailed, but having spent so much time on the water, between crossing the Atlantic on my way to and from Britain and going down the Ohio and Mississippi rivers, I'd had my fill of aquatic adventures for the time being.

I took my time walking back home, pondering my interests and things I desired to learn to do. New Orleans was not quite awake yet. A few people were heading off to work, going home from work, or going home from an all-night party. Occasionally, I would come across a person asleep in a doorway, in an alley, or in the middle of the street. This certainly was a city that put fun first and work second. It was like an adolescent version of Europe.

When I got back to the apartment, Raul was sitting at the table by the liquor cabinet, writing frantically on a piece of paper. Last night, after we got Miriam settled into her apartment, Raul and I had a few drinks while we talked and got to know each other. Tired from traveling and in a half-drunken euphoria, I had gone to bed before ten. Raul looked as if he had not been to bed yet. He did not look up from his writing as I entered the room.

"Good morning," I said awkwardly. Raul groaned and raised

his hand with his index finger pointed up, signaling to give him a moment.

I looked around awkwardly and walked over to the bookshelf, careful not to make my steps too loud. I looked over the books for a few moments. Then Raul clapped his hands together once.

"All right! All done!" he said excitedly as he stood up. "Have you had breakfast?"

"Have you slept?" I asked.

"Who needs it? Let's go downstairs."

We went down to Leon's directly below us where a small breakfast crowd was enjoying their coffee as they waited for their meals. Raul and I took a seat at the front next to the windows. The waitress brought us coffee and a few fresh biscuits. Raul introduced her to me. Her name was Claire, and she was in her mid to late thirties. She was a very kind and sweet woman who was always smiling. Raul obviously knew her well, for they talked as if they had been friends since childhood. He made inappropriate comments and jokes that would not sit well with most women, but Claire would just laugh and slap him on the shoulder. Raul ordered for the both of us without looking at a menu, and Claire left to give the order to the cooks.

"I imagine you must come here a lot," I observed.

"Every day and every night," Raul said. "From breakfast time to about nine at night or so, it's just a typical restaurant, but at night it's a great place to drink and talk to people. It doesn't become a wild bar crowded with a hundred people. It's very quiet and relaxing. But you're a young man and would probably enjoy the crowded bars and loud parties."

"Not really. Actually, I much prefer a calm, relaxed environment," I said.

"That's good. You're mature," Raul said.

"I wouldn't go so far as to say that. It's just a preference. Oh, I almost forgot to tell you that we are all invited to the opera this Saturday."

"Ah! *Les Huguenots!*" Raul said excitedly. "I was planning on going to that. Who extended the invitation?"

"A man we met on the steamboat on our way here. His name is Charles Devereux."

"The steamboat tycoon! What a good person to befriend!"

"Do you know him?" I asked.

"I haven't had the pleasure. Is he a good man, or is he a typical, pompous businessman?" Raul asked frankly.

"He's a good man. Not pompous in the least. Miriam has taken quite a liking to him."

"I see. I've been meaning to ask if you and Miriam have a relationship that extends beyond friendship, or is it simple?"

"It's simple. We kissed once out of curiosity, and it made us realize that our chemistry doesn't extend beyond friendship."

"That's good. No need to complicate things, especially in this city where there are so many beautiful women to choose from! They'll go crazy for a fresh Yankee like you!" Raul joked.

I laughed and shook my head. "We'll see. I'm not really looking for love right now."

"Who said anything about love? Besides, you don't find love; it finds you. Certainly, you're old enough to know that cliché by now."

"Yes, that's true. We'll see what happens. This coffee is fantastic."

"It's the best in town," Raul promised. "How did it go down at the docks this morning?"

"Not so good. When I got there, I realized that I don't want to be a fisherman, not right now at least. I want to stay on dry land for a while," I explained.

"Well, it's good that you realized it now rather than in the middle of the Gulf," Raul pointed out.

Our food arrived, and Claire refilled our coffee. We had Andouille sausage, eggs, and headcheese, which was meat from the head of a pig served in aspic with many flavorings. It was all very good. It was my introduction to Cajun food, and I instantly fell in love with the intense mixture of flavors.

"What do you think?" Raul asked.

"It's amazing — all of it. I love it," I said with a full mouth.

"Good! New Orleans has some of the best food in the world, and I know all the hidden gems of cuisine in the city. I will show you them all."

"I can't wait," I said, as I took another bite of head cheese. "You know, I've always wanted to learn to cook."

"Have you?" Raul asked, very interested. "It's a wonderful art to know."

"After traveling around Europe, trying all the different kinds of food and the different ways they are prepared in each country, I became very interested."

"Well, then, learn to cook — Claire!" Raul yelled. Claire smiled and came strolling over to our table.

"How is everything?" she asked.

"Fantastic. In fact, Konrad here likes it so much, he wants to learn how to make it," Raul said.

"Is that so?" Claire asked me with a surprised look on her face.

"Um… yes. Absolutely," I said, feeling a bit awkward with the situation.

"Now, Claire, this is a young man who is just dying to learn all he can about cooking, and he would do anything for the chance to learn — anything! He'll take out the garbage, scrub the floors, and do the dishes. He'll even bathe the goddamn dog that eats the trash out back! What do you think, Claire? Do you have any work for this strong, capable, hard-working young man?"

"Well, if all of that is true, then I think we can find some work for him," Claire said. "Why don't you come in tomorrow morning at the same time as you did today? We'll put you to work."

"That sounds wonderful, ma'am. Thank you very much!" I said graciously, still trying to digest what had just happened.

Claire smiled mischievously and said, "We'll see if you're still thanking me after tomorrow. Welcome to Leon's!" She took our empty plates and walked back to the kitchen.

Raul paid for the meal, and we went back upstairs to our apartment. Raul walked over to the liquor cabinet and poured himself a glass of whiskey. He asked me if I wanted one, but I declined. It wasn't even close to noon yet! I walked over to the piano and looked it over.

"Do you play the piano?" I asked.

"Me? No. A woman I used to know played. I bought it for her," Raul said. He took a big sip of his whiskey and sat down at the table. "Do you play?"

"I used to. I took lessons from Henry Christian Timm for a few years when I was a child. He's a conductor now at the New York Philharmonic," I explained.

"Why don't you play something for me?" Raul asked.

"It's been so long since I've played. I don't think I remember how."

"Playing the piano is a skill one never forgets. Come on! Do you know Beethoven's *Sonata Pathetique*?" Raul asked.

"That's Piano Sonata Eight, right?"

"Yes," Raul confirmed.

"I used to play it. I don't know if I remember. Do you have the sheet music for it?"

"It's under the seat. Just lift it up."

I lifted up the seat of the piano bench where there was a storage compartment for sheet music and songbooks. I rummaged through the papers and then noticed that Piano Sonata No. 8 was on top. I took it out, placed it on the piano, and sat down. I looked it over and imagined the sound of the piece in my head. It was coming back to me. I began to play, but Raul quickly stopped me.

"No, no! Play the second movement, the *Adagio Cantabile*," Raul instructed.

I turned to the next page and looked over the notes of the second movement. I played the first note and hesitated, then I played the next two, and slowly the fourth, and so on until it came back to me as if I had never stopped playing. I missed a few notes here and there, but I played well, considering. Raul listened with his eyes closed.

"More pain," Raul instructed.

I stopped playing. "What?" I asked.

"Play with more pain, more emotion. Don't just press the keys and play the notes. Concentrate all of your pain and sorrow into your fingertips, and let the weight of your emotions guide your hands," Raul instructed, as he pretended to play the piano with one hand while holding his drink in the other.

I was taken aback by his instructions. I had not been expecting to receive a lesson. However, I liked his thoughts, and I tried my best to apply them as I started again from the top. It flowed much more naturally out of me this time, but it was still not to Raul's liking. He stopped me only a few measures into the piece and gave me the same instruction. Why was he so passionate and so critical about this piece? I tried again. This time I thought about the last image of my parents the day I left New York as they stood in the doorway, waving goodbye. Raul liked this attempt much better. I got almost halfway through the movement before he stopped me once again with the same instruction, "More pain."

XII

THE NEXT DAY, I started work at Leon's. My job entailed everything Raul told Claire I would do. I cleaned the tables, washed the dishes, scrubbed the floors, took out the trash, and did all the other "dirty work" imaginable. I did everything but bathe the dog that ate the scraps out back (there really was a dog that ate the scraps out back). I also spent a lot of time shucking oysters. I was very slow and clumsy at first. I cut my hand at least half a dozen times. Claire told me that shucking oysters took a couple of days to get used to, but after that it would be fluid and natural like second nature. It was hard work, but it felt good to get my hands dirty with some real manual labor for the first time in my life.

There was always something for me to do whether the restaurant was busy or not. I would work as quickly as I could while still doing the job right, and, in turn, I created a fair amount of free time for myself. I spent all of my free time in the kitchen with Emilio, the head chef. The first time I met him, I was surprised to see that he was Hispanic and even more surprised when I learned that he was only twenty-four years old. I had assumed that the chef at a Cajun/Creole restaurant would be one of those two ethnicities and much older, but Emilio was a pureblooded Mexican. He had been born and raised in Mexico near Monterrey. When he was fifteen, he had left home to become a fisherman. He spent six years fishing in the Gulf of Mexico before finally ending up in New Orleans where he began working as a *saucier*. Being a fisherman, Emilio, with his healthy curiosity for seafood preparation, spent a lot of time experimenting with seasonings, marinades, and cooking styles for seafood dishes. He quickly gained a reputation in New Orleans as being a great chef with a great imagination. Three years later, he became the head chef at Leon's.

73

He was more than patient and willing when it came to showing me how he prepared and cooked his dishes. He had no hesitation in telling me his "secrets", for he did not consider them as such. His philosophy was that great food was meant to be shared. If another chef used his recipe, it just meant that more people were getting the opportunity to try it. He was very short, but he had the biggest laugh I had ever heard, and he was always laughing. Even when the restaurant was at its busiest and he was rushing to make a dozen dishes at once, he was laughing the whole time. Half the time, I didn't even know what he was laughing about.

The other cook was more like what I had pictured a New Orleans chef to be. His name was John, and he was Cajun. He was tall, lanky, and in his mid-fifties, yet he looked much older. He was very hard to understand, and most of the time it was a good thing. Every time I walked by him, he'd yell, "You're a good man, you know that?" which he said to everyone, unless it was a woman. If a female employee walked by him, he'd either say, "You're a good woman, you know that?" or, "You're lookin' mighty lovely today." He was a little on the crazy side, but he could cook, and that's all that mattered.

Martha was the wife of the owner of Leon's, but she ran the place herself. She was a tough, no-nonsense kind of woman with a dry sense of humor. She never smiled, but she made lots of jokes at everyone's expense. It was all in good fun though. They were a close family who loved to tease one another. It didn't take long for them to accept me as one of their own.

After working twelve-hour days for my first four days, Martha let me go at four on Saturday to go to the opera. Before going upstairs to the apartment, I walked a few blocks over to Miriam's apartment. I knocked on the door. A faint voice yelled, "Come in!"

I opened the door and walked into her apartment. I looked around, but I did not see Miriam anywhere.

"Where are you?" I called.

"I'm in the bath!" she called back.

I walked into her bedroom. The sliding door to the bathroom was half opened, and I could see Miriam's legs, sparsely covered in bubbles, resting on the foot of the bathtub. I walked over to the door and slid it all the way open. Miriam did not open her eyes as she relaxed in the warm bath. The bubbles covered everything of value but were sparse enough to make my imagination wander. I smiled and leaned against the wall.

"I hope I'm who you were expecting," I said with a smirk. She opened her eyes and looked at me.

"I knew it was you. Stop smiling; you can't see anything," she pointed out.

"I see you're getting ready for the opera," I commented.

"Mentally and physically."

"I just wanted to stop by and let you know that Raul and I will come by to get you at six-thirty," I told her.

"Make it a quarter after six, will you? I want to get to the theatre early enough to mingle and meet people," Miriam said.

"There's a party afterward, you know. There will be plenty of time to mingle then," I informed her.

"How will I mingle with people at the party if I don't first meet them at the theatre?" Miriam asked.

I rolled my eyes. "You make a good point. A quarter after six it is."

"Good. You smell funny, Konrad," Miriam said.

"It's the restaurant," I replied.

"You need a bath. Why don't you join me?" Miriam teased.

I shook my head and smiled. "No, thank you. I'll take one at my apartment."

"Oh, Konrad, don't you want to take a bath with me?" Miriam pressed with a playful smile.

"That 'quarter after six' nonsense turned me off," I said with a smirk as I walked out of the bathroom. Miriam splashed water at me, but it fell short.

"I'll see you at six-thirty!" I called to her as I opened the door to leave the apartment.

"You'd better be joking!" Miriam yelled back.

I closed the door behind me and walked back to my apartment. When I got there, Raul was pouring a drink at the liquor cabinet. He was already dressed for the opera.

"There you are! I drew you a bath because you always smell like seafood when you come home, which is fine, but I don't think it will go over too well at the opera," Raul said.

"Why, thank you," I said.

Raul walked over and handed me a glass of whiskey. "Relax for a while, but be quick. I want to leave by six so we can get there early."

I smiled and rolled my eyes as I walked into the bathroom. As I was undressing, I noticed a very handsome suit hanging behind the door.

"What's this?" I called out to Raul.

"It's my gift to you," Raul answered. "I know it's no saber like your other uncle gave you, but it's certainly better than the clothes you have."

I chuckled and admired the fine suit. "Thank you."

"Sure," Raul called.

I sat down in the bath with my glass of whiskey. It seemed that Raul had been expecting me earlier, for the bath was just a little warmer than lukewarm. It was no matter. The whiskey warmed me up just fine.

After I had bathed and shaved, I put on my new suit and looked at myself in the mirror. It was a fine suit, and I looked quite good in it. I combed my hair to the side and adjusted my jacket. Satisfied with my appearance, I walked out of the bathroom and into the living room where Raul was pouring whiskey into a flask. At five till six, we left and walked over to Miriam's apartment. Raul knocked on the door.

"Open up, princess! Your chariot awaits!" Raul yelled.

"Come on in! I'm not quite ready!" Miriam called.

Raul made a face at me to indicate he was not surprised, and we walked into her living room. The door to her bedroom was shut, and we could hear her scrambling around, so we sat down and waited.

"Just have a seat! I'll only be a moment," Miriam called from her room.

Suddenly, her bedroom door opened a little bit and Miriam poked her head out.

"Didn't I say a quarter after six?" Miriam asked, looking at me.

"What can I say? I'm just so anxious to mingle," I said sarcastically.

"Very funny. It was you, Raul, wasn't it?" Miriam asked.

"Guilty," Raul admitted.

"I knew your were a fellow mingler! How nice!" Miriam slammed the door shut and quickly opened it again to poke her head out. "Can one of you fine gentlemen tie me up," she asked.

Raul smirked at me as our minds drifted into sinful thoughts. Raul gestured for me to go. I stood up with a mischievous smile on my face as I walked toward her.

"It would be my pleasure to tie you up, my lady," I said.

Miriam rolled her eyes. "You had your chance earlier," she said.

Miriam stood in front of the mirror looking herself over as I stood behind her and tied up the back of her dress.

"You look quite handsome," Miriam complimented.

"Thank you," I said without looking up from my task. "The suit was a gift from Raul."

"Oh? He bought me this dress as well," Miriam said.

"Generous man."

I finished tying the back of her dress and stared at her in the mirror. I looked her over carefully before giving her a compliment. I could see that she was waiting for it.

"You look absolutely gorgeous," I said sincerely.

Miriam smiled graciously. "Thank you, Kon."

We stood there for a moment, looking at one another in the mirror. Finally, I gave her a light slap on the rear end, but my hand did not penetrate the many layers of petticoats on her skirt. Miriam jumped.

"Hurry up!" I said, as I walked out of her room, closing the door behind me.

"I just have to put on my jewelry, and then I'll be ready!" Miriam called.

Ten minutes later, Miriam finally came out of her room, ready to go. I took out my father's pocket watch and checked the time.

"What do you know? It's six-thirty," I teased.

"I guess I'll just have to mingle extra fast!" Miriam returned. She posed in all her glory and asked, "How do I look?"

"You look stunning, my darling!" Raul said. "You'll be the belle of the ball!"

"Why, thank you, Raul. Now, are you two handsome gentlemen ready to escort me to the opera house?"

We walked outside and down the stairs. Miriam stood between us and took both our arms. She looked around in confusion as we started walking down Bourbon Street.

"Where's the chariot you said awaited me?" she joked.

We laughed and walked toward the Theatre d'Orleans.

XIII

WE WALKED DOWN BOURBON Street to Orleans Street and went half a block east to the theatre where a large crowd of people were socializing outside while others went into the theatre. We went inside and picked up the tickets that Charles had left for us. Just as the usher was about to show us to our balcony seats, Charles came over to greet us and told the usher he would handle it as he handed him a few coins.

"I'm so glad you all came!" Charles said joyfully. "This must be Mr. Quintero de Leon."

"Please, Raul will be just fine. It's a pleasure to meet you, Mr. Devereux," Raul said.

"If I'm to call you Raul, then you must call me Charles, and the pleasure is all mine. Miriam, you look heavenly!"

"Thank you, Charles," Miriam said with a slight bow of her head. "And you look quite strapping yourself."

"You're too kind. We have a few minutes before it starts. Let me buy you all a drink at the bar," Charles invited.

We all walked over to the bar. Charles bought us each a mint julep. Miriam and I had never had this cocktail before, and we both liked it very much. Charles introduced us to a few of his friends in the lobby, and Miriam got her chance to mingle. The atmosphere was nothing like it had been at the New York Philharmonic last December as I was expecting it to be. Unlike the Philharmonic or any social event in New York, for that matter, it was not a stiff, ostentatious display of aristocrats attending an event simply to show their upper-class status rather than their appreciation for the arts. The people I saw and met at the Theatre d'Orleans did not care about their status. The theatre was filled with both rich and poor, and there was no pressure to pretend to be someone else. It seemed to me that the show itself was of second priority. What these New Orleanians seemed to love most about social events was socializing. Everyone was laughing and talking in big groups. They really loved being around one another and enjoying the moment. There was much touching, hugging, and kissing. Their time together was not taken for granted.

As I was being introduced to one of Charles' friends, Jeffery, I noticed the figure of a woman in the background moving more graciously than any creature I had ever seen. There were too many people, and I could not get a good look at her. Jeffery was asking me questions, and I tried my best to pay attention to him and answer his questions, but I could not help but to look past him to get a glimpse of this angelic woman gliding across the room in a jade gown. Finally, I caught a brief glimpse of her profile. Her jaw line was profound, her cheekbones high, and I believe I caught a sparkle of hazel in her eyes, but I could have just been imagining it. Her copper hair was worn in a style I had never seen before. Her shoulders were bare and extended from a slender neck. That was all I could observe before she disappeared into the crowd again.

"I apologize, Jeffery," I said, as I gave him back my attention. "I seem to have been distracted by a beautiful woman, but she is gone now."

Jeffery laughed. "Well, then I suppose I can't hold it against you! It is the fault of man, not yourself. At least women are a healthy distraction!"

"That's true, I suppose," I admitted.

"Konrad!" Charles yelled. "I have someone I'd like you to meet."

"Excuse me, Jeffery," I said.

I walked over to the bar where Raul and Miriam where already talking with this man whom Charles wanted me to meet.

"Konrad, this is James Morrison," Charles introduced. "James, meet Konrad Quintero de Leon."

"It's a pleasure to meet you, Konrad," James said.

"The pleasure is mine, Jim," I responded.

"James, please."

"Of course, James."

James had not smiled yet. He immediately came off as the very stuck-up, pompous type that I had known in New York. In fact, he reminded me a little of Jonathan Shaw without the fake friendliness. James was a snob and did not try to hide it. He seemed very out of place with all the happy, fun-loving people around him, for he did not seem to be enjoying himself one bit.

"James is a business associate of mine," Charles said. "An investor of sorts."

I had been wondering why Charles kept James's company, and this made sense. They were merely business acquaintances — not friends.

"Where's your fiancée, James?" Charles asked.

James did not attempt to locate her. He stared off idly and said, "Who knows with that woman. She's always running about."

"Sounds like someone I know," I said, looking at Miriam.

Miriam smiled and batted her eyelashes. "We social butterflies can't deny our instincts to interact with others!"

"Of course not!" Charles said. "Who can deny their instincts?"

James looked at Miriam distastefully for a brief, discreet moment. He rolled his eyes and made a strange grunting sound in his throat. Miriam and I were the only ones to notice. Miriam looked at me with confusion and discomfort. I shrugged.

"I believe the opera will be beginning soon," Charles said. "Let's take our seats, shall we?"

"That sounds great," Raul agreed.

"I'm going to track down my fiancée," James informed us. "I'll see you after the show." He turned and walked away.

We walked up the stairs to the balcony level, all the while I was looking down to the lobby in search of the beautiful woman of whom I had only caught a glimpse. She was nowhere to be found. We took our seats in the balcony. Miriam sat between

Charles and I, and Raul sat next to me. Most of the balcony and floor seats were full, but a few patrons were still making their way to their seats. The orchestra was in the pit below the stage warming up on their instruments. I looked around for the woman in the jade gown again, but it was impossible to get a good look at anyone. Raul took his flask out of his jacket pocket. He took a sip and handed it to me. I took a sip and handed it back.

"I saw the premier of this opera in Paris in 1836, with Cornelie Falcon as 'Valentine' before her beautiful voice failed her," Raul said. "It was spectacular. It's a phenomenal opera. It's too bad you don't know French."

"I will soon enough. Just keep teaching me," I said.

"I will. I will, indeed," Raul promised. "It's an absolute necessity. Now, do you know about the Saint Bartholomew's Day Massacre that took place in Paris in the late sixteenth century?"

"Yes, when thousands of Protestants were slaughtered by Catholics," I recalled.

"Precisely. What you are about to see is all building up to the massacre of the Protestants, or Huguenots," Raul explained. "The story opens at the chateau of Count Nevers who is a Catholic. He will be the baritone. Nevers and his noblemen are awaiting the arrival of Raoul, our hero, who is a Huguenot. He will be the tenor. When he arrives, he tells the men of a mysterious beauty with whom he rescued and fell in love. Then enters Valentine, the soprano, who Raoul recognizes as his mysterious love whom he rescued. Turns out she is to marry Nevers. Now, knowing that, you should be able to understand the rest."

As I was about to speak, cheers and applause filled the theatre as the maestro took his place before the orchestra. He bowed humbly to the audience and then turned to the orchestra and began the "Prelude". The first act began, and I was quite impressed. The voices of the singers, the magnificent set, and the music were all at their very best and at the highest level of grand opera. Raul was right. After his explanation of the first act, I was able to follow the rest of the opera, even though I could not understand what was being sung. The story was not too complex but quite deep. I especially loved the fourth act where Raoul goes to see Valentine at Nevers' home after she and Nevers had married. As Raoul and Valentine meet in secret, they hear the approach of Catholic nobles and monks who swear to kill the Huguenots, but Nevers takes no part in it. Now, Raoul must make a decision: Does he stay with his true love who begs him not to go, or does he go to warn his fellow Huguenots? Raoul chooses duty over love and leaves to give warning to his friends. In the final scene of the fifth act, Nevers is killed while protecting Raoul's servant, Marcel. Valentine becomes a Protestant so she can marry Raoul, but soon after their union, Raoul and Valentine are murdered by Valentine's father, who realizes all too late that he has killed his own daughter. I am not afraid to admit that I shed a few tears at this part. Then enters the queen and a chorus of soldiers singing, as the curtain closes on this tragic tale.

I wiped my tears away, stood in applause, and yelled "Bravo!" with the rest of the audience. Dozens of roses were thrown onto the stage, as the cast bowed graciously. It was a truly marvelous opera.

After a half hour of mingling in the lobby again, everyone at the theatre began to head over to the Orleans Ballroom for the party. The ballroom was quite large. The dance floor was surrounded by many tables, which were big enough to fit fifteen people at each. Many people attended the party, and the tables filled up fast. Fortunately, we got there early enough to lay claim to a table in the corner. Many people were already dancing to the music of a small chamber orchestra.

Raul, Miriam, and I sat at a table with Charles and many of the people to whom we had been introduced at the theatre, including James — and Jeffery, who sat next to me and was extremely talkative. He was a very nice man, but one just could not get a word in with him. James, of course, was quiet and stiff.

He nursed the same glass of whiskey all night. As we all sat around the table laughing, drinking, and telling stories, more and more people would pull up chairs to join us. Miriam and Raul were both naturally very social people and were certainly the life of the party, despite the fact that they had only just met all of these people. When they spoke or asked questions, nothing seemed trivial or forced. It especially pleased me to see Miriam adapting so well to her new environment. The more I watched her interact with this new crowd of people, the more I believed that I had done the right thing by bringing her with me. She had not become a new person — but rather the person she always had been. This was just the first time she could really be that person.

Then, all of a sudden, the music stopped. The dancers stopped dancing, and everyone began to applaud as they directed their attention to the front of the room. I turned around in my chair and saw that the performers of the opera had made their entrance. I clapped along with everyone else. Everyone began to stand in ovation. The performers bowed graciously, smiled, and waved to their admirers. Many people began walking up to the performers to shake their hands and congratulate them.

"Pull up a few more chairs, will you," Charles said, addressing the men at our table. Then Charles quickly walked over to the performers and began speaking with Camilla Bianco who had played the female lead of 'Valentine'. Jeffery, and a couple of others, pulled three more chairs up to the table. Jeffery, who had been sitting next to me, put one of the chairs between us and smiled at me.

"Hopefully," Jeffery said with a wink, "Lady Camilla will sit next to us."

I laughed and looked back at Charles who was now leading Camilla toward the table, along with Andrea Santoro, who played the male lead of 'Raoul', and Maurice Lavoie, who played 'Nevers'. When they arrived at our table, Charles introduced them and everyone stood to greet them. After formalities were out of the way, we passed around the champagne. Camilla sat between Jeffery and I, just as he had hoped. She was an extraordinarily beautiful woman. She was just barely thirty-five and looked absolutely radiant. Her skin was olive; her hair was as black as the night, and her eyes were a deep ocean blue. Her smile was captivating and bright.

Once everyone had been poured a glass of champagne, Charles raised his glass and everyone joined him.

"To the limitless bounds of the human voice!" Charles toasted.

"Here! Here!" everyone yelled in unison, and we all touched glasses.

While Camilla and I were touching glasses, she smiled at me. I believe there was a hint of seductive mischief in her eyes as they locked onto mine. Maybe it was just my hopeful imagination, mixed with a nice buzz from the alcohol. However, her attention was quickly turned away from me to a bombardment of questions about her career and praises for her performance. She handled it all very smoothly and with profound grace. She had certainly done this many times.

"You know," Raul began, leaning in to Camilla, "I saw the premier of *Les Huguenots* in Paris with Cornelie Falcon as 'Valentine', and I must say, I was much more impressed by *your* performance."

"Why, that is quite a compliment," Camilla acknowledged in her sensual Italian accent. "Thank you very much."

"No, thank you for gracing us all with your wonderful voice," Raul corrected her.

Camilla laughed and bowed to Raul. "You're too kind." She then looked at me, and I was quite taken by surprise when she put her hand on my leg briefly to get my attention.

"Now! Do you sing, Konrad? You look as if you could be a singer or a performer of some kind."

I chuckled. "No, not at all. However, my mother sang in the opera."

"Oh! Did she?" Camilla asked, very interested, as she shifted her torso to face me and leaned in slightly.

"Yes, she performed at the Theatre d'Orleans in fact, when it first opened, before it burned down."

"Really? What is her name?" Camilla asked.

"Back then it was Lenora Mann. She was with a German opera company. I don't recall the name."

"Ah, yes! I've heard of her! I've never heard her sing, but my vocal teacher knew her and spoke of her on many occasions. He raved about her voice."

"Small world," I said.

"Small opera world," Camilla corrected. "Now I see why you look like a singer. Your sensual lips must have come from your mother. All singers have very sensual lips, don't you think?"

"Of course," I said. "It's the last thing their voice touches before dispersing to the ears of the listeners. The audience hangs on the lips of the singer."

"Well put," Andrea Santoro said to me. He raised his glass for a toast. "To the lips!"

"To the lips!" everyone yelled in unison, and we all touched glasses.

"To the lips," Camilla whispered to me. She smiled with her seductive eyes, and we touched glasses again. Maybe, earlier, it had not been my imagination.

"Now, what is it that the chorus of soldiers is singing at the very end?" Miriam asked.

"They are singing, 'God wants blood,' my dear," Santoro replied.

"My goodness. What interesting subject matter for an opera; wouldn't you say?" Miriam suggested.

"Indeed," Santoro agreed. "That's why I was so attracted to it when I was approached to play 'Raoul'. It's very moving — very tragic. Although the love story between Raoul and Valentine is all a creation of Eugene Scribe, the events that were taking place during the time, the Saint Bartholomew's Day Massacre, adds so much more depth to this forbidden love."

"And Giacomo Meyerbeer's composition of the music is just absolute brilliance," Maurice Lavoie added.

"I just can't believe that all those people were killing each other over religion," Miriam said in disbelief. "God wants blood? What an awful thing to believe!"

"Well, it certainly is a pattern in history," Lavoie pointed out. "Look at the Crusades — or the missionaries coming over to the Americas to convert the natives to Christianity and killing all who would not obey them, while destroying all of their historical records so that future generations may not know anything of their previous existence. Entire cultures were destroyed in the name of God. Quite hypocritical, wouldn't you say?"

"Certainly! I couldn't agree with you more," Raul said. "I hope there are no religious fanatics at this table whom we might be upsetting!"

Everyone laughed at Raul's flippancy.

"We're all godless hedonists here," Camilla joked.

Everyone began to slip into their own private conversations. Charles and Miriam were growing very friendly. She was being shamelessly flirtatious, and he obviously did not mind. Jeffery was talking Camilla's ear off, so I leaned toward Raul who was sitting next to me and asked him to pass me the caviar. I had been eyeing it all night but was too embarrassed to ask for it. Now, since everyone was wrapped up in their own conversations, I made my move. Raul set the caviar before me. He was also kind enough to pour me a glass of red wine. He said that he had been wanting to get his hands on the caviar all night as well. We took our spoons and sampled the salted sturgeon roe. It was very good. As Raul and I talked and ate, there was a bit of a commotion as my recent acquaintances welcomed a new guest at our table.

"For those of you who have not met her," James began, "this is my fiancée, Anastasia Carriere."

"It's lovely to see you all," Anastasia said in a soft, French accent.

I looked up to see this woman being introduced and could not believe who stood before me in the grasp of that awful, aristocratic snob, James Morrison. It was the mysterious woman I had been searching for at the theatre and had since forgotten, the woman in the jade dress, my healthy distraction. Anastasia was her name. What a wonderful name! I was finally getting a good look at her. I felt myself staring with raised eyebrows, but I did not care. She more than exceeded the mysterious vision of perfect beauty I had imagined when I could only see her profile for that brief moment. She was a bit thinner than I had thought. She looked firm — yet ever so fragile. She was the kind of woman a man must caress very softly and slowly to absorb every ounce of her beauty and cherish it in his fingertips. Her copper-colored hair contrasted perfectly against her smooth, light, caramel skin. Her rose petal lips looked soft and sensual and put all singers to shame. Oh! And her neck! Her beautiful, slender neck! And her collar and her shoulders. Her figure was just breathtaking!

Finally, she looked at me and our eyes met. However, I do not believe she was looking at me and falling in love as I was with her. She was probably wondering why I was staring so obviously at her, which Raul brought to my attention when he leaned in to me and whispered, "You're staring!"

"I don't care!" I whispered back. "I can't help it!"

"You may not care, but I'm sure her tight-ass fiancé won't be too pleased!"

I finally blinked out of my daze, as Anastasia took a seat between James and Miriam. James whispered something to her that I could not hear, but he did not seem pleased, and I noticed Anastasia's mood change from joyful to slightly irritated.

Miriam began talking to her, so I whispered to Raul, "Have you met her?"

"Who? Anastasia? Yes, of course! Everyone in town knows her."

"How do you know her?" I pressed.

"I painted her portrait once."

"Really? How can the human hand mimic such heavenly perfection?" I asked.

"It can't. I'm not proud of the painting at all. Now, just come off it, Casanova. She's engaged to one of the richest men in New Orleans."

"But it's not meant to be. Anyone can see that. She's too free for him."

"Most marriages aren't meant to be. And what do you know of her being free? You don't even know her."

"I know enough," I stated confidently.

"My God! What a fitting opera we saw tonight. It certainly turned you into a blind, romantic fool."

I smirked and gave Raul a nudge. "Shut up and pour me some more wine, will you?"

"As long as you promise to stop talking about Anastasia, and for God's sake, stop staring!"

"I promise," I said, while Raul refilled my glass of wine.

"My dear Camilla," Andrea Santoro said loudly, "I think it is only appropriate that I have my first dance with my leading lady!"

"Of course, my leading man."

Camilla and Andrea went off to the dance floor hand in hand and joined in with the other dancers doing the Viennese Waltz. I overheard Anastasia ask James to dance.

"You know I don't dance, Ana," James said bitterly.

"Oh, come on, James! Dance with your fiancée!" Charles said.

"Why don't you do me the honor," James said, looking at Charles with an annoyed expression.

"Very well," Charles said, standing up. "Anastasia, it would be my pleasure to dance with you since your boring fiancé has clumsy feet," Charles teased, winking at Miriam. James rolled his eyes and folded his arms.

"I would love to, Charles," Anastasia accepted, her face lighting up again. She took Charles' hand and they headed off to the dance floor.

Jeffery looked at Miriam and smiled. Just as he was about to ask her to dance, she quickly asked me to dance. I obliged her and we also headed off to the dance floor.

"You and Charles seem to have become very friendly," I commented as we waltzed.

"He wants to kiss me. I can tell by the way he keeps looking at my lips."

"Lips seem to be quite an obsession tonight," I remarked.

"I noticed you staring at James' fiancée. That's not polite," Miriam teased. "But I can certainly see why you would stare. She's quite pretty."

"I noticed you talking to her," I said.

"Yes, I was. Are you asking me what she's like?"

"I didn't ask anything."

"Well, she's very lovely and quite charming. She's adorably sweet. Oh! And she has the most wonderful French accent I have ever heard."

"You sound more taken by her than I," I teased.

"I just think she'd make a good friend. It's a shame she's engaged to that horrid James fellow."

We danced in silence for a few moments. Then Charles walked over and asked if he could cut in.

"Of course!" I replied. I stepped back and gave way to Charles as he took Miriam in his arms.

"Why don't you dance with Anastasia, Konrad," he said, gesturing with a nod to where he had left her alone.

"Oh! Sure." I looked at Miriam with wide, nervous eyes. She smiled and raised her eyebrows.

I walked over to where Anastasia stood alone. She looked at the people dancing around her and then turned her attention to me as I approached.

"It looks as if we've both lost our dancing partners," I observed.

"It looks that way," Anastasia agreed.

"Well, would you like to dance?" I asked nervously.

"Sure."

At the moment my hand slid into hers, my heart began to race. I was sure she could hear it thumping like a drum in my chest. As I put my other hand on her waist and slid it softly up her side to her shoulder blade, I felt as if I was melting. The first time I touched her, I felt like a blind man who was seeing for the first time in his life. As she put her hand on my shoulder and touched me for the first time, a tingling sensation forming in the pit of my stomach rose to my chest and exploded throughout my body. We began to move with the music quite naturally. We were fluid and graceful. I do not know how, for my knees were weak and my feet felt heavy.

I looked into her eyes, and she looked back into mine, drawing me in. Her eyes were emerald green as I had thought, with a hint of gold stemming off from her pupils like a star. What had started off as awkward became so naturally comfortable, as we stared into each other's eyes. My feet became lighter. We were dancing on air. We spun our webs around the dance floor until it became so thick there was only the two of us locked in a forbidden moment of passion stolen by a necessity to touch — or to simply be near each other.

Then, the song ended. We hung in our web for a moment longer, as it began to disappear into the air.

"I'm Konrad," I finally said, our eyes still locked.

"I'm Anastasia."

"It's wonderful to meet you," I said.

"And you," she said, taking a deep breath.

And that was it. Anastasia let out a shivering sigh, looked at her feet, and walked off the dance floor to our table. I watched her as she sat back down next to James. I stood there in the middle of the dance floor, unable to move, as the next song began and everyone started to dance.

"I hope you saved a dance for me," a familiar voice said behind me. I turned around to see Camilla standing before me.

"Why, of course. I was just looking for you," I lied.

"How flattering," she said.

I took her in my arms and we danced. She asked me where I had learned to dance so well, and I told her that my mother had taught me. She asked me many other questions and told me many things about herself, none of which I remembered. I hardly remembered dancing with her. All I could think about was Anastasia. The smell of her sweet breath still teased my nostrils. Her eyes were all I could see.

After Camilla and I danced and had sat back down at our table, I suddenly realized how rude I must have been to her. We had been dancing and she had been talking, but I was still in a daze of childish love from my dance with Anastasia and probably seemed uninterested. However, if that was in fact the attitude I had presented, it made her like me even more. As we sat next to each other at the table, Camilla flirted with me audaciously. She was constantly touching my arm, my leg, or my chest. Despite her boldness, she was in complete control of the situation. Any attempt I made to flirt back was ignored. If I touched her, she discreetly shied away. I was only trying to humor her flirtatiousness, for I was in no way interested in the same sense she seemed to be interested in me. She was a beautiful woman, and any man in his right mind would die for one night with her, but I was not in my right mind at the time. My mind was on another woman and an innocent, yet forbidden, love affair, and that is never a right mind. I looked across the table at Anastasia occasionally. Once or twice, I caught her looking at me through my peripheral vision.

"I think I've had my fill of this place," Charles announced as he stood up.

"It *has* been a long night," Miriam agreed.

"A long night?" Charles asked in confusion. "My dear, the night has only just begun. Shall we move this party elsewhere?"

"You are all welcome to come to my humble home," a man named Nathan suggested.

"That sounds wonderful," Anastasia agreed as she stood up.

"Good! Everyone is coming then?" Charles asked the group.

Everyone at the table was excited to go to Nathan's house. We all quickly finished our drinks, and as everyone else began to head for the door, Charles picked up a bottle of whiskey and a bottle of champagne from the table.

"Grab those two bottles of wine, would you, Konrad?" Charles asked with a wink.

I grabbed the bottles of wine and followed Charles outside, where everyone from our table was waiting. We began walking through the French Quarter, which was full of drunk people laughing, yelling, kissing, and having a good time. The Quarter was even more lively at night than during the day. I looked at my father's pocket watch. It was half past two.

"Do they always party this late?" I asked Raul.

"Until the wee hours of the morning, my friend. This is when the real fun begins."

XIV

WE SAT IN THE enormous living room of Nathan's mansion on the river, which was anything but humble. The walls were decorated with paintings, the curtains were made of the finest cloth, and elaborate candlesticks were abundant. Sculptures were placed randomly, yet thoughtfully, around the rooms, and glimmering chandeliers hung from the ceilings.

Our numbers had more than doubled on the way to Nathan's mansion, as we met people in the streets. Everyone was gathered around the fireplace, some drinking from glasses, and some drinking straight from the bottle. The candles as well as the fire dimly lit the room and gave it sort of an eerie feel, but somehow that made it even more beautiful. Some people sat in chairs and on the couch, while the rest sat on pillows on the floor or just lay on the Persian rug in front of the fireplace. All were bellowing with drunken laughter, including myself. I was sitting on the floor with my back resting against Miriam's legs, while she sat on the couch with Charles and Anastasia. I didn't know where James had gone, but I didn't really care. Miriam and Anastasia had been talking together ever since we had arrived at the house, and they seemed to be hitting it off well. They were constantly laughing at one another. Anastasia's laugh was a sweet, happy tune from Heaven's harp. It was the "Hallelujah" angels sing.

I spoke mostly with Charles, Jeffery, Santoro, Lavoie, and, of course, Camilla, who sat so close to me on the floor that she was practically in my lap. I hoped I was not giving Anastasia the wrong impression, but I suppose by the way Camilla and I were sitting that it could only look one way.

Santoro was lying on his back on the floor with his head resting in the lap of a beautiful woman who was feeding him grapes as they laughed hysterically. The woman then held a bottle about a foot above Santoro's head and poured the wine into his mouth. Some of it splashed on his lips and all over his face. Everyone laughed.

On the other couch, four of the women who had been at our table at the hotel squeezed together, fitting snugly between the arms. Raul stood behind them, leaning on the back of the couch, with his face close to theirs, as he seemed to be telling an entertaining story. The four women were hanging on his every word and laughing very often.

In one of the chairs, a couple was kissing quite passionately, while the man sat in the chair and the woman reclined across his lap. Another couple had gone off to another room, and I could only imagine what they were doing. I had been to a party like this in Paris. I had always admired and enjoyed the freedom and open-mindedness of the Parisians, but there were certain things that were a little too free for my taste.

Camilla excused herself from me to get us a drink. I watched her as she walked over to Nathan who was leaning against the fireplace. He was talking with James who had returned out of nowhere. I couldn't hear what she said to him. Then the two of them walked out of the room to return a few minutes later with a pitcher of water, a tray of glasses, and an all too familiar green bottle.

"I think it's about time for a proper drink, wouldn't you all say?" Nathan asked the group. Everyone cheered excitedly. The couple who had snuck off to the other room returned in a daze of drunken lust. Their hair was messy and their clothes a bit ruffled.

Nathan poured the green concoction into the glasses and then added a splash of water to each. The glasses were passed around. Camilla walked over to me carrying two glasses filled with the milky, green liquor. She handed me one and sat down next to me on the floor. There was no toast. Everyone just started drinking as soon as they got their glass.

"Have you ever had absinthe before?" Camilla asked me as she took a sip, and I nodded. "Ah, good! So you know its powers. You know it's a love potion," she said, as she touched her glass to mine.

"Something like that," I replied.

She took another sip, while I put the glass to my lips and tilted it, but I did not drink the absinthe. That was how it had started in Paris that summer a few years earlier. It was my first time trying absinthe and one of the worst experiences of my life. I'd had a full glass at a party, which had started out much like this one. When things started to get a little too free for my taste, I left while I was still coherent. I began walking the streets of Paris in a drunken stupor. I did not hallucinate as many people claimed they had when drinking absinthe. However, everything around me seemed all too real. Everything was so vivid and clear that it felt like a dream. I would be laughing like a child for a moment, and then all of a sudden something, a building, a dog, or a carriage would strike me the wrong way and I would become as paranoid as a man who had just committed murder. After about an hour of wandering around, I lost consciousness. I don't know how long I was unconscious, but I do know that it was for quite a bit of time, for when I became coherent again, my legs felt as if they had needles stuck in them. I was still quite drunk and far from any place recognizable, and I knew I must have been wandering for a very long time. I was no longer walking the glamorous streets of Paris but was somewhere on the outskirts of the city by the river and in a poor neighborhood that reeked of decay and filth. There were drunkards passed out in the alleys and on the streets with rats crawling all over them. The drunkards who were still awake and roaming around as was I were crude and yelling obscenities at me. I was stalked by a man whom I still believe was a serial murderer waiting for me to go into a dark alley. There were prostitutes on every corner begging for my business. None of them had a full set of teeth and looked as if they were crawling with disease. It took me three hours before I was sober enough to find my way home. After that night, I swore to never drink absinthe again.

Camilla finished her glass quite quickly. Raul had also finished his glass and was becoming quite friendly with two of the women on the couch. I looked behind me to see if Miriam was drinking hers. She was halfway done with it, and I noticed that Anastasia was not drinking absinthe, only wine. That pleased me. It led me to believe that she was innocent.

The minutes passed and the absinthe was consumed. People were dancing alone and together. Everyone was laughing for the sake of laughing when nothing was being said. Conversations lost substance. Everyone was becoming more affectionate toward one another. What had started out as a very enjoyable gathering of friends in a beautiful mansion had turned into something quite boring to me.

"I want to dance," Camilla said, looking at me with glassy eyes. "Do you want to dance with me? You're such a great dancer."

"You go ahead," I told her. "I'll come dance with you in a little bit."

Camilla stood up and walked over to the middle of the room where people were dancing in a very sensual manner. The women were moving their bodies like belly dancers. I shifted into a more comfortable position and looked back at Miriam. She looked as if she was on the verge of falling asleep. Then I noticed that Anastasia was no longer sitting on the couch with her. I stood up and looked around the room for her, but she was nowhere to be found.

Leaving Miriam in the care of Charles, I began to roam the house in search of Anastasia. I didn't see her anywhere. As I came to the end of a long hallway, I heard the laughter of a group of people coming from behind a closed door. I opened the door to a smoke-filled room where a dozen men and women were passing around a long pipe. James was among them. It didn't take me long to see that they were smoking opium. They were all in a sleepy, euphoric daze. James was sitting on a couch with a woman lying across his lap. I looked around and did not see Anastasia in the room. Without saying anything, I closed the door and walked back to the living room. Not much had changed. Miriam and Charles were still sitting on the couch, looking quite innocent compared to all that was going on around them. I decided to go outside to see if Anastasia had gone out for some air. I saw a silhouette standing at the end of the porch staring off at the full moon. I knew it was Anastasia, and I began walking toward her. She did not hear my footsteps until I was only a few feet away. She turned around quickly; I had startled her a bit.

"I'm sorry," I apologized.

"It's all right. Did you need to get out of there as badly as I?"

"I was looking for you," I said, rather honestly. I couldn't help it. She looked absolutely radiant in the moonlight. The blue glow against her skin was so soothing that even the most chronic of liars would tell her his deepest secrets. She looked at me with a slight smile as she seemed to be summing me up.

"We danced together earlier, didn't we?" she asked. She was playing with me. Certainly she had not forgotten those precious moments that had felt like an eternity.

"Yes, I believe we did."

"You're not drunk like the rest of them, are you?"

"No. I had absinthe once and promised myself never again," I said.

"That's good. My fiancé loves to drink."

"That's strange. He seems like such a stiff fellow."

"That's probably because he hadn't had a drink in a while."

She seemed a little upset. We stood there for a moment, staring off at the river in silence.

"Why are you marrying him?" I finally asked.

"Excuse me?" She looked at me in surprise.

"If you don't mind my asking. It's just that he... well... he's just so stodgy. He never smiles. And you say he's a drunk—"

"I never said he was a drunk," she interrupted.

"He just doesn't seem right for you," I continued.

"You don't know me."

"You can learn a lot about someone when you dance with them," I argued.

"And what did you learn about me?"

"I learned that you long to be touched, by the way you trembled when I placed my hand on your back."

"It was your imagination," she said, looking away from me.

"I know you're not in love with him. I could tell by the way you looked into my eyes. No woman in love would look into another man's eyes the way you looked into mine."

She chuckled. "And I suppose your imagination told you that I'm in love with you?"

"No — not yet, anyway."

"You must be drunk. No man would be so forward with a woman who is engaged to be married. I don't want to talk about it anymore. I see that you have a weakness for sopranos," she said, changing the subject.

I laughed. "Not at all!"

"You've been all over each other all night."

"I didn't know you were paying attention," I said with a smirk. Anastasia ignored the comment. "Well, I'm afraid it is only one-sided. I was only trying to humor her to not seem rude."

"You certainly go out of your way to be polite."

"Well, I am a gentleman," I said.

"I'm sure you are. So, if sopranos aren't your weakness, then what is?"

"What do you mean?"

"All men have a weakness when it comes to women. If a beautiful opera star like her isn't your weakness, then what is?"

I thought about it for a moment. "Subtleties," I finally said.

"Subtleties?"

"Yes. The way a woman smiles when a certain mood strikes her, the way she tilts her head when she laughs, the way the right side of her mouth goes up higher than the left when she smirks, the way she scrunches her nose when someone makes a joke at her expense, and the shape of the curve where her neck and collar meet."

"The curve?" she asked in confusion.

"Yes, here." Slowly, I raised my hand to her neck. I gently slid my index finger down the side of her neck, along the curve and along her collarbone to her shoulder, all the while looking into her eyes. Goosebumps formed on her skin, and she shivered as I touched her. I softly grasped her shoulder and stepped closer to her, while pulling her toward me until our bodies were touching. She looked into my eyes as I began to run my finger along her collarbone and up her neck. I ran my thumb across her cheek and put my other hand on her waist. She didn't say a word or give me a look of protest. She stared into my eyes longingly. I slowly leaned in. She closed her eyes, so I closed mine. Finally, my lips touched hers, and we kissed under the light of a full moon. She smelled of lilac. Her lips tasted like the sweetest nectar from the brightest rose. Her lips were as soft as clouds, and I felt as if I was evaporating into them. She trembled in my arms. What a kiss!

Slowly, she began to pull away from me. She hung on my lips for a moment longer, and then it was over. She stared into my eyes, but her gaze was broken by the sound of the door opening. She stepped away from me as Charles walked onto the porch.

"Ah, Konrad! There you are! I think Miriam is ready to go," he informed me.

I still couldn't take my eyes off of Anastasia. "All right; let's go."

"I'll get Miriam," Charles said, and he went back inside.

"I should go back in," Anastasia said, suddenly feeling guilty. She started to walk away.

"Wait," I said, grabbing her arm. "We'll walk you home."

"That's very kind of you, but I'll go home with my fiancé," she said.

I let her go. She got to the door just as Charles was walking out with Miriam who could barely walk.

"Goodnight, Anastasia," Charles said.

"Goodnight," Anastasia said quickly, as she walked past him and into the house.

"Ga night, Ana," Miriam said drunkenly.

"You ready, Konrad?" Charles asked.

"Sure," I said, as I walked over to them. "Where is Raul?"

"I think he'll be staying here for the night," Charles answered.

"There's Kon!" Miriam said. "Lemme hold your arm, Kon. I'm having trouble walking."

Charles and I held Miriam up and began walking her back to the French Quarter. By the time we got to Miriam's apartment, the sun was rising. We put Miriam to bed, and I thanked Charles for helping me get her home safely. He was a good man. He began walking home and I ran to my apartment. I quickly changed my clothes for work and rushed downstairs to Leon's, arriving right on time. My body was weak and exhausted, but I had never felt better. Anastasia's kiss sustained me all day long.

XV

FOR THE NEXT FEW weeks, I worked constantly from sunrise to late into the night. I spent my days doing my typical duties. At night I was the bartender's assistant — so to speak. I wiped down the bar every so often, collected glasses and washed them, and even served drinks when it got real busy. Raul was there almost every night to poke fun at me and give me a hard time while he had a few drinks.

I had started cooking my own food for my lunch break. I experimented with different recipes, but nothing ever turned out well. I always took my meals out back to eat so no one could see my reaction when I tasted it. I would often take just one bite, cringe in disgust, and spit it out. The remainder usually went to feed the dog who I had named 'Scrappy'.

In those few weeks, I had not seen Anastasia since the night at Nathan's mansion when we had kissed. I was always looking for her though. Every time the door to Leon's opened, I checked to see if it was her. I would wander around the French Quarter to look for her walking the streets, dining in the restaurants, or browsing the shops. I didn't know what I would say if I did see her or if she even wanted to see me, but every day I longed for her. I smelled her lilac scent everywhere, even when my nostrils were being stung by the intense aromas of Emilio's cooking in the kitchen of Leon's. I tasted her every time I licked my lips. She haunted my every thought and sense, and I could not escape her. Was she experiencing the same? I doubted it, but I hoped. How could I feel this way so strongly and she not? No, she had to feel the same way.

One night after work, I went over to visit Miriam whom I had not seen in a few days. I found out that she had been spending a fair amount of time with Charles. He had been showing her around the city and taking her to nice dinners.

"Well, it sounds as if love is blossoming," I commented.

"I don't know about that," Miriam dismissed. "We will see. He did kiss me the other night."

"Oh? And how was it?"

"It was nice. It felt right. It was very romantic. Charles is a very confident man, but I could tell he was nervous."

"Well, I'm happy for you, Miriam. I really am."

"Thank you. But don't be too happy for me. Who knows what will come of it?"

"Marriage?" I teased.

"Stop it! You know I never want to get married. What a useless institution."

"Have you seen Anastasia lately?" I had wanted to ease into the question, but I just blurted it out without thinking.

Miriam looked at me strangely. "Yes, I've seen her quite a few times actually. We have lunch together a couple of times a week. Sometimes we go shopping or to a salon. Why do you ask?"

"No reason," I lied. "Has she mentioned me?" I was not being as subtle as I had meant to be.

"Konrad, you haven't fallen for her, have you?" Miriam asked, still looking at me strangely. "Have you been thinking of her since that night at the opera? After that one dance? Don't be silly, Konrad. That was a month ago!"

"Who's being silly? I just asked a question."

"Well, she hasn't mentioned you. Well, not in the sense I believe you mean."

"In what sense then?" I asked.

"Just friendly conversation, Konrad. I can't very well talk about how I came to be here in New Orleans without talking about you."

"So, you talked about me. She didn't ask?"

"Well, when I told her how we came here together, she asked

what you had been doing before and why you decided to come to New Orleans."

"That's it?" I asked.

"Yes, that's all I can recall. She's an engaged woman and quite happy."

"I don't think she's happy."

"Just forget about it," Miriam coldly advised me.

"Well, we kissed that night at Nathan's, you know. She didn't happen to mention that, did she?" I asked bitterly.

"No, she did not. Did you really kiss her, Konrad?"

"Yes, and she kissed me back, and quite passionately, I might add."

"Well, you shouldn't have done that. I dislike James as much as you do, and I don't know why Anastasia is with him. But she *is* with him, and if this is just some selfish infatuation with a pretty girl, you should leave it alone."

"Of course it's selfish, Miriam. Love is the most selfish thing in the world! Well, I should get going," I said and then stood up to leave. I walked over to Miriam to kiss her goodbye. Then a clever idea hit me. "Why don't you and Anastasia have lunch at Leon's sometime?"

"Konrad, I won't have any part in your scheme to steal Anastasia away from James."

"What scheme? I'm just saying that you should have lunch at Leon's."

"I know what you're saying, and you know what I'm saying."

I dropped to my knees at Miriam's feet and grabbed her hand. "Please! Just ask her to meet you there for lunch this week. All you have to do is show up a little late, and while she's waiting for you, I'll talk to her for a bit. I'll see if there's anything there, but if not, I'll leave it alone and never mention it again."

"I'm not going to lie to her or hide anything from her. I'm going to tell her that you work at Leon's. If she says she won't go, then you'll know she doesn't want to see you and you'll never mention it again."

"You have my word. But she'll come."

"Fine! Wednesday then, two o'clock," Miriam agreed.

I kissed her hand excitedly. "Thank you!"

"All right. Go on, now. I need my beauty sleep."

"You don't need it," I said, as I stood up and headed for the door.

"Thank you, but I already agreed to your scheme," Miriam said. "And please bathe before you come over here next time. The smell of that restaurant is negatively nauseating."

"You mean *positively* nauseating?" I corrected her as I opened the door.

"There's nothing positive about it," she replied.

I laughed as I walked out the door. "You're a strange woman," I said.

I shut the door and walked back home, full of excitement and hope. I knew Anastasia would come to Leon's. She had to. But if she didn't, I would be true to my word and leave her alone. But I knew she'd come. I couldn't possibly feel this way about her unless she was feeling the same way. She'd come.

* * *

I waited impatiently for Wednesday to arrive. When it finally did, I spent the entire morning at work an excited, nervous wreck. I shucked oysters, madly searching for a pearl. I don't know why I thought one pearl would impress Anastasia, but I felt an urge to give her one — or two, if I was lucky. I carried out my regular duties as needed, but my priority was finding a pearl. Martha got mad at me, since I was shucking far more oysters than what was being ordered, but I promised to pay for them. Whatever oysters didn't sell, I ended up eating or feeding to Scrappy. Between Scrappy and I, we probably ate close to four dozen oysters. By the time it neared two o'clock, I was feeling quite sick to my stomach. Scrappy seemed very happy, however.

I did finally find a pearl, and at that moment it seemed like the most beautiful jewel in the world. I kissed it thankfully and put in my pocket. I walked through the kitchen to the dinning room to see if Anastasia had arrived. I immediately saw her sitting alone at a table for two. I quickly backed out of sight, exhaled a deep breath, and licked my fingers to fix my hair. I took one more deep breath and walked out into the dinning room. Anastasia was reading the menu, so I could not rely on her noticing me as I pretended to casually walk past her.

As I walked by her table, I stopped and looked at her in confusion. It was quite pathetic.

"Anastasia? Is that you?" I asked.

She looked up at me and smiled a bit awkwardly. "Konrad! Miriam said you worked here."

"Yes. How are you? Are you here alone?"

"I'm fine. Miriam is meeting me here for lunch."

"May I?" I asked, gesturing to the chair.

"Well, like I said, Miriam is meeting me," Anastasia repeated.

"I'll just sit until she gets here," I said as I sat down. I cringed in confusion as I felt my leg. "What's that in my pocket?" I reached into my pocket and took out the pearl. "Oh, I almost forgot. I happened upon this pearl today when I was shucking oysters," I said.

"It's very pretty," Anastasia commented.

I smiled at her while admiring the pearl. "You should have it," I said, as I held it out to her.

"Oh, no..." Anastasia responded.

"Go on — take it — I insist. A pearl as beautiful as this deserves to be with someone as beautiful as you," I said.

"Please, don't."

"Come on. What am I going to do with it?"

"It's one pearl. What is anyone going to do with it?" she said.

I took my hand away and put the pearl back in my pocket. "You're right; it's silly."

There was an awkward silence. "Why don't you collect a few more and make me a necklace?" she suggested, probably feeling bad for declining my gift so rudely.

"Sure. When's your birthday?" I asked.

"July fourteenth — why?"

"Just so I know when I need to have gathered all the pearls."

"Now it won't be a surprise," Anastasia pointed out with a frown.

"You suggested the necklace, so it wouldn't be a surprise anyway," I returned.

"That's true. Now, why are you working here? Miriam told me you went to Oxford. I don't imagine that you went there to learn to shuck oysters."

"No, I studied physics and philosophy. I've just always wanted to learn how to cook, so I do all the dirty work here while I watch the chefs and try to learn as much as I can."

"A philosopher and a chef, an interesting combination." Anastasia picked up her menu, and as she browsed it she asked, "So, what do you recommend?"

"Emilio makes an phenomenal *Etouffee*," I suggested.

"Wonderful! I love *Etouffee*. Is the shrimp fresh?"

"Of course."

"Good! I'll take that."

"What time is Miriam supposed to meet you?" I asked.

"A few minutes ago."

"She's always late," I said.

"She never has been with me," Anastasia commented.

"Oh! Well, that's strange."

"Yes, indeed it is," she said with a thoughtful squint and a slight smirk as she looked at me.

"Do people ever call you Ana or Stasi?" I asked after a few moments of silence.

"Yes, some do. James calls me Ana. Why do you ask?"

"Anastasia is just such a beautiful name. It would be shame to shorten it."

"I agree. I've always loved my name, but I don't mind people shortening it if it's easier for them."

"It's not easier; people are just lazy. Where does your name come from?"

"From my great grandmother. My father wanted to name me after her," Anastasia said.

"Where is your father, if you don't mind my asking?"

"I don't mind," she said. "He and my mother live in Paris."

"Oh? So what brought you here?"

"My father. We moved here when I was sixteen. He's a shoemaker, you see, and my grandfather was already very successful in France, so he decided to try and expand the family business here. Two years later, my grandfather died, so my father and mother moved back to Paris to take over the business there. When James found out that we were leaving, he asked me to marry him, so I could stay. He bought me my own apartment, and my parents agreed to let me stay."

"I see. Do you remain close with your parents?" I asked.

"As close as one can be through letters."

"Will they come for the wedding?"

"They want to have the wedding in Paris. James wants to have it here."

"Where do you want to get married?"

"It doesn't matter to me," Anastasia said.

"Really? I don't believe that."

"Why not? It's the truth."

"All women have their weddings planned out when they're little girls," I said.

"Well, not me."

"Have you set a date for your wedding yet?" I asked.

"No, not yet. James is very busy. Once things slow down, we'll set the date."

I nodded and tried not to show too much emotion. "Your English is very good. When did you learn?"

"I started learning when I was a little girl. I was fluent long before I moved here, not that I really needed to be, since everyone here seems to speak French."

"I'm learning French. My uncle is teaching me," I said. "It's a beautiful language."

"I like Italian much more. I started learning it when I was a little girl as well as English, but I never stuck with it. Do you know any other languages?"

"My mother is German and my father is Spanish, and I learned both languages when I was very young. I learned Latin while I was at Oxford."

"Latin? That's a language you don't hear very much. Say something."

I thought for a moment. "*Ut mos ego aspicio vos iterum?*"

"And what does that mean?"

"When can I see you again?"

Anastasia smiled and shook her head. "I don't know."

I looked out the window and saw Miriam crossing the street. "When? Just for coffee or lunch — anything."

"I can't. It's not appropriate," Anastasia said.

"It's not appropriate to have friends? Don't be ridiculous."

Anastasia leaned forward. "I think we both know that we overstepped that boundary the night we met."

"Ah, so you remember?" I said with a proud smile. She looked away and smiled. "Coffee? For an hour, for a minute! Just let me see you again."

"Why?" Anastasia asked.

I sighed and thought for a moment. "Because there are things about you I don't know, and that upsets me."

She looked at me with interest as she thought about her answer. "Coffee tomorrow morning then."

"I can't tomorrow. Have to work. Friday?"

"Friday then. There's a cafe on *Rue Royal* near Orleans. It's by the Saint Louis Cathedral," Anastasia said, as Miriam walked into the restaurant.

"Eight?" I asked.

"Nine."

"I'll see you Friday at nine," I said, standing up as Miriam approached. "I'm sorry; I'm in your seat. How are you, darling." I kissed Miriam on the cheek.

"I'm just fine, thank you," Miriam said as she sat down. "I see you've kept my friend company for me since I was so horribly late. I'm sorry, Ana."

Anastasia and I shared a look at Miriam's shortening of her name. "It's quite all right, dear. Konrad and I had a nice talk."

"Well, it seems we're all happy then," Miriam said, looking at me with a smile.

"I'll let you two ladies dine. Anastasia, it was wonderful seeing you again." I took her hand in mine and kissed it softly.

"Until we meet again," Anastasia said.

I winked at Anastasia and nodded to Miriam. "Ladies."

I turned and walked back to the kitchen, letting out a great sigh of relief. I had not realized how tense I had been. I walked out back for a deep breath of fresh air. Scrappy was sleeping in front of the door and quickly jumped to his feet when I walked out. I breathed out all the tension I had let build up inside of me. I had felt fine talking with her. After the first few awkward moments of dialogue, I began to feel very relaxed. I breathed out another deep breath and smiled excitedly. I knew she would come.

XVI

FRIDAY MORNING WOULD NOT come fast enough. Work on Thursday had been slow, which gave me too much time to reminisce about my conversation with Anastasia the day before and too much time to grow anxious for Friday. I tried to keep myself as busy as possible, but there just wasn't enough to do to keep my mind off of her. Emilio taught me how to make risotto, which I found to be an entertaining dish to make. Toward the end of the preparation of the dish, in order to get the rice to the right creamy consistency, the chef quickly pushes the bowl out and up, causing the rice to fly almost two feet into the air and then land nicely back in the bowl. The first couple of times I tried this, I could not even make the rice fly out of the bowl. When I finally got the rice to jump into the air, it did not go straight up. Instead, it came right back onto me, splashing onto my face and shirt.

After I cleaned up, I started making my dinner. Emilio watched me but did not help. I finished cooking my meal and went out back as usual to take a bite and feed the rest to Scrappy. However, it actually turned out to be edible. Scrappy watched me eat with confused, sad, puppy-dog eyes. I could have eaten the whole thing, but I felt bad for the dog and gave him the last half of my meal.

The late-evening crowd came in to get their night started with a few cocktails. It was quite busy, so I helped out behind the bar. Three young men about my age strolled into Leon's full of laughter as they headed to the bar. They had been coming in every night for about a week, but I had not seen them before that. I had not met them properly, but they seemed like nice enough fellows. They were a bit rough around the edges and could get rowdy from time to time, but it was all in good fun. They sat down at the bar, so I asked them what I could get them. They asked for a bottle of whiskey and three glasses. I uncorked a bottle and poured them their first glass.

"Appreciate it, partner," the tall, muscular one with fine, light-blond hair said. His strong, bulky figure was intimidating, but his face was kind and welcoming. It had a nice oval shape and came down to a pointed chin. His mouth was small, and his cheeks looked as if they had never lost their baby fat. "I've seen you around here a lot, but we haven't been properly introduced. I'm Will Mason. Everyone just calls me Mason, though."

"I'm Konrad Quintero de Leon," I said, while shaking hands with Mason.

"Damn! That's quite a name. You don't look Mexican," Mason observed.

"I'm Spanish and German."

"My mother's German," Mason informed me. "These two knuckleheads are Kyle Ripley and Cole Jackson." I shook their hands, and they said they were pleased to meet me.

"You don't sound like you're from around here," Cole said. "You from up North?"

"New York City," I replied.

"That's up North alright! Damn, partner! What brings a Yankee like you to New Orleans?" Mason asked.

"Curiosity, I suppose," I admitted. "Boredom — adventure."

"Well, I will certainly drink to that," Mason said. "Pour yourself a drink, Konrad." I grabbed a glass and filled it from their bottle.

We raised our glasses to one another and drank down our whiskey in one gulp. Mason refilled their glasses and then looked at me to see if I wanted a refill. It was not busy, so I shrugged and held out my glass as he filled it.

"Now, I know New Orleans must seem like a big adventure to a Yankee like yourself, but I'll tell you where the real adventure is," Mason said. "It's the West, my friend, the frontier. We just came back from a five-month expedition not four months ago. You've heard of John Fremont?"

"John Charles Fremont? The explorer?" I asked.

"Well, there's no other!" Mason answered.

"I read a newspaper article about him. I believe the subheading was, 'A Report on an Exploration of the Country Lying between the Missouri River and the Rocky Mountains on the Line of the Kansas and Great Platte Rivers'."

"Yeah, something like that." Mason lit a cigar. "I'll tell you what, partner; that was one hell of an adventure. You're just riding along, seeing all these things for the first time. You see one thing, and you think it's the most beautiful place in the world. You go another hundred miles further, and you see something even more beautiful. You ever seen the Rocky Mountains?"

"I've only seen paintings," I admitted sadly.

"Leonardo da Vinci couldn't do the Rockies justice. You have to see them, Konrad," Mason insisted. "On our way back from the South Pass, we climbed to the highest peak in the whole range and Fremont planted an American flag at the summit. You're on top of the world up there. You can damn near see the Pacific Ocean!"

"The Pacific Ocean, huh?" I asked, very interested. "Have you ever seen it?"

"Sure have. I swam in it. Cleanest, clearest, freshest ocean in the world — warm, too."

"I'd like to see it one day," I confided.

"Every man should see it at least once," Mason said in a daze, as he recalled the image to his mind's eye. "We saw grizzly bears in the mountains. Huge, angry monsters they are. I killed one myself with my rifle. Shot him right through the eye. I made a coat out of his fur. Made this necklace with one of his claws." Mason showed me the claw hanging from a leather strap tied around his neck. "The meat wasn't anything to write home about, but I'll tell you what meat *is* delicious — buffalo. You ever seen a buffalo, Konrad?"

"No," I said.

"Best meat in the world. When we were crossing the plains, we saw herds of them. Thousands! So many you couldn't even see the end of them. They darkened the plains for miles."

"That sounds amazing," I said.

"You should come with us next time," Mason invited. "If it's adventure you want, you're not going to find it here. You've got to get out of the city and onto the frontier."

"When are you going back out?" I asked.

"Don't know," Mason replied. "There's word going around that John Fremont is leading another expedition with Kit Carson as scout again. I hear that this time they want him to map the area from the South Pass to the Columbia River. You'd get to see the Pacific Ocean."

"That would be fantastic. When will you go?" I asked.

"It's just rumors right now. I'll let you know when I hear more, partner," Mason promised.

My imagination and excitement ran wild, as I pictured the great expedition across the frontier. For the first time that day, Anastasia was not on my mind.

* * *

On Friday morning, I walked to the café where Anastasia had asked me to meet her. I arrived nearly an hour early to give myself a chance to calm my nerves. I sat outside at a table in front of the café and drank two cups of coffee and had a cigar while I read the first volume of *Encyclopedie nouvelle*, which I had found on Raul's bookshelf. From where I sat, I could see the Saint Louis Cathedral and Jackson Square. It was an exceptionally nice day in March. The temperature was moderate, and the humidity was comfortable.

By the time I saw Anastasia walking up the street toward me, I was feeling quite relaxed and in the mood for a nice conversation with a beautiful woman. I put out my cigar and finished my second cup of coffee. I stood up and greeted her with a kiss on each cheek, and then we sat down and I signaled to the waitress for two more cups of coffee.

"That's a heavy bit of reading you're doing," Anastasia commented.

"I happened upon it while looking over my uncle's bookshelf," I said. "Have you read it?"

She shook her head. "What is it about?"

"Socialism," I said with a smile.

"I see. Are you a socialist?" Anastasia asked.

"I don't believe so. It's an interesting idea, but merely a stepping stone to something greater. But I don't believe it would work in modern times," I said, as the waitress brought our coffee.

"What's this 'something greater'?"

"*Utopia.* Have you ever read it? It's by Thomas More."

"Yes, I have. And I believe it's called 'Communism'," Anastasia said with a smirk.

"Well, however you wish to call it," I said, returning her smirk, "I'm actually reading it because I met the founder."

"You met Pierre Leroux?" Anastasia asked.

"I did, the summer I lived in Paris. I met him at Café Procope. I had just read his treatise, *De l'humanité*, and I overheard him speaking about it with a couple of other men who seemed to be philosophers as well, though not known, as I suppose is the case with many philosophers. I joined in the conversation and had a fruitful argument with *monsieur* Leroux," I explained.

"That must have been an interesting experience," Anastasia said. "I saw Alfred de Musset at Café Procope once."

"Really? Did you have the pleasure of speaking with him?" I asked.

"Unfortunately not."

"I'm surprised he did not come to your table and write you

a poem. A woman like you could inspire great poetic verse," I said.

"Well, he did not. However, my grandfather met Voltaire at Café Procope. He met Thomas Jefferson there as well. My father was there, but he was too young to remember."

I raised my eyebrows in surprise and interest. "How incredible! What did he talk to them about?"

"Well, he talked to Voltaire about religion and why he put chocolate in his coffee."

"Why did he put chocolate in his coffee?" I asked.

"To cure hangovers," Anastasia said with a confused smile.

"Interesting — and Jefferson?"

"I'm not sure what he talked to Jefferson about, but I do know he made a pair of shoes just for him."

I laughed excitedly. "Your grandfather made shoes for President Thomas Jefferson! That's amazing!"

Anastasia laughed with me. "Isn't that something?"

"Your grandfather sounds like he was a very interesting man," I said.

"He was. I wish you could have met him. You would have gotten along wonderfully."

"I'm sure we would have. After all, I get along quite well with you."

"We do get along well, don't we?" Anastasia agreed.

We had a few more cups of coffee as we conversed for a good hour and a half. We talked about her life in Paris and New Orleans. I asked her what she wanted to do in the future, and she said she would like to see New York City and Philadelphia. She also expressed a great desire to see Havana, Cuba, which I found interesting. She said she had heard it was a beautiful city with the most gorgeous beaches and waters of the brightest blue. When she told me this, she seemed to be in a dreamy daze, but there was a hint of sadness in her eyes, as if she did not believe it would ever happen.

I told her about meeting William Mason and the possibility of a westward expedition with John Fremont and Kit Carson. She thought it sounded like a "lovely adventure". She was much more interested in me and my past and future than she had been in our last conversation. She asked me about my family and my dreams. Our meeting went very well and seemed very fluent and comfortable. She smiled much more this time. It was nice.

When she said she had to be going, I told her that I would like to see her again and asked if that would be all right. She said she would love to see me again, so we decided to meet at the same place Monday morning. I walked her home to her apartment in the French Quarter. It was not far from the café. I kissed her goodbye on the cheek, and she kissed me on the cheek back.

I felt wonderful as I was walking home. Then, I suddenly began to feel guilty. It did not feel as if there was anything more than friendship blooming between Anastasia and I, for the time being, although I knew very well that I had loved her from the moment I first saw her. We were just two people getting to know each other, but my intentions were not so innocent. Though I was sure Anastasia would make a very good friend, friendship was not what I wanted from her. She was an engaged woman, but that was to an awful man who did not love her, show interest in her, and was most likely unfaithful to her. James did not know what he had. Therefore, was what I was doing really immoral? I would be doing her a favor, as well as a favor to her fiancé. But does that justify my attempts to break a loveless engagement? I had no answer to my questions. I must listen to my heart, as I had in New York when it told me to go to New Orleans. That was my only answer. It was my answer to everything.

XVII

ON MONDAY, I MET Anastasia at the same café and at the same time as before. I did not arrive early to calm my nerves this time, for I felt quite comfortable and relaxed. When I arrived, she was already sitting at the same table outside at which we had sat during our last meeting. A cup of coffee was already waiting for me. We talked for about an hour, this time getting to know the little things about one another. I found out that her favorite scent was lilac, which was the smell of her skin. Her favorite color was emerald green, which was the color of her eyes. Her favorite song was Mozart's *Madamina, il catalogo e questo* from his opera, *Don Giovanni*, which was also her favorite opera. Her favorite food was roasted duck. Her favorite beverage was *blanc de noirs* champagne. Her favorite book was *Notre-Dame de Paris* by Victor Hugo. I asked her if she had read *Don Quixote,* and she said she had not. I told her it was my favorite book and that I would loan her my copy. After three cups of coffee, I paid our tab and walked her home.

"Would you like to come in for a moment," she asked me as we stood at her door. "There's something I want to show you."

"Of course," I said with surprise. "I would love to."

She opened the door, and we walked inside. It was a nice, cozy place. It was not large, but quite humble. There was only the one bedroom and the living room, but it all came to life with the finest décor. It smelled of lilac and jasmine from the scented candles placed carefully throughout the apartment. The lace drapes were emerald green, and all of the furniture matched them in the most subtle way.

"What is it you wanted to show me?" I asked.

"Did your uncle ever tell you that he painted me once?" Anastasia asked.

"He has told me, actually. I would love to see it."

"It's right up there," she said.

She pointed to a painting hanging on the wall above the fireplace. My jaw dropped slightly as I gazed upon her nude portrait. She was watching my reaction with a faint smile on her face. I walked over to the fireplace without saying a word. I did not take my eyes off the painting. It was almost a recreation of Francisco de Goya's, *The Nude Maja*. Lying on a white bed with pillows embroidered with emerald green and a deep lilac violet, the pose was almost the same as the *Maja*, except that in Anastasia's portrait her head was on the left side of the canvas rather than on the right, and instead of both hands being behind her head, only her left was, looking as if she was running her fingers through her hair. Her right arm lay at her side with her hand resting naturally just above her hip. Her legs were together and slightly bent, leaning toward the viewer. Unlike *The Nude Maja*, her hair was up to expose her beautiful neck and shoulders. The strokes used for the curves of her womanly figure were subtle, for she was more petite than the *Maja*. Her expression was that of playful seduction as opposed to the mysterious seduction of the *Maja*. The color of the background was brighter, therefore making the portrait seem more innocent and more inviting than Goya's. It was truly a masterpiece, and it captured her beauty about as well as I imagined any painter could. It would be impossible to capture the perfection of beauty in a recreation of the masterpiece God had made in Anastasia.

"It's beautiful," I finally said, not taking my eyes off the painting.

"Do you think it's a good likeness of me?" she asked.

"Well, I can only speak of the shoulders and up since I have not seen the rest of… you. But, yes, Raul captured your beauty as well as one could in a painting, especially your eyes and bone structure. It's truly magnificent. I love it."

"Yes, I do too. I think it's quite lovely and tasteful. Raul is a fantastic artist. I really wish he would sell his work or at least show it. I had to beg him to paint my portrait. I offered him money, but he would not take it. I finally convinced him by promising that I would not show it to anyone. Don't tell him I hung it above my fireplace. Don't even tell him I showed it to you."

"I won't. I'm glad you showed it to me. I feel honored to have had the pleasure of seeing it. It's a work of art captured in a work of art."

Anastasia smiled at me. "Thank you. I'm glad you like it."

I could see that she was going to invite me to stay, so I told her I should be going, and she walked me to the door. I opened the door and stepped outside.

"Will you be attending the ball tomorrow night?" Anastasia asked.

"Which ball is that?" I asked.

"The Mardi Gras Ball at the Orleans Ballroom, of course," she explained.

"I haven't heard about it. It sounds like fun."

"It will be. It's a masquerade, so it will be an adventure trying to find each other," she said with an excited smile.

"I'm sure it won't be too hard to find you," I said. "You'll be standing next to the man too grumpy and smug to wear a mask."

"Be nice, Konrad," Anastasia said, smiling playfully. "Besides, James won't be there. He hates the Mardi Gras."

"Really? I'm so surprised," I said, sarcastically.

"Stop it! So, you'll be there?"

"I will," I promised.

"Good. I hope we find each other. Have a good day!"

"You, too, darling," I said, and I kissed her cheeks.

I went back to my apartment and asked Raul where I could find a costume for the ball. He told me not to worry and said he had a costume for me. When I asked to see it, he said that I had to wait until tomorrow.

* * *

On Fat Tuesday, I started work early in the morning as usual. It was busy all day long, and everyone was in a festive mood. Many people started to celebrate early by having morning cocktails. There were many orders for oysters, and I found three more pearls. It was a particularly good day.

At dark, the festivities began with hundreds of people celebrating in the streets, dressed in beautiful, unusual, and disturbing attire. There were more varieties of masks than I could count. The most common costume and mask combination I saw was that of a jester with the bright, multi-colored suit, pointy-toed shoes, a strange mask, and cap 'n' bells headwear.

We closed Leon's down at nine, for it was not a popular destination for this sort of celebration. When I finished my closing duties, I quickly ran upstairs to my apartment, where Raul, Miriam, and Charles were already dressed for the ball and having drinks. They seemed a little drunk already. They greeted me with great excitement and told me to hurry and get ready. Raul had already drawn me a bath and had hung my costume on the door. I bathed quickly and got dressed. I wore a long, gold coat with a dark-green trim, over a white, oversized blouse. My velvet trousers were the same green as the trim on my coat and only reached to my knees. Underneath the trousers I wore white stockings. My shoes were black with big gold buckles. I liked the audacious outfit. I combed my hair and walked into the living room, where Raul was pouring another round of drinks for the four of us.

"That is a fantastic costume!" Charles said with a big laugh.

"You look quite handsome," Miriam complimented.

"Why, thank you," I said with pompous sarcasm, as I grasped the lapels of my coat. "You look quite lovely as well, my dear."

Miriam was wearing a very elaborate yet traditional gown of the style of Seventeenth Century dress. Her mask was in her lap.

It was silver with a flowery design and was sparkling with crystals and pearls. Long, white feathers came from the top and bent out to the sides with two feathers sticking straight up. Charles was dressed like a Spanish bullfighter. Raul's costume seemed surprisingly simple in comparison to his eccentric taste. He was wearing a black suit with a tricorne hat.

"Where's your costume, Raul?" I asked.

"I haven't put it all on yet," he replied. "You do look dashing in my old clothes. You wear them well. I can't believe I used to be your size. I wore that at Mardi Gras in Nice, France, thirty years ago! Damn! I'm old!"

"No, you're in your prime," I said. "Don't I need a mask?"

"Ah! Yes!" Raul said, taking a drink while handing me mine. I took a sip of the brandy while Raul ran into his room. He came back a moment later with my mask in hand. "Here you are. Try it on."

I took the mask in my hands and looked it over. It was a combination of green, gold, and black to match the rest of my outfit. The eyeholes were narrow and oval and came to a sharp point on the outsides, which curved up slightly. It covered from the top of the forehead to three-quarters of the way down the bridge of the nose. It curved down just over the cheekbones. On either side, two curving points came down to the jaw line and went inwards an inch and a half before curving upwards and around. I put the mask on, and it fit snugly against my face.

Raul laughed excitedly. "It looks great on you! Just one more thing." He proceeded to mess up my nicely combed hair. He let my hair fall over the mask and my ears, sticking up sporadically in places. He then untied the top of my blouse so that the neck was open down to the middle of my chest. "There! You're all set." He finished his drink and set the glass on the table. "All right! Finish your drinks, and let's go to the ball!"

Raul went back into his room, as Miriam, Charles, and I quickly finished our drinks. When Raul came out of his room, he was wearing a black cape with red trim that went all the way around his body and came together in the front. His mask was black on one side and red on the other, with contradicting patterns, and went from under his tricorne to the tip of his nose and over his cheekbones. The long nose of his mask extended out about four inches and curved down slightly. He carried a black cane with a gold handle. He looked sinister, but playful.

Miriam and Charles stood up and put on their masks. Charles' mask was a small, black, leather strip that only covered his eyes and half his nose. We walked out the door and into the crowded streets, quickly blending into the masqueraders. We slowly made our way through the crowd of drunken, dancing, laughing people toward the Orleans Ballroom. It took us nearly an hour before we finally arrived at the ball. There were probably a hundred people standing outside the doors of the Orleans Ballroom waiting to be let inside. The Ballroom was already overcrowded, and the doormen were not letting anyone else inside. Fortunately, Charles was able to use his name and a few coins to get the doorman to let us in. I immediately began searching for Anastasia. As I looked over all of the women in their similar flamboyant gowns and similar flamboyant masks, I realized what a difficult task finding Anastasia would be.

We walked down the long, wide hallway where many people were mingling with their cocktails in hand. Everyone seemed much more relaxed wearing masks over their faces. Nobody was recognizable; therefore, they could be whomever they wanted to be. Nobody had to be shy or afraid. The aristocratic stiffness, which usually accompanies social gatherings of the wealthy upper class was non-existent tonight. The atmosphere was relaxed, and the people's attitudes were inviting. Complete strangers conversed comfortably, and old friends met for the first time without knowing it. It was quite refreshing, but, on the other hand, it was sad that it took a mask to show one's true self. If only people could be this way without the shelter of illusion.

We walked into the main ballroom where all the masqueraders were dancing to the joyful music of a chamber orchestra. They were playing Mozart's *Quartet, K.370*, and everyone was dancing in synchrony. I looked around for Anastasia, but it seemed a hopeless task. There were probably a thousand people in the ballroom alone, not to mention in the other rooms. Charles and Miriam went to dance, and Raul went to the bar for a drink. I began walking around the ballroom to get a look at the people mingling around the dance floor. After two laps around the ballroom and two long quartets, I'd had no luck. A new song began. It was a quick, upbeat number. The dancers would waltz with one partner for a few moments and then switch partners. This would be a good opportunity for me to get a look at many of the women on the dance floor. I rushed into the dance and was quickly grabbed by a lively, old woman with a wonderful smile on her face. I gave my full attention to each woman I danced with as not to be rude, but in-between partners, I looked at as many women as I could. After six partners, I had not seen a woman who even resembled Anastasia in the slightest. How would I ever find her?

My next partner was a very drunk, young woman who could barely stand on her own two feet. I practically had to hold her up as we danced. When we spun, she nearly fell out of my arms. She leaned back, looking up at the ceiling with her arms out like wings as if she thought she was flying. She was laughing hysterically. I flung her into the arms of some poor, young gentlemen at the switch of partners. It was like a game to try and pass her off to the next man before she vomited.

Suddenly, a familiar figure landed in my arms. "Hello, stranger!" It was Miriam.

"Have you seen Anastasia?" I asked.

"It's nice to see you, too," Miriam said bitterly but with a smile.

"I'm sorry. How are you?"

"You can't pretend to be nice now. I haven't seen Anastasia.

And if I had, I wouldn't tell you. It would ruin the game. Well, it's time to give me away, love!"

I passed Miriam to the next fellow. I looked around, growing irritated with myself for not being able to spot my swan in this pond of ducks. That was a bit of an exaggeration. These women were all beautiful. I just had not thought that it would be so difficult to find her. My next partner fell into my arms with a pleasant smile on her face. For a moment she looked like Anastasia. My mind was playing tricks on me now. I looked past my partner, and for a moment I saw Anastasia across the dance floor. It was as brief as the first time I had seen her when I had caught a glimpse of her profile in the lobby of the Theatre d'Orleans. I knew it was her, not because I recognized the distinguished jaw line, the aesthetic neck, or those sensuous shoulders. I knew it was her because of the way my stomach jumped when she danced across my line of sight. I let my partner go and began to make my way across the dance floor. It was nearly an impossible task. I could only walk a few feet at a time before a woman landed in my arms from out of nowhere. I kept my eyes on her as she moved from partner to partner. Each woman I danced with brought me closer to Anastasia. As I felt the song drawing near its chaotic conclusion, another woman fell into my arms just as I was reaching out for Anastasia. She was in the arms of another partner, as well. As we danced, she was close enough to touch. The partner switch would not come soon enough. Anastasia's partner let her go, and I let my partner go. Just as she was about to fall into the arms of another man, I took her swiftly into mine. She looked at me with surprise.

"I found you," I said, sighing a breath of relief.

"I'm sorry, but I don't believe we know each other. We're all strangers here." She had a playful smile on her face. She was wearing an elegant dress of green, which made her emerald eyes shine through her gold mask, which was designed to look like leaves with violet feathers flowing gracefully out of the top.

125

"We're all strangers, huh?" I asked, returning her playful smile.

"Oh, yes."

"Well, you feel strangely familiar in my arms," I said. The song was in its final measures.

"Well, that is strange. I'm sure we've never met."

"Then please forgive me, stranger," I said. The song ended. The dancers stopped dancing and applauded the orchestra.

"Forgive you for what?" Anastasia asked.

I leaned in to kiss her. She smiled and quickly met my lips with hers. This kiss was brief but passionate. She pulled away just as quickly as she had leaned in to meet my lips. She smiled that playful smile of innocent seduction.

"It was a pleasure meeting you, stranger," she said as she walked away.

"Where are you going?" I asked with a confused smile.

"If I stay with you, we won't be strangers anymore," she said.

"I don't understand." I tried to go after her, but everyone was leaving the dance floor to take a break after such an exhausting number, and that made it impossible for me to go after Anastasia. She disappeared into the crowd as quickly as she had appeared before me. I searched for Anastasia for the rest of the night with that confused smile frozen on my face until three in the morning when Raul and I finally left with Miriam and Charles, but I never found her.

XVIII

I SPENT THE NEXT two months working, reading, and continuing my French lessons with Raul, in which I had become quite proficient. I had become a decent cook after learning from Emilio and could make a few dishes of which I was quite proud. I was doing less of the dirty work and helping out more in the kitchen preparing meals. I still shucked oysters, but mostly because I was searching for pearls. I found a half dozen more pearls and almost had enough to make Anastasia's necklace, though I had not seen her since the Masquerade Ball, formally that is. I had seen her at a few dinners and parties, but only across the table or across the room. She did not attempt to look at me or make eye contact, let alone speak with me. I did not understand why. I asked Miriam many times if Anastasia had mentioned me during their outings. She had not.

Three nights a week, I worked as the bartender. William Mason and his friends had become regulars at the bar, and I had become good friends with them, especially Mason. On my nights off, I would go out on the town with them. We would go to the less classy bars or just buy a couple of bottles and sit by the river. It was a nice break from the aristocratic lifestyle of the rich upper class, which I had been trying to get away from in New York but had not quite succeeded. Granted, the rich upper class of New Orleans was much more relaxed, open, and genuinely polite and accepting, but I was beginning to grow tired of it all as I had in New York. I liked most of the people, but the fancy dinners, parties, and balls were becoming tedious and growing old. I was beginning to feel as if I had traded one prison cell for another. My last cell had not had a window, but my new one did, and with a wonderful view. However, it was still a cell, and I was ready to escape. Coming to New Orleans had been an adventure, and getting to know the city and its people had been a grand experience, but my adventure did not end here. It was time for something new. My heart was restless once again. I felt the walls closing in as I squandered my time on the silly, lavish parties. I was growing anxious. My knees bounced rapidly when I sat, and I could not stop cracking my knuckles. Occasionally, I would find myself short of breath for no physical reason. I began pacing a lot. It seemed that I could not keep still for the life of me. I felt my mind turning cynical and depressed.

On a cloudy, humid day in late April, Raul and I were sitting out on the balcony, doing a French lesson when the mailman started walking up the stairs to our door. Since the balcony of our apartment was so close to the stairs, the mailman stopped three-quarters of the way up and handed Raul the mail over the iron railing. Raul thanked him, and they had a few laughs at one another's expense. The mail was only one envelope, which was addressed to both Raul and me. Raul opened it with a knife and read it aloud.

"On behalf of Mr. James Morrison and Ms. Anastasia Carriere, you have been cordially invited to an evening of fine dining and conversation at the grand Saint Charles Hotel. Please arrive no later than eight o'clock on Saturday, the Twenty-Ninth of April. Your presence is greatly appreciated." Raul closed the letter and handed it to me. "Quite an invitation for a dinner party."

"Indeed," I agreed. "What do you think it is?"

"A presentation of their status. That's what these things usually are," Raul suggested.

"Yes, I suppose so," I said, still pondering the possibilities of what it could mean. "The twenty-ninth is this Saturday. Are you going?"

"Of course. For free food and free drinks, I'd be crazy not to go. Besides, the Saint Charles Hotel is amazing. You will love it."

We went back to our French lesson, but my mind was on that

invitation of peculiar formality. It was a special occasion of some sort, and my mind wandered over the possibilities. I feared the worst.

* * *

Martha gave me the night off on Saturday so I could attend the dinner party. I drank half a bottle of wine in the bath that evening to calm my anxiety, for I had been growing more and more inquisitive every day, as I waited to find out the occasion for which the dinner was being held. The wine did not calm me, however. It only made me more skeptical. I put on the fine suit Raul had bought for me when Miriam and I had first arrived in New Orleans. I combed my hair carefully, making sure each strand sat exactly as I wanted. I dabbed a bit of perfume on my neck and took a sip from my glass of wine as I looked myself over in the mirror. I did not know why I was being so particular about my appearance that night. Anastasia would probably not talk to me or even look at me, just as she had not at the other dinners and parties we had gone to since the Masquerade Ball. It seemed like a childish game, and I was growing weary of it. We had talked that day at Leon's when she had told me that she would like to see me again. We had met twice for coffee at the café by Jackson Square where we'd had wonderful conversations on many topics. She had invited me into her home where she'd showed me a very personal painting. She'd told me to search for her at the Masquerade Ball where, once I found her, we'd had a very sweet kiss. Why was she being so cold all of a sudden? Why this peculiar invitation to this mysterious dinner?

Maybe I was just thinking too much. Maybe she was afraid that we were moving too fast and getting along too comfortably. Maybe she felt guilty. I was wasting my time trying to figure out what she was thinking and what game she was playing, for what lucky man would God bless with such a gift? A man's life is too easy as it is. The man who could decipher a woman's intentions through her actions would have to be God Himself, for I don't believe even His Son worked such miracles.

Raul and I had a glass of whiskey together and then left for the dinner. Raul had arranged for a carriage to pick us up. Miriam had gone with Charles, so for the first time, it was just Raul and I arriving together. Miriam and Charles had developed a very close relationship. They had been spending much time with one another, and I rarely saw her. She had even stopped attending Raul's French lessons with me. But she seemed happy, and I was happy for her.

Raul and I arrived at the Saint Charles Hotel precisely on time. The door to our carriage was opened for us, and we were escorted to the door where we showed our invitation. Another man came to escort us to the dinning hall and showed us to our seats at the table where Charles and Miriam sat, along with two men and two women I had never met. It was a table of couples except for Raul and I. The entire dining room had been reserved for this event, and all the tables were full. Anastasia and James sat at a table, which was strategically positioned to show it was the head of the room. I had an unobstructed view of Anastasia, but she, of course, did not look at me.

The dinner was rather boring. Miriam and Charles were in their own world of new, young love, and they could not keep their hands off one another. The other two couples at our table were full of tedious conversation. Raul humored them, but I did not. I sat quietly in my seat and drank my wine. I was beginning to realize that these were the same pointless conversations I had been having in New York. I had only thought it was different and new and grand because I was in a new city. Now it was old to me.

I constantly looked across the room at Anastasia, trying to read her thoughts. She smiled and conversed with the people at her table, but when she was not involved in the conversation, her face went cold and expressionless. Time went by quickly from the time Raul and I arrived to when the waiters were taking away our dessert plates. After dessert, the champagne was brought out. Raul poured the champagne for everyone at our table, and as I raised my glass to my mouth, James stood up, tapping his glass with a spoon. I rolled my eyes irritably and lowered my glass.

"If I could please have everybody's attention! I have an announcement!" James said. The room quickly went silent. I was about to find out the answer to the question that had been driving me crazy since I'd received the invitation, but I no longer cared. "Well, *we* have an announcement." James smiled at Anastasia and gestured for her to stand up with him. She obediently did as he asked. "The reason we have invited you all here tonight is because… well… we have set the date for our wedding! It will be on Friday, the twenty-sixth of May at the Saint Louis Cathedral!"

Everyone clapped and cheered joyfully as James kissed Anastasia, everyone except me. My question had been answered, and my fear of the worst had come true. I felt Miriam's compassionate eyes judging my reaction as I stared at the table. I drank my glass of champagne down in one big gulp.

"To the future Mr. and Mrs. Morrison!" one man yelled.

"Here! Here!" everyone yelled, raising their glasses.

"Thank you!" James said, raising his glass to everyone. He and Anastasia touched glasses and drank. Everyone else followed.

I looked across the room at Anastasia. Her eyes finally met mine, but only for a brief moment. She showed no reaction. I did not know what to make of it. I did not know why she was marrying James. I did not know when they had discussed the wedding date. I did not know when they had made the reservations for the Saint Louis Cathedral. All I knew was that I could not be here anymore. Not at this dinner, and not in this town. I took my napkin off my lap and tossed it on the table. I excused myself and stood up. Miriam reached for my hand and asked me to wait. I ignored her plea and walked quickly out of the dining room and out of the hotel.

I stumbled onto the street and stopped to catch my breath. I was beginning to feel as if I was suffocating. This feeling was all too familiar. I regained my breath and began walking toward my apartment. When I got there, I did not go upstairs. Instead, I went into Leon's and sat down at the bar. I ordered a shot of whiskey. I drank it quickly and ordered another. I had not noticed until then that William Mason was sitting at the end of the bar with Kyle Ripley and Cole Jackson. I took my drink and moved next to them.

"Look at you on this side of the bar for once," Mason quipped.

"You get fired?" Kyle asked.

"No, I have the night off," I informed him.

"You seem upset, Konrad," Mason remarked.

"I'm fine."

"Well, then cheer up and drink up. We're celebrating tonight!" Mason motioned to the bartender. "Can we get another round over here?"

The bartender grabbed a bottle of whiskey and walked over as I finished my shot. He refilled our glasses.

"What are we celebrating?" I asked.

"John Fremont's expedition got the go-ahead. He's outfitting in St. Louis, and we head out in June. We're going out West, partner, and you are coming with us!"

"Really? How do I get hired on?" I asked.

"Don't worry about that," Mason said. "Just come to St. Louis with us, and we'll make sure you have a place in the outfit."

I thought about it for a moment, but only a moment. There wasn't much to think about. I had no reason, nor desire, to stay in New Orleans. An expedition out West was exactly the adventure for which I had left New York.

"When do we leave?" I asked.

"Two weeks, partner. No need to pack your bags. You'll be given everything you need, and it's all funded by the government."

"To the West!" Cole yelled, holding up his glass.

"To the West!" Mason and Kyle yelled in unison.

We all touched glasses. They took their shots quickly. I held my glass to my mouth as my imagination wandered. "To the West," I said softly to myself, and I drank my whiskey.

XIX

THREE DAYS AFTER DECIDING to join Mason and the others on an expedition westward, I invited Miriam and Charles over for dinner, which I had made myself. It turned out quite well, and everyone seemed to enjoy it. I had gone down to the market that morning and handpicked the fresh fish from the morning's catch.

"What's this all about, Kon?" Miriam asked, as we enjoyed a glass of wine after the dinner. "You invite us over and cook us this wonderful dinner. There must be some occasion."

"Well, I just wanted to share a bit of news with all of you," I began. "I've been talking with William Mason and a few others, and it turns out that John Fremont and Kit Carson will be embarking on an expedition out West in June. I've decided to join the outfit."

Miriam looked at Raul. He shrugged, indicating that I had not mentioned my decision to him.

"How will you be hired? Mustn't you have experience in exploring or be a mountain man or a soldier?" Miriam asked.

"Or a scientist?" Charles added.

"Not necessarily," I said. "Though I did study physics at Oxford. Mason said he could get me hired on."

"Well, that sounds as if it will be quite an adventure," Charles commented. "I'm happy for you."

"Thank you, Charles."

"It seems quite dangerous, Kon," Miriam said fearfully. "Aren't there Indians and bears on the frontier?"

"Of course it will be dangerous, Miriam," Charles said. "It wouldn't be an adventure if it wasn't. But Konrad is a resourceful man. He will be just fine."

"When will you be leaving?" Raul asked.

"We'll leave for St. Louis in a week and a half. We'll outfit the expedition and head out on the trail in June," I explained.

"I hope you're not running away because of Anastasia," Miriam interjected.

"Don't be ridiculous. I've been talking about this with Mason and the boys for a while now. They knew another expedition was coming up. Now it's official."

"Well, I think it's great," Raul said. "It will be a once in a lifetime experience."

"I agree," Charles said. "Good for you, Konrad."

"Yes, I'm happy for you, as well," Miriam said. "I'm just worried — that's all."

The next day, I went into work at Leon's and told everybody I would be leaving for the expedition in a week and a half. Martha said she would be sad to see me go and that there would always be a job for me when I came back. Emilio told me I had come very far as a chef, but I still had much to learn, so we would pick up where we left off when I returned.

I spent the next week working every day and preparing to leave during my free time, although there was not much preparation necessary. As Mason had said, everything I needed for the expedition would be provided. I practiced fencing by fighting shadows with the saber Uncle Friedrich had given me. There was a possibility of confrontation with Indians on this expedition, and I knew I could not count on my skill with a rifle or pistol in the event of an attack. I had not practiced with my saber since I had arrived in New Orleans, so I was a bit rusty; however, it came back to me very quickly. A skill such as fencing is not easily lost, especially after the extensive amount of training I had received from Friedrich.

As excited as I was, the day I was to leave for St. Louis did not arrive quickly enough, but when it finally did arrive, I was more than ready. I packed a few books to read by the nightly campfires.

I put my father's watch in my pocket and strapped my saber to my hip. I did not need to hurry, for it was only eleven in the morning and the steamboat for St. Louis did not leave until noon, but I could not wait. I had everything I needed and was ready to go. When I walked into the living room, Miriam and Charles were there with Raul to say goodbye. I had not heard them come in.

"You look like you're ready for an expedition," Raul said.

"Aww, my little explorer is off on another adventure," Miriam said in a motherly, babying voice, as she adjusted the lapels of my jacket.

"Very funny," I said, rolling my eyes.

Miriam smiled sadly as she looked into my eyes. She threw her arms around my neck and hugged me tight.

"I'm going to be all right. I promise," I assured her

"I know you are, but I'm going to miss you so much," Miriam said.

"I'm going to miss you, too, but I'll be back before you know it."

Miriam released her hold and backed away to look at me. "And you'll be careful?"

"Try not to worry, darling," I said.

"I'll try," Miriam promised.

I began making my way to the door. I shook Charles' hand firmly, and he patted me on the back.

"Good luck, Konrad," Charles said. "Try your best to remember every little detail so you can tell me all about it when you return. Lord knows, I'd be lying if I said I wasn't a little jealous."

"I'll take good notes for you," I promised. I walked over to Raul and shook his hand. "Are you going to be all right without me for a little while?"

"I'll probably cry myself to sleep every night, but, other than that, I'll be fine," Raul joked. "You have fun out there, Konrad. It should be a great experience."

"Thank you," I said. I opened the door and stood in the doorway. "I'll see you all in a few months."

"Oh, wait!" Charles said, as he quickly walked over to me while reaching into his jacket pocket. "I nearly forgot." Charles took out four steamboat tickets and handed them to me.

"What's this?" I asked.

"You are good friends with the owner of a steamboat line. You didn't think you'd have to pay for your ticket, did you? There are four of you, right?"

"Yes. Thank you, Charles," I said.

He smiled and nodded. "We'll see you soon."

I walked out the door and waved as I made my way down the stairs. They stood in the doorway and watched me walk down the street until I disappeared around the corner.

Before going to the docks, I had one stop to make that was on the way. I walked up to Anastasia's apartment and stopped at her door. I did not knock, for I did not want to see her. I reached into my pocket and took out the oyster pearl necklace I had made for her. I'd finished it only a few days earlier. I had collected enough pearls for the necklace to fit around her neck with a little bit of slack. It had turned out quite well, and I was proud of the finished product. I hung it from her doorknob. I paused a moment as I thought about knocking to see if she was home and to say goodbye, but I quickly regained my senses and decided that it would be best not to see her. I turned and walked to the docks. When I returned, she would be a married woman and our relationship would not be as it had been.

As I waited for Mason, Kyle, and Cole, I stood on the docks watching the men load supplies onto the steamboat I was to ride to St. Louis. They arrived ten minutes before noon, and they were full of excitement. I handed them their tickets and told them a friend of mine had done the honors. They were very grateful. We boarded the steamboat, and soon we were heading up the Mississippi River toward St. Louis.

XX

WHEN WE ARRIVED IN St. Louis, we went straight to the outfitting office to sign up for the expedition. The office was a small rented building next door to a saloon in the middle of town. Inside this tiny office was only a desk with one man sitting behind it, lazily looking over a stack of papers.

Without looking up from the papers, the man asked, "What can I do for you boys?"

"You can start by looking me in the goddamn eye, you rude bastard!" Mason said.

I looked at him in surprise, and so did the man at the desk. Then the man smiled and stood up.

"Will Mason!" the man exclaimed. "I was wondering if you boys would be coming back for round two!"

"Wouldn't miss it," Mason said, shaking the man's hand. "How are you, Tom?"

"Good! I'm good! Just getting this expedition ready to go as soon as possible." Tom looked past Mason to Kyle and Cole and reached out to shake their hands. "Kyle, Cole, glad to see you." Tom then looked at me, trying to recognize my face and put a name to it.

"Sorry, Tom. This is Konrad Quintero," Mason said. "He's a physicist."

"Nice to meet you, Tom," I said, shaking his hand.

"Likewise, Konrad," Tom returned. He sat back down in his chair. "Well, I'll tell you what, boys; you're gonna be the last to join the outfit. I started signing people up three days ago, and we're already filled up."

"Well, John Fremont's a celebrity now," Kyle said. "Everybody wants to be a part of his legacy."

"I guess so," Tom agreed. He flipped a piece of paper around and pushed a feather and ink forward. "Here you go. Just put your marks on this piece of paper here."

Mason signed his name first and then gave the feather to Kyle. Cole signed next and gave the feather to me. I signed my name and handed the ink and paper back to Tom.

"You boys are all set," Tom said. "You got horses?"

"Sure don't," Mason answered. "Guess the government will have to oblige us."

Tom smirked and nodded. "Go down to the stables and tell them I sent you. Pick out your ride and then get a room at the hotel across the street here. That's where the rest of the boys are. You'll probably have to share a room. Again, just tell the desk clerk I sent you, and he'll set you up."

"Thanks, Tom," Mason said. "We'll be seeing you later."

"All right. Good to have you boys on board."

We left the office and walked down the busy main street through the heart of St. Louis. When we got to the stables just outside of town, the stableman seemed to already know that we were with John C. Fremont's outfit. He showed us his horses, and Mason, Kyle, and Cole looked them over very carefully, studying every inch of the creatures and asking the stableman many questions. I really had no idea what to look for in a horse. They all looked the same to me other than color and size. I paid close attention to Mason and the others to see how they chose their horse. When they had each picked out their horse, the stableman asked me which one I wanted. I had noticed another group of horses in a separate corral and was captivated by a beautiful white horse with an exceptional build. He was smaller than the others, but he looked strong and fast. There was a wildness in his eyes that caught my attention.

"What about that white one over there?" I said, pointing to the other corral.

The stableman looked to where I was pointing and chuckled.

"Those are all mustangs, kid. Aaron rounded them up and brought them in just yesterday. They ain't been broke yet."

"When will they be broken in?" I asked.

"Hell, I don't know. When Aaron feels like it, I suppose," the stableman replied.

"Well, is Aaron around?"

"Who knows? He could be anywhere. Why don't you just pick one of these horses I just showed you?"

"I like that one," I said, lifting my chin toward the white stallion.

"Well, if you like him so much, then break him yourself," the stableman suggested.

"Can I?" I asked excitedly.

The stableman looked at me with surprise. "I don't know; can you?"

"I'd like to try."

"Have you ever broken a horse before?"

"No…"

The stableman raised his eyebrows and tilted his head. "Well, you can try. Come on."

"You've never broken a horse before?" Mason asked, as we walked toward the corral.

"Nope. Is it hard?" I asked.

Mason laughed and shook his head. "This should be interesting."

There was an empty corral connected to the one that contained the wild horses, forming the shape of a figure eight. In the middle of the empty corral, there was a thick post about seven feet tall driven into the ground. The stableman opened the gate to the empty corral and gestured for me to follow him inside. Mason, Kyle, and Cole leaned against the fencing of the corral, waiting with excited anticipation. The stableman led me over to the gate, which connected the two corrals and handed me a lasso. I unraveled the rope and held it questionably.

"Just rope your white stallion, and then I'll open the gate and close it back up," the stableman said.

"Then what?" I asked.

"Haven't you ever seen this done before?" he asked with a confused look on his face.

"No, not exactly," I admitted.

He chuckled and shook his head. "Well, you bring that stallion in here and keep that post between you. Get that rope around it and let that son of a bitch run around and buck until he gets tired. When he's settled down, you grab that saddle sitting on the fence there and put it on his back."

"Then what?"

The stableman shook his head and smiled. "I don't think there's gonna be a 'Then what?', kid. Now, go ahead and rope your mustang."

I held the lasso in my hands and waited for the white stallion to come into range as the horses ran around. When he did, I tossed out the lasso, side-armed, and missed horribly. Mason and the guys laughed. I pulled the lasso back in and prepared to throw it again. This time, I swung the lasso over my head and threw it out. I missed my stallion, but I had gotten closer. I pulled the rope back in and swung it over my head, as I waited for the white stallion to come back around. I threw the lasso out again, and the rope fell around the neck of the wrong horse. The mustang I had lassoed jerked violently and kicked. I held onto the rope as tightly as I could as it slid through by bare hands. The fighting horse riled up the rest of the horses.

"Just let it go! — Let go!" the stableman yelled, so I let go of the rope. "I'll get it later," he commented.

The stableman handed me another rope and noticed that I was not wearing gloves. He gave me his gloves. I put them on and took the rope in my hands. I swung it over my head and threw it out. The lasso fell over my white stallion's head and tightened around his neck. I pulled him toward the gate as the stableman opened it up. The white stallion ran angrily into the empty corral, kicking and bucking his legs wildly. The stableman quickly shut the gate and climbed out of the corral.

I held the rope tightly in my hands as I let the stallion throw a fit. I kept the post between us and wrapped the rope around it. This made it much easier to hold the horse. He ran madly around the corral for a good ten minutes before finally settling down to a steady trot. When he finally stood still, I wrapped the rope around the post a few more times. Then I walked over to the fence and grabbed the saddle.

"Now, don't just throw that saddle on his back," the stableman advised. "You got to talk to him first. You got to pet him. You got to make him trust you. Be his friend. Be calm, and don't act scared. Be confident. Horses are like women; if you approach them with confidence, they'll respond positively."

I nodded and began walking slowly but confidently over to the white stallion, holding the saddle by the horn. He was breathing loudly through his flared nostrils. He watched me closely as I approached. When I was close enough to touch him, I stopped and let him absorb my presence. After slowly setting the saddle on the ground. I took a step closer to the stallion and stood next to his face. He looked me in the eyes.

"Hello, my friend," I whispered in a gentle voice. "Everything is all right. Don't worry. May I pet you?"

I slowly raised my hand to his cheek and gently touched him. He jerked his head away but stayed calm. I told him it was all right and that I was not going to hurt him. I petted him again, this time on the neck. He did not pull away. I continued to pet him softly and speak to him in a soothing voice.

"You know," I told him, "I saw you when I was looking at those other horses, and there was just something about you that made you stand out from the others. I see a little bit of myself in you, I think. We're both wild creatures trapped in a cage, and we need to be free. We need to run with the wind and see places we've never seen before. We're the same, you and me. Don't you think?" The stallion breathed out loudly through his nostrils, as if he was sighing. "So, what do you say? Do you think we could be friends?" I petted him on his neck a few moments longer. "I'm going to put a saddle on your back now. It's going to feel a little strange, but I promise that it's all right. It's nothing to be afraid of. You ready? Here we go."

I reached down and picked up the saddle. As slowly as possible, I hoisted the saddle into the air. The stallion quickly jumped away and began running around wildly once again. I dropped the saddle and went to grab the rope around the post, but the rope had come lose. The stallion was running around the corral, jumping and kicking, with the rope hanging from his neck. I sidestepped beside him, keeping my distance, as I waited for an opportunity to grab the rope. He suddenly stopped and quickly changed direction, coming right for me. I dove out of the way and rolled onto my stomach. I reached for the rope and grabbed it with both hands as he ran past me. I let his momentum pull me off the ground and onto my feet. My weight on the rope caused him to turn around swiftly, and he began running toward me again. I quickly stepped behind the post and wrapped the rope around it. I let him run around a bit more until he finally calmed down. He trotted around in circles for a few moments and then stood still. I wrapped the rope around the post about ten times, grabbed the saddle, and confidently walked over to the hard-breathing stallion.

"Calm down, my friend," I said softly, as I gently petted his neck. "I know this is strange to you, but I promise that there is nothing to worry about. I'm just going to put this saddle on your back. It's not going to hurt. You might even like it." I started to pet his cheek. This time he did not pull away. I petted his nose and felt his moist breath on my hand. "You need a name, don't you, my friend? It would be rude of me to ride you without first giving you a name." I thought for a moment as I continued to pet his nose. He seemed to be warming to me. "How about... I call you 'Renegado'? I think that would be fitting. Do you like that?" The white stallion stomped his right front foot as he let out a loud, rumbling breath. His head jerked up and came back down. It seemed to be a positive acknowledgement. "Renegado it is. And I am Konrad Quintero de Leon. I'm going to put this saddle on you now."

Gracefully, I once again hoisted the saddle into the air, and it came down snuggly on Renegado's back. He stepped away from me fearfully, but he did not run away. I told him it was all right, as I stepped toward him and petted his neck. I talked to him as I secured the saddle onto his back.

"That wasn't so bad, was it?" I asked him. "Now, I'm going to sit on your back. It's going to feel even stranger, but it's all right. Here we go."

I slowly put my left foot in the stirrup. I pushed my foot down to judge Renegado's reaction. He was calm. In one swift, fluid motion, I grabbed the saddle horn, pulled myself up, and threw my right leg over his back. He began jumping around wildly before I was sitting in the saddle. I held the saddle horn with both hands, as I tried to get my right foot into the stirrup. When I finally had both feet in the stirrups, I squeezed my legs into Renegado's sides as hard as I could. I let go of the saddle horn and held on to the reins, trying my best to control him. There was not much I could do but hold on and wait for him to tire himself out. Just as I was getting used to his bucking and jumping, Renegado kicked his back legs high into the air and pivoted around on his front legs, sending me flying off his back. I landed hard on my shoulder and quickly opened my eyes to look for the stallion, but I was blinded by the cloud of dust that had formed around me. As the dust cleared, I saw Renegado running straight at me. I quickly rolled out of the way and jumped to my feet. I backed up to the fence and watched him run around until he finally tired himself out again.

When he had quieted, I walked up to Renegado and began to pet him gently. I told him he had given me a good throw but that I wasn't giving up. I grabbed the saddle horn and put my left foot in the stirrup once again. As I started to throw my right leg over his back, he bucked and then leaped forward. I pulled my leg back and jumped onto the ground, landing smoothly on my feet. I followed him as he trotted around to the other side of the corral and stopped as if waiting for me to catch up. It was beginning to seem like a game. I climbed into the saddle and let him buck, kick, and run me around. I stayed in the saddle much longer this time before I was thrown hard into the dirt once again. I stood up, dusted myself off, and climbed back into the saddle. This pattern continued for a while with my being thrown another dozen times. I was beginning to feel bruised and beaten, but most of all, tired. I let out a heavy sigh as I walked over to Renegado. I wondered if he was laughing at me. Then I realized that he was probably just as exhausted as I was. He was probably asking himself the same question that I was asking myself, which was, "When is he going to give up?"

The sun was beginning to go down, and the white half-moon had appeared in the darkening sky. I pulled myself into the saddle once again, and Renegado began to throw his usual wild fit. I held on tight with determination. I stayed in the saddle far longer than any time before. I could hear Mason, Kyle, and Cole cheering. Renegado put up a wild fight, but I stayed on his back. Finally, he grew tired and began trotting calmly around the corral. Mason, Kyle, Cole, and the stableman clapped at my victory. I pulled on the reins, and Renegado quickly halted. I climbed off his back and petted his neck. I thanked him and told him that he was a good horse and that I looked forward to us being partners. I walked over to the fence of the corral with a proud smile on my face despite the pain and exhaustion I was feeling.

"Well, it seems we've come to an understanding," I said to the stableman. "Is he my horse now?"

"He's all yours, kid," the stableman agreed, shaking my hand. "Good work. I've never seen a first-timer break a horse that fast."

"I didn't break him. Like I said, we came to an understanding."

XXI

WE RODE BACK INTO town on our new horses. Though Renegado was not bucking and trying to throw me, he was quite difficult to control. He walked with a mind of his own from the stables to the hotel. He would not go in the direction I pulled the reins, and he never walked in a straight line. Every now and then he would start trotting ahead of the other horses. Mason, Kyle, and Cole laughed at the sight of Renegado and me all the way to the hotel.

When we arrived at the hotel, we tied off our horses and went inside. We told the hotel manager that we were with the Fremont Expedition, and he did not seem pleased. He rolled his eyes, which appeared quite large behind his glasses, and grabbed the room key as we signed the ledger. The manager handed the key to a young girl sitting behind the front desk, who I assumed was his daughter. The manager was a very short man with sparse, gray hair, but he had a very young, peculiar face. He was probably no older than forty. Unfortunately, he was just cursed with bad genes. However, his daughter was quite lovely with a very symmetrical face. When she stood up to take the key from her father, they were nearly the same height. She must have been blessed with her mother's genes. I imagined the manager's wife was quite tall and broad with a chiseled face. They would certainly be an odd sight standing side by side. I saw that Mason had also noticed the beauty of the manager's young daughter. He stared at her and smiled his charming grin as he leaned against the desk.

"Is this a family run hotel?" Mason asked the manager.

"Yes, it is," the manager replied awkwardly.

"I bet y'all sure are getting tired of us explorers coming in here and taking up all your rooms while you wait for the government to reimburse you," Mason said sympathetically.

The manager chuckled and nodded. "I'm sure they'll pay us soon enough."

"They will," Mason vouched for the government. "But I'm sure it puts you in a tight spot for the time being. No income or anything."

"Sure, but it's fine. We do all right," the manager lied.

"Tell you what," Mason said, leaning toward the manager. "Why don't you let us go ahead and pay for our rooms?" Kyle and Cole looked at Mason inquisitively. I thought it was a nice gesture.

"Oh, no. You don't need to do that," the manager said.

"I insist. It's not fair that the government sends all of us here but can't seem to get a damned accountant out here to reimburse you in a timely fashion." Mason began to reach into his pocket for money.

"No, no, sir! I really appreciate the offer, but I really can't accept it. Thank you! Really! I just can't!"

"You sure?" Mason asked.

"I'm sure," the manager replied. He grabbed another key from the desk drawer and handed it to his daughter. "Why don't you show them to their rooms, darling."

"Thank you kindly, sir," Mason said, tipping his hat to the manager.

"Enjoy your stay, boys," the manager said with a gracious smile.

We followed the manager's daughter up the stairs and down the long hallway of doors. She stopped, unlocked one of the doors, and opened it. She smiled and handed the key to Mason who was closest to her. He handed the key to Kyle and told him and Cole to take the room. Mason and I continued to follow the daughter down the hallway as she led us to our room. She unlocked the door, which was four rooms down from Kyle and Cole's room and handed the key to Mason. He thanked her for her help and gave her a generous tip. She bowed thankfully, and we went into our room.

We put our saddlebags on the floor, and I took my saber off my hip and placed it on the dresser. Mason asked me if I had stolen it or had taken it off a dead officer, both of which I found to be strange assumptions. I explained the history of the saber and how it had been passed down to me. Mason seemed disappointed with my explanation. I think he was hoping for a more interesting story.

We went to Kyle and Cole's room, and then we all went next door to the saloon. Mason, Kyle, and Cole instantly began shaking hands and embracing friends they had not seen in a while, most of whom they had met on the previous expedition. I was introduced to about two dozen rough-looking men in the short span of about ten minutes. They all looked the same, and I would probably forget most of their names, but there was one man who I knew would be impossible to forget. He stuck out in a curious way and captivated my attention before we had even been introduced. I had never seen him before, but I instantly knew who he was. He was Kit Carson. I watched as Mason, Kyle, and Cole walked up to him and shook his hand. They shared a joke and slapped each other on the shoulder. While Mason, Kyle, and Cole laughed hysterically as they reminisced about something that had happened during their last adventure, Carson just smirked dryly with a look of mischievousness in his eyes.

"Konrad, come here!" Mason yelled over to me. I walked over and stood before Carson. "Kit, this is Konrad Quintero," he introduced. "Konrad, this is Mr. Kit Carson."

I shook his hand and said, "It's nice to meet you, Mr. Carson."

"Call me Kit, and welcome to the outfit," he said in a strangely expressive monotone.

At first glance, Carson did not look like a tough, rugged adventurer and Indian fighter. He stood no higher than five and a half feet tall, and he did not look to have an ounce of muscle or fat on his body. His brown hair was stringy and thin, just barely reaching to his shoulders. He looked unhealthy, but his eyes made up for it. His metallic-blue eyes told all of his stories. They were penetrating, worn, distant eyes full of wildness, experience, determination, and a frozen look of inquisition. Peering into them, one could see the hundreds of rivers he had crossed, the mountain ranges and deserts he had traversed, the men he had killed, the friends he had lost, the near death experiences he'd had, and the women he had loved. He told it all in his eyes.

Mason introduced me to a few more friends of his from the previous expedition, and we all got acquainted with the men he did not know. They seemed to be a nice bunch, but they were all very rough looking — sporting scars, long hair, and various styles of scraggly facial hair. Their attitudes were either extremely quiet and unexpressive or extremely loud and eccentric. Based on my clean-cut appearance and curious, polite attitude, I did not feel as if I fit in with these rugged men at all, but they seemed to accept me as one of their own. It was probably because Mason had vouched for me. However, it was obvious that I would have to prove myself as one of them to truly *be* one of them.

* * *

In the next week and half, our outfit was supplied and ready to begin the expedition. It was a hot morning in June when the outfit secured their saddles and checked and double-checked supplies. Citizens of St. Louis watched excitedly as we prepared to embark on what we all believed was to be one of the most important expeditions of the century. After all, the newspapers were calling John Fremont "The American Magellan". We had close to seventy horses and mules and a supply wagon, which contained a mountain howitzer, and this large parade was stopping all activity on the main street of St. Louis.

I petted Renegado's nose, as I took in the crowd of citizens, which was growing larger by the minute. I looked around at our outfit, and it seemed that we were just waiting on our leaders, John Fremont and Kit Carson. Tom Fitzpatrick, another well-known mountain man working as a guide on our journey, was already sitting atop his horse, impatiently looking around for Fremont and Carson.

"You ready?" Mason asked me as he backhanded me on the shoulder.

"Never been more ready in my life," I responded.

Mason checked his rifle to make sure it was loaded and then stuck it in his saddle scabbard. He checked his pistol as well and then stuffed it in his belt. As I watched Mason check his weapons, I put my hand on the pommel of my saber, making sure it was secured well in my belt. I had not loaded my rifle or pistol and did not know how. I was too embarrassed to ask. I anxiously took out my father's gold pocket watch and checked the time. It was nearly nine o'clock. As excited as I was to leave, I knew I should appreciate the late start, because for the next few months we would be waking up a good hour or two before the sun and riding hard through rough conditions until the sun had long given way to the moon.

I petted Renegado again and looked around for John Fremont. I was growing overwhelmingly anxious. Excited butterflies flew wildly around in my stomach. I could feel my heart beating faster and faster. I couldn't wait to be on the trail, hundreds of miles away from civilization. I imagined the Great Plains and the buffalo that roamed them. I imagined the mountains and the forests, the deserts and the rivers. I could almost smell the salty, wet air of the Pacific Ocean.

The audience that had gathered to see us off began to clap and cheer. I looked to see John Fremont and Kit Carson walking out of the office where we had signed up for the expedition. Carson walked straight to his horse without acknowledging the huge crowd that had formed in his honor. Fremont took off his hat and stopped to wave to the crowd. He walked to the front of the outfit where his horse waited for him. He climbed into his saddle, looked over the outfit, and then said something to Tom Fitzpatrick who was sitting atop his horse next to him. Carson checked over his supplies and climbed into his saddle. Fremont raised his hand to silence the crowd, indicating that he wished to say something. The crowd quickly hushed and waited for him to speak.

"I want to thank all of you fine people of St. Louis for coming out to see us off on this historic occasion," Fremont began. "I remember two years ago when we gathered in this great city to embark on our first expedition westward that the crowd was not even a quarter of this size. None of us realized the spark we would ignite at that time. We were opening a new chapter in the history of our nation, and now we're off to continue writing that chapter as we explore the second half of the Oregon Trail from South Pass to the Columbia River. This is an even longer and more ambitious expedition than our first, and I am more than confident that it will be an even greater success. With the two greatest scouts in America and a fine outfit of brave, selfless men, together we will pave the way for the expansion of this great country we live in, so that you may have the opportunity to start a new life in the West and be a part of this chapter with us. Thank you all for keeping us in your prayers. God bless you and God bless America!"

The crowd roared in applause and cheers. Fremont gestured to the outfit, waving his hand and pointing westward. We climbed onto our horses and began riding slowly out of town. The crowd followed us all the way to the edge of the city until the plains opened up before us. We were on our way.

Before long, we had left civilization behind, and the wild stood before us. My heart jumped with excitement. My next adventure had begun.

XXII

IN A FEW SHORT days, we were riding out of Missouri and crossing over into the wild territory of the West. It was well known to the experienced men of the outfit that we had moved into Indian country, but everyone seemed to remain at ease. I asked Mason why nobody seemed to be worried about Indians, and he said there wasn't much to worry about. He said we probably wouldn't even see any, and if we did, it would most likely be a friendly meeting. He assured me that there was very little to worry about during the first half of the expedition. The land was quite navigable and had been crossed many times by most of these men. He told me to enjoy this part, for we would pass through it quickly and would soon be traversing the rugged mountains and dense forests. Despite Mason's assurances, I was still filled with a fair amount of anxiety and fear of the unknown.

But my anxiety was calmed when we began riding across the Blue Stem Hills, where we were greeted by the rolling, vibrantly green mounds of gently blowing grass with colorful wildflowers sparsely arranged throughout. Resting above the hills was a magnificent display of fluffy, white clouds moving slowly beneath the bluest sky I had ever seen. It felt dreamlike at first — as if I was looking at a painting. I soaked it in with a smile of awe on my face, as I began to realize that I was part of this masterpiece painting, this dream — I was living in it.

We passed through the Blue Stem Hills all too quickly, and we briefly followed the Arkansas River into the Great Plains. Once again, I was overwhelmed by the beauty of the seemingly endless expanse of steppe and prairie. The wheat-colored grass leaned to the south due to a steady wind blowing from the north. The sun was hidden by a thick layer of gray clouds, which stretched across the vast sky, casting a heavenly, white glow upon the plains.

I observed the beautiful land coolly, but inside, my soul was screaming with excitement and awe at the sheer magnificence of what I was seeing. The clouds parted, forming a small opening in the sky. The sun cast down its angelic, white rays through the opening and shot a single beam of light onto a small section of the prairie about a mile ahead of our outfit.

As we rode along, I noticed a shallow, circular depression in the soil. It was about ten feet in diameter and about a foot deep. It was a strange scar in the middle of the grassy prairie.

"What is that?" I asked Mason.

"That's a buffalo wallow," he said. "The bison roll around in the dirt, and that's what it makes. Looks pretty fresh, too."

"Is there a herd nearby?" I asked.

"Probably. If there is, Kit will find it. We could be having buffalo for dinner tomorrow night."

The next day, Kit Carson and Tom Fitzpatrick rode off to search for the herd. They were gone from sunrise until late afternoon. When they returned, they informed the outfit that they had found the herd and had killed four bison about ten miles away. Carson and Fitzpatrick led the outfit to where they had left their kills. We arrived about an hour before sundown. There was a long strip of torn-up earth as far as I could see where the herd had stampeded after Carson and Fitzpatrick had begun firing. We set up camp and got our fires started. A group of men skinned the bison and cut up the meat for the rest of us. This was done in a very timely fashion.

By dark, Mason, Kyle, Cole, a couple of others, and I were sitting around our fire cooking our buffalo steaks. The meat smelled amazing. It had been a long time since we had fresh red meat. My mouth watered as I watched the flames kiss the lean steaks. Mason had seasoned our steaks with salt and gunpowder. He said that was the only way to eat buffalo.

Our steaks cooked quickly, and soon we were taking them off

the fire and putting them on our plates. Mason said buffalo taste best when it's cooked rare. As we began cutting into our steaks, Kit Carson walked over to our campfire with his plate and a raw slab of buffalo.

"You boys mind if I eat with you?" Carson asked.

"Not at all, Kit," Mason answered, scooting over to make room for the grizzled scout. "Have a seat."

Carson sat down between Mason and Cole. He put his steak over the fire. We held our plates awkwardly, not sure if we should cut into our steaks or wait for Carson's to finish cooking.

"Go ahead and start eating, boys. You ain't got to wait on me," Carson said.

We started cutting into our steaks as Carson flipped his over. I had my first bite halfway to my mouth when Carson said, "Ain't no one going to bless the meal?" We looked around at one another awkwardly, wondering who was going to do the honors. "Ah, hell, I'll do it," Carson said. He bowed his head and closed his eyes. The rest of us did the same. "Bless us, O Lord, and these your gifts, which we are about to receive from your bounty, through Christ our Lord. Amen."

"Amen," we said, somewhat in unison.

Carson made the sign of the cross over his chest, raised his head, and opened his eyes. He took his steak off the fire and put it on his plate. He had barely let it cook. We all began to eat. My first taste of buffalo was not particularly revolutionary. I certainly enjoyed it more than beef. I liked how lean it was and the gamey flavor it had. The gunpowder spiced it up a bit.

"What do you think?" Mason asked.

"It's good," I said. "I really like it."

"Of course you do. Gunpowder makes for a good seasoning, doesn't it?"

"Yeah, I never would have thought," I said.

Carson looked at me strangely as he chewed up a bite of his rare steak. "You never had buffalo before?"

"Nope."

Carson nodded and cut another bite off his steak. "You know, the best way to eat a buffalo steak is with red chili. Ain't nothing better."

Everyone nodded and groaned with full mouths in agreement. Red chili would certainly liven the steak up a bit.

"Are you Catholic, Kit?" I asked.

"Yep. I sure am," Carson said. "Just converted not too long ago."

"What inspired that?" I asked.

"My wife. The padre said I had to be baptized into the Church in order to marry her, so I did. You Catholic?"

"I was raised that way. I haven't practiced it in years," I said. "I've always liked the theatrics of it though."

"Yeah, me, too," Carson said.

"I heard you got married a little while ago," Mason said. "Who's the gal?"

"Josefa is her name. She's a sweet, young girl. Comes from the Jaramillo family in Taos."

"I see," Mason said. "Well, congratulations."

"Thank you."

"How many wives have you had now, Kit?" an older, raspy-voiced man named David Johansen asked, as he cleaned the juice from his steak off his mustache and the corners of his mouth, smiling as he gave Carson a mischievous look.

"Josefa is my third, David," Carson said as he ate his last bite of steak.

"Damn! I'm still trying to find my first," Kyle said, shaking his head in disappointment. Everyone laughed.

We finished our steaks and added a couple of logs to the fire. Carson stuffed some tobacco into his pipe and had a smoke. David did the same. Mason, Kyle, Cole, and I smoked cigars. We conversed around the fire and had a few laughs. Carson removed his hat and pushed his long, stringy hair back. His fingers got caught in the tangles of his unkempt hair, and he put his hat back on. In the light of the flickering flames of the campfire, I noticed a scar on Carson's neck, just below his left ear. I asked him how he got it.

"This old thing?" Carson asked, feeling the scar with his fingers. "I thought everyone knew that story."

"Konrad doesn't," Mason said. "Tell him, Kit. It's a good story."

"Well, it was the summer of 1835, and I was up at the Green River for the annual rendezvous. I was feeling particularly inclined to be womaned after nearly getting myself killed by the Blackfoot the season before. I ended up letting myself fall for this pretty, young Arapahoe girl named Singing Grass. Turned out, a big Frenchman named Joseph Chouinard had fallen for her, too. When she ended up choosing me over him, he said some unkind words to her and went on a drunken rampage for a few days too many. He terrorized everyone who got in his way. He was looking for a fight, but everyone tried their best to ignore him. One day, he finally came over to my camp and insulted my friends and me. I'd had enough of this drunken Frenchman. It was a fight he wanted, so I decided to oblige him and shut him up. I don't remember what I said to him—"

"You said you were the worst American in the camp, and if he didn't stop his foolishness, you were going to rip his guts out," Cole interrupted.

"Yeah, something like that," Carson continued. "So, we go get our weapons. I grab me a pistol, get on my horse, and ride out to meet this son of a bitch. He comes back with a rifle. We charged each other on horseback until we were right up on each other. Our horses' heads were touching. He yelled some things, and I yelled some things. And then, from point blank, we shot at each other. I hit him in his hand and blew off his thumb. His horse shied at the last moment, so he just grazed me here." Carson pointed to the scar on his neck again. "Had his horse not shied, I wouldn't be sitting here with you boys now."

"What happened after you shot off his thumb?" I asked.

"I went and grabbed another pistol to finish him off. When I came back, he was on his knees, holding the bloody stump that used to be his thumb and begging for his life. He didn't bother anyone else after that."

Everyone laughed.

"Speaking of big, loud drunks, where the hell is John Dawkins?" Jeremy McAvoy asked. He was a young man with a thick layer of scruff on his leathery face. He always seemed to be squinting. "I thought he of all people would join back up with our outfit."

"I heard he got killed in San Antonio not long after we got back from our first expedition," David Johansen said in an emotionless, raspy voice, as he sharpened a stick with his hunting knife.

"Really? That true?" McAvoy asked.

"That's what I heard," David said, without looking up from the stick he was sharpening. "Got into a scuffle with a few Mexicans over a card game. Took on four guys with his fists. One of them pulled a gun and shot him in the back."

"No, no," Mason said, leaning forward. "He was hanged. The fight happened like you said, but he was the one who pulled the gun. He shot at one of the guys, but he missed. The bullet ended up hitting some poor fellow at the bar in the back of the head. He was tried and hanged a month later. At least that's what I heard from Charlie Bent when I was in Taos back in January."

"Well, if you heard it from Charlie Bent, then it's probably the truth," David said, still not looking up from the stick he was sharpening. "Either way, he's dead."

"That's too bad," McAvoy said sadly. "Why didn't I hear anything about it?"

"Well, 'cause you got mud in your ears half the time, Jeremy," Mason teased.

"Shut up, Mason," Jeremy returned.

"You didn't hear nothin' 'cause John Dawkins was a raging drunk like Chouinard, and nobody gives a damn about guys like that."

"Speak kindly of the dead," Carson said. "He can't defend himself."

David gave Carson an irritated look and then went back to sharpening his stick. "Well, I guess he couldn't defend himself when he was alive neither."

Everyone was silent for a while as we finished our cigars. The world of mountain men and adventurers like the men I was sitting with was a small and violent one. It was very different from the world I knew, which made it very appealing to me. They were certainly a different breed. In the world I came from, men were driven by money, work, and status. In the world I was living in now, men were driven by the moment and by instinct. Money was not essential to their lifestyle. They followed their hearts wherever it took them in a constant search for adventure and excitement. These men were rough and wild and did not have the best of manners. They were charming in an effortless way, not feeling the need to impress anyone. It was a violent world and a very real world, but there was an innocence to it, a purity that came from the very core of man's most basic desires. It was a world of men simply being men and not a world of men being what they were told they should be. This was the world to which I knew I had always belonged.

We finished our smokes and laid out our bedrolls. Mason put a few more logs on the fire to keep it going all night, for the open plains got quite cold after the sun disappeared. I lay under my Mexican blanket, staring up at a midnight sky speckled with more stars than I had ever seen. Long after the men of the outfit had fallen asleep, I remained awake, wide-eyed and in a euphoric contentment, as I listened to the sounds of the plains. The wind blowing the grass, the howls of the coyotes, the flapping wings of the night birds, the crackle of the campfires, and even the snores of the men were soothing to me.

I finally allowed myself to drift off to sleep. I awoke a few hours later to the sound of a fresh log catching fire and the heat of the rising flames warming my back. I rolled over, and Kit Carson was kneeling next to the fire, preparing a pot of coffee. I sat up and took a sip of water from my canteen.

"Is it about that time?" I asked Carson in a whisper.

"Yep. The sun will be coming up in a couple hours," Carson said in a soft voice that was not quite a whisper.

"Getting an early start on the coffee, I see."

"Nothing raises the morale of a man more than waking up to a fresh pot of coffee," Carson revealed. "You get any sleep last night?"

"Not much. I don't really like sleeping," I said.

"Yeah, me neither," Carson admitted. "Feels like a waste of time."

"I'm always too excited for the next day."

Carson nodded in agreement, as he reached into his pocket and took out two strips of jerky. He tossed one to me. I thanked him and took a bite.

"You ain't never done anything like this before, have you, kid?" Carson asked.

"Is it that obvious?" I asked with a chuckle.

"No, you do just fine. You carry your weight. You just ask a lot of questions. That's a good thing though. You should never be afraid to ask questions."

"I met Mason, Kyle, and Cole in New Orleans, and they told me about the expedition, so I signed on. No questions asked," I explained.

"Yeah... well, you don't need a lot of experience for this sort of thing. You just sort of follow your basic instincts. This sort of thing just comes natural to a man, I think."

"It feels natural," I said.

"Not to say anybody can do it. It's certainly not for everybody. You got to be in the right state of mind. It takes a special kind of person to follow their basic instincts."

"Yeah, I guess it does," I agreed.

"You from the North?" Carson asked, holding out his hand and gesturing for me to hand him my cup.

"Yeah, New York," I said, handing him my cup. He took the coffee off the fire, filled my cup, and handed it back to me. "Where are you from originally?" I asked.

"I was born in Kentucky, but my family moved to Missouri when I was a year old."

"When did you decide to come out West?" I asked.

"When I was sixteen, I signed on with a merchant caravan heading to Santa Fe. I just tended to the horses and whatnot. But that's what set me off. After that, I lived in Taos for a while where I learned how to be a trapper. I signed on to a trapping party in the spring of '29, and up until I met John Fremont, that's what I did."

"Sounds like an exciting life," I commented.

"Sure," Carson said, not seeming completely convinced.

I took a sip of my coffee. Men around the camp were beginning to get up and move around. I looked to the east and saw that the sky had turned from nearly black to a lighter blue, indicating that the sun was preparing to make its grand entrance. Soon, all of the men were up and getting ready for the day. We rolled up our bedrolls and threw dirt on the fires. Just as the sun began to peak over the horizon, we saddled our horses and rode out of camp.

At about noon, we reconnected with the Arkansas River. We stopped to refresh our canteens and to let our horses drink. I decided to ride a little farther upriver and have a look around. As I rode along the riverbank and peered into the clear, calm water, I noticed a fair number of trout swimming about. I followed along the bend of the river and could no longer see the outfit, though I could still hear them. They were a loud bunch.

When finally out of hearing distance from the outfit, I stopped to soak in the solitude. After climbing off Renegado's back to let him drink from the river, I kneeled down next to the water and filled my canteen, took off my hat, splashed water on my face, and ran my wet hands through my hair. I exhaled a loud sigh of contentment while observing the beauty around me. Suddenly, I noticed a figure on horseback at the top of a hill across the river. Quickly rising from my kneeling position, I squinted into the sunlight and immediately realized that it was an Indian. He sat atop his horse and did not move as he stared at me. I stared back at him and did not feel afraid or nervous. He was the first Indian I had ever seen. I was more curious than anything. We stared at one another for a few moments. Finally, I raised my hand in the air as a friendly gesture of greeting. The Indian stared at me a few moments longer and then returned my greeting by raising his hand. He lowered his hand and grabbed his reins. He quickly turned his horse around and disappeared down the other side of the hill. I stood there for a while longer, smiling, and realizing that I had just had my first encounter with an Indian.

I heard the crunch of hooves on the grass behind me and spun around to see who it was. It was Kit Carson.

"Didn't mean to startle you," Carson apologized.

"No, it's okay. You didn't startle me. I just saw an Indian," I said.

"Did you? Where?"

I pointed to the top of the hill where the Indian had been sitting his horse. Carson looked up to the top of the hill while shielding his eyes from the sun with his hand. He nodded and looked down at me.

"Well, I can smell the buffalo herd. If you'd like to join me, I was going to go look for them. Figured a greenhorn like you has probably never seen a massive herd of buffs before."

I shook my head.

"Then come on. They ain't too far."

I climbed onto Renegado's back and rode up next to Carson. We rode across the plains, heading south and angling slightly west. A breeze blew from the south, bringing with it a peculiar, animalistic smell. I assumed it was the buffalo herd. Carson and I rode for about twenty minutes before coming to the base of a large hill that stretched far across the plains. I could hear the grunts of the herd on the other side.

We began climbing the hill, and I was filled with anticipation as I prepared to gaze upon the great herd. We came to the top of the hill, and in the broad valley below was a sight like nothing I had ever seen. The grazing herd stretched for what seemed like miles and was so dense that I could not see the ground on which they walked. There had to be thousands of them. It was an incredible sight. I stared at the herd in awe.

"It's something else, ain't it?" Carson asked.

"It's unbelievable!" I replied, still trying to take in the massive number of buffalo.

"The sight of herds like this never ceases to amaze me," Carson commented.

"Are we going to hunt them?" I asked.

"No," Carson replied. "It ain't our herd to hunt. You say you saw an Indian earlier, probably an Arapaho. This is their herd. They're probably on the other side of this valley, getting ready for the hunt right now."

We sat there at the top of the hill, watching the herd for a while. I hoped to see the Arapaho hunting party charge out and attack the herd, but they did not. Carson and I turned out horses around and rode back down the hill to rejoin the outfit.

That evening, after we set up camp for the night, I walked off on my own to sit by the river and watch the sunset. I smoked a cigar as I watched the orange sun slowly descend into the horizon. The last sliver of the sun disappeared behind the hills, but the fiery glow hung in the sky a while longer.

XXIII

OUR JOURNEY WESTWARD THROUGH the Great Plains continued smoothly as we followed the Arkansas River. I rode along, nearly oblivious to everything except the beautiful scenery around me. The plains had pretty much looked the same for the past few days, but every inch of it was new to me. With every step we took, I was reminded that I was sitting on the back of a good horse while riding through the wild lands of the frontier, not knowing what dangers or beauties lay ahead of me as I lived off the land and my instincts. I felt just as I had always imagined a man should feel.

"How are you doing, Konrad?" Mason asked, as he rode up next to me, snapping me out of my daze.

"I'm good. How are you?"

"Good, my friend. I'm good."

"How much longer before we get to the Rockies?" I asked.

"Well, we're only a few days away from Bent's Fort. You'll be able to see the Rockies from there. Then it's just another couple days."

"What's Bent's Fort?" I asked.

"It's a trading post on the Santa Fe Trail. I used to work there as a hunter. That's how I met Kyle, Cole, Kit, and some of these other lunatics."

"Where were you before that?"

"Taos. Went straight there after leaving home when I was seventeen. I heard it was the capital of the Southwestern fur trade, and that was where I wanted to be. I wanted to be a trapper, a mountain man." Mason became lost in his thoughts for a moment. "Damn! That was six years ago!"

"How did your parents feel about that?"

"They didn't care too much. I got six brothers and sisters, so they had plenty of other children to worry about. They were probably glad to have one less mouth to feed," Mason said with a chuckle.

I took a deep breath and felt a slight vibration in my chest that caused me to suddenly start coughing violently. The episode lasted a few moments. I spit out the mucus that had come up with the cough.

"You all right?" Mason asked, a concerned look on his face.

"I'm fine. Just something caught in my throat."

The truth was, I had been feeling slightly unwell almost all day long. The night before, I had awakened in a cold sweat, shivering beneath my thick blanket as I lay next to the warm campfire. I felt fine in the morning, but by about noon, that general feeling of tiredness and weakness in the muscles caused by a fever began to creep over me. I prayed that it was nothing and that it wouldn't get any worse. Now I was coughing. I began to fear that I had caught a cold. I drank three canteens of water that day in the hope that keeping myself well hydrated would put off whatever I had caught.

That night, I awoke once again in a cold sweat, shivering under my blanket. This time, my fever was accompanied by abdominal pains and a headache. The next day, I didn't feel any better. It no longer felt like a typical cold, and I began to fear that it was something worse. I hid my fear from the outfit, but I could not hide my symptoms. My cough had gotten worse and now accompanied me steadily throughout the day. The abdominal pain caused me to hunch over as well as lose my appetite. The color in my face had faded, and the headache caused me to squint in pain. Mason, Kyle, Cole, and a few others told me at various times throughout the day that I did not look well. Mason told me to drink lots of water. I already had been, but I drank even more.

As soon as we stopped to set up camp for the night, I laid out my bedroll and went to sleep in hopes that a good rest would cure whatever illness I had contracted. Mason woke me up in what felt like the middle of the night, but I noticed that the men were still up and huddled around their campfires, indicating that it was still evening.

"What is it?" I said.

"How are you feeling?" Mason asked, kneeling over me. David Johansen was with him.

"I'm fine. Just a little tired," I lied.

"I brought David over to have a look at you. He's knowledgeable about illnesses," Mason explained. David knelt down next to Mason and studied me thoroughly.

"I'm fine. It's just a fever. It will probably be gone in the morning if you'd just let me sleep."

"All right — enough of this tough-guy talk," David said bluntly. "I'm going to need you to be honest with me." David felt my forehead with the back of his hand. "You're pretty warm. Do you feel like you're temperature has been getting higher?"

"I don't know. Maybe a little," I said. I had a sudden, short coughing spell.

"I see you got a cough," David remarked. "Headache? Stomach pain?"

"Both."

"You been getting bloody noses?"

"No."

David put his fingers to the left side of my neck, just under my jawbone, to check my pulse. "You been having diarrhea?"

"Yeah."

"How many times a day?"

"A couple."

David nodded and wiped his hands on his pants. "Looks like you got typhoid fever."

"Yeah, that was my first thought," Mason said.

"Is that bad?" I asked. "What does that mean?"

"It means you ate someone's shit, partner," Mason said.

"What?"

"It was probably in the water you drank or something you ate," David said.

"Is it bad?" I asked.

"It can be. Just drink as much water as you can," David instructed. "We'll get you looked at by a real doctor when we get to Bent's Fort tomorrow."

David stood up and walked away. I tried to thank him but began to cough when I opened my mouth to speak. Mason handed me my canteen and told me to finish it before I went back to sleep. When I finished drinking, he took my canteen and said he would go fill it up for me. I thanked him and almost instantly fell back to sleep.

I woke up sporadically throughout the night, feeling just a little worse each time. Mason woke me up in the morning when the outfit was preparing to leave. He handed me my canteen and told me to drink as much as I could. Mason, Kyle, and Cole gathered my things, saddled Renegado, and helped me climb onto his back. It was kind of them to help but quite embarrassing. I felt like a poor, helpless greenhorn who didn't have what it took to survive on the frontier. I think Mason knew that I must have been feeling as if I were a burden, for he kept reassuring me that it could happen to anyone. I'm sure that was true, but it did not happen to anyone; it happened to me, and I happened to be the only greenhorn in our outfit. It made me look weak. It made me look as if I didn't belong among these men.

* * *

Shortly after crossing into the High Plains, we came upon the adobe citadel on the north bank of Arkansas River that was Bent's Fort. The double doors of the fort's entrance opened up, and two men walked out to meet us.

"I was wondering when you boys were going to get here,"

the short, round-faced man with gray, receding hair said as he approached.

"Good to see you, Charlie," John Fremont said.

The other man, young and lean, looked like a mountain man. He was dressed in buckskins and had a sharp, bird-like face. His beak of a nose and pronounced cheekbones pushed the corners of his mouth down into an over-emphasized frown. His curly, blond hair puffed out under his wide-brimmed hat.

"Dick Wootton!" Carson called to the mountain man. "Surprised to see you're still here. How did you manage to tie him down, Charlie?"

"Tie him down?" Charlie said. "I've been trying to get him to leave!"

Dick shook his head at Charlie Bent. "You wouldn't know what to do without me." He walked over to Kit and shook his hand. "How are you, Kit?"

"Well, I could use a hot meal," Carson replied.

"You're in luck. Charlotte's just started lunch," Dick informed him. He looked over to Fremont and extended his hand. "You must be John Fremont. It's an honor, sir. I'm Richard Wootton."

Fremont shook Dick's hand. "It's a pleasure to meet you, Mr. Wootton."

"Take your horses around back to the stables and come have some lunch," Charlie invited.

We rode around the fort to the stables where we were met by half a dozen men who were there to tend to the horses.

"Who were the two men who met us out front?" I asked Mason as I climbed off Renegado.

"The older one is Charles Bent. He and his brother, William, built this fort," Mason explained. "The other one is Dick Wootton. He works as a hunter and trader around here. Now, let's see if we can't find a doctor."

Charles Bent walked out to the stables to make sure everything was going smoothly. I saw David Johansen walk over to him. He said a few words and pointed at me. Bent nodded, and he and David began walking toward Mason and me.

"Will Mason, it's good to see you," Bent said, shaking Mason's hand.

"You, too, Charlie," Mason returned. "This here is Konrad Quintero."

"Good to meet you, Konrad. How you feeling?"

"I've been better," I said.

"We think he has typhoid," Mason explained. "You got a doc around?"

"Yeah, Bill Thompson is here. Why don't you take Konrad to St. Vrain's room, and I'll go find the doc."

"Thanks, Charlie," Mason said.

Bent went off to find the doctor, and David and Mason led me out of the stables and into a narrow hallway. We walked past the general store and through a walkway that led into the main courtyard of the fort where there were about five-dozen mountain men, Indians, and Mexicans intermingling. We walked under the overhang of the second level of the fort and stopped at one of the rooms where David opened the door. The room was small and empty except for a bed in the far corner, a chair next to a fireplace, and a buffalo-hide rug in the middle of the room. A crucifix hung on the wall above the bed.

"Why don't you lay down, Konrad," Mason suggested.

I walked over to the bed and lay down under the covers. I was sweating profusely and had been all day. I drank a few big gulps of water from my canteen.

A few minutes later, Bent walked into the room with the doctor, Bill Thompson. He was a tall man, with short, brown hair who looked to be in his early forties. He grabbed the chair, pulled it up next to the bed, and sat down.

"I'm Bill Thompson," he said.

"Konrad," I said, my eyes barely open.

"I hear you're not feeling very well," the doctor said.

"Yeah," I managed.

The doctor turned to Mason and David who were standing behind him. "You boys think he has typhoid, huh?"

"He's got all the symptoms," David answered, "High fever, cough, headache, stomach pain, diarrhea, slow pulse."

The doctor felt my head and checked my pulse. "I'm just going to open up your shirt, Konrad." He pulled the blanket down to my waist and unbuttoned the top five buttons on my shirt, pulled it open, and looked at my chest. "Yep. It's typhoid fever all right."

I looked down at my chest to see what the doctor had seen. Rose-colored spots had formed all over my torso.

"What does this mean, Mr. Thompson?" I asked. "How long before I'm better?"

"It's going to last about a month, son," the doctor responded. "You're going to need to stay in bed and keep yourself hydrated and fed."

"A month?" I asked. "No, I'm on an expedition. I've got to stay with the outfit."

"I'm afraid you're going to have to stay behind," the doctor told me. "I'll be honest with you, son; right now, you may be able to push through the pain, but in about four or five days, you're not going to be able to get out of this bed without someone carrying you, and that's how it'll be for three weeks. I'm going to go get you a cold washcloth to keep you cool." The doctor and Bent then left the room.

I shook my head bitterly.

"I'm sorry, partner," Mason said sympathetically. "This is just real unlucky."

"Yeah," I said shortly, turning my head to stare at the wall.

"You need anything? Want to try to force down some food? Charlotte makes some great flapjacks. I could tell her to make you some. I bet they'd go down easy with some water."

"No, thanks. You go on and eat," I said, still staring at the wall.

"You sure?" Mason asked.

"Yeah — go on."

"All right. I'll be back in a little bit to check on you," Mason promised.

David and Mason walked outside and shut the door behind them. I clenched my jaw in anger and frustration. I gripped the sheet as hard as I could until my knuckles turned white and then began to punch the bed over and over until tears fell down my cheeks. I wouldn't get to cross the Rockies or the desert. I wouldn't get to see the Columbia River or the Pacific Ocean. Mason, Kyle, Cole, and the rest of the outfit were going to go on without me, while I was stuck in this damned fort.

The next morning at dawn, Mason, Kyle, Cole, David, Kit Carson, and John Fremont all came to my room to say goodbye before they continued their journey westward. I put on the best smile I could fake and wished them luck on their expedition. They wished me a speedy recovery and promised to see me in a few months when they returned. Mason stayed behind after the others had left the room.

"I'm sorry this happened to you, partner," he said. "I know how bad you wanted to be a part of this."

"Yeah, well, you're just going to have to enjoy it for the both of us," I said.

"I will, and when I get back, we'll find ourselves another adventure, all right?"

"I'll be waiting," I said. "Be careful out there."

"Will do, but not too careful. Got to have some fun!" Mason shook my hand and patted my shoulder. "Get better, partner. I'll see you soon."

"All right. See you soon."

Mason tipped his hat to me and walked out of the room. I

stared at the door and sighed hopelessly. The frustration had left me, for there was nothing I could do now. They were gone, and I was stuck at the fort and getting worse. I dipped my washcloth in the cold water beside my bed and laid it on my forehead, and then I quickly drifted off into a feverish sleep.

* * *

The next two weeks were a blur. By the end of my second week of illness, I had slipped into a state of delirium accompanied by spells of delusion. The doctor came in to check on me daily, but because of the state I was in, I had to be constantly looked after by a Cheyenne woman named Quahneah, who, in my delirious state, I often mistook for Anastasia, Miriam, or my mother. The poor woman sat by my bed all day and all night, listening to my incoherent rants about God knows what, as she force-fed me and gave me water. She bathed me, cleaned my sheets, and took me outside for fresh air. She soothed me when I became restless or irritated by singing to me in her native tongue. On a couple of occasions, she had to bring in Bill Thompson to restrain me when I would try to leave to rejoin Fremont's outfit.

By the beginning of the fourth week, the delirium had passed, and my fever began to drop. I was finally able to get some decent sleep, and my appetite returned. The red spots on my torso vanished, and the color returned to my skin. The pain in my abdomen and head faded, and my cough subsided. I remained in bed a few days after my temperature had returned to normal, for I was very tired from the lack of sleep my illness had caused.

Once my energy returned, I took a warm bath and shaved off the patchy beard that had grown on my face. After walking out of my room and into the courtyard of the fort, I closed my eyes and let my head fall back as I embraced the rays of sunlight. I took a deep breath of fresh air and exhaled it slowly. The fort was lively with traders and adventurers.

"I almost didn't recognize you standing up," a familiar voice said. I turned to see Bill Thompson walking toward me.

"Hello, doc," I said with a big smile.

"I'm surprised you know who I am. So, this is what you look like when your not withering away," the doctor teased. "It's good to meet you."

I laughed and shook his hand. "I appreciate all of your help, Mr. Thompson. And I apologize for any trouble I might have caused you. I really don't remember much."

"No apology is necessary. Besides, I didn't do much; I just checked on you from time to time. Quahneah is the one who took care of you."

"Right. Where is she? I'd like to thank her."

"She's setting the table for lunch," the doctor said. "Why don't you come eat with us, and you can thank her then. You could use a substantial meal. You must've lost twenty pounds!"

I had lost a lot of weight. My clothes that had once fit snuggly hung quite loosely from my frail body. Almost all of the muscle I had developed during my active four years in Europe was gone. I felt as if I had deflated.

"Yes, a big meal sounds wonderful," I said.

I followed Bill to the dining room where Quahneah was setting the table. The fort's somewhat permanent staff was sitting at the table, waiting for the food. Quahneah looked at me and gave me a big smile. I walked over to her, and she stopped what she was doing. She was quite beautiful. No wonder I had confused her with Anastasia.

"You look much better," Quahneah said.

"Thank you. And thank you for taking care of me. I really couldn't be more grateful. If there's anything I can do to repay you, please tell me."

"You don't need to do anything for me. I was glad to look after you," she said sincerely.

"Well, thank you. We never properly met. I'm Konrad," I said, extending my hand.

"I'm Quahneah," We shook hands. Her hand was tough, yet still quite delicate. Her grip was firm. "Not Anastasia, or Miriam, or Mother," she teased with a wonderful laugh.

I smiled and nodded in embarrassment. "Yes, of course. I'm sorry about that."

"Please, sit down and eat," she invited.

I thanked her again and sat down next to the doctor.

"Is Charles Bent around?" I asked Bill. "I'd like to thank him for housing me."

"He went down to Taos last week," Bill answered. "Not sure when he'll be back."

Bill introduced me to everyone at the table. Among the men at the table was Dick Wootton, who I remembered from the day I had arrived at the fort. He remembered me, too, and told me that I looked a hell of a lot better but could certainly use some fattening up.

The meal was substantial. We ate large buffalo steaks with rice and a hearty potato and pork stew. To finish it off, we had coffee and the most amazing pumpkin pie I had ever tasted. Bill told me that the cook, Charlotte, who was William Bent's slave, was famous throughout the West for her pumpkin pies.

"What are your plans, Konrad, now that you're healthy?" Bill asked me as we sat around, finishing our coffee.

"Well, I don't know who's in charge, but I was hoping I could stay here until my outfit returns," I said.

"You can stay as long as you want, so long as you put in some work," Dick Wootton said.

"I'll do anything you need me to do," I offered gratefully.

"Good! What's your trade?" Dick asked.

"Well, I don't really have one," I said honestly.

"What are you good at?"

"I can cook."

"We got plenty of those, but I'm sure they wouldn't mind a little help in the kitchen," Dick said. "You a good shot?"

To save myself time and embarrassment, I explained my situation to the men, that situation being that I was quite inexperienced in this sort of life.

"Well, you've come to the right place," Dick said when I finished my explanation. "Every greenhorn's got to start somewhere. We all did. Tomorrow, I'll take you hunting with me, and we'll go from there."

"That sounds great," I said. "Thank you."

After lunch, I went out to the stables and found Renegado, surprised that he hadn't jumped the fence and escaped. The poor fellow had been stuck in the stables for a month. I petted him for a while and apologized for keeping him locked up. I then found my saddle and put it on Renegado's back. I climbed onto his back, and the stableman opened the gate for us. As soon as we were out of the stables, Renegado started to gallop away from the fort toward the hills. Suddenly, he broke into a dead sprint, nearly causing me to roll off his back. I leaned forward and held on tight to the reins, as I let him release all of the energy that had been building up inside of him. I screamed with excitement, as I clenched my legs against his sides, holding on for dear life. I had never ridden a horse running at full speed. It was exhilarating. Renegado ran at a dead sprint for over a quarter of a mile before finally slowing down to a steady trot and then eventually a slow walk. I inhaled a deep breath to slow the adrenaline pumping through my veins.

I brought Renegado to a stop and looked to the west. Far off in the distance stood the massive, bluish-purple peaks of a seemingly endless mountain range. It was the Rockies. I gazed upon them in awe. They were daunting even from a great distance. They stood wild and magnificent, cutting into the sky with great ferocity, both disconcerting and inviting.

I wondered where Fremont and the men were. They were probably still traversing the Rocky Mountains. I was envious as I stared at the glorious mountain range, imagining all the things I might have been seeing had I not grown ill and been left behind at Bent's Fort. But there was nothing I could do about it now. I was stuck at the fort, and the outfit was probably riding out the other side of the mountains. All I could do was make the best of my situation and learn and experience as much as I could at the fort while waiting for Fremont and the men to return from the expedition.

XXIV

THE NEXT MORNING, I awoke before the sun. I was still used to the early mornings on the expedition. The fort was quiet except for a few traders getting an early start on the day. I walked across the empty courtyard, climbed the stairs to the second level, and walked along the narrow walkway that wrapped around the fort. While leaning up against the eastern wall and watching as the sun began to rise, I could smell the cottonwood smoke and spices as breakfast was being prepared. A rooster crowed from the stables. Of all the places I could have been stranded, I was glad I was stuck at Bent's Fort. The land surrounding it was beautiful. The fort itself was exciting and full of interesting, friendly people. And it was life on the frontier.

The sound of a harsh whistle startled me. I turned around and looked down into the courtyard where Dick Wootton was standing.

"Glad to see you're up," Dick said. "Come get some breakfast, and then we'll head out."

We ate cheesy eggs and bacon for breakfast, which we washed down with coffee. After breakfast, Dick and I walked out to the stables where the rest of the hunting crew was saddling their horses and getting the wagon ready. Dick introduced me to the three men. The man hitching the horses to the wagon was Stephen Fletcher. The other two men were skinners. One was a Mexican named José Sanchez, and the other was a French-Canadian named Andre Labonte. José was a friendly young man about my age. He had a light mustache and kind, light-brown eyes. Andre was a brawny bear of a man. His face was covered in a thick layer of whiskers that reached from his Adam's apple almost to his eyes, and he wore a thick mustache that curled at the ends. He was quiet and had an expressionless face, but he didn't come off as rude or unfriendly. We climbed onto our horses while Fletcher took the wagon, and we headed west along the Arkansas River in search of game.

We wandered around the plains for an hour while Dick studied everything around him very closely for signs of wildlife. We came to a buffalo wallow, and Dick stopped and climbed off of his horse. He told me to get down as well. I stepped into the wallow where Dick was kneeling down, digging around in the dirt. He picked up a clump of hair and rubbed it between his fingers. He handed it to me, and I did the same.

"You see how the hair is still wet? Greasy? It ain't dead and dry," Dick said.

I felt the hair in my hands and nodded.

"That means the wallow is fresh. The herd probably ain't too far from here." Dick stepped out of the wallow and studied the ground carefully. "See his hoof prints here?" he indicated, pointing to the ground. I walked over and looked where he was pointing.

"Yeah, I see it."

"So, we can see that he walked out of the wallow this way and headed northwest. We're on the right track. I don't think the herd will be too far from here."

We got back on our horses and rode northwest. Dick's first hunting lesson taught me that tracking animals was not a science. In fact, it was quite simple once one knows what to look for. It's just a matter of paying close attention to the small details. When it comes to telling if something is fresh, whether it be hair, dung, or a print in the dirt, it's pretty cut and dry.

We rode through the plains for another half-hour until we suddenly came upon a small herd of whitetail deer. Dick quickly stopped and held up his hand as a signal for the rest of us to do the same. As he climbed off his horse, he told me to get off of mine and grab my rifle. I grabbed the loaded Hawken rifle Dick had given me and followed him as he crept closer to the herd. He stopped when he thought we were in a good position and laid down. I did the same.

"This is your chance to get your first kill," Dick said. "Have you ever shot a rifle before?" I shook my head. "I didn't think so. It's pretty simple. Just point your muzzle at your target. See that buck closest to us?" Dick pointed at the buck he meant. He was about one hundred and fifty feet away. I nodded as I aimed my rifle. "Good. Now, rest the stock on your left hand. Don't grasp the stock or the weight of your arm will pull it down. Since we're lying down, you don't have to worry about that."

I rested the rifle stock on my hand and adjusted myself into a comfortable position. I peered down the top of the barrel. The buck was in my sights, unaware of my presence, as he grazed.

"You're looking good," Dick said. "Now, get the butt of the rifle snug against your shoulder — real snug. Good. Now, you're going to want to aim for the deer's heart, just behind his shoulder." Dick leaned over my shoulder and peered down my rifle to check my aim. "Good."

Dick lay down on his stomach and positioned his rifle. He took aim at a buck off to the left and further away.

"Make sure you squeeze the trigger. Don't pull it, or you'll jerk your rifle and miss your target," Dick said. "Just squeeze it gently and smoothly. On the count of three, we're going to fire. You ready?"

"Yeah, I'm ready," I said, closing my left eye.

"One," Dick began, "two — three."

Dick and I fired simultaneously. The rifle kicked hard against my shoulder and collarbone. I winced in agony and surprise. When I opened my eyes and peered through the cloud of smoke, I saw my buck fall. I had hit him.

"You got him!" Dick said, as he stood up and watched the herd of deer run away. The echo of our rifles was still hanging in the air. "Good shot! Let's go get our kills!"

I stood up proudly and walked over to the buck I had shot.

He was dead all right. My bullet had hit almost exactly where I had aimed.

"Damn!" Dick said, looking at the bullet hole. "Good shooting, Konrad."

"Thanks. Not bad for my first time, I guess."

"Not bad at all. Damn near perfect. I'm going to go check on my kill."

Dick walked over to the buck he had shot. I knelt down next to my buck and looked into his open, lifeless eyes. A sudden wave of sadness came over me. I touched his thick fur, admiring the beautiful animal.

"Good shot, *amigo*," José complimented in his thick, Mexican accent.

Startled, I stood up quickly and turned to face José. He had brought Renegado and Dick's horse with him. He climbed down from his horse and observed my kill.

"Real good shot," he repeated.

"Thanks," I said.

Andre was riding over to Dick and his kill.

"You see? Hunting is easy! Now, I get to do all the hard work," José commented, and then he took out his big knife, knelt down over the buck, and quickly cut its throat. The blood began to trickle onto the grass, quickly creating a red pool next to the deer.

"Why did you do that?" I asked, stepping back as the blood inched toward my feet.

"It makes skinning him easier. Makes the skin looser," José explained.

Fletcher drove up in the wagon and complimented me on my kill. I looked over and saw Andre slit the throat of the other buck as Dick walked toward me. José began the process of skinning my buck, and Fletcher climbed down from his wagon to help him. Dick patted me on the back and stuffed his rifle into his saddle scabbard.

"Let's go," Dick said, climbing onto his horse.

"Where are we going?" I asked, walking over to Renegado and putting my rifle in my saddle scabbard.

"We still got to find that herd of buffalo," Dick said.

I climbed into my saddle, and we rode northwest in search of the buffalo herd, while José, Andre, and Fletcher tended to our kills. Dick and I rode for about three miles before I started to smell the familiar scent I had smelled when Kit Carson had shown me my first herd of buffalo. A few minutes later, the herd came into view. It was not nearly as large as the herd I had seen with Kit Carson, but it was still an intimidating and extraordinary sight. We climbed off our horses and tied them to a tree, grabbed our rifles, and walked out toward the herd. As we got closer, we knelt down and approached them slowly, stopping every now and again to make sure we weren't seen. When we were about three hundred feet away from the herd, we stopped and took our positions.

"Do you know how to load your rifle?" Dick asked.

I told him I did not know how, and he showed me by slowly demonstrating while giving me a detailed description of what he was doing. It seemed simple enough but somewhat tedious.

"All right," Dick began, handing me back my rifle. "What we're going to do now is simple. We're going to shoot as many as we can before they start running away. They ain't very smart animals, and since there are so many of them, it will take them awhile to become all the wiser. You saw how I loaded your rifle. It's pretty simple. You're going to have to reload as fast as you can. We should be able to knock down about twenty of these sons of bitches."

"Really? That many?" I asked.

"Sure! I've gotten as many as twenty-five in one sitting," Dick bragged. "If they start stampeding toward us, just hightail it back to the horses as fast as you can. Got it?" I nodded, and Dick said, "All right; let's shoot some buffs!"

Dick raised his rifle and took aim. I did the same. Dick fired and I quickly followed. The butt of my rifle kicked hard against my already bruised shoulder. My bullet hit the buffalo I was aiming at, and he dropped to the ground next to the buffalo Dick had shot. When I looked over at Dick, he was already halfway done reloading. I reloaded as quickly as I could. I was quite clumsy. As I fumbled around with the gunpowder, Dick fired again. The explosion startled me and I jumped, for I was deep in concentration as I tried to load my rifle. I looked over at Dick as he quickly reloaded his rifle. I finally finished loading my second round just as Dick finished loading his third. I took aim and fired. Dick fired immediately after me. My shoulder and collarbone were really beginning to hurt.

I reloaded my rifle much more quickly the third time. I was still clumsy and slow, however. Dick fired off another shot, and I fired a few moments after him. We continued to shoot and reload over and over again, and I eventually lost count of how many shots I fired or how many buffalo I had shot. We sat there, firing shot after shot for about ten minutes before the herd began to stampede away from us toward the south. Dick rose to his feet, after swiftly reloading his rifle, and took aim at the stampeding herd. He fired and dropped a buffalo. I finished reloading my rifle and stood up to fire as Dick reloaded. I got off two more shots before the herd was out of range. Dick had gotten off four more.

Dick smiled at me and patted me on the back. "That was fun, wasn't it?"

"Yeah." I massaged my shoulder and rotated it around. "My shoulder is killing me though."

"You'll get used to that. It'll be sore the first couple of times, but soon you won't even notice it. Let's go see what we got."

We walked out to where the herd had been grazing. The land was littered with big, dark-brown mounds scattered sporadically over the grassy plain. We walked around, counting our kills and making sure they were dead. We ended up dropping twenty-eight buffalo. Dick said that it was a real good take and that I had done very well on my first buffalo hunt. He said I was a natural hunter.

Soon, Fletcher was driving the wagon toward us, with José and Andre riding out in front of him. They complimented us on our hunt. Andre took a long, metal spike out of his saddlebag, walked over to the buffalo closest to us, and hammered the spike through the nose of the buffalo and into the ground. He slit its throat, and made a few other quick cuts. Andre and José then hooked their horses up to the buffalo hide and pulled their horses forward until the buffalo hide ripped away from the carcass. I watched, wide-eyed in shock and disgust. It was a very brutal process.

Fletcher took the buffalo hide, cleaned it, and put it in the wagon, while José and Andre went on to the next dead buffalo. Dick and I got on our horses and began riding in the direction the herd had stampeded in search of any wounded buffalo that may have fallen.

We rode around for two hours and found no wounded buffalo, nor did we locate the herd. We rode back to the site of our slaughter, where José and Andre were finishing up their gruesome job. The wagon was filled with buffalo hides. They packed as much meat into the wagon as possible and covered it with salt. However, the wagon only held the meat of about ten buffalo. The rest of the naked carcasses were left to rot. This did not sit well with me.

"Why didn't we take the meat from the rest of the buffalo?" I asked as we rode back to the fort.

"Couldn't fit it all in the wagon," Dick said.

"Why don't we take out more wagons then?" I pressed.

"Well, it wouldn't do any good. It would all just spoil. Hell, some of the meat we're bringing back with us is just going to spoil. We can't use it all, but the hides are worth plenty," Dick explained.

We arrived back at the fort in the late afternoon. We carried the hides to the general store where most of the trading took place. The man who ran the store counted the hides and recorded our day's take in his ledger. We then went back to the wagon and took the meat to the kitchen. Once our wagon was unloaded, we unsaddled our horses, gave them a brushing, and fed them.

"Well, Konrad," Dick started, as we walked across the busy courtyard of the fort. "Today you had your first kill and your first buffalo hunt. That calls for two drinks."

We walked into the billiard room, which was simple and just big enough to play billiards without hitting the wall with the cue stick. Dick headed straight for the modest, unattended bar in the corner. He grabbed four glasses and a bottle of rum off the shelf above the bar, filled the glasses, and handed three of them to José, Andre, and me. We all touched glasses and drank, and then Dick refilled our glasses.

"You play billiards, Konrad?" Dick asked, as he grabbed a cue stick and walked over to the table.

"I've played a little," I said. I had actually gotten quite good while living in Europe. I grabbed a stick and joined Dick at the billiard table.

"How about a game of English Billiards then?"

I accepted his challenge, and he set up the game. We decided that the first player to reach 100 would be the winner. I broke to start the match. José and Andre watched and commented as we played, calling us "lucky" on our good shots and making fun of our poor shots as they shared a bottle of rum.

After twenty minutes, the score was 30 to 26 in Dick's favor. I was not at my best, and Dick was much better than I had expected. After a devastating miss while trying to pot the red ball, I held out my empty glass to José, while he and Andre made fun of me for my embarrassing shot. José refilled my glass, and I drank the rum down in one gulp, as Dick potted the red ball for a three-point shot. I shook my head, took the red ball out of the pocket, and put it on the spot, which happened to be right next to Dick's cue ball. I took careful aim and took my shot. My cue ball hit both the red ball and Dick's cue ball. Dick's cue ball was potted in the corner pocket. The red ball bounced off the top rail and rolled into the corner pocket on the opposite end, making it a seven-point combination shot to tie the game. Andre and José laughed and clapped for my extraordinary shot. I bowed graciously and shrugged at Dick who was shaking his head.

We continued to play billiards and drink for about thirty more minutes. I finally made the winning shot that put me at 101 points against Dick's 97 points. Dick congratulated me on my win, and we walked over to the kitchen for dinner, which was the deer I had shot. I enjoyed the taste of venison very much. It was lean and gamey but quite flavorful, especially when prepared by Charlotte's hands. I found that I liked the deer meat more than beef, buffalo, or pork, but not as much as I liked lamb. After dinner, Dick and I went outside and sat at the top of the steps that led to the second level of the fort while we each had a cigar.

"Did you enjoy your first day as a hunter?" Dick asked.

"Sure. It was an interesting experience," I said.

"You did good, and you'll get better every time we go out," Dick promised.

"I'm sure I will," I said, looking up at the millions of stars above me. The moon was full and casting a beautiful, blue glow onto the fort. "Will we be doing any trapping?" I asked, as I exhaled the smoke from my cigar. "I've always been interested in how that works."

"No, we won't be doing any trapping," Dick said, shaking his head as he stared at his feet. "No, that's a dead business."

"Why is that?"

"Well, fashion has changed, for one. The top hat made from the beaver hides we used to take is no longer the style. Even if they were still in demand, there's hardly any beaver left to trap. I left Bent's Fort awhile back to go live in the mountains as a trapper, but there was just nothing left. So, I came back here to work as a hunter. Now, here I am, killing buffalo 'cause their hides are in demand, but that demand will be gone one day. That is, if the buffalo ain't gone first."

"Then what? That's the end of hunters, too?" I asked.

"Buffalo hunters, yes, but there will be something else to hunt. Something else will come into demand, and we'll just hunt that till it's gone."

Dick spoke with no emotion but rather bluntly, as if it was just a matter of fact. I figured hunters and trappers like Dick chose their profession less for the money it provided, which was not much, but more for the adventurous lifestyle it allowed. I had not particularly enjoyed the hunt earlier that day, but I knew it was a skill I needed to know for survival, and being proficient with a rifle was necessary on the frontier. I had not minded shooting the deer, since it had provided the employees of the fort with meat for the evening. The buffalo slaughter was harder to swallow, and I could not get out of my head the image of those naked carcasses left on the plains to rot. However, I knew I had to work to earn my stay at the fort, for I had no place else to go. They had been good to me, and if hunting buffalo was what I had to do to repay them, then I would reluctantly do so.

XXV

SUMMER ON THE HIGH Plains was beautiful, with the bluest skies, endless in their magnificence, and rarely did the clouds hinder the sun from casting down its glorious rays to give brightness and heat to the earthly life below the heavens. The dry heat was soothing yet energizing.

I spent my days doing any work that needed to be done around the fort. I helped Charlotte in the kitchen on a number of occasions and even learned a few new recipes. Quahneah taught me how to tan a buffalo hide and make it into a robe. The first robe we made together, she allowed me to keep for myself, telling me I would need it during the winter. I also went on many walks with Quahneah, where she showed me the different types of plants that could be used for medicinal remedies.

I continued to hunt with Dick, José, Andre, and Fletcher. We went on many buffalo hunts and would bring in as many as forty hides in a single day. I had become a very good shot with both my rifle and my pistol and had grown quite efficient and swift when it came to reloading.

I accompanied Dick, José, Andre, and Fletcher on their occasional trips to Taos to buy supplies for the fort. Taos was a small adobe village amongst the sage of the plains at the base of the Sangre de Cristo Mountains. Being the capital of the Southwestern fur trade, the town was full of wild adventurers and mountain men. There was a welcoming restlessness in the air that blew in tune with my heart. It was a gem of a town, full of wonderful, accepting people. We would arrive in the evening and spend the night drinking at the saloons and gambling with the adventurers who had many stories to share. Many of their stories sounded embellished, unbelievable, and often just strange enough to seem true. I was introduced to an awful poison the locals called

"Taos Lightning", which was their infamous moonshine. I drank one glass and lit up like a firefly. It was absolutely terrible, and I felt that more than one glass would be enough to kill a man, but these men drank it as if it was water.

After a night of drinking and gambling, we would find comfort in the warm, welcoming beds of the brothel girls. In the morning, we would get the supplies we needed for the fort, either through trade or regular purchase at the general store, and begin our short journey back to Bent's Fort.

I also accompanied Dick and his team on supply trains headed north to trade with the Cheyenne and Arapaho Indians. My first encounter with the Natives was quite unnerving but went very well, as Dick said it always did. The trading was very professional and friendly. The Natives joked with us and told stories. They seemed to have a wonderful sense of humor. We traded them guns and the accessories to go with them, as well as blankets, beads, trinkets, coffee, liquor, flour, sugar, and tobacco. In return, they gave us buffalo hides, buckskins, and sometimes horses.

Almost every evening, when all my work was done, I would ride Renegado westward to the highest hill and stare off at the Rocky Mountains. I often wondered where the outfit might be and what they were doing. I thought of my parents, Uncle Friedrich, Raul, and Miriam. I tried not to think of Anastasia, but she always managed to find her way into my thoughts. Anastasia was synonymous with beauty, and I was surrounded by it. Her image was bound to appear in my head from time to time.

However, the long, hot days of summer began to fade. A coolness found its way into the wind and began to nibble at the trees, and the leaves began to fall. The days grew colder, and in late October the first snow of winter fell. The plains were blanketed beneath the thin, white layer of powder, and it was beautiful sight.

That thin layer of white on the plains grew thicker as November gave way to December. In the winter, the fort continued to function, and business went on as usual. We did not make as many trips to trade, and fewer traders came to the fort for business.

The buffalo hunts with Dick and his team became even more frequent in the winter, for the hides were much thicker and were worth a great deal more. We went hunting almost every day. Sometimes we would return with no success and sometimes with great success. From the middle of November through February, the only work I did for the fort was hunting, and I was growing weary of it.

Almost every night there was a "get together" in the dinning room, shortly after dinner. People drank, socialized, and danced to the scratchy tune of a fiddle. I grew weary of the parties as well. I found myself spending much of my free time alone in my room, sitting next to the fire while reading a book from Doctor Thompson's extensive library or going on long rides across the snowy plains.

As I approached my twenty-third birthday at the end of the year, I began to grow restless again, but not in the same way I had in New York or New Orleans. It was a calm restlessness, deeply internal and causing an aching pain in my heart. It was a restlessness I felt I could do nothing about. I was stuck at the fort. The heavy snows of winter and the unpredictable weather that could often be unforgiving felt like a temporary wall. Even if the weather had been good, I could not leave. I had to wait for my outfit to return from the expedition.

Along with feeling restless and trapped, a gloomy loneliness had swept over me with the arrival of the bitter cold. Maybe it was the sad sight of the naked, leafless trees or the prairie grass flatted beneath the heavy blanket of snow. Maybe it was the absence of the sun hidden behind the gray clouds, aching to break through. Maybe it was the cold, slowing the beat of my heart, that caused me to ache for the warmth of Anastasia's presence. It was probably just the weather, but Anastasia haunted my thoughts and dreams. I often found myself sitting in my room at my desk next to the fire, trying to summon the words I wished to write to Anastasia in a letter, but they would not come to the paper as they had come to my heart.

The winter brings out the cold sense of loneliness in people. I had felt this cold loneliness before, whether I was missing a love I had lost or just longing for the companionship of love. It always felt the same; the crisp, sharp, biting cold of winter was like the lonely spirits of summer love, which once were combined as one in a sweaty entanglement with their counterparts, dancing on clouds and rainbows with the warm sun at their backs. But their flame went out like a candle at the end of its wick, with the black smoke of their lonely, cold souls wisping through the trees and streets in a desperate search for their lost love, thus creating winter. As people become aware of the bitter loneliness, they become inspired, more than ever, to search for love. The lucky and the hopeful find somebody, thus giving birth to spring when love blooms with the flowers. With gentle nurturing, these flowers grow radiant and hot, and the summer breathes its wet heat upon them. They grow too hot much too quickly, and they begin to wither. The sun grows sad and ashamed, and it hides away behind the clouds, allowing fall to deliver the final blow. The leaves fall, as do the lovers' hearts, as they slowly become untangled, until each becomes their own again. They drift apart, growing lonelier and colder. Their spirits are swept up into the wind to blow cold for the winter. I missed Anastasia greatly.

* * *

March arrived, bringing with it the spring to lift the cold and my spirits. The snow melted, and color returned to the Earth and the sky. As the days grew warmer, birds and other wildlife that had been absent for the winter returned to their habitats. The fort became busier as conditions along the trails improved. Traders arrived daily in great numbers to do business.

The spring air was refreshing, and the sun shined proudly with its fervent rays as if making up for lost time. The warmth pushed my cold, lonely depression back into the dark depths of my heart. But my sadness was not replaced with happiness. By April, I was beginning to grow quite worried for the outfit, as I anxiously awaited their return. I rode to the west daily, each day riding further and further westward, in hopes of seeing the outfit far off in the distance. As I gazed upon the Rockies, I wondered if they had become lost in the mountains upon their return, but I quickly dismissed the thought, for Kit Carson knew every inch of those mountains and would not have allowed the outfit to become lost. My next thought was that they'd had a terrible run-in with the Indians and had been slaughtered. The men of the outfit were tough, and some were even trained soldiers, but could they fight off the attack of an Indian war party? I quickly dismissed this idea as well, for if an outfit of nearly seventy men had been slaughtered, there would have been word of it in the mountain man community. I did not know what had happened to the outfit, but I knew the expedition was not supposed to take this long. When I told Dick Wootton of my concern for the outfit, he quickly denied any grisly possibilities. He assured me that if anything had happened, we would have caught word of it. However, I remained skeptical.

Spring passed in the blink of an eye and gave way to a summer much hotter than the last. Toward the end of June, Dick asked me to accompany him on a supply run to Taos to get fireworks and liquor for the Fourth of July celebration. It was at that moment I realized it had been over a year since I had embarked on Fremont's expedition. I couldn't believe I had been at Bent's Fort for that long. I found it even harder to believe that the outfit had still not returned. Or had they? Was it possible that they had taken a different route upon their return and had passed the fort completely? Had they forgotten me? If they had taken a different route, I was confident that Mason would return on his own to the fort. Surely he had not forgotten me. Though it was unlikely, it was a possibility. If there was no one coming for me, then I would have to leave on my own, for I had no desire to remain at the fort any longer. I decided that if the outfit had not returned by the first of September, then I would go back to New Orleans on my own.

* * *

Dick and I returned to the fort on the first of July after an uneventful trip to Taos with a wagon full of fireworks and liquor. I had expressed my concerns to Dick, and he doubted that Fremont and Carson had led the outfit back to St. Louis on a different route. He also said that if I were to travel back on my own, it would be a pretty easy trip. The weather would be mild, and Indians would not be a great threat, but if I was not confident in traveling alone, then I could always hire a guide in Taos to take me to St. Louis. That was reassuring to me.

Dick and I unloaded the barrels of liquor and left the fireworks for José to set up. He was the only one at the fort who knew anything about fireworks.

The next day, Dick, Andre, Fletcher, and I went hunting without José. He stayed behind to fiddle with the fireworks and make sure they were ready for the Fourth of July. Apparently, the Bents threw a great celebration. I did not recall the Fourth of July the year before, for I was bedridden and delirious with typhoid fever.

Our hunt was unsuccessful. We did not locate a buffalo herd, nor did we see any other game. We returned in the afternoon, and I went to my room to read. I dozed off and was awakened by a commotion in the fort. I got out of bed and calmly walked out of my room. Everyone was leaving the courtyard and heading to the rear of the fort. Many had gathered on the second level and were staring off into the west. I looked up to the watchtower where a guard was always present. He was standing with Charles Bent and pointing westward with one hand as he shielded his eyes from the sun with the other. Was it Indians? Mexicans? Were we under attack?

I ran up the stairs to the second level and rushed to the western wall of the fort. I looked out over the plains and quickly saw what everyone was fussing about. An organized force of about seventy well-armed mounted men about three hundred feet away rode toward the fort. It took me only a moment to see that it was John Fremont and his men. I laughed excitedly and ran back down the stairs to greet them at the stables with everyone else.

"I told you they were all right," Dick said as he walked up next to me.

Charles Bent walked out of the stables to meet the outfit as they arrived moments later. Fremont and Carson were at the front of the outfit. I could see David Johansen and Jeremy McAvoy a little ways behind them. The faces of the men were worn and dirty. They were tanned and dry from the sun. Bent waved to the stablemen, signaling for them to take care of the outfit's horses. Eight men pushed through the crowd as the outfit began to dismount.

I walked out of the stables to greet them as they entered the fort. The men who remembered me shook my hand, patted me on the back, and told me it was good to see me again.

"I see you survived the fever," David said. "You look a hell of a lot better. How are you?"

"I'm well, thank you. You all look exhausted," I commented.

"We'll be all right. Just get us a few drinks, and we'll be as good as new."

David patted me on the back and went into the fort. I continued to look over the men in search of Mason. Finally, I spotted him giving the reins of his horse over to one of the stablemen. He patted his mare's rear as the stableman led her to the stables. Mason saw me, smiled, and began walking over. He looked very worn out. His eyes seemed as if they might suddenly shut at any moment. His clothes were dirty and torn. He walked toward me slowly, seeming a little saddle sore. Kyle and Cole were right behind him.

"You're still here!" Mason asked as he approached. "Good to see you, partner!"

Mason shook my hand, grabbed my shoulder, and shook me a little bit. His spirited attitude did not match his miserable appearance. I told Mason that I was glad to see him, and I greeted Kyle and Cole and shook their hands.

"Well, you're a little late," I suggested.

"Yeah, we'll tell you all about it once you get us a bottle of whiskey and show us to your room," Mason promised.

I showed Mason, Kyle, and Cole to my room, and then I went to the billiard room for a bottle of whiskey. When I returned to my room with the bottle, they were all lying on my bed, their feet hanging off the side. I uncorked the bottle and handed it to Mason as he sat up on my bed. He took a swig and passed it on.

"Well, aren't you going to tell me about the expedition? Why were you gone for a year?"

"Right," Mason said, taking another swig of whiskey before handing the bottle to Cole. "Well, it started out just fine. Everything was going according to plan. We crossed the Rockies with no problems. We got to the Great Salt Lake and stayed around there for a while to study it. We found no evidence of subterranean rivers connecting the lake to the Pacific. We continued on to the Oregon Country where we stayed for a while, mapping the Columbia River and its tributaries and exploring the mountains and the forests. It's really beautiful up there, Konrad."

"I wish I could have seen it," I said.

Mason went on to explain how Fremont had not been satisfied with the expedition once they had completed their mapping assignment. Instead of returning, they stayed put for a few days before Fremont decided to lead the outfit on a spontaneous trip southward into Alta California in a desperate search for Buenaventura, a waterway that supposedly connected the Great Lakes with the Pacific Ocean. The discovery of this speculated waterway would have been the greatest discovery of the century. Shortly upon their arrival in Alta California, the outfit was caught in the snowdrifts of the Sierra Nevada Mountains. Mason described it as "the most miserable experience" of his life. He said they were certain that they were either going to starve or freeze to death, and each day it seemed they were just waiting to find out which it would be. He said they ate the leather off their saddles and cut small incisions in their horses to drink their blood. Almost all of the men were frostbitten to some extent. Mason had lost his little toe on his left foot. One of the men, a scientist named Paul Stevenson, had become completely deranged from starvation. However, by some miracle, Kit Carson had found a way out of the mountains and had led the outfit to safety before anyone died.

They rode through the Central Valley into the Mojave Desert. The Mexican government had gotten word of their presence in California and had threatened to send an army after the outfit. Fremont reluctantly led the outfit out of Mexico, and they slowly made their way back to Bent's Fort without finding Buenaventura, which was a discovery in itself.

Mason asked me what I had been doing at the fort while they were gone, and I explained my duties as we passed around the bottle. I told them I was working as a hunter with Dick Wootton and had become quite efficient with my rifle and pistol. We sat in my room for a while and shared stories.

That night, Charles Bent decided to throw the Fourth of July celebration early in honor of Fremont and his men for their brave expedition and safe return. We ate a hearty meal that Charlotte, Quahneah, and a few others had spent the afternoon and evening preparing. After dinner, the celebration began in the dinning room with dancing and drinking and expanded throughout the fort. Everyone got good and drunk. The men from the outfit were obviously happy to be back in civilization.

The celebration carried on through the night and grew louder and wilder. I was having a laugh with David, Kyle, and Cole when I noticed that I hadn't seen Mason in a while. I began looking around for him and finally spotted him on the second level by himself. I climbed the stairs and walked over to him.

"What are you doing up here?" I asked, as I leaned up against the wall next to Mason.

"Just thinking," Mason said, taking a sip of whiskey.

"What about?" I asked.

"About what's next. The expedition is over. We'll be back in St. Louis in a few days. I'm just trying to figure out what to do next. God knows, I don't want to sit around and wait for the next expedition if there is one."

"I know how you feel. Do you have any ideas?"

"Yeah, I was thinking about Texas," Mason said.

"What's in Texas?" I asked.

"A lot, my friend. It's a wild place — untamed. Plenty of trouble for a couple of crazy bastards like ourselves to get into," Mason promised, slapping me on the back. He took a sip of his whiskey and set it on the ledge of the wall. "I got a friend there... in Texas, Jack Burton. Met him when I first arrived in Taos. He kind of took me under his wing. He got me work and a place to stay. He eventually brought me up here to Bent's Fort and got me work as a hunter. He's a good guy. He was on the first expedition with Fremont, too. Now he's in Texas working as a Ranger, running off Indians, chasing Mexican bandits, and saving villages from marauders. It seemed like an exciting place, the way he talked about it in the last letter he sent me. What do you think, Konrad? Want to go to Texas?"

"Sure," I said. "Why not?"

Mason laughed and threw his arm around my shoulder. "You

ain't a greenhorn anymore, partner! Let's get back to the party, huh?"

Mason and I rejoined the celebration, which carried on late into the night. At midnight, José began lighting the fireworks. Colorful explosions of light burst against the starry sky, and everyone began shooting their pistols into the air as they cheered.

The next day, I packed up my belongings with the rest of my outfit and saddled Renegado as we prepared to leave for St. Louis. I said my goodbyes to everyone. I thanked Charlotte for her wonderful meals, and I thanked Quahneah and Bill Thompson for taking care of me while I was ill. I thanked Charles Bent for allowing me to stay and for giving me a room. I said goodbye to José, Andre, and Fletcher and thanked them for all they had taught me. I found Dick in the billiard room, shooting the balls around by himself.

"We're getting ready to take off," I told him, standing in the doorway.

"Oh, yeah?" Dick set down his cue stick and walked over to me. "Finally leaving, huh? Thought I'd never see the day."

"Yeah, me neither," I said with a chuckle. "I want to thank you, Dick, for all you taught me and your patience with me."

"Patience? I've never seen a faster learner," Dick said.

"Well, thank you all the same. You turned this greenhorn into a man who can take care of himself, and for that I'm forever grateful."

Dick nodded and extended his hand. We shook, and I told him I hoped to see him again soon.

By one o'clock, we were on our horses and riding away from the fort. I looked back at Bent's Fort as it slowly got further and further away. Soon, it disappeared behind the hills of the Great Plains. I looked ahead to the east as we rode toward St. Louis, and I began to think about my next adventure.

BOOK II

Justice by God

I

I ARRIVED IN NEW Orleans at the end of July after an uneventful ride across the Great Plains to St. Louis and an even more uneventful trip down the Mississippi River. I stepped off the steamboat and quickly made my way through the madness on the dock, leading Renegado by the reins. William Mason had gone home to Memphis to visit his family, and Kyle Ripley and Cole Jackson had stayed in St. Louis with many of the other men from the outfit. We had not made any solid plans as far as where we would go next, but Mason said he would write to Jack Burton in San Antonio and see about the possibility of being Texas Rangers.

I imagined that Mason, Kyle, and Cole were exhausted after such a long and grueling expedition and were looking forward to relaxing for a while. However, I had just spent a year at Bent's Fort and was ready for something new. I was not ungrateful for the opportunities my year at the fort had provided. I had learned a lot and had become much more self-sufficient, but I was still restless. I thought that Texas sounded like a wonderful idea, and I hoped it would work out. For the time being, I was happy to be back in New Orleans to see Miriam and Raul. I had missed them very much.

After dropping Renegado off at the nearest stables, I went to Miriam's apartment to invite her to Raul's so I could tell them both of my adventures, or lack thereof, at the same time. I walked up the stairs and knocked on the door. I heard her quick footsteps inside as she paced to the door. The door opened, and Miriam stood before me, looking as beautiful and elegant as ever. As soon as she saw me she screamed in excitement.

"Konrad!" she yelled, as she threw her arms around my neck.

We hugged each other tight. "I can't believe you're back!" she exclaimed, as she continued to embrace me tightly.

"Neither can I," I said. "I fear I won't be here for long if you continue to stop the blood from flowing to my head."

"Oh! I'm sorry!" Miriam said as she released her embrace. "I'm just so excited to see you! I had no idea you were coming back or *if* you were coming back!" Miriam slapped my shoulder playfully and gave me a stern look. "I thought you would be back months ago. Why didn't you write to me? I've been worried!"

"There wasn't much of a postal service where I was. Otherwise, I would have written you every week."

"I see." Miriam touched the whiskers on my cheek with the back of her hand. "Look at you! You look so different! I don't think I've ever seen you without a clean shave. And your hair is so long!" I had not cut it since I left New Orleans for the expedition. When it was not pushed back under my hat, the front of my hair reached to the tip of my nose, and the back was nearly to my shoulders.

"There weren't many barbers either," I explained. "But you look as gorgeous as ever."

"Well, we will need to get you cleaned up as soon as possible," Miriam said. "Though I do like the rugged frontiersman look on you!"

"Thank you," I said with a chuckle. "Why don't you come with me to Raul's apartment, and I'll tell you both all about my trip."

"That's sounds wonderful!"

Miriam closed her door and took my arm as we walked down the street toward Raul's apartment. She talked constantly all the way there, telling me all she had been up to over the past year. She and Charles were still a couple and had gone on a trip to St. Louis at the beginning of the summer. She said it had been a wonderful vacation and that she had really enjoyed the city. She said that she and Charles were also planning a trip to France and that she was almost fluent in French, thanks to Raul. She told me about all of the shows she had been to; the theatre, the opera, and the art exhibits. She seemed to have been enjoying herself. I was happy for her.

We knocked on Raul's door, and he opened it promptly, looking the exact same as he did when I first met him; wild hair, black silk robe, and a loose white blouse.

"There he is!" Raul yelled boisterously. "I was just about to send a search party after you! What took you so long?"

"I'll tell you all about it," I said.

Miriam walked inside and sat down, while Raul poured us all a drink. Everything was the same. Raul handed us our drinks and took a seat, and I proceeded to tell him and Miriam of my adventures and of my misfortune. They listened intently as I described the beauty of the Great Plains, the magnificence of the Rocky Mountains, and the gigantic herds of buffalo.

"Well, that sounds like a wonderful adventure," Miriam said. "Other than getting typhoid fever, that is."

"Yes, that's too bad, but you made the best of it," Raul added. "It sounds as if you learned a lot at that fort — and got to do a lot as well."

"Sure," I agreed. "I would have preferred to go on the expedition and see the Pacific Ocean, but I did get to do many things that I otherwise might not have done."

"I know it's cliché, but everything happens for a reason," Raul said. "Your experience at the fort was preparing you for something greater, I'm sure. You'll get to see the Pacific soon enough. There's plenty more adventures to be had."

"Yes, of course," I agreed.

"What are your plans now?" Miriam asked.

"Texas is a possibility," I said, and I finished my drink and set it down on the table.

"Texas?" Raul asked in surprise. "That's even wilder than where you just came from! What do you want to do in Texas?"

"Not sure. Maybe join the Rangers. Mason has a friend there. It's just an idea right now."

"What will you do for now?" Miriam asked.

"Stay around here, I suppose. Maybe go back to work at Leon's. We'll see."

"Please stay for a while," Miriam begged. "I missed you dearly."

"I missed you, too, Miriam, and you, as well, Raul."

"It's good to have you back, Konrad," Raul said.

"It most certainly is," Miriam agreed. "And I'm sure Charles will be very excited to see you. He talks about you all the time. I think he was a little jealous of your adventure."

"Well, we should all go out to dinner tonight then," I suggested. I stood up and walked over to the liquor cabinet to pour myself another drink. "Did you go to James and Anastasia's wedding?" I asked as I poured my drink.

"No, we didn't. Actually..." Miriam said, hesitantly. "The wedding was called off."

I looked at Miriam in surprise as I sipped my drink. "Really? What for?" I sat back down in my seat.

"Well, everyone thinks James called it off, but I know that it was Anastasia who decided not to go through with it," Miriam explained. "She wouldn't talk to me much about it. She just said she couldn't marry James. She just couldn't. She wasn't in love with him."

I nodded and thought for a moment. "Where is she now?"

"She went back to Paris to stay with her family for a while," Miriam said.

"Why?"

"She was ashamed and humiliated. When she broke it off with James, he said all sorts of awful things about her — hurtful things — lies, things no man should ever say about a woman. A few people believed him and began to look at Anastasia like she was filth, so she thought that everyone felt that way. I tried to talk her out of leaving. I told her it would all be forgotten gossip in a few weeks, but she wouldn't listen and went back to Paris anyway. She said that it was only temporary, but she's been gone for a year now."

I was silent for a moment as I tried to comprehend what Miriam had told me. I had hoped that Anastasia would not go through with the engagement, but I never imagined she would leave. I wanted to kill James for slandering Anastasia's name just because he couldn't handle the embarrassment.

"Konrad, why don't you walk me home so I can get ready for dinner tonight?" Miriam asked.

Miriam and I walked down Bourbon Street, her hand holding my arm. I was lost in thought as I pondered what had happened to Anastasia.

"You should write to her, Konrad," Miriam suggested. "I have her address. We've been keeping in touch."

"What would I say to her?"

"Ask her to come back. Ask her to come back for you."

"What are you talking about? Why would she come back for me?" I asked.

Miriam stopped and stepped in front of me so that we were facing each other.

"Konrad, don't you know? Anastasia called off the wedding because she was in love with you!"

"Did she say that?"

"She didn't have to. It was obvious. I just know these things; I'm a woman."

"And you think that if I just write her a letter, she will come back?" I asked.

"Just send her a letter telling her you are back in New Orleans, and tell her you want her to come back."

"All right, I'll do that," I assured her.

"Good! I'll give you her address, and you can write the letter before dinner."

I went back home after dropping Miriam off at her apartment and poured Raul and myself another drink. We sat outside on the balcony and had a cigar with our drinks.

"You must write a letter to your parents as soon as possible. In fact—" Raul grabbed a blank piece of paper from the stack, which was weighted down by a rock, on the balcony table. He gave me ink and a feather as well. "Your parents have sent me four letters since you have been gone. Your mother is worried sick. You need to write them and tell them you are all right and that you have returned safely to New Orleans."

I quickly began to scribble a letter to my parents. I had written to them before I left for St. Louis to sign on with the outfit and had told them of my plans to go on Fremont's expedition, but I had not written to them since. I was sure they were worried. I quickly explained all I had been doing for the past year and how an illness had kept me from going on the expedition. I explained why it had taken me so long to write and apologized for any worry I might have caused them. It ended up being about a page long. I folded it, put it in an envelope, and sealed it. Raul put his cigar out in the ashtray and took my letter.

"I'll take this to the post office for you," Raul said. "I'm going to the store now, and it's on the way."

"Thank you."

Raul winked and went inside. He came out the front door and started walking down the stairs, humming a joyful tune. I watched Raul walk down Bourbon Street with a goofy pep in his step. He tipped his hat to everyone he passed on the street and gave them a friendly greeting. He skipped around the corner and disappeared. I smiled and shook my head. He was a strange man.

As I sat there, finishing my cigar and my drink, I thought about what I might say in a letter to Anastasia. Should it be a confession of my love? An honest attempt at describing my feelings for her and what I believed they meant? Should I beg her to return so that we could be together? Or should it be a friendly letter? Should I simply inform her that I had returned from the expedition and was back in New Orleans? No, a friendly letter would be degrading. If she truly did call off her wedding because she was in love with me, then to speak to her as a friend would be humiliating.

I took another blank piece of paper out from under the rock on the table, dipped the feather in the ink, and began writing a letter to Anastasia.

My dearest Anastasia,

I have just returned from a yearlong expedition under the command of John Charles Fremont and was greatly disappointed and heartbroken to find out that you had returned to Paris. However, I was glad to hear that you had called off the wedding, though I'm sorry for the pain it caused you. I'm sorry you felt that leaving was the only way to escape. I know that feeling very well. But I have returned, and there is nothing I want more than to see you again. We do not have to stay here if you do not wish to. We can go anywhere you like. Just come back for me. I have not stopped thinking about you. Since the very first moment I saw you, you have been swimming through my thoughts. Since the first time we kissed, your taste has been on my lips. The smell of your lilac skin lingers in the wind everywhere I go and teases my senses. Our time together was brief and unfinished. There are still so many things I do not know about you... so many pieces of yourself that make you the extraordinary woman you are, and I will gladly spend two lifetimes learning every single detail. Please, come back. I have missed you so. Come back. I beg you, my love, please, come—

I crumpled up the letter and threw it away. I began writing another letter, this time in a more friendly tone, but I threw it out as well. For some reason, I could not bring myself to write her a letter. It just did not feel right. It was not that my feelings were not genuine, though I did begin to question whether it was love or infatuation. It was true that she had been on my mind since the moment I first saw her. I had tried to forget her when I ran away to join Fremont's outfit for the expedition, but forgetting her was an impossible task. It only made me miss her more. If she really had called off her wedding because she was in love with me, and if she were to come back to New Orleans because of a letter I wrote, begging for her to come back to be with me, then I would be putting myself in a very committed position. If she returned for me, then I would have stay for her. There would be no running off to embark on an expedition out West. There would be no going to Texas to join the Rangers. There would be no spontaneous adventures. I would be committed to Anastasia, and I would be forced to ignore my restless heart. I knew that Anastasia was a supportive woman and that she would encourage me to follow my heart and embark on adventures when the opportunity was presented. She was a free-spirited woman herself and would probably want to go with me. But she was a woman who deserved one hundred percent of a man's attention, as all women do, and despite my love for her, I was afraid that I would not be able to give that to her. No, it would be unfair for me to ask her to return. No matter how much I loved her and how badly I wanted to see her, I was too selfish and too young to make that commitment. If she was to return, it must be because her heart told her to do so and not because I did. So, for now, I would still my hand and wait for Anastasia's heart to speak to her.

That night at dinner, Miriam asked me if I had written Anastasia a letter. I told her I had tried but had decided that it was best not to.

"Don't you love her, Konrad?" Miriam asked.

I replied simply, "Yes."

II

I SPENT THE NEXT month trying to readjust to civilized life in a large city and found it quite difficult. I went back to work at Leon's, but I only worked three or four days out of the week, for I did not want to get tied down to a job. I attended a few social gatherings but tried to avoid them as much as possible. I often found myself riding Renegado up the Mississippi until all civilized life disappeared and I was alone with nature. I knew Renegado needed to stretch his legs after being cooped up in the stables, just as I needed to stretch mine from being cooped up in the city. I would sometimes spend as many as three nights alone in what was the closest thing I could find to the wilderness. A regular escape into the solitude of nature was the only way I could keep from going crazy due to the routine and the pressures of the narrow, civilized society.

I began doing the strength and agility exercises I had learned from Uncle Friedrich when I studied gymnastics and fencing under his direction and quickly began to rebuild the muscle mass I had lost during my illness. I also practiced fencing on a daily basis, for that was a skill I had worked hard to attain and did not want to lose.

I did what I could to pass the time as I waited to hear word from Mason. I even began writing poetry. My poems were mostly dark, sad verses about unattainable love or love lost and misplaced, or I would write angry verses about my distaste for society and aristocracy.

I began my French lessons with Raul again, picking up where we had left off. I was surprised at how much of my previous lessons I had retained after not practicing for a year, and I progressed rather quickly.

As the summer faded into the fall, my heart only grew more

restless. Sleeping became a difficult task, as my dreams were haunted by visions of the frontier and the adventures I would have. I could hear the waves of the Pacific Ocean calling to me.

In the middle of December, Gaetano Donezetti's French opera, *La Favorite*, came to the Theatre d'Orleans. Charles had reserved seats in the balcony for Miriam, Raul, and myself as an early birthday present to me. Despite my disdain for the social gatherings of the elite, I could not deny my love for the arts, especially the opera. I put on a smile and the fine suit Raul had bought for me. Charles and Miriam came to Raul's apartment a couple of hours before the opera to have a drink.

"I got a letter from Anastasia today," Miriam said, looking at me to judge my reaction. I did not allow my expression to change. "I wrote to her after you returned, Konrad, since you would not, and I told her you had come back."

"Well, what did she have to say," I asked.

"She said she's glad you have returned safely and was sorry to hear of your illness. She said she would like to come back to New Orleans and that she misses you very much, but, unfortunately, her father has grown ill and she must stay in Paris to help her mother take care of him."

"That's too bad," I said. "Did she say if her father's illness was very serious?"

"No, but I imagine it's somewhat serious if she has to stay and take care of him." Miriam paused and looked at me. "She said she would love to hear from you."

I finished my glass of Cognac and refilled it. "Well, maybe I will write her."

After we finished our drinks, we walked to the Theatre d'Orleans and began to tediously socialize in the lobby. A chill came over me as I remembered that it was here I caught that first brief glimpse of Anastasia as she glided across the room in her jade gown. She was so beautiful that night and even more beautiful every time I had seen her since, which was not nearly enough to quench my thirst for her. While Raul, Miriam, and Charles talked with a group of their friends, I walked over to the bar and ordered a glass of red wine. While leaning up against the bar, I tiredly sipped my drink and began to slip into a daze as I recalled the night when I had first met Anastasia, but my daze was interrupted by an all too familiar loutish voice.

"Well, look who it is!" James Morrison said, as he stumbled up to the bar and stood next to me. "Konrad 'The Adventurer' returns!"

I looked at him irritably and then looked away, for his nose looked all too appealing to break, and I did not wish to make a scene.

"You're not going to say 'hello' to an old friend?" James asked. He seemed a little drunk.

"I don't recall us being friends," I said, bluntly.

"Oh, you're not still bitter about Anastasia choosing me over you, are you?"

I looked at him strangely but did not reply.

"Yes, of course I knew about you two," he said. "I'm not a fool. But, not to worry; I called it off. Not because of you, though. You weren't the only one she was fooling around with. There were many others."

"I'm not getting into this with you," I said. "You know as well as I do that your words are slanderous lies, so don't try to sell me your nonsense. It may work on the rest of these fools, but not on me." I turned my back to James and sipped my wine.

"Do you think you knew her better than I did?" James pressed. "You fool! You don't really think she ever loved you, do you? She just used you like she used half of the other men in the city. She was addicted to the company of men. There's a name for women like her. I believe they call them 'whores'."

My temper was rising and my blood was boiling. I tried to

calm myself, for I knew he was trying to provoke me. I tried my best to be a gentleman and ignore his empty words.

"But I'm sure you won't take my word for it," he went on. "I'm sure you'll just believe that whore friend of yours, Miriam, who is a more useless waste of space than Anastasia ever was."

I'd had enough. I slammed my drink down on the bar and quickly turned around to face James.

"I'm sorry, Konrad. Did I up—"

I threw my fist into James' nose before he could finish his sentence. I didn't really want to be a gentleman anyway. While the force of my punch was still pushing James back, I quickly grabbed the back of his head and slammed it down onto the bar. I let him fall to the ground. Leaning over him, I grabbed him by the collar of his shirt and pulled him up to me. I punched him three more times before Charles and Raul pulled me off him. Somehow, James was still conscious. His friends got him to his feet and held him back as he tried to charge me, blood gushing from his nose and spraying from his mouth as he spoke.

"You gutless coward!" he yelled, amongst other slurred obscenities I could not hear over the quick, deafening beats of my heart as adrenaline pumped rapidly through my veins.

"A duel!" I heard James yell. "I challenge you to a duel! Tomorrow at dawn!"

"I accept!" I yelled, as Charles and Raul dragged me out of the theatre. Miriam quickly followed us outside. "I'm fine! Let me go!"

Charles and Raul reluctantly let go of me, and I began pacing on the street as my heart began to slow to a normal beat.

"What happened, Konrad?" Miriam asked.

"He was provoking me and I snapped."

"What did he say?" Miriam pressed.

"He called you and Anastasia whores," I said, putting my hands on my knees as I stopped pacing to catch my breath.

"Why, that son of a bitch!" Miriam said angrily, as she began marching back into the theatre. Charles quickly grabbed her and stopped her.

"Miriam, dear, I think Konrad more than defended your honor. Let's just leave it be," Charles said, and Miriam sighed and crossed her arms irritably. "He challenged you to a duel, Konrad," Charles reminded me.

"Yes, I know, Charles! Did you not hear me accept?"

"Yes, I did hear you. I'm just making sure you know what you accepted," Charles said. "Have you ever been in a duel, Konrad?"

"No. Has James?" I asked.

"Just one time that I know of," Charles replied.

I nodded and was silent for a moment. "How exactly does it work?"

The next morning, Charles and Miriam arrived at Raul's apartment an hour before dawn to accompany me to the duel. I had not slept at all that night, for I was very anxious. I asked Charles if I would need to bring my pistol, and he said that one would be provided for me. That made me a little nervous. What if James set me up with a pistol that did not work? I wouldn't put it past the weasel.

Raul, Charles, Miriam, and I took a carriage to the site where the duel was to take place, which was near the Spanish Fort by the Lake Pontchartrain entrance of the Bayou St. John just north of the city.

"This is just barbaric," Miriam protested. "This is below you, Konrad. The frontier has turned you into a barbarian."

"I was challenged, Miriam," I justified, although I knew she was right. "I'm defending my honor as well as yours and Anastasia's."

"Nonsense," Miriam said, crossing her arms and looking out the window.

"I don't wish to kill him," I said. "If I merely wound him, will that satisfy the judges?"

"It depends on what is decided beforehand," Charles said. "Request that the duel end at first blood. Are you a good shot, Konrad?"

"I am," I said confidently.

"Good, because James is mediocre at best. Just wound him and it will be over."

We soon arrived at the site of the duel. A thin layer of fog hung over the grass amongst a small gathering of spectators. We stepped out of the carriage, and I saw James waiting next to an out of place table in the middle of the small, grassy opening.

"All right. What do I do?" I asked, not taking my eyes off of James, as I took off my jacket and rolled up my sleeves. I hid my anxiety behind an over-confident demeanor, which I hoped would be intimidating.

"Go out and meet him," Charles said. "The rules will be explained, you'll pick your weapon, and you will have your duel. Would you like me to go with you?"

"No, I'll go on my own," I replied.

"Very well. Good luck, Konrad," Charles said as he shook my hand.

"You'll do fine," Raul said. I shook his hand.

Miriam was beginning to cry. "Oh, Konrad, don't get yourself killed! You don't have to do this!"

"Oh, stop it, Miriam," I said coldly.

I turned and began walking confidently toward James. My face was frozen with an intense look of anger, yet I seemed calm and collected. Inside, however, I could not have been more the opposite. I arrived at the table in the middle of the grassy opening and stood before James. He had two black eyes; his nose was swollen and bruised, and it looked to be broken. He had a small cut on his cheek and one on his chin. An old man stood behind the table while James and I stared each other down.

"Are you gentlemen ready to begin the duel?" the old man asked.

"Yes," James answered, speaking for the both of us.

"The challenged will choose his weapon first," the old man said, opening the fancy box sitting on the table. Inside the box were two pistols. They were very lavish, single-shot pistols that looked to be from the Eighteenth Century. "You may pick your weapon now, sir."

I took one of the pistols out of the box without much thought. I looked it over and held it at my side while James took the other pistol.

"Before we begin, I would like to request that if a non-fatal wound occurs before death, that be the end of the duel," I suggested.

"Challenger?" the old man said, looking at James.

"I accept," James said.

"Then whomever draws first blood, whether it be fatal or not, shall be the victor of the duel," the old man said. "Now, will the gentlemen please step out into the center of the green with your backs turned to one another." James and I did as he said. "Now, walk ten paces on my command. Then, turn and fire at your opponent," the old man instructed from behind the table.

The old man counted off our steps so that we would arrive at ten at the same time. My heart was racing. For some reason, it wasn't until step five that it suddenly occurred to me that I could be killed. As that reality became apparent to me, my breaths grew short and fast.

"Eight!" the old man yelled.

I took a deep breath and exhaled slowly. It helped. I felt my heart slow slightly.

"Nine!"

"I will not die here today," I said quietly to myself. "I will not die here today. I will not die today." As I repeated these words, I began to believe them. A sudden wave of calmness melted over me and relaxed my entire body. My heart slowed drastically.

"Ten!"

I took my tenth step, quickly turned, and aimed my pistol. James was immediately in my sights. I fired at the exact same time as James. I heard his bullet cut through the air just inches from my head, and then I saw James fall beneath the smoke from his pistol. I lowered my pistol and watched as James squirmed around, holding his shoulder as he cried out in pain. He would live. I dropped my pistol, turned, and walked back to the carriage where my friends awaited my return. They congratulated me as we got into the carriage. I sat down and exhaled a deep, shaky breath. The confidence and calmness that had been the reason for my victory suddenly left me as I began to comprehend what had just happened. My hands began to shake, and I chuckled nervously, grateful to be alive, and just as grateful to have not taken James' life. I found it comical that the greatest danger I had yet encountered in my life after spending a year on the frontier was a silly duel in New Orleans. It seemed as if luck was on my side for the time being.

III

On the eve of the New Year, I sat outside on the balcony of Raul's apartment, reading a newspaper article about John Fremont and his latest expedition. The headline read, 'JOHN C. FREMONT IS "THE PATHFINDER" ', a nickname referencing Natty Bumppo, James Fenimore Cooper's character from *The Leatherstocking Tales*. The article also called Fremont 'The American Magellan'. I sipped a cup of coffee with my legs propped up on the table, as I read about the adventure of which I should have been a part. In the streets below me, the New Orleanians had already begun the festivities and celebrations, as they said goodbye to 1844 and prepared to welcome 1845, though it was still early in the afternoon. Events of this scale were all-day celebrations in New Orleans. I poured a shot of whiskey into my coffee and continued reading the article about Fremont's expedition.

A familiar voice yelled up from the street below, "You sure look comfortable up there!"

I peered down over the railing of the balcony to see Mason, Kyle, and Cole making their way across the crowded street.

"I was wondering if I'd ever hear from you!" I yelled back.

Mason, Kyle, and Cole walked up the stairs leading to my apartment. Instead of going through the front door, they jumped from the stairs to the balcony and climbed over the railing. I stood up, shook their hands, and patted them on the back.

"It's good to see you, gentlemen," I said. "Would you like a drink?"

"Sure — fill us up," Mason replied.

There were already four glasses stacked on the table. I turned them over and filled them from the bottle of whiskey I had used for my coffee. Cole grabbed the bottle when I finished pouring and looked at it curiously.

"Damn! This looks fancy," Cole commented.

We all touched glasses and drank.

Mason nodded in satisfaction. "This *is* good," he said. He looked at the newspaper I had been reading. "Are you reading this nonsense?" Mason laughed.

"Yeah, I just read it."

"'The Pathfinder'?" Mason said in confusion. "Fremont led us into snow drifts in the Sierra Nevadas and nearly got us killed. Carson is the one who found the path and got us out of there alive."

"That's politics," I pointed out. "They're trying to sell Fremont to the people. They're saying he might run for president."

"Well, if Kit Carson is his vice president, then he should do just fine!" Cole commented, and we all laughed.

"Now, what's the plan?" I asked. "I've been going crazy here for the last few months."

"Yeah, you look like you've been going crazy," Mason said sarcastically. "You're sitting up on your balcony, feet propped up, while you read your newspaper and sip your fine whiskey."

"Yeah, all right; it may not look like it, but I'm painfully bored. I need a great change of pace."

"Well, it sounds like Fremont's got another expedition in the works for this year," Kyle announced.

"Yeah, I heard about that," Mason said, seeming uninterested. "They want him to map the source of the Arkansas River and explore the eastern slopes of the Rockies."

"What about your friend in Texas, Mason? Did you ever hear from him?" I asked.

"I did. We came here as soon as we got his letter," Mason said. "He wrote that the Rangers are recruiting as many men as they can, so now is the time to join. He said that if it's excitement and adventure we want, then the Texas Rangers might be exactly what we're looking for," Mason explained. "And that was it. It sounded like he had copied a newspaper ad. He ain't much for writing letters."

"Well, what do you think?" I asked.

"I'd go tomorrow," Mason said. "Hell, I'm getting bored just looking at you, Konrad."

"I thought I heard guests," Raul said, walking out onto the balcony.

"This is my Uncle Raul, gentlemen," I introduced. Mason, Kyle, and Cole introduced themselves and shook his hand.

"It's a pleasure to meet you, boys," Raul said, taking a seat. "Are we celebrating yet?" Raul held out his wine glass, and I poured him some whiskey. "To the New Year!" We all touched glasses and drank.

"Have you started without us?" Miriam's playfully angry voice bellowed from the street.

I looked over the railing at Miriam and Charles. "My dear, you know nothing really begins until you arrive," I said. Miriam smiled proudly, tilting her head to the side.

Miriam and Charles walked up the stairs, into the apartment, and came out onto the balcony. Introductions were made, and Miriam's hand was kissed by all as if she was royalty.

The afternoon progressed into evening, and we continued to converse on the balcony while the celebrations continued in the streets below. Miriam was her usual talkative, charming self. She asked Mason, Kyle, and Cole many questions about life on the frontier. She was very fascinated by the lives of these rugged adventurers who lived freely off the fat of the land and rarely had a dollar to their name. These were men whose only possessions were the clothes on their backs and the weapons they carried. I could tell that she was finding it all very romantic as she listened to the stories they told and their vivid descriptions of the beautiful, rugged West. The conversation was certainly a change-of-pace from the dull, boring, repetitive conversations of the wealthy elite to which she was accustomed. Of course, Miriam never saw them as such.

Charles was quite fascinated as well, although his fascination was closer to desperation. As I watched him become taken in by these stories of adventure on the frontier of the West, I noticed a longing in his eyes. There was a dull twinkle of desire and restlessness in them, but it was quickly fading. A wave of sadness came over me as I watched Charles live vicariously through the stories of Mason, Kyle, and Cole. I had always thought of Charles as a good and noble man, but, at that moment, I lost a great deal of respect for him. All men have restless hearts, but most are ignorant and deaf to the promptings of their truest and most basic self. This ignorance is not the fault of these men but of man and the cage he has built. I always thought of Charles as one of these men, but I realized that he was the worst kind of man. He was a man who heard the strange beat of his restless heart but chose to ignore it. He was a man with the desire and the capability to follow his heart, but he lacked the courage to do so. I looked at him and saw the man I could have been, the man I had been groomed to be and then had denounced. The man who follows the world is a shell and sees only himself. The man who follows his heart sees the world and is the yolk that nourishes it.

"Did you hear me, Konrad?" Miriam asked.

I snapped out of my thoughts. "I'm sorry — what?" I asked.

"I said, Charles and I are going to France in the spring!" Miriam announced.

"That sounds wonderful," I said. "I'm sure you'll love it."

"Of course you will!" Raul said. "You might not come back!"

"Oh, we'll be back," Charles assured him. "I've got a business to run."

"Well, that sure sounds like a great trip. I'd like to see Europe one day," Mason commented.

"How long do you plan on being in France?" I asked.

"We'll leave in the spring and return in the winter," Charles said.

"I'm hoping Anastasia will return with us," Miriam said. "I just sent her a letter telling her that Charles and I were coming to kidnap her."

"Do you think she will come back with you?" I asked.

"I think so. I think traveling alone back to Paris was very hard for her," Miriam said. "I imagine it must have been quite scary."

"Does anybody know what time it is?" Cole asked. "Ain't it close to midnight?"

I checked my gold pocket watch. "It's not even ten o'clock," I said.

"Well, we could head over to the Orleans Ballroom," Charles suggested. "I'm sure it's quite the party."

I rolled my eyes at the suggestion.

"Oh, I'm so bored with those parties," Miriam said. "I'm enjoying our little party right here. Unless, of course, you all want to go."

"I'm not really sure it's our cup of tea," Mason said.

"In that case, I'll go get us a couple more bottles of wine," I said while standing up.

"I'll go with you," Miriam offered.

Miriam and I walked inside and headed to the wine cabinet. I studied the bottles carefully as I tried to decide which ones to pick.

"I really like your friends, Konrad," Miriam said.

"I'm glad. They seem to like you as well."

"Do you think so? You don't think they find me boring?" Miriam asked.

"Miriam, I don't think anyone could find *you* boring," I said, as I held up a bottle of pinot noir. "What do you think of this?"

"Oh, no! How about a cabernet?" Miriam suggested. "And take a chardonnay. You really don't think they find me boring? They've had such exciting lives!"

221

"Of course not, Miriam. In fact, I've never seen them so engaged in conversation before." I pulled out two more bottles and showed them to Miriam.

"Really? Oh, those look fine."

I stood up and began uncorking the bottles. "You have an unequaled ability to relate in conversation to people of all sorts, whether they be adventurers, smug aristocrats, or the Pope."

"Thank you, Konrad," Miriam said. "Won't you come to France with Charles and me?"

"I don't think so, Miriam."

"Well, why not?" Miriam asked disappointedly. "How romantic it would be if you showed up in Paris at Anastasia's door to bring her back to America with you!"

"Don't do that, Miriam."

"Why don't you come? Charles and I both really would love you to join us," Miriam pressed.

"Well, the boys and I were planning on going to Texas," I said.

"Texas? But Texas is just around the corner. Why would you rather go there instead of France?"

"I've been to France, Miriam. I've never been to Texas."

Miriam frowned and folded her arms. "What's there to do in Texas that's so exciting?"

"Plenty. It's a wild place. It's an untamed frontier," I replied.

"Of course! It's all adventures and danger and peril—"

"Yes, adventures, Miriam! Why are you so excited to hear about all the danger Mason, Kyle, and Cole put themselves in, but when I suggest something of that nature, you turn into my mother?"

"Because I don't love them, Konrad! I love *you*! I worry about *you*!" She began to cry a little. I sighed and put my arm around her shoulders.

"I'm sorry, darling, but I'll be fine. You don't have to worry," I comforted her.

"You always say that. You don't know if you'll be fine. You can't promise me that. And telling me not to worry isn't going to stop me from worrying. I'll worry about you from the day you leave until the day you return, just as I did the last time you left and were gone for a year. When you invest feelings in a person, and when you care about someone, worrying is inevitable. That's just how it is. Didn't you ever worry about me while you were gone?"

"Of course," I said.

"Then don't tell me not to worry!"

Miriam pushed my arm off her shoulder and walked back to the balcony, wiping away her tears. I sighed and shook my head. I grabbed the two bottles of wine and walked out to the balcony. When I got outside, Miriam had already put on her happy face and had jumped right back into a lively conversation.

We continued to celebrate and have a merry time on the balcony, and the celebrations in the streets below grew bigger and wilder as the New Year approached. Just moments before midnight, Charles presented the expensive bottle of champagne he had brought for the occasion. He opened the bottle and began to fill our glasses as the bubbles began to overflow. At the stroke of midnight, we touched glasses and toasted the New Year. A fine display of fireworks lit the midnight sky with a beautiful array of colors above the banks of the Mississippi River.

IV

In the morning, on New Year's Day, Mason, Kyle, Cole, and I awoke early and went downstairs to Leon's for breakfast. After our meal and four cups of coffee, we decided that we would leave for Texas at the end of the week to join the Rangers. A new adventure was upon the horizon, and I began to get that familiar feeling of anxiety and excitement that stirred my stomach and made my imagination run wild with visions of the unknown. My heart raced eagerly with contentment.

Later that afternoon, I sat out on the balcony and wrote a letter to my parents to inform them of my plans. Remembering Miriam's reaction to my leaving and what she had said about worrying for those we care for, I was much more sympathetic toward their feelings than I had been in the letter I had written informing them of my plans to go on the expedition with Fremont. Miriam, being as worried as she was, made me realize how worried my parents must be, especially my mother. In my letter, I did my best to make my plans seem safe and well thought out. I explained in great detail the experience and character of the men with whom I was traveling. I even went as far as saying that they took care of me like I was their little brother. I promised to write them every chance I got.

* * *

Mason, Kyle, Cole, and I had decided to leave early Friday morning, so on Thursday evening, Raul, Miriam, and Charles took us out for a very nice dinner. Miriam sat next to me and was quite affectionate throughout the evening. She was always touching my arm or my leg or brushing my hair back off my face, but strictly in a platonic sense. I knew she was very worried about me and the dangers I might encounter in Texas while working as a Ranger. She loved me, and I loved her dearly. My relationship with Miriam was one of the most important and most special relationships I had ever had in my life. There was a special bond between the two of us that had stemmed from coming together at a transitional and very vulnerable point in our lives. From those points, we grew together and impacted one another in a way that shaped, and would continue to shape, who we were together as well as individually. It was a bond much like a brother and sister in some ways and like lovers in other ways. I would miss her greatly while I was gone and would feel like a piece of me was missing until we were reunited once again.

After dinner, Charles took Mason, Kyle, and Cole to the Saint Charles Hotel where he had rented a room for them as a parting gift. Raul went back to his apartment, and I walked Miriam back to hers. She invited me in for a nightcap.

"What would you like to drink?" Miriam asked, as she walked over to the liquor cabinet. "I just got a really nice bottle of rum from Barbados."

"That sounds wonderful," I said, sitting down on her couch.

Miriam opened the bottle and poured our drinks. She walked over to the couch and sat down next to me, making sure to leave no space between us. She leaned up against me and rested her head on my chest. I put my arm around her. She handed me my drink and held up hers.

"Cheers," she said, simply.

"Cheers," I added, and we touched glasses and sipped the rum.

"It's good, isn't it?" Miriam asked.

"Very good. When did you start drinking rum?"

"Raul introduced me to it. One night he opened a bottle of rum that had been given to him by Jean Lafitte — the pirate."

"Yes, I know who Jean Lafitte is. Raul knew him?"

"Apparently so."

T. William Phillips

"Interesting."

Miriam sat up so she could look at me. "You're really leaving tomorrow?"

"Yes, I am."

"You've only been here a few months. I wish you'd stay longer. You're sure you won't come with us to France?"

"I told you; I've been there before."

"But you've never been there with me," Miriam persisted. I smiled sympathetically. "You will write this time, won't you?" she asked.

"Yes, of course, every chance I get," I promised. "And when you write to me, just send your letters to the San Antonio post office. I'll check it when I'm in town, all right?"

"All right."

"And I want you to write me as soon as your boat arrives in France, so I'll know you got there safely. And write me as soon as you get back to America."

"Will you be worried about me?" Miriam asked, looking deeply into my eyes.

"Of course I will."

"Really?" she persisted.

"Yes, Miriam, I'm going to worry about you!"

Miriam leaned back against me and finished her drink. "It's just… I feel like your always running away, and people don't run away from the people they care about."

I gently grabbed Miriam's shoulders and turned her so that I could see her eyes. "Miriam, I'm not running away from you or anybody or anything. And I care about you and love you very much. You mean the world to me, darling, you know that. I hate to leave you—"

"Then why do you? Why are you always leaving? If it's not running away, then what is it?"

"It has nothing to do with you. It's just something inside of me… It's hard to explain. It's this feeling I get, this restlessness. It's the reason I went to school at Oxford and traveled around Europe. It's the reason I left New York to come here, and it's the reason I left here to go out West. It's the same reason I am leaving now. I just have to. If I don't, I'll go crazy, and that has nothing to do with you. I have this insatiable thirst to see and touch and taste everything. I want to experience and learn as much as I possibly can — while I can. I would love to go to France with you. I loved Europe. But America is wild! And it's one of few wild places left. But it won't be wild forever. Soon, it will be like the rest of the world — tamed and domesticated. Do you understand?"

"Yes, I think I do. I'm sorry for being so stupidly emotional," Miriam said.

"You're not."

"I'm just going to miss you."

"I'm going to miss you," I said, kissing her forehead.

"But, it should be much easier for me this time since we'll be able to write each other."

"Yes, much easier."

Miriam cuddled up next to me and laid her head on my chest. I put my arm around her and held her tight. We stayed like that in silence for an hour. When I noticed that she was asleep, I slowly stood up and softly laid her down on the couch. She curled up and sighed. I took the blanket off the back of the couch and put it over her, and then I kissed her on the cheek and left, locking the door behind me.

It was just about midnight when I got back to Raul's apartment. He was having a drink on the balcony. I joined him, and he poured me a glass of whiskey. We raised our glasses to one another and took a sip. I let the smoky tones from the peat linger on my tongue before I swallowed.

"Miriam told me you knew Jean Lafitte," I said.

Raul laughed. "Yes, I knew him. I did a little business with him. He owned a couple of warehouses where he would disperse his... plunder, I suppose. I often went down to his stores and told him what I thought certain items were worth, and he'd pay me for my troubles. We'd also get drunk together quite often. He was a good man. Would you like to try some of the rum he gave me?"

"Sure."

Raul went inside and came back with a less than ordinary looking bottle and two shot glasses. He poured us each a sip.

"He gave me this bottle more than thirty years ago, but I've only drunk from it on four occasions, and never more than a sip. It is the best rum I have ever had the pleasure of tasting. To Jean Lafitte."

Raul and I touched glasses and drank the rum. It was very good — and very strong. I don't think I could have handled more than a sip. Raul put the cork back in the bottle.

"That is very good," I said.

We went back to sipping our whiskey and lit a couple of cigars. The city was quieter than usual, and it was quite calming.

"Do you ever feel like I'm running away from you?" I asked after a long silence.

"What do you mean?" Raul asked, looking at me with great interest.

"Miriam seems to think that I leave because I don't care about her or value our friendship."

"Well, she's a woman," Raul said simply. "They tend to over-analyze and exaggerate such things. I've never felt that way. I know you're a young man. I was a young man, too, once. Of course, that was about eight thousand years ago." I laughed. "But I know how you feel. You're young and you want to explore and see the world. I understand that. All young men feel that way at one point, but few ever act on it. But you do, and for that, I hold you in the highest respect."

"Thank you," I said graciously.

"With that said, I also think you're very naïve."

"What do you mean?" I asked, taken off guard by the criticism.

"Your plans are to go to Texas and join the Rangers, right?"

"Yes."

"James Polk has just been elected president, and during his campaign he made it quite clear that his plans were to expand America from the Atlantic to the Pacific. He will most certainly annex Texas, which will put us at war with Mexico. You're not a stupid man, Konrad, so I'm sure you know this already."

"Yes, I suppose it's possible."

"No, not possible — inevitable. We *will* go to war with Mexico, and you're going to Texas, the front lines, to join a company of Rangers that will be very active in the war effort." I nodded but said nothing. "I know that at your age war sounds like a romantic display of honor, sacrifice, and defending freedom. I felt that way, too. That's why I joined the New Orleans Militia and fought with Jean Lafitte in the Battle of New Orleans thirty years ago. But it wasn't romantic. There's nothing romantic or honorable in watching another man die, no matter what side he's fighting for."

"I didn't know you fought in the Battle of New Orleans," I said.

"Indeed, I did."

I thought for a moment about what he said. "Well, I don't know what's going to happen, but I do know that I don't want to live my life based on what I think might happen. If we go to war, then I'll defend my country."

"Defend your country? Your country is the one who will be attacking. Mexico is the county that will be defending itself. Listen, Konrad, all I'm saying is, I don't want you to allow yourself to be used by the government. They take advantage of young, restless, adventure-seeking men such as you to fight for their greed and lust. I just don't want you to regret the decisions you make."

"I don't believe in regret," I said.

Raul shook his head and leaned back in his chair. "All right. I've said my peace."

We sat and drank all night long and spoke on less serious topics. However, as we joked and laughed, Raul's words were resonating in my head and challenging my thoughts. *I don't believe in regret.* What a silly thing to have said. I wished I could take it back.

* * *

About an hour before dawn, I began gathering the few belongings I planned to take with me. I strapped my saber to my hip and felt in my pocket for my father's watch. I stuck my pistol in my belt and sat my rifle and a small bag of random possessions next to the door. I heard a whistle from outside. I walked out onto the balcony and peered down at the street where Mason, Kyle, and Cole were sitting atop their horses, waiting for me. They had brought Renegado for me as well. I waved down to them.

"You off?" Raul asked, walking out of the bathroom.

"I am. They're waiting downstairs."

"All right. I'll walk you down."

Raul grabbed my bag and rifle and carried them down to the street for me. I thanked him and stuffed my rifle into Renegado's saddle scabbard. I tied my bag onto the back of the saddle and petted Renegado's neck.

"Well, good luck, my friend," Raul said. "Keep your eyes open and be careful out there."

"Thank you, Raul — and I will." I stuck out my hand. He shook it and pulled me in for a hug.

"Take care of yourself. You're like a son to me, now. I don't want you getting yourself killed, all right?"

"All right." I didn't know what else to say.

"Goodbye, my boy," Raul said, releasing me from his embrace.

I patted Raul on the shoulder and smiled. I climbed on my horse, and Mason, Kyle, and Cole said goodbye to Raul and thanked him for his generosity. Raul nodded and waved goodbye to us as we gave our horses a kick and rode away. As we rode further and further away, I looked back and saw Raul still standing there at the bottom of the stairs, watching sadly. He lowered his head and started walking back up the stairs. We turned the corner and rode northwest out of the city.

V

WE TOOK A FERRY across the Mississippi River and continued riding along the Gulf Coastal Plain of Louisiana. We rode along next to the swamplands and marshes and crossed the many rivers draining into the Gulf of Mexico.

At the end of the third day, we set up camp on the west side of the Calcasieu River just north of the lake. After we set up camp, Mason shot a twelve-foot alligator, which we ate for dinner. The next day, we crossed the Sabine River into Texas. We rode on, heading southwest, and stopped for the night on the banks of the Trinity River. We woke up two hours before sunrise the next morning to make up for time lost in the Louisiana wetlands. We passed south of Houston rather than through it, for none of us had any desire to see the city. We set up camp in a beautiful pine forest, and I shot a deer for dinner. The next morning, we awoke two hours before dawn once again. We crossed the Brazos River and the Colorado River that day and were dead tired by the time we stopped for the night. On the seventh day of our trip, we crossed the Guadalupe River in the rain. It rained throughout the day, but it was mostly drizzle. However, it made for a very cold and uncomfortable day of travel. I enjoyed it very much.

At noon on the eighth day, we arrived in San Antonio. I immediately liked the town. It was not too big or fancy, nor was it too small or simple. The Texians walking through the streets nodded and tipped their hats to us as we rode along. The town was small enough that everyone seemed to know we were strangers. It was quite busy as we rode through. There were many wagons hauling supplies or being loaded with supplies. Despite the busyness of the town, it had a very relaxed atmosphere.

We rode slowly past the Alamo where the legendary battle had taken place. The abandoned mission was a ruin. Weeds and grass grew on the walls. It was a depressing sight.

"Where do you reckon we should go?" Kyle asked.

"My guess is a saloon," Mason said. He noticed a man crossing the street. "Excuse me, sir. We were wondering where we might find the Rangers."

"The market square, at the inn," the man said, pointing in the direction he meant.

"Thank you, sir," Mason said.

We rode through the town until we came to the market square at the center of town. We rode into the *Plaza de Armas* where the market was teeming with life. Vendors stood by their wagons and oxcarts full of goods, joyfully trying to sell their products to the many potential customers walking about the square. The market smelled of the most wonderful assortment of foods being prepared and cooked right before us. We climbed off our horses and tied them to a post. We walked through the market, observing the venders and their products, and watching as they prepared their meals. We had not eaten all day, and our mouths were watering as our senses were teased by the wonderful aromas. Our stomachs growled, begging us to satisfy their needs.

A skinny, young Mexican boy walked by, and Mason gently grabbed him by his shoulder. He asked the boy where we might find the inn where the Rangers stayed. The boy was talkative and had a great big smile. He told us he would show us where they were, and we followed him across the market. When we got to the inn, the boy held out his hand, waiting for his payment.

"What? You want me to pay you for taking us fifty feet?" Mason asked. "I don't think so."

"I help you! You pay!" the boy insisted.

"You're out of your mind, kid!"

"All right, all right," I said, reaching into my pocket. I took out a coin and gave it to the boy. "Is that enough for your troubles?" I asked the boy in Spanish.

"*¡Sí, senor! Gracias.*" The boy ran off and disappeared into the market.

"You're a softy, Konrad," Mason said with a smirk.

We walked into the inn, which had a saloon on the first floor. It was filled with a variety of men in different styles of dress. Some wore *sombreros* and were dressed like Mexicans. Others wore buckskin shirts and leggings, and some were dressed in a regular American fashion. They all looked rough and wild. They sat at the tables, playing cards and having laughs as they drank and smoked cigars and Mexican *cigarittas*. Some looked at us for a moment as we stood at the door and then went back to what they were doing. We walked up to the bar and ordered a round of whiskeys. The bartender set the glasses in front of us and poured our drinks.

"Are these the Rangers?" Mason quietly asked the bartender. The bartender nodded. "You know where I might find Jack Burton?"

"Who's askin'?" one of the men at the table behind us asked without turning around. I don't know how he heard Mason. He had spoken so quietly that even I could barely hear him. Mason turned around.

"A friend of his," Mason said. "You know him?"

The man laid down his cards, stood up, and walked over to us. He was tall, lean, and wore a thick, black mustache with a small, black patch of hair under his bottom lip against the shadow of a day's growth of stubble. His dark, squinting eyes observed us carefully.

"What do you want with him?" he asked.

"I'm Will Mason—"

"All right," the tall man said, uninterested.

"I wrote Jack a little while ago and told him me and my friends here want to join the Rangers. He told us to come here. So, here we are," Mason explained.

"Here you are," the tall man repeated. "You want to be Rangers, huh? Well, we can always use some fresh meat." He stared us down for a moment. "Jack's in his room upstairs. Second door on the left." The tall man turned and sat back down at his table.

Mason looked at me with raised eyebrows and a confused smirk. We drank our whiskeys and headed upstairs. Mason knocked on the door of the second room on the left. I heard footsteps pounding toward the door. The door opened, and before us stood a shirtless Jack Burton. His face lit up at the sight of his old friends.

"I was wondering when you boys were going to get here," Jack commented. He shook Mason's hand and patted him on the back. He gave Kyle a light slap on the face and backhanded Cole in the belly. "Get the hell in here! How are ya?"

"Good, Jack. What are you doing in here?" Mason asked, as we walked into the room.

"I was just reading," Jack said. I noticed *The Deerslayer* sitting on his bed stand. I liked him already.

"Jack, this is Konrad Quintero," Mason introduced. "Konrad, Jack Burton."

Jack and I shook hands. "It's good to meet you," Jack said.

"You, too, Jack."

"How did you end up running around with these goons?" Jack asked me.

"I met them in New Orleans. They told me about Fremont's expedition."

"Oh, you went on the expedition?"

"Well, not really. I got sick with typhoid fever and had to stay behind at Bent's Fort."

"I see. I had typhoid a few years ago. Miserable. Bent's Fort isn't a bad place to be stranded though. They put you to work there once you got better?"

"Yeah, I hunted, ran supplies, and did anything else that needed doing," I explained.

"Good! Interesting," Jack said, staring at me for a moment.

His eyes were sharp and inquisitive. He seemed to be peering into my soul. "So, you boys want to be Rangers, huh?"

"Yeah, we just met one of your comrades, I believe," Mason said.

"Yeah? Kind of a mean fellow?" Jack asked, as he put on a shirt and began to button it.

"Yeah, dark hair, mustache, angry eyes," Mason described.

"That sounds like Gavin Callaghan," Jack said, tucking in his shirt. "I'm sorry you had to meet him first. He's not the most polite person in the world. Just ignore him. He's one of those types who keeps a chip on his shoulder just for the sake of having a chip on his shoulder." Jack brushed back his greasy, shoulder-length, dirty-blond hair and put on his hat. "Let me buy you boys a drink."

We went downstairs into the saloon. Jack led us to the bar and ordered a round of whiskeys for us. He turned around, leaned up against the bar, and scanned the room. Then he took a *cigaritta* out of his pocket and lit it.

"Almost all of the gentlemen you see here are Rangers," Jack stated.

"Gentlemen, huh?" the bartender questioned with a chuckle as he poured our drinks.

"You know you love us, Pete," Jack said, turning around to face the bar. "Thanks for the drinks, partner." He put a few coins on the bar.

"The rest of the boys here have credit, Jack. Why don't you let me write you up a tab? I know you're good for it."

"I don't like owing people money. Debt is just one more thing to worry about," Jack said. "Besides, I might die tomorrow and you'd be shit out of luck." Pete laughed and went to tend to another customer. "Cheers, boys," Jack toasted, and we touched glasses and drank.

"Did your friends find you, Jack?" Gavin asked without turning around in his seat to look at us.

"They did, Gavin," Jack said, leading us over to Gavin's table. "Thanks for sending them in the right direction. By the way, gentlemen, these boys are Mason, Kyle, Cole, and Konrad, and they're looking to sign on with us."

The men at the table nodded and grunted simple greetings. Gavin did not look up from his cards.

"Have y'all eaten?" Jack asked us.

"No," Mason replied.

"All right, then let's go get some grub, huh?" Jack suggested. He led us outside into the market square. "Let me explain how this works," Jack began, as we walked by the vendors through the busy square. "Like I said, most of those men in there are Rangers, and we're all part of the same company under the command of Jack Hays. But our company has many smaller detachments. Those detachments can have from ten to thirty men. Our detachment is commanded by Lieutenant Walter Smith, and we get paid thirty dollars a month."

"Is Gavin in your detachment?" Kyle asked.

"Unfortunately, yes. He may be a son of a bitch, but you'll be glad he's with us when the fighting starts. The man fights like the devil," Jack said. He stopped at one of the vendors where a plump Mexican woman was stirring a large clay pot resting over hot, glowing embers. "Here we are, boys. The most wonderful concoction you will ever taste. Five bowls, please, ma'am," Jack said in Spanish. The woman smiled a great big smile and began filling our clay bowls with a delicious-looking chili. "When it comes to San Antonio cuisine, this is what most people think of. We call these fine ladies 'Chili Queens', and they make the best chili you will ever taste."

The Chili Queen handed us our bowls and Jack paid her. She gestured for us to eat.

"Try it!" she said in Spanish.

"She wants you to try it in front of her," Jack said. "I think she can tell it's your first time."

We filled our spoons with the chili and blew on it to cool it down, and then we took a bite. It was fantastic. It was a wonderful combination of beef and beans mixed with tomatoes, onions, and garlic, along with an array of peppers to spice it up and give it a nice kick. Mason, Kyle, and Cole nodded and smiled in satisfaction. The Chili Queen smiled proudly and thanked us.

"This is unbelievable," I complimented in Spanish. "What do you put in this?"

"No, no! It's a secret," she said in Spanish. I smiled and nodded in understanding. I thanked her for the chili, and we continued walking through the market square.

"You speak Spanish, Konrad?" Jack asked, though his tone made it sound like a statement.

"Yes, my father is Spanish, so I learned from a very young age," I explained.

"What's your mother?" Jack asked with much interest.

"German."

"And do you speak that as well?"

"I do. I also speak Latin and French," I said, trying not to sound like I was boasting.

"That's fantastic," Jack said. "You must have one of those minds that can absorb new languages."

"I suppose. I've always enjoyed learning other languages, which I think makes it easier to learn."

"Certainly. I can speak Spanish pretty well. I know a little Comanche and some Kiowa. Where are your horses?" Jack asked.

"Toward the front of the square," Mason said.

"Show me."

We ate our chili as we walked over to our horses. When we got to the horses, Jack looked them over very carefully. He petted them and studied their physiques, but he spent a great deal of time looking into their eyes. He studied Renegado the longest.

"Whose horse is this?" he asked.

"He's mine. I call him 'Renegado,'" I said.

"He's beautiful," Jack observed, not taking his eyes off of him. "Looks like y'all will be fine. One of the make or break requirements in becoming a Ranger is that you have to have a good horse. Now, let's go see if we can't find the lieutenant and get you signed on."

We walked back to the inn and went upstairs to Lieutenant Smith's room. Jack knocked twice.

"Who is it?" the lieutenant grunted from inside the room.

"It's Jack, lieutenant."

"Come in, Jack."

Jack opened the door, and we walked into the room. Lieutenant Walter Smith was standing at the dresser with his Colt pistol in hand. He looked at us and set it down, then poured himself a glass of whiskey. He was a brawny man with a thick mustache and a clean shave. His eyes look tired and uninterested. His skin was tanned and leathery and showed quite a few wrinkles, though he didn't appear to be very old. He couldn't have been more than thirty-five.

"What can I do for you boys?" he asked. He took his glass of whiskey and slowly sat down on his bed.

"I got a few new recruits here for you," Jack said. "They're friends of mine. They were on Fremont's first expedition with me and just got back from his latest expedition."

"And now you boys want to be Rangers, huh?" Lieutenant Smith asked.

"Yes, sir, lieutenant," Mason answered for all of us. "We're all fine shots, and we certainly aren't strangers to roughing it on the frontier."

"I'll be the judge of that," the lieutenant said coldly. "Got good horses?"

"Yeah, I just checked them out. They've all got admirable mounts," Jack informed.

"All right. Welcome aboard," Smith said. "Get them fixed up

239

with everything they need, Jack. You boys be present for training tomorrow at dawn. We'll see how you stack up."

We thanked him and left to head to the gun shop where we each received two Colt thirty-six caliber revolvers, one Colt eight-shot carbine rifle, and a large Bowie knife, as well as a belt to hold it all and a wallet full of ammunition. At the general store, we were equipped with a Mexican blanket and a month's supply of salt, parched corn, and tobacco, along with a few other little necessities and luxuries. Once we were equipped, Jack got us rooms at the inn. We put our supplies in our rooms and went downstairs to the saloon to have a few drinks. We ended up getting quite drunk with our new comrades. They all seemed like a good bunch of men, all of them except for Gavin Callaghan. There was something off about him. At about midnight, we went to our rooms in a dizzy daze and went to bed.

The alarm on my pocket watch started ringing at five-thirty the next morning. I did not feel as poorly as I had expected to feel after a night of excessive drinking. Maybe I was still a little drunk. I drank an entire canteen of water and began to dress. As I was buckling my belt, which carried my pistols and my Bowie knife, there was a knock on the door. I opened the door, and Jack and Mason stood before me. I grabbed my rifle, and we walked over to Kyle and Cole's rooms. Kyle was not awake, and Mason practically had to pull him out of bed and dress him.

We went downstairs to the saloon and sat down at a table, which already had five plates waiting for us. To make sure we got to training on time, Jack had awakened early and had ordered our breakfast. The breakfast was very good. There was bacon and sausage, a sourdough biscuit, and three eggs smothered in a green chili sauce. We washed our meal down with a quick cup of lukewarm coffee and headed out to our horses. We stuffed our rifles in our saddle scabbards and began riding north out of town.

Soon, civilization disappeared and we were riding through the beautiful Texas Hill Country.

It took us about twenty minutes to get to the Ranger camp from San Antonio, and we arrived just as the sun began to cut into the sky. There were twelve Rangers at the camp, not including Jack, Mason, Kyle, Cole, and myself. There were two fires going. One was being used to cook breakfast, and the other was being used for coffee. One man was tending to some biscuits being cooked in a Dutch oven buried in the ground. Many of the men were cleaning their guns and smoking cigars or *cigarittas*. They wore long, scraggly beards and a variety of other styles of unkempt facial hair. I had never seen a rougher-looking group of men.

We rode over to where the rest of the horses were tied off to a rope, which was tied to two trees. There was a short, stocky man grooming his horse. He looked up at us as we approached and then went back to his grooming and said, "Morning, Jack."

"Morning, Ned."

"Are these the new recruits I heard the boys talking about?" Ned asked.

"Yeah. This is Mason, Cole, Konrad, and Kyle. Boys, this is Ned Riley. He's short and may not look like much, but he's the toughest son of a bitch in this outfit. I've never seen a better fist-fighter in my life. Unfortunately, he can't shoot worth a shit, so his combat skills only really apply to drunken barroom brawls."

Ned laughed and shook his head. His face was smooth and round, with a beard that only grew under his chin and up to his earlobes. He had a light layer of blond fuzz for a mustache and was kind of an awkward-looking fellow, but he certainly had a fire in his eyes, which made me believe that Jack wasn't joking when he said Ned was the toughest man in the outfit.

We tied off our horses, grabbed our rifles, and walked over to the fire where the coffee was being prepared. A scrawny young man with stringy, brown, shoulder-length hair and a patchy beard was telling a story.

"He had his men stick three hooks in each'a his ears and a coupl'a hooks in his tongue. All them hooks was tied to ropes, and then them ropes was tied to a limb on a tree. Then they just let um hang there 'til the hooks ripped off his ears and tongue," the scrawny, stringy-haired young man explained.

"I doubt that's true," a man lying down with his head on his saddle and his eyes closed said in a slow, laconic drawl. "Them hooks would just rip through his ears and tongue. They wouldn't pull them off."

"They was real deep, and right in the middle. And they was real thick hooks."

"What are y'all talking about over here?" Jack asked, grabbing the coffee and pouring himself a cup.

"Dan here heard some rumor about Vicente Montes hanging one of his own men with hooks in his ears and tongue," the man lying down said, still not opening his eyes.

"Montes' man talked too much about what he heard. It's a symbolism, right, Jack?" Dan, being obviously uneducated, asked Jack, a known reader.

"Yeah, that's right, Dan."

Jack introduced us to the men around the fire. The young man who had been telling the story was Dan Sanders. The slow-talking man lying down was Joe McLeod. He was broad-shouldered and well built, and he looked quite strong. He had a lazy demeanor that made him seem as if he had not a care in the world. The other three men were Pat Collins, Dalton, and Javier Martinez, who everyone just called Javi. They were all tough, battle-hardened men. Dalton had a mean-looking scar down the side of his face. But despite their rough and wild appearance, they were all quite friendly.

"Here comes the lieutenant and his protégé," Dan indicated by nodding toward Lieutenant Smith and Gavin Callaghan as they rode into camp.

"Damn, Dan," Dalton said with a chuckle. "What's with you and these big words today? 'Symbolism' — 'protégé'."

"I been readin' them books Jack give me. I'm tryin' ta get an education," Dan replied.

"What the hell do you need to get educated for?" Pat asked. "You wanna be president or something?"

"Maybe I do. I'd make a good president, I think," Dan predicted.

"If you ever become president, I'll move to Mexico," Joe promised.

"If I became president, I'd exile you *to* Mexico," Dan jested.

Joe chuckled without opening his mouth or making the effort to form a smile. He still hadn't opened his eyes.

The lieutenant and Gavin rode past us. We all greeted Lieutenant Smith respectfully. He nodded but only briefly glanced at us. Gavin coldly stared at Mason, Kyle, Cole, and me. I watched Smith and Gavin ride over to the horses where Ned was still grooming his, and Ned stopped what he was doing to tend to the lieutenant's horse.

Lieutenant Smith and Gavin walked over to the other campfire where a couple of the men handed each of them a plate. Smith and Gavin took their plates and walked away from the camp to eat by themselves.

"What do you think they talk about?" Dan asked.

"The weather," Joe said blandly.

When Lieutenant Smith and Gavin finished their breakfast, the training began. We broke up into three groups, with Mason, Cole, Kyle, and I forming our own group. Jack was there to walk us through the drills. We went to three different stations, but before we began training, Jack sat us down and gave us an extensive lesson on our weapons. He taught us how they worked, how to load them, how clean them, and then, of course, how to use them.

The first exercise was basic marksmanship on foot. First, we shot with our pistols at targets carved into trees. We practiced from ten yards, twenty yards, thirty yards, and forty yards away. Jack was a fantastic shot with his pistol, hitting the center of the target from every distance with little or no time to aim between shots. Mason was quite good, as well, and Kyle and Cole were decent. I was certainly the worst of our group, but I still was not bad. I was much better when we did the same drill with our carbine rifles from fifty, one hundred, one hundred and fifty, and two hundred yards away. While working at Bent's Fort as a hunter, I had become deadly accurate with my Kentucky Long Rifle. The smaller carbine rifles were less accurate and took some getting used to. However, I adapted quickly and was the best shot after Jack. We practiced marksmanship on foot with pistols and rifles for two hours before moving on to the next drill — horsemanship.

The Rangers were trained to ride like the Comanche Indians. This was not a simple task. I had watched the other Rangers of our detachment practice horsemanship while I was practicing marksmanship, and it was an incredible display of skill. With their horses running at full speed, they could lean over the side of their horse and pick up a hat off the ground. They could hang off the saddle and fire their pistols from under the neck of their horse, swiftly pull themselves upright, slide over to the other side, and fire in the opposite direction. The athleticism that these men displayed from the backs of their horses was a spectacle at which I marveled. Jack assured Mason, Kyle, Cole, and me that in just a few short months we would be able to do that as if it was second nature.

The next drill was marksmanship from the back of a sprinting horse. It was quite difficult but very fun to practice. There were two posts the size of an average man driven into the ground and spaced forty yards apart. We would ride toward the first post at full speed while shooting our rifles at it. Once we reached the first post, we would drop our rifles, draw our pistols, and shoot at the second post while riding at full speed. Some of the Rangers were simply remarkable at this drill. There was a circle drawn at the top of the post about the size of a man's head, and Jack, along with many of the other Rangers, could hit it dead center every time. In fact, most of them were better marksmen while riding full speed on their horses than they were while standing still on the ground.

After spending two hours on each of the three drills, we took a break for lunch. We took an hour and a half to eat, drink coffee, and smoke tobacco while our horses rested. By about half-past two, we were back to training. We spent another hour on each drill and finished our day's training at six in the evening. Some of the men stayed at the camp and spent the night there, while the rest of us rode back into town. For dinner, we went to a vendor in the market square famous for his *tamales con chili*. It was a very good meal. I was surprised at how great the food had been in San Antonio. I had not expected it to be bad, but I had certainly not expected it to be so good.

After dinner, we went back to the inn for a few drinks at the bar. At the end of the day, I was glad I had decided to become a Ranger. It seemed as if it was going to be an exciting experience.

VI

WE TRAINED FOUR OR five days out of the week, and, as time progressed, Mason, Kyle, Cole, and I improved rapidly. We adapted quickly to the lifestyle of the Rangers, and we molded into our outfit quite well. After a week with them, we were treated as veterans and not greenhorns. They were a very accepting group of hardened, rough men.

In training, I had excelled faster than the others. My marksmanship, both on foot and on horseback, became incredibly accurate from all distances. My skill and acrobatics on my horse became so natural and so profound that I even surprised myself. I suppose it was not too hard to believe; I had always been very disciplined when I set my mind on accomplishing a certain skill or acquiring knowledge of a certain thing. The discipline I had learned from fencing translated well to my quick development as a marksman, and the strength and agility I had acquired while practicing gymnastics translated well to my horsemanship.

I could tell that Lieutenant Smith was impressed by my speedy development as a Ranger. He never said so or complimented me, for he was not the kind of man to give praise for an accomplishment, but I noticed him watching me quite a bit, more so than he watched the others.

We had not been assigned any missions yet, and I could tell that the Rangers were growing restless — as was I. I looked forward to venturing out and away from the comforts of civilization into the frontier in search of renegade bands of rustlers, thieves, and murderers. I thought a lot about what combat would be like. I had read about wars and firsthand accounts of what it was like to take a life, but words did not satisfy my curiosity and my romantic ideas. I asked Jack what combat was like, and his answer was simple, "In combat, a man finds out who he really is."

I had no desire to kill a man for any reason. As a lawman and a man, my desire was to track down criminals and capture them. 'Justice by God' was the inscription on the sword Uncle Friedrich had given me, and that was how I wanted it to be. However, I knew the reality of the matter, and I was not naïve to the possibilities and the likelihood on the wild Texas frontier of violent skirmishes between outlaws and lawmen such as myself and my fellow Rangers. I also knew there was no way to prepare for it.

On a miserably hot day in the middle of spring, I lay on my bed reading and unsuccessfully trying to keep cool. It was one of our days off from training. While most of the men were downstairs in the saloon drinking and playing cards, I read *Paradise Lost* by John Milton, which had been recommended and loaned to me by Jack. He ordered a shipment of books from New Orleans every couple of months and had practically created a library in the lobby of the inn. I expressed to him my love for books, and we browsed over the many titles he had collected over the past couple of years. He would pull one book after another off the shelf, telling me that I absolutely had to read each one, and then he would change his mind when he would find another book he thought was essential. I had read many of them, but there were also many I had not read. I settled on *Paradise Lost* after Jack promised it would change my life. I loaned him my treasured copy of *Don Quixote*, which he surprisingly had not read.

I finished book four of the epic poem and decided to go downstairs to visit with my comrades. I saw Mason and Jack at the bar nursing a glass of whiskey. As I walked over to join them, a disgruntled man with a bulging gut burst into the room. Everyone stopped to look at him.

"I'm looking for Lieutenant Walter Smith," the fat man said. "I was told I could find him here."

Lieutenant Smith stood up. "I'm Lieutenant Smith. What do you want?"

The fat man walked over to him quickly. "My Negro ran away, and I'm sure he's on his way to Mexico. I was told you and your Rangers would be able to retrieve him before he crossed the border."

"Yeah, we can catch your slave. What's the reward?" Lieutenant Smith asked.

"Fifty dollars," the fat man responded.

Lieutenant Smith thought for a moment and briefly looked at Jack. "All right. I'll put my best men on it."

"Thank you, lieutenant!" the fat man said.

"Just wait outside. You're going to need to show my men the trail."

The fat man went back outside in a hurry. Lieutenant Smith called Jack over to him, so Jack finished his drink and walked over to Lieutenant Smith. The lieutenant spoke to Jack briefly, but I could not hear what he was saying, and then Jack turned and walked over to me.

"Get what you need, Konrad," Jack said, gesturing for me to follow him upstairs as he walked past me. "Smith wants you and me to catch that slave."

I followed Jack up the stairs, confused. "What do you mean, you and me? Just the two of us?"

"Well, it doesn't take a whole outfit to catch one slave."

"Why me though?" I asked. A wave of excitement came over me.

"He thinks it'll be a good first experience for you," Jack replied. "Pack light."

Jack went into his room, and I ran down the hallway to mine. I grabbed the only things I imagined I would need — my guns, my knife, and my saber. The saber was really just for show. I guess I also felt superstitious about it. I just did not feel right without it at my side. I met Jack outside his room and we went downstairs. Mason, Kyle, and Cole wished us luck.

We met the fat man outside. His name was Henry. He

explained the situation, struggling to keep up with us as we paced quickly toward our horses. Henry owned a cotton plantation in East Texas just north of Houston. The slave who had escaped had been one of his strongest. Henry said he talked to a man in Gonzales who said he saw a lone slave walking through town the day before, probably trying to find a horse to steal. No horses had been stolen in Gonzales, so, as far as we knew, the slave was still on foot. Jack told Henry that we would find him and that he should stay in San Antonio and wait until we returned with his slave. Henry thanked us and watched as we rode quickly out of the city.

We headed south across the San Antonio River toward the Nueces. About a mile past the San Antonio River, Jack slowed his horse to a calm, steady, unhurried pace. I did the same and looked at him in confusion.

"What are we doing?" I asked.

"Slowing down," Jack said.

"Why?"

"Because I have no intention of catching that slave," Jack said. "If we do end up finding him, I'll just escort him to the border."

"You're an abolitionist?" I asked, stating it more as an observation than a question.

"Well, I don't write pamphlets or anything, but, yes, I don't believe it's right."

"Well, I feel the same way. What do we do now?"

"Just ride around. Enjoy the scenery. You've never seen the Rio Grande before?" I shook my head. "All right, then let's go have a look."

We changed our course westward toward the Rio Grande and Mexico. We roamed around the brush country, which was quite beautiful in a rough, rugged way. The dry, hard land was covered in mesquite, blackbrush, cacti, and deciduous tree life. We rode through thickets and forests and to the tops of hills that overlooked spectacular views. A couple of hours before dusk, we stopped to set up camp. We unsaddled our horses and let them graze while we built a fire, made a pot of beans, and ate some jerky for dinner. We had seen a deer, but we decided not to shoot it since there were only two of us and we would just end up letting most of it rot. Jack promised me a good, Mexican meal when we got to a village called Montilla near the Nueces River.

The night fell upon us quickly, as we continued to feed the fire and smoke *cigarittas*. Jack reached into his saddlebag and pulled out a small bottle of whiskey. He tossed it to me, so I took a drink and tossed it back to him.

"Mason told me the two of you met in Taos," I stated.

"Yeah, we did. Poor kid was as green as an emerald. I saw him wandering around town for three days, wide-eyed and amazed while he scrounged for food and looked for work, so I finally decided to help him out." Jack took a couple of swigs from the bottle of whiskey and passed it to me.

"How'd you end up in Texas?" I asked. I took a sip of whiskey and passed the bottle back to him.

"That's a good question." He stared blankly at the whiskey bottle for a few moments and then finally took a sip. "I had gone back to Taos after the first Fremont Expedition and then decided I wanted to go to New Orleans. I guess I just ventured off course and ended up in San Antonio. I had a few drinks with some guys who turned out to be Rangers and decided to join them." Jack took a swig of whiskey and exhaled a deep breath. "You're from New York?"

"Yes, I am," I answered. "Where are you from?"

"Philadelphia."

"Really? I didn't realize I was in the company of a fellow Yankee," I said.

"Well, I haven't been a Yankee for years now."

"When did you leave?" I asked.

"June 2nd, 1833, when I was eighteen."

"Why?"

"Well, I imagine it was the same reason you did, Konrad," Jack said. "I was bored. I wanted to travel. I was tired of the city and the people. I didn't want to be a lawyer like my father. I wanted excitement and adventure. So, after my first year at the University of Pennsylvania, I just left."

"Just like that, huh?"

"Just like that."

"Our stories are quite similar," I said.

"Oh? And where did you get sent off to? Harvard? Yale?"

"Oxford."

"Really?"

"I wasn't sent there though. I chose to go. I wanted to see Europe."

"Hell, I might have finished school if I had studied in Europe. I didn't have a choice in the matter though. I had spent my whole life in Philadelphia. By the end of my first year at the university, I felt like I was losing my mind."

"I know what you mean," I sympathized.

"Then what? You came back from school in Europe, realized why you left in the first place, and started heading west?"

"That about sums it up," I replied. "Where did you go after you left Philadelphia?"

"I headed down to Virginia, worked in Richmond for a month, and hated it. So I started making my way west. Got to St. Louis where I worked as a carpenter. When I got tired of that, I headed down the Mississippi to New Orleans and got a job on a sloop of war, essentially, as master's mate. We sailed to Brazil and spent some time in Rio de Janeiro, and then we chased pirates off the coast of Africa. By the time I got back to New Orleans, I had lost all taste for the sea."

"That sounds amazing," I said.

"It wasn't as exciting as you think. It was rather uneventful."

"What did you do after that?" I asked, intrigued by his life.

"I went back to St. Louis for a short time and worked as a

carpenter again until I had enough money to buy the best horse I could find. That's how I got Carolina," Jack said, gesturing to his dark-brown mare grazing with Renegado. "Once I had a good horse, I decided I needed to take her for a good, long ride, so I rode the Santa Fe Trail and ended up in Taos. I worked as a trapper, trader, hunter, shoed horses, broke wild mustangs, you name it. Spent a lot of time in the mountains. Eventually, I met Mason, and you know the rest of the story."

"It's quite a story," I said. Jack laid down on his bedroll, using his saddle as a pillow.

"What set you off, Konrad?" Jack asked as he stared into the night sky.

"What do you mean?" I asked.

"What made you leave everything you know, everything that was comfortable to you, and caused you to set out for a life like this?"

"Well, I guess it was when I realized that the things I thought made me comfortable made me uncomfortable."

"Yeah?"

"Yeah." I thought for a moment as I stared at the fire. "I've always loved reading, ever since I was a little boy. As I matured, my taste for literature matured. I started reading books with more depth, books that made me ponder life, its meaning, and its mysteries. I read what others had learned throughout the course of their lives, and that was all good and well for a while, but soon the restlessness began to overwhelm me. The books could no longer satisfy my thirst for knowledge and adventure. One can only learn so much from the words of others before they must begin to learn through their own experiences. And that's why I had to leave."

"The Lockean idea that knowledge is obtained through the senses," Jack said. He smiled and looked at me through the flames of the fire. "There's no happiness for men like us, you know — the restless thinkers, the wandering contemplators. Happiness is for the people back in those cities we left, for the civilized societies and for the people who let others do their thinking for them. Ignorance is bliss, so leave happiness for the ignorant."

"Why can't *we* be happy?" I asked.

"We can be happy, but for us, happiness comes in small doses, just for a fleeting moment. Then we have to run to something else. It's like searching for water in a desert when you're trying to get to the Garden of Eden. You walk around, hot, exhausted, and desperate, until you finally find some water. It may be a puddle, or it may be an oasis. Either way, you're still in the middle of the desert, so you fill your body with all that it can take, and then you have to move on to find your way to the Garden of Eden or the next watering hole."

"Well, what happens when you find the Garden of Eden? Isn't that happiness?" I asked.

"You don't find the Garden of Eden," Jack said. "It doesn't exist. It's a mirage."

Jack closed his eyes to go to sleep. I lay down under my blanket and rested my head on my saddle. I lay awake for a while, thinking about what Jack had said. It was a bit depressing and cynical, but it was an interesting point of view and one I felt was worth pondering.

We woke up at dawn, and Jack quickly got the fire going again. He prepared the coffee while I went looking for our horses. I found Renegado and Jack's mare, Carolina, grazing in an open field of dirt and shrubs. I approached them calmly with a lasso in each hand. I petted their noses, slowly put the ropes over their heads, and led them back to camp. The coffee was ready, so I poured myself a cup. We smoked and sat by the fire in silence as we sipped our coffee and took in the new day. It was a pleasant morning. There were no clouds in the sky, and the sun was not too hot yet. The birds chirped in the woods around us, singing in harmony with the cool, morning breeze.

After we finished the coffee and put sand on the fire, we packed up our belongings, saddled our horses, and rode out of camp toward the Rio Grande. At about eleven o'clock, we crossed the Nueces River, and, soon after, we arrived at the small village of Montilla. As we rode into the village, we were welcomed by big smiles and courteous greetings. The village was only a few intersecting rows of small, whitewashed adobe homes. The population was made up solely of Mexicans and could not have numbered higher than one hundred people. Jack smiled and greeted everyone he saw by name.

Smoke rose from the houses and filled the village with aromas that teased my nostrils and made my mouth water.

"What a lovely village," I commented.

"Yeah, it is. When we're out patrolling the border and the frontier, we'll come here every now and again to trade for supplies and get a good meal."

We stopped at one of the adobe homes and climbed off our horses. As we tied them to a post, a short, old woman with white hair and wrinkled, leathery skin walked out of the home. She smiled a beautiful smile, and her brown eyes lit up with excitement.

"Hello, Jack! I had a dream you would come today," she said in Spanish.

"Well, your dreams have come true, my dear," Jack said, in Spanish as well. "How are you, Felipa?" Jack kissed her on the cheek and embraced her lightly, not to crush her fragile bones.

"I'm well. And how are you, my boy? Who is your friend? I haven't met this one."

"This is Konrad," Jack said. "Konrad, this is my second mother, Felipa."

"It's a pleasure to meet you, ma'am," I said in Spanish. We shook hands.

"It's always nice to meet new people," Felipa said. "Well, you boys are just in time for lunch. Come inside! I'm still cooking."

We walked into her home, which was just one big, open room with a single bed in the corner. In the middle of the room, there were two fire pits with a few stools around them that sat low to the ground. Both of the fire pits were going. One was cooking *tortillas*, and the other was roasting *carnitas*.

"It smells wonderful, Felipa," Jack said, still speaking Spanish. The people of Montilla did not speak English. Most of the White people they came into contact with spoke Spanish to some degree, so it was never necessary to learn English.

"This is only the beginning," Felipa said. "You just wait."

A young girl, no older than ten, with a long, braided ponytail, walked into the room, carrying two plates of assorted sliced vegetables and seasonings. A beautiful young woman followed behind her, carrying four plates of more assorted foods. She carried two of the plates in her hand and balanced the other two on her forearms.

"Hello, girls!" Jack greeted them.

"Thank you, my dear," Felipa said, taking the two plates off the beautiful woman's forearms. The little girl set down her plates and hugged Jack tightly around his neck.

"Konrad, these are my granddaughters," Felipa introduced. "The one suffocating Jack is Gabriela, and this gorgeous woman is Anita. She looks just like I did when I was her age."

"Hello!" Gabriela said loudly, as she thrust her hand in front of my face. I smiled and shook her hand.

"It's good to meet you, Gabriela," I said. "And you, Anita." Anita smiled and nodded.

Felipa took a handful of diced tomatoes and a handful of diced onions and sprinkled them on the *carnitas*. She added some cilantro and told us to grab the *tortillas*. Since I was closest to the other fire, I grabbed the *tortillas* and set them down. Felipa handed me a plate on which I placed the *tortillas*. As Jack and I teased our growling stomachs with a hearty appetizer of *carnitas* wrapped in *tortillas*, Felipa, Anita, and Gabriela began preparing the main course, which was *enchiladas*. Anita made the red chili pepper and tomato sauce while Felipa prepared and began cooking the beef. Gabriela cut up some *nopales*, which was peeled segments of a prickly pear cactus, for us to snack on while we waited. It was my first time to have *nopales*, and I found it very tasty.

"Do you like your chili sauce spicy?" Anita asked.

"Sure," I replied.

"You know I do," Jack said.

"All right. I'll make it spicy then," Anita said.

"Do you like it spicy?" I asked.

"I do. I only asked because a lot of White men can't handle it," Anita said with a playful smile. "I'm going to get a *habanero*, Grandmother."

"All right. Will you bring the cheese as well, dear?" Felipa asked.

"Yes, Grandmother."

"And one more onion, please," Felipa added.

"All right." Anita started walking out of the house.

"I'll help you," I offered as I stood up.

Anita smiled as I followed her outside. We walked through the village toward her house.

"Were you born in this village?" I asked.

"Yes, I've lived here all my life," Anita responded.

"Really? Have you traveled anywhere?" I asked.

"What do you mean?"

"Have you ever visited another place?"

"I went to San Antonio with my uncle once," Anita said.

"When was this?"

Anita thought for a moment. "Six years ago, when I was fourteen," she replied.

"You're twenty years old, and the only places you have been are Montilla and San Antonio?"

Anita smiled and looked at me strangely. "Yes?"

"Well, haven't you ever wanted to go see other places?" I asked.

"What is there to see?" she asked. "Come, this is my house."

We walked into her modest adobe home, which was very similar to Felipa's, only this one had two beds.

"What is there to see?" Anita repeated, as she began gathering what she needed.

"The whole world — everything. You've never wanted to go somewhere else?"

"I don't know. Where have you gone?"

"Well, I grew up in New York City," I began.

"Where is that?"

"Northeast, on the Atlantic Ocean," I explained.

"It's a big city?"

"Yes, very big. I went to school in England and traveled around Europe. I went to France, Germany, Italy, and Spain."

"Where is Europe?" Anita asked, handing me a plate of cheese.

"It's across from New York, on the other side of the Atlantic Ocean," I said.

"Close?" Anita asked.

"No, not really. You have to take a long boat ride to get there. Do you have a map?"

"A map?"

"Yes, a map of the world. I'll show you where I've been."

"I don't have a map."

I nodded and looked around the house while Anita quickly diced an onion. "Where is your mother and father?" I asked.

"My mother died eight years ago while giving birth to Gabriela," Anita said emotionlessly.

"Oh, I'm very sorry," I said empathetically.

"It's all right."

"And your father?" I asked.

"I never knew my father."

"I see… so you're grandmother takes care of you and your sister?" I asked.

"Yes, she's wonderful," Anita answered.

"She seems wonderful. And what about this uncle of yours who took you to San Antonio?"

"He lives in San Antonio and comes here to visit from time to time. Are you ready?"

I nodded, and Anita carried the plate of diced onion and the *habanero* pepper back to Felipa's house, while I carried the plate of cheese. Soon, the *enchiladas* were ready and we all ate. It was a very good meal. It was certainly one of the best meals I'd had in long time. As we ate, I caught little Gabriela staring at me a few times. When I looked at her, she made a goofy face and laughed. She was missing a tooth, and a new one was just beginning to grow in its place. She was an adorable child. I caught Anita staring at me a couple times as well, but not in a playful sense.

After lunch, we sat around and conversed for about half an hour, and then Jack and I announced that we had to be leaving. Felipa begged us to come back soon and expressed how much she enjoyed cooking for handsome, young *Americanos*. We said our goodbyes, and then we climbed onto our horses and waved goodbye as we rode out of town.

Jack and I arrived at the Rio Grande just as the sun was beginning to set. We rode onto the rocky banks of the big river and stared across to Mexico. We sat there, simply observing, listening, and allowing our minds to comprehend the beauty, which our senses were gathering.

"Well, we better set up camp," Jack said when the sun disappeared behind the hills to the west. "We'll start our long ride back to San Antonio tomorrow."

"It's a shame we didn't catch that slave," I said sarcastically.

"A damn shame," Jack agreed. "But we tried our best."

VII

IT TOOK JACK AND I two days of steady riding to get back to San Antonio. When we arrived, we were immediately greeted by Henry, who was quite upset to find out that we had not caught his slave. We apologized and assured him that we had done our best, but the slave must have been well into Mexico by the time we reached the border.

The next day, training continued as usual. In the evening, we returned to town and ate dinner at the inn. I sat at the bar with Mason, Kyle, Cole, and Jack to have one drink before retiring to my room to do a little reading and to write letters to Raul, Miriam, and my parents. Just as I stood up to leave, Ned rushed into the inn. He had been out scouting for the past two days.

"Lieutenant, I need to talk to you," Ned said. Lieutenant Smith stood up, and he and Ned walked outside.

Lieutenant Smith and Ned returned a few moments later as we were speculating with one another as to what Ned was telling Smith. We watched Lieutenant Smith anxiously as we waited for him to address us. We were informed that Vicente Montes and his men were in Seguin, so we quickly got what we needed and prepared for a quick ride.

Just as the night began to darken the sky, we galloped quickly out of town, heading northwest toward Seguin. We rode swiftly through the night without stopping or slowing our pace to anything less than a light trot.

"Who is this Vicente Montes?" Mason asked Jack.

"He's a thief and a robber and a murderer," Jack said. "And he's the worst of them. He's been terrorizing and marauding towns and homes in Texas for years, but we've never been able to catch him. He's kind of a sore spot with these guys. They've been trying to capture and kill him long before I joined the outfit. He's a very talented and clever thief, and he completely lacks morality."

Jack went on to explain how Vicente Montes had grown up on a ranch just outside of Seguin. His father was a peon who worked for the wealthiest family in the area, which also made Vicente a peon. From birth, he had been essentially treated as a slave. When he was seventeen, he killed his master while the man slept and immediately fled. Lieutenant Smith and his men were given the assignment of catching this murderer and bringing him to justice. Vicente fled to Mexico where he joined a team of bandits. His talents did not go unnoticed by their leader, and he quickly created an infamous reputation amongst the fearful citizens of Texas as a clever thief and a sadistic murderer. After a few years with the band of marauders, his ambition grew, and he turned the men of his outfit against their leader, Antonio Sanchez. Vicente gave Sanchez the option of disappearing into obscurity or death. Sanchez, angered by this mutiny and disrespect, drew his pistol to kill Vicente, but Vicente was quicker and shot him dead. The band of marauders was then under his command, and they grew even more violent and raided homes and towns more frequently. The citizens of South Texas began to live in fear, and it seemed that the country was at the mercy of this man who could not be caught by the Rangers.

As we drew closer to Seguin, I began to grow nervous, for it seemed that if we did encounter Vicente and his men, a violent exchange of bullets would be inevitable. My duel with James Morrison was the only combat experience I'd had, and I'd thought that was a terrifying ordeal. The prospect of engaging a large number of well-armed men with much combat experience and who were as ruthless as they were skillful made my heart race with fear and excitement.

We arrived at Seguin well after midnight and entered the town silently. It was quiet, and there was no one to be seen. We knocked on the door of the first house we came to and asked the fearful man who answered where Vicente and his men were. The man said they were in the saloon. Lieutenant Smith thanked the man and told him to stay inside. We rode back behind the buildings, and under the cover of darkness we slowly made our way toward the saloon. As we began to hear the ruckus from the saloon fifty yards away, we climbed off our horses and covertly made our approach toward the building.

When we arrived at the saloon, Mason, Kyle, Cole, and I were told to surround the building to make sure no one escaped while the rest of the Rangers went inside to engage the enemy. Cole and I stayed at the back of the saloon and guarded the rear door. Mason and Kyle went up either side of the building toward the front just in case any of the bandits got past the Rangers inside.

As the Rangers prepared to enter the saloon through the front, Cole and I held our pistols pointed at the door, ready for anything. I could tell that Cole was as nervous as I. Suddenly, the back door opened, so we quickly fixed our pistols on the man who walked out. Seeing our pistols in his face, he dropped his bag of trash and put his hands in the air. It was just the bartender. I pulled him out of the doorway and pushed him against the wall. I told him to sit down and be quiet. My heart was working hard to make up for the beats it had missed. I exhaled a deep breath and shook my head at Cole as we both regained our composure. Then we heard the Rangers barge through the front door, screaming commands to surrender as they quickly took positions around the room. There was a brief period of yelling from both parties, and then the gunshots began.

I could not see the gunfight, but it sounded like madness. Cole and I looked at one another, not sure if we should go in and help or stay put. Then we heard the quick footsteps of a man running toward us. Cole stepped into the doorway just as a man came running out, tackling Cole hard to the ground. Just as I was about to step in and help him, I heard another set of feet running toward me. I holstered my pistol and picked up my rifle as the man drew near. Just when he was at the doorway, I stepped into his path and struck him hard on the forehead with the butt of my rifle. He fell unconscious to the ground.

I quickly rushed over to Cole who was wrestling with the man who had tackled him. The bandit was on top of Cole with a knife, trying to stab him. Cole used every bit of his strength to hold back the knife as it inched toward his face. I kicked the bandit in the ribs as hard as I could, knocking him off of Cole. I pointed my rifle at his head and told him to drop the knife. Cole stood up, picked up his pistol, and pointed it at the bandit. With two guns on him, the bandit threw his knife away and lay still.

The gunfight inside ceased after less than a minute, though it seemed much longer. Cole and I dragged our two prisoners inside the saloon where the rest of the Rangers were holding the surrendered bandits at gunpoint. I looked around the room and saw that eight of the Mexican bandits were certainly dead and six were wounded. None of the Rangers had been killed, and none had been wounded. The remaining twelve bandits had surrendered and had thrown their weapons away. Their hands were in the air, while the Rangers kept their guns pointed at them. Gavin was angrily questioning one of the bandits. Apparently, Vicente Montes and his right-hand man, Mateo Cabrera, were not present, and Gavin was trying to find out where they were.

"I don't know!" the bandit kept saying.

Gavin brutally beat the bandit after each answer that was not to his liking. Gavin's dark, hawk eyes raged with anger and hatred as he yelled questions and threats at the man. The violent questioning seemed to be going nowhere. Gavin suddenly drew his pistol and pointed it at the bandit's head. Then he turned to Lieutenant Smith. Smith nodded once, as if giving permission. Gavin turned back to the bandit, squinting his eyes as a slight smirk came upon his lips. He pulled the trigger, and an explosion of red sprayed from the back of the bandit's head. He collapsed to the ground, and Gavin stared down at him with the cold smirk on his face as a pool of blood inched toward his feet.

Gavin asked the bandits, "Does anybody else want to lie to me, or is someone going to start telling the truth?"

They remained silent, so Gavin pointed his gun at the next bandit, pulled back the hammer, and shot him in the throat. The bandit grabbed his wound with wide eyes while choking on his own blood and gasping for air. The other bandits watched while their comrade was slowly dying.

"Where is Montes?" Gavin yelled. He pointed his gun at the next bandit.

"I'll tell you! I'll tell you!" the bandit yelled, closing his eyes and turning his head with Gavin's pistol pointed at his face.

"Good boy," Gavin said. "Talk!"

The bandit quickly explained that Vicente Montes and Mateo Cabrera had left to return to Mexico right after they had taken control of Seguin. Montes had gone to gather the rest of his men for a future raid. When asked where this future raid would take place, the bandit said he was not sure for Vicente did not reveal his plans to anybody other than Cabrera until the plan was already in action. However, he said he believed that Vicente planned to attack San Antonio. When asked how big a force Vicente had waiting in Mexico, the bandit informed us that he had as many as two hundred men upon which he could call at a week's notice.

Lieutenant Smith sent Ned Riley and Mark Spencer back to San Antonio to pass this information along to Captain Jack Hays and to let him know that we were holding sixteen of Vicente's men prisoner in Seguin. We escorted the prisoners down the street to the jailhouse, where we found the sheriff and his deputy locked and chained in their own cell. We released them and locked up the ten unwounded prisoners in one cell and then locked the six wounded prisoners in another. We sent the deputy to fetch the doctor for the wounded men who were wincing and crying out in pain.

All we could do now was wait for instruction from Captain Hays. Lieutenant Smith sent Kyle, Cole, Mason, and I to the saloon to clear out all of the dead bodies and lay them in the street, which was a very unpleasant task. I had not had any real experience with death, and carrying bloody, dead bodies into the street was grotesque and sobering. The rest of the Rangers were sent to search the town for any bandits that might have been hiding and to patrol the outskirts of Seguin. Lieutenant Smith and Gavin stayed at the jail to guard the prisoners.

Though we had not caught Vicente Montes or Mateo Cabrera, our mission had been a success. We had taken the town back from the terrorizing bandits and had returned it to the citizens. We had also locked up the prisoners and obtained good information about the whereabouts and plans of Vicente Montes. However, the manner in which the information had been obtained was not sitting well with me. That — mixed with the nauseating task of carrying dead bodies out of the saloon — made my stomach turn. I was not pleased with Gavin's actions, nor was I pleased with Lieutenant Smith condoning such actions. I did not know if the rest of the Rangers felt the same way I did. If they did, no one said so.

Mason, Kyle, Cole, and I helped the bartender clean up the saloon and did our best to get it back in order after the chaos of the gunfight that had taken place a few hours earlier. I did my best to clean the blood off the wood floors and walls, but it was an impossible task. Jack, Dan, Joe, Dalton, Pat, and a few other Rangers strolled into the saloon after checking over the town and talking with the citizens about what had happened.

The bartender thanked us all for relieving him and the town of the "uncivilized horde of thieves" and offered a drink for everyone. Of course we all accepted, and he poured a round of drinks for us. Javi Martinez walked into the saloon with a concerned look on his face.

"Is your family all right?" Jack asked. Javi's parents and sister lived in Seguin, and he had been very worried about their safety when he found their home empty.

"They're fine," Javi said, removing his hat. "They were at the Murphy's house, along with some other folks."

"Can I get you a drink, son? It's on the house," the bartender offered.

"No, thank you," Javi declined. "I don't drink."

"Well, then, I guess I'll have your drink for you," the bartender said, refilling his own glass.

"What did they say?" Jack asked Javi.

"Well, Montes and his boys came into town around noon," Javi explained. "Four men tried to make them leave, but they were killed. Three women were raped. One of them was my sister's best friend, Elizabeth. I've known that girl almost my whole life."

"How is she now?" Dalton asked.

"Not good. Not good at all. She ain't talking to nobody. She can't stop shaking. She's got a crazed look in her eyes, and she's real pale. She won't let nobody touch her. She won't even talk to my sister."

"Is she hurt physically in any way?" Jack asked.

"Well, when they cut her dress open, the knife cut her breast a little. She's also got a split lip from where someone hit her," Javi said.

"Damn!" Dan yelled angrily. "Goddamn those sons of bitches! We should hang every last one of them — right now!"

I found myself growing quite enraged as well. The murder of innocent citizens was an awful crime that deserved a harsh punishment, but the rape of an innocent woman was a vicious, sordid act of the most inhumane nature. I did not think what Gavin had done to those unarmed bandits after they had surrendered was right, but now I certainly did not feel as strongly against it as I had earlier.

About an hour and a half after sunrise, Ned and Mark

returned from San Antonio with orders from Captain Hays to have the prisoners tried in Seguin and to carry out their sentences swiftly. As soon as we had done that, we were to ride south and patrol the border.

Lieutenant Smith brought many of the citizens into the jailhouse to identify the bandits who had shot the four men who had tried to stop them and also to identify the men who had raped the three women. The bandits were quickly and confidently identified. Four of the men were found guilty of murder, and nine more men were found guilty of rape. These crimes, on top of robbery and marauding, resulted in the punishment of death. We drew straws to decide who would carry out the executions. There being only eighteen men in our Ranger outfit, all but five of us would have to carry out the executions. I desperately hoped I would draw a short straw, for I did not want to have to kill a man this way. These men were guilty of horrendous crimes for which they deserved to be put to death. However, I did not have the stomach to be an executioner. To defend myself by killing a man when he was threatening my life was one thing, but to shoot a bound and unarmed man was a very different thing.

Lieutenant Smith walked over to me, holding the straws in his hand. My heart pounded as I took one. I stared thankfully at the short piece of straw in my hand. Lieutenant Smith stared at me for a moment. He seemed a bit disappointed by the relief in my eyes. When all of the men had drawn straws, Kyle, Ned, Dan, Lieutenant Smith, and myself were the only ones who would not be executing a prisoner.

Lieutenant Smith ordered us to bring the sentenced prisoners to the back of the town. We did so quickly. We took a long, wooden beam and nailed it to the wall of the building. We then tied the prisoners to the beam.

"Our Father, who art in Heaven, Hallowed be thy name . . ." the bandit prayed as I tied him to the wooden beam. He was the same man who had told us where Vicente had gone. He trembled as he recited the Lord's Prayer. I briefly looked him in the eyes as I finished tying his hands and then quickly turned and walked away.

Once the prisoners were tied to the beam across the back of the building, the Rangers who had drawn the long straws lined up for the mass execution. Mason seemed calm and unaffected by what he was preparing to do. Cole seemed a little nervous. Jack stepped into the line reluctantly. I could tell from his expression that he did not want to do what he was about to do. Gavin seemed quite happy with the orders. The rest of the men were like Mason — calm and unaffected. Kyle, Dan, Ned, Lieutenant Smith, and I stood behind them.

"Ready!" Lieutenant Smith ordered. The Rangers raised their rifles and took aim at their targets.

"You're aiming too low!" one of the bandits yelled. It was Gavin's target.

"Aim!" Lieutenant Smith yelled.

"You're aiming too low!" the bandit yelled to Gavin. Gavin did not adjust his aim.

"Fire!"

The explosion of gunshots was deafening. I turned away as the prisoners dropped dead to the ground, hanging from the beam by their hands. One of the men screamed out in pain. It was a scream that was more deafening than the gunshots. It was the man who had informed Gavin that he was aiming too low. He had been right; Gavin's bullet had struck him in the gut.

"Damn, I missed," Gavin said with a smirk.

"Just finish him, Gavin," Dan said.

"I will — hold on. Just let me get my pistol." Gavin took out his pistol and opened the cylinder. "Shit, my pistol ain't loaded. Hold on, partner!" he yelled to the bandit who was dying a very slow and very painful death. Gavin began to load his pistol.

"Just take mine, Gavin," Javi said, holding out his pistol.

"No, that's all right. Thanks though."

"Stop fooling around! We ain't barbarians!" Dan pleaded.

Gavin just smiled and slowly reloaded his pistol as the dying prisoner continued to cry out in pain, begging for someone to finish him. Jack quickly drew his pistol, aimed, and shot the dying man in the head. Jack holstered his pistol and angrily walked away.

"Why'd you do that, Jack?" Gavin asked. "I was almost ready!" Jack ignored Gavin and continued to walk away. "He was my kill, Jack! You had no right!" Jack disappeared around the corner.

"All right, men," Lieutenant Smith began. "Let's load up and move out. We got some bandits to catch."

I stared at the dead prisoners against the wall as the rest of the Rangers began to leave. Lieutenant Smith walked over to me with a cold look in his eyes.

"Don't worry," Smith said. "You'll get your chance." He stared into my eyes for a moment and then turned to follow the rest of the Rangers back into the middle of town.

We climbed onto our horses as the citizens of Seguin came out to thank us for what we had done for them. They stuffed food, tobacco, and whiskey into our saddlebags and wished us a safe journey. We rode out of town and headed south toward the border in search of Vicente Montes and Mateo Cabrera.

VIII

WE RODE SOUTH TO the Rio Grande toward Ciudad Guerrero where we suspected Vicente might be gathering his army of guerillas. We asked settlers in the area if they had seen or heard any word of Vicente Montes. Many of them believed he was further north, up the Rio Grande.

We made our way north toward Laredo, stopping at every village and town in-between. Everyone we spoke to seemed very worried and desperately wanted us to stay and protect them. Texas was in the process of being annexed into the United States, and many Texans were worried that the violence from the Mexican robbers and bandits would become even greater. We did our best to relieve their fears with confident words and promises of protection and peace. We certainly knew that they were merely words and that our promises were nowhere close to guaranteed.

We roamed South Texas from the Nueces River to the Rio Grande in search of Vicente and his marauders. Each evening, about two hours before dark, we would stop and set up camp. Some of the men would tend to the horses, and others would gather wood for fires and begin preparations for dinner. Jack, Javi, Gavin, and I would often be in the hunting party who brought in dinner for the outfit. After we ate, and after the night had set in, we would put out the fires, pack up camp, and ride away from our trail for about an hour to bed down for the night. We did this because the smoke from our cooking fires could easily be spotted by watchful enemy eyes.

Each morning, we would wake before sunrise and set out in search of bandits and gather intelligence from every source we came across. We did not have much luck, and our excursion seemed fruitless. However, the fact that the border had been so quiet meant that word of our patrol along the Rio Grande had reached the ears of Mexican bandits and had made them wary of embarking on any raids. That was an accomplishment in itself.

After riding up and down the border for about two weeks, we made our way to Montilla. We arrived at the pleasant village in the late afternoon, and Lieutenant Smith requested a hearty meal for his men. The inhabitants of the village went to work preparing dinner. Jack, Mason, Kyle, Cole, and I went to Felipa's home. She was very happy to see us. Anita and Gabriela were there to help Felipa prepare dinner for the Rangers. I had drawn a very detailed map of the world when I returned to San Antonio after my last visit to Montilla, and I took it out to show Anita where I had been. Gabriela was very interested as well. I showed them where we were in Texas in relation to the rest of the world. I showed them New York, where I had come from, and ran my finger across the Atlantic Ocean to England to show them where I had gone to school. I showed them France, Germany, and Italy. When I pointed out Spain and told them that it was where my ancestors and their ancestors had come from, they were stricken with awe. They began to ask many questions, and I gave them a very brief lesson in geography. They were quite interested, for the only world they knew was the small village of Montilla. Their eyes lit up as I described the lands of afar. When Anita asked me how our ancestors got to America, I gave a short history lesson on the discovery of the New World.

By the time I finished giving my broad lesson in history, dinner was ready. We made our plates, and as we scooped up the food, I noticed that Felipa had not made enough for Anita and herself.

"Why are you not eating?" I asked.

"We ate a big lunch," Felipa said.

"Yes, but it's dinner. You should eat," I insisted.

"We're fine — really," Anita said, but from the look in her eyes, I knew that she and Felipa were sacrificing their meal in order to feed us. I imagined many of the people in the village were sacrificing meals in order to meet the demands of Lieutenant Smith and the Rangers.

I took an extra plate and put some of my food on it. I told Jack, Mason, Kyle, and Cole to do the same, and they were more than happy to sacrifice a little bit of their meal. I handed the full plate to Anita and did the same with another plate, which I gave to Felipa. They thanked us and began to eat.

After dinner, the Rangers began to assemble to move out of the village and find a place to camp nearby. We thanked Felipa, Anita, and Gabriela for their hospitality and prepared to leave. Anita and Gabriela insisted that I come back soon to teach them more about the world. I told them that I would be more than happy to and promised to return with great stories about the history of the world. I let them keep the map I had drawn for them, and they were very grateful.

At dusk, we rode out of Montilla and continued riding for about two miles before stopping to bed down for the night. The next day, we rode south toward Laredo. We were all beginning to grow frustrated with the fact that we had not yet found Vicente or heard any word of his whereabouts.

In the middle of the afternoon, when we were about thirty miles north of Laredo, a man on a horse came speeding toward us, frantically waving his hands in the air. We sped up to meet the quickly approaching rider.

"What's wrong, sir?" Lieutenant Smith asked the man when he arrived.

"Laredo is under attack!" the man said.

"By who?"

"Vicente Montes and his men!"

"How many are there?" Lieutenant Smith asked.

"I don't know — at least a hundred."

We began riding quickly toward Laredo, pushing our horses as fast as they would allow. Night fell as we neared the town. As midnight approached, we began to see the flames of burning homes in Laredo. We entered the town cautiously, as the citizens frantically tried to put out the fires. We quickly discovered that Vicente and his men were no longer in Laredo and had ridden northward out of town hours earlier.

We helped the citizens put out the fires and began asking questions. We found out that Vicente and his men had ridden into town and had been met by the opposition of a few armed citizens. A brief gunfight ensued, and all nine of the armed citizens were killed. Vicente and his men began terrorizing the town and looting from the stores and homes. They went through the town on a rampage that lasted about two hours before they finally left, making off with many goods and supplies as well as about twenty horses.

We listened as the citizens cried and yelled angrily while telling their horror stories. Many men and women had been beaten and were badly hurt. One woman suddenly approached me, bellowing the most horrific cry I had ever heard. Tears streamed down her face as she told me that they had killed her thirteen-year-old daughter. I tried to soothe her the best I could, while also trying to find out what had happened, but the woman was hysterical and incoherent. She fell to her knees, and I held her as she cried. Her husband came over and took her from me. His eyes were red, but he was in control of his emotions for the time being. I asked him what had happened.

"They came into our house and began throwing everything around. We cooperated and told them to take whatever they wanted, but that didn't matter. Then they saw my daughter." The father began to choke up as he hugged his wife. "My beautiful, happy, young daughter! They took her, and I tried to stop them, but there were too many. They held me and my wife down and made us—" The man had to struggle to continue. "They made us watch as they raped our daughter." He was crying hard now. "She was screaming for me to help her, but there was nothing I could do! There was nothing I could do! She was screaming and crying! Her eyes — she was so scared. She looked into my eyes as they took her over and over again. When she realized that there was nothing I could do, she tried to fight them herself. She bit the man's nose as hard as she could, and he began to bleed very much. He yelled at her, and then he began to beat her. He punched her over and over again, long after she had stopped moving. When I went to her after they let me go, she was already dead." The husband and wife held each other as they cried.

"Do you know which one it was? Do you know his face?" I asked.

"Of course," the man said. "It was Mateo Cabrera."

Mateo Cabrera, Vicente Montes's right-hand man. I promised the poor couple we would catch these men and bring them to justice, but my words brought them no comfort. I left them there in the street, holding on to one another as they sobbed uncontrollably.

We did not stay in town for long. Vicente and his men had left only a few hours before we had arrived, and we needed to go after them while they were still on the run. We rode quickly out of Laredo and headed north on the bandits' trail.

We traveled all through the night without stopping. When morning came, we picked up the bandits' trail again. They had turned slightly east, which led Lieutenant Smith to believe that they were planning to attack San Antonio from the north. Just before noon, we came to a point where the trail split in two different directions. One trail was heading northeast, and the other was heading west toward the border. According to Javi's trained eye, the trail heading northeast looked like a force of about a hundred and fifty men. The trail heading west looked to be about forty men plus about twenty unmanned horses.

Lieutenant Smith suggested that Vicente Montes was on his way to attack San Antonio with his larger force and had sent a smaller force back to Mexico with the stolen horses. Javi, being the best mounted, was sent to San Antonio to inform Captain Hays of the impending attack on the city, while the rest of us followed the trail heading west toward the border, for we did not want the murdering thieves to cross back into Mexico. More importantly, it was our duty to retrieve the stolen horses and goods and return them to the citizens of Laredo.

We rode quickly toward the border, which was about ninety miles away, desperate to catch Vicente's men before they crossed the Rio Grande. Since Jack and I were the best mounted after Javi, we were sent ahead of our outfit to try to get a visual of Vicente's men.

Jack and I rode at a swift pace all through the afternoon. Renegado and Jack's mare, Carolina, were champions. We had been riding them hard for the past few days with little rest, but they showed no sign of fatigue.

Dusk began to fall upon us as we slowly made our way through a thicket. When we came to the end of the dense stand of trees and shrubs, Jack held up his hand and stopped his horse. He squinted as he peered through the trees where a small abandoned fort stood alone in the middle of an open plain. There was smoke coming from inside the fort. Outside the fort, there were about forty saddled horses, ready to go at a moment's notice, and about twenty unsaddled horses, probably the stolen horses. We had found Vicente's men, and the fact that they had built a fire told us that they had expected us to follow the larger force and not them. Jack and I turned our horses around and quickly made our way back through the thicket to find Lieutenant Smith and the rest of the Rangers.

When we found our outfit, we told them what we had seen and the whereabouts of the thieves. Lieutenant Smith decided that we would attack the fort at dawn. We continued riding until we were only a quarter of a mile from the fort. We bedded down and got only a couple hours of sleep before waking to move in on the fort under the cover of darkness.

We waited in the thicket where Jack and I had spotted the fort. We climbed off our horses and tied them off. About half an hour before dawn, we began creeping stealthily across the open plain toward the fort.

The sun began to light up the sky, as we stood at the entrance of the fort and prepared to attack. Lieutenant Smith nodded to Gavin and Joe who then pushed open the two doors. We immediately began to fire as we poured into the fort. The bandits quickly scattered while returning fire. I was near the back of the outfit as we rushed into the fort, and we took cover where we could find it. I had yet to get a clear shot at any of the bandits. It was chaos as bullets flew all around me. Smoke and dust from riddled adobe walls hung in the air. As I ducked down beside one of the doors, I noticed a bandit running up the stairs to the walkway that went around the top of the fort. I fired at him as he climbed over the side of the fort, but I missed.

I ran outside and turned the corner just in time to see the bandit jump from the fort and land on the back of one of the saddled horses. I fired at him as he rode off, but I missed. I quickly jumped onto the back of one of the horses and began to chase after him. As I closed in on him, I raised my pistol and took careful aim at the horse, for I wanted to take the bandit alive. I fired, and my bullet hit the horse's rear. The horse stopped quickly and kicked his front legs into the air as he fell over. The bandit fell from the horse's back, quickly stood up, and began to fire at me. I leaned over the side of my horse to take cover. I peeked under the horse's neck as I closed in on the bandit. When I was only a few feet away, I pulled myself back up, jumped from the horse, and tackled the bandit to the ground. I rolled off of him and quickly got to my feet. I tackled him again before he could get to his feet, and we wrestled on the ground. I was stronger than him and soon had him pinned. I punched him until he was barely conscious and had lost the strength to fight back. I stood up, keeping my pistol pointed at him as I grabbed the horse I had been riding. I took a rope from the horse's saddle and bound the bandit's hands. As I looked at his face, I noticed a gash on the bridge of his nose and another just below his nostrils. It looked as if his nose had been bitten. I quickly made the connection and realized he was Mateo Cabrera. The poor girl from Laredo had bitten his nose while he was raping her, just before he had beaten her to death. I clenched my teeth as an intense wave of rage came over me. I tied to the saddle the other end of the rope that bound his hands, climbed onto the horse's back, and began riding back to the fort, dragging Mateo Cabrera behind me.

The gunshots in the fort had ceased, and the Rangers were bringing out the prisoners. Of the forty bandits in the fort, twenty-six had been killed. Not a single Ranger was killed, and only three were slightly wounded. We bound the fourteen prisoners to their horses. Lieutenant Smith complimented me on my capture of Mateo Cabrera.

"What's the plan, lieutenant?" Gavin asked Smith.

"Well, we've got to return these horses to Laredo and get these prisoners locked up," Lieutenant Smith said. He paused for a moment to think. "But I want to get Cabrera and Gomez to San Antonio." Roberto Gomez was another infamous bandit amongst Vicente's thieves. Lieutenant Smith looked at me for a moment and then turned to Joe. "Joe, I want you and Konrad to escort Cabrera and Gomez to San Antonio, while we take the rest of the prisoners and these horses back to Laredo."

"Yes, sir, lieutenant," Joe replied.

"Can you handle that, Konrad?" Gavin asked. He seemed a little bitter that he had not been asked to escort Vicente's two most infamous thieves. He was also probably jealous that I had been the one who had captured Mateo Cabrera.

"Yeah, I can handle it," I said confidently.

"Good," Lieutenant Smith said. "Y'all take your prisoners and get moving. The rest of you, round up these horses and let's get our prisoners back to Laredo."

Joe and I went to the thicket and climbed onto our horses. We rode back to the fort, took our prisoners, and began heading toward San Antonio.

IX

JOE AND I MOVED our prisoners, Cabrera and Gomez, slowly along the trail to San Antonio. It was supposed to be a fast trip, but we had not checked Gomez's horse carefully enough. The horse we had put him on was old and slow. He walked as if he was tired and his joints ached. This was discomforting to me, for I had hoped to make it to San Antonio that night. I did not want to spend the night on the open plains with these clever thieves and murderers. However, as we slowly rode along, the sun crept toward the western horizon, and it seemed that we would have to stop to bed down for the night.

Just before nightfall, we came to a grassy plain with a fair amount of shrubbery. It seemed like a place where we could be well hidden. We kept our horses saddled and did not make a fire. We took Cabrera and Gomez off their horses, bound their hands behind their backs, and bound their feet as well. We covered our prisoners in buffalo robes as well as ourselves to camouflage us better amongst the shrubs. Joe took out a bottle of whiskey and gulped down a big swig.

"Take it easy with that, will you?" I said. "You're going to need to have your wits about you if something happens."

"Don't worry about me. It's going to take a lot more than this for me to lose my wits," Joe insisted.

"Can I have some of that, my friend?" Mateo asked Joe.

"Shut up," Joe answered. Mateo chuckled and laid his head down.

"Why does Lieutenant Smith want us to take these two to San Antonio, anyway?" I asked. "Why can't they go to Laredo with the rest?"

"Because these two are the most famous," Joe explained.

"Smith wants them tried and executed publicly and in front of as many people as possible. He wants to make a statement."

Mateo laughed at what Joe said.

"What's so funny?" I asked.

"Killing us won't stop Vicente," Mateo answered. "It will only feed the beast."

"Well, it will stop you," I reminded him.

"Yes, but it won't undo what I've done," Mateo responded. "Do you know how many people I've killed? Too many to count, and I'd do it all again if I could."

"You killed a thirteen-year-old girl," I said.

"Yes, yes I did, and I raped her. I enjoyed it very much."

"There's a special spot in hell for people like you," I said emotionlessly.

"Oh, yes! Right by Satan's side! Satan and his demons will welcome me with open arms. I will join his army, and we will battle God and his little angels and throw them out of Heaven, and then evil will rule the world!"

"You're insane, Mateo; do you know that?" Joe said blandly. Mateo squealed in laughter. Joe took a swig of whiskey.

"Do you want to take the first watch?" I asked Joe.

"Yeah. You go to sleep."

"Wake me in four hours," I said.

Joe nodded. I put my head under my buffalo robe and closed my eyes. I did not think I would be able to sleep, being so close to two mass murderers, especially one as sadistic and sick as Mateo Cabrera. I could not believe the things he had said. His sick words and awful laughter haunted my thoughts as I listened to him breath only a few feet away from me. He even breathed like a mad man. However, I was very tired from the excitement and activity of the past couple of days, and even if my mind would not rest, my body began to force itself to sleep. I dozed off as my exhausted body shut down.

I awoke to the sound of chirping birds. As my mind shifted from dreams to reality, I tried to remember where I was. As I became aware of my situation, I realized that Joe had not roused me for my watch. I quickly pulled the robe off my face and looked at the sky. It was almost dawn. I looked over at Joe and saw that he was asleep and snoring loudly. I quickly looked over at Mateo Cabrera and Roberto Gomez. They were still under their buffalo robes. Frustrated, I kicked Joe in the shoulder and he awoke angrily.

"What?" he asked without opening his eyes.

"What do you mean, 'What'?" I said. "You fell asleep on your watch!"

Joe looked at Mateo and Gomez. "Well, no harm done. They're still here."

I looked around, still not satisfied with the situation. Something felt wrong. I looked at the horses. Renegado and the old horse Gomez had ridden were right next to me. I spotted the Spanish gelding Cabrera had been riding, but Joe's horse was nowhere to be seen.

"Joe, where is your horse?" I asked, quickly rising up.

Joe looked around in confusion. "I don't know. He was tied off right next to me."

I looked at Mateo carefully. He was sleeping soundly. I looked past him to Gomez. The buffalo robe appeared to have a body under it, but I saw no legs or arms. I jumped to my feet and lifted Gomez's robe to find only a shrub beneath it.

"Shit!" Joe exclaimed, quickly jumping to his feet. "How the hell did he get away with my horse so quietly?"

I ignored Joe. I pulled Mateo to his feet violently and dragged him to his Spanish gelding. Mateo laughed and mocked our situation, as I lifted him onto the horse. I took a rope and was preparing to bind him to the horse as the sun began to light the sky.

"Oh, shit!" Joe said urgently. "Konrad, look!"

I rushed to Joe's side to see what he was looking at. Across the prairie to the east, I saw upon the edge of the horizon the silhouettes of a large company of horsemen about a mile away. They numbered at least one hundred. I immediately knew it was Vicente and his band of marauders. Gomez had escaped and found them, and now Vicente was returning to retrieve his right-hand man.

"Have my friends come for me?" Mateo asked with a sinister chuckle.

"I won't be able to outrun them on that old pony," Joe said.

My mind raced as I assessed the situation. Joe was essentially without a horse, the pony being useless under the circumstances. I looked up at Mateo upon the back of the Spanish gelding. He was smiling smugly as if he had outsmarted us. He looked to the horizon and watched as his comrades rode to his rescue. As I thought of the options, of which there were few, I began to realize that there was only one thing I could do.

"We got to go now, Konrad!" Joe yelled.

I looked at the quickly approaching company of horsemen and looked back at the sick, sadistic, thief, murderer, and rapist sitting upon the Spanish gelding. I glared at him angrily as he smiled down at me. I imagined that smile upon his face as he beat that poor thirteen-year-old girl to death. I heard his heavy, perverted breathing as he raped her. I had made my decision, and I executed it quickly. I drew my pistol and promptly shot Mateo Cabrera in the head. He fell from the back of the horse and landed hard on the ground. I climbed onto Renegado's back, and Joe climbed onto the back of the Spanish gelding where Mateo had been sitting. We rode away, pushing our horses as fast as they would go.

My heart raced, pumping adrenaline rapidly through my veins. We rode hard for about five miles until Vicente and his men could no longer be seen behind us. We continued to push our horses as fast as they would go until we finally arrived in San

Antonio after a few hours that passed as if they were only a few minutes.

Joe and I went straight to the Ranger headquarters and informed Captain Jack Hays of our situation. He immediately began to mobilize the Rangers. Javi came to greet Joe and me as we mounted with Hays' company of Rangers. By the time all of the Rangers had mobilized, we numbered about sixty or seventy men. Captain Hays led us out of town to meet Vicente's band of outlaws, which was certainly greater than our forces, maybe twice as great — or more. My heart had not slowed since I had awakened that morning. Now, my heart was beating faster than it ever had. I was anxious, and a little fearful, as we rode across the prairie. I had been in only two engagements before, but those engagements were hardly worth mentioning and of completely different circumstances. For one, I had not even fired my weapon in the first engagement, nor had I faced a bullet. In the second engagement, I had spent the whole fight chasing Mateo Cabrera. Furthermore, my previous engagements had been surprise attacks in an enclosed space. Now, I was riding out with a force of sixty men to face a larger force on an open plain.

"You look nervous, Conrado," Javi commented as he rode next to me.

"Why do you say that?" I asked.

"Because you look like you just came from a swim in the river," Javi explained. "I know it's hot, but it's not that hot."

"I'm just a little anxious," I admitted modestly.

"Why? You just killed one of the most infamous bandits in Texas! You should be riding into battle like a king! Don Conrado!" Javi exclaimed. "Joe here is the one who should be anxious after falling asleep on his watch. What a fool!"

"Shut up," Joe said, not making much effort to defend himself.

"I'm to blame as much as Joe is," I said. "And I'm certainly no Don."

281

"You killed Mateo Cabrera. That makes you a Don in my book," Javi said.

"The scout is returning," I said, gesturing ahead as a man rode quickly toward us.

The scout gave a brief statement to Captain Hays. Hays then ordered us to ride at double time, informing us that Vicente's force was not far away and that they were riding out to meet us head-on. I took a deep breath and exhaled slowly. We rode another mile or so before Vicente's army of bandits appeared on the horizon. They were approaching us quickly. Hays ordered us to speed up, and the distance between our forces quickly began to close. Just as we were nearing shooting range, Hays ordered us into a different formation. Our force divided into three sections, and each section spread out, forcing our enemy to aim rather than fire blindly into a mass of men. Joe, Javi, and I were on the right flank.

I leaned down on Renegado's neck and whispered into his ear. "I know you're nervous, Renegado. This is my first battle, too. Do not be afraid. We will make it through this alive. We will not die here today. We will not die here today."

Renegado let out a deep breath and shook his head as if working himself up for the battle. His pace quickened. He was ready — and so was I. I pulled my rifle out of the scabbard and cocked it.

The first shots exploded from the bandits. Hays immediately gave the command to fire. I fired in unison with the Rangers and saw many bandits fall as I rode out of the cloud of smoke. We fired at will, as did the bandits. Sticking my rifle in its saddle scabbard, I took out my Colt pistol and began to fire. Once I fired my five bullets, I took out my second pistol and emptied it into the bandits as we charged forward. We were now close enough to see the whites of one another's eyes. While the Rangers around me reloaded their pistols in preparation for the collision between our two forces, I drew my saber. I bellowed a ferocious battle roar as I stared at my target not ten yards away. He was aiming his pistol at me, but there was not an ounce of fear in my body. Had there been any before, I had just screamed it out of me. My target fired, and I felt the bullet blow my hair. I swung my sword across my body, right through the ribcage of my target.

The forces of Rangers and bandits collided in a chaotic array of gunshots and hand-to-hand combat. Some men fought with knives, and some swung their empty rifles into the skulls of their enemy. The officers fought with their sabers, as did I. My skill with the saber was unmatched by any on the battlefield, and from the looks in my enemies' eyes, I could tell that they had not encountered a man nearly as handy with a sword as I. Battles such as this on the frontier were fought with guns and knives. My mode of hand-to-hand combat, especially in the style in which I used it, was foreign to them, thus making it impossible to defend against.

The battle was a blur to me, as I swung, stabbed, and chopped with my sword while I rode through the mass of bandits. It was a blur, yet, I had never felt more alert in my life. It seemed that I knew exactly what was going on around me. I could tell when I was about to be attacked before I even saw my attacker. This awareness was intoxicating in the most sobering way, but it quickly passed. After only a few minutes, the bandits retreated with less than half the number with which they had engaged us. As I looked over the mass of Rangers still standing strong, I saw that our numbers had not diminished. Looking down at the dead bodies that littered the battlefield, I saw that they were all bandits.

Hays and about forty of his Rangers regrouped and began chasing after the retreating bandits. The rest of us assessed the damage and tended to our wounded comrades. By the end of our assessment, we found that only three Rangers had been killed and six wounded, and their wounds would not be fatal if they received proper care. Vicente Montes had not been among the bandits left dead on the battlefield. He had led the retreat to salvage what men he still had left.

I petted Renegado's neck and told him what a great job he had done. He was breathing hard, and so was I. His white coat was stained with the blood of our enemies, and he looked like a menacing creature, standing proud and stoic amongst the slain bodies. I looked at my blood-covered saber. I took out my handkerchief, wiped the blade clean, and put the saber in its sheath.

While Hays and his men chased the bandits back to the border, the rest of us rode back into San Antonio. I unsaddled Renegado at the Rangers' stables and washed him down thoroughly for half an hour. I brushed his hair for another half an hour, all the while praising him and thanking him for his grace, his ferocity, and his serenity under pressure. When I finished grooming him, I kissed his cheek and gave him over to the stableman.

I headed to the inn at the market square, where the rest of the Rangers were having a drink at the saloon and toasting their wellbeing and having lived to fight another day. I desperately needed a drink now. The adrenaline was gone; my heart had slowed, and I was beginning to comprehend all that had happened during that eventful day. I sat down at the bar next to Joe and Javi and ordered a whiskey.

"Don Conrado!" Javi exclaimed. "The hero of the day has graced us with his presence!"

"Enough with this 'Don' nonsense," I said, gulping down my shot of whiskey and ordering another.

"What? You don't like it? It's a honor," Javi said.

"Well, I don't deserve to be honored," I said.

The bartender refilled my glass, and I tried to ignore Javi as he praised me for my bravery and skill in battle. His attention was suddenly drawn away elsewhere, and I was left alone with my thoughts. I had killed many men in battle that day, well near a dozen. But the men I had killed in battle did not bother me as much as I imagined it would. We had engaged those men to defend the city and its innocent inhabitants. They were an army of thieves, murderers, and rapists who would have raided the city and killed many innocent people had we not met them in battle. We had prevented what had happened in Seguin and Laredo from happening in San Antonio. However, my execution of Mateo Cabrera was not sitting well with me. I tried to justify it in my mind as I had with the men I had to kill in battle, but I could not. I told myself that Cabrera had murdered more people than he could count and was unapologetic about it. He had raided many towns and had stolen from hardworking, innocent people. He had raped that thirteen-year-old girl and had beaten her to death. Who knew how many other women he had raped? Who knew how much innocence he had stolen? I thought over and over again about the circumstances, which had led me to execute him. Had I not done what I had done, what would have happened? What had been my options? Joe and I could not have both ridden upon Renegado's back and gotten away from Vicente and his well-mounted bandits, while dragging Cabrera on the Spanish gelding, and I certainly could not have left Joe behind to be killed while I rode away with our prisoner. Nor could I have left Cabrera behind to be reunited with his cold-blooded marauders only to pillage and murder and rape again. The only reasonable choice had been to execute Cabrera on the spot, for that was the fate that awaited him in San Antonio anyway. However, it had not been my place to carry out his punishment.

Given the circumstances, I realized that no matter what choice I could have made, it would not have been a pleasant one, and no other choice would have rested easier on my conscience. I was doomed to suffer the torments of a bad situation. I drank my whiskey and ordered another.

"I'm sorry, Konrad," Joe said, staring down at the bar. I had forgotten he was sitting next to me. "I shouldn't have fallen asleep. None of this would have happened."

"It would have happened regardless. It was just set into action in a different way than we planned," I said.

"Maybe you're right, but I still shouldn't have fallen asleep." It was the first time I had ever heard any emotion in Joe's voice.

"Don't worry about it," I comforted. "We improvised and made do with the circumstances. It turned out to be a very successful day. I'm going to bed. Goodnight, Joe."

I drank my whiskey and put some money on the bar as I stood up. Then I took my glass and the bottle to my room and left Joe to torment himself as I walked upstairs to do the same.

X

THE DAY AFTER THE battle, Lieutenant Smith and my fellow Rangers returned from Laredo. I was in my room, lying on my bed and smoking a *cigaritta* when there was a knock on my door. I told them to come in, and Jack, Mason, Kyle, and Cole walked into the room. I stood up to greet them and asked them about Laredo. They said they had tried and executed the prisoners as we had done in Seguin.

"Don Conrado, huh?" Jack said with a smirk.

"You've been talking to Javi," I said.

"It's fitting," Jack complimented.

"He said you were like a warrior from the old times, fighting with that saber of yours," Mason said.

"I always thought that thing was a goofy decoration, but it sounds like you actually know how to use it," Cole said.

I poured myself a drink from the bottle by my bed. "Would anyone like a drink?"

"Yeah, but let's go downstairs and have it," Jack suggested.

I nodded, set my drink down, and followed them down to the saloon. Jack ordered us a bottle, and we took it to an empty table and sat down. Jack filled our glasses.

"I don't know if you heard, Konrad," Mason began. "But Polk has ordered four thousand troops to Texas from Louisiana. They'll be coming here and to Austin and Corpus Christi."

"Really?" I asked. "What for?"

"Well, as soon as the annexation of Texas into the United States is official, Mexico will probably declare war on us."

Jack and I sat quietly, sipping our drinks, as Mason, Kyle, and Cole talked about the war as if it had already begun. They romanticized the glory, the honor, and the adventure of war, as all young men do. I certainly had romantic ideas of war, as well.

I had read many books that praised the glorious battles, the warriors of freedom, and the duty of the soldier to defend the innocent. I had also read the more realistic perspectives on war. However, young men do not pay attention to the darker realities of war. At the moment, my ideas of war were not romantic, for I had killed my first man the day before and had fought in my first real engagement. I felt nothing romantic about it. I finished my drink and excused myself from the table to go to the post office and check my mail.

When I arrived at the post office, I had two letters waiting for me. One was from Raul, and one was from Miriam. Miriam had sent me a letter not long ago, informing me that she was a day away from boarding a ship bound for France. The letter I had gotten today meant she had arrived safely. I took the letters back to my room at the inn and lay in bed while I read them. I read Miriam's letter first.

My dear Konrad,

Charles and I have arrived in Paris! We took a riverboat from Le Havre to Paris and stopped at all of the wonderful places along the way. It is so beautiful here. I wish you had come with us. We are staying at the Hotel de Crillon, and it is just magnificent. We went to see Anastasia, and she is doing very well. Her father has overcome his illness, so I'm trying to convince her to return to New Orleans with Charles and me. I think she will. Anastasia has been the most wonderful tour guide.

At this point in her letter, Miriam began to ramble on about the sights she had seen, as Miriam tended to do when she got excited about something, which was just about everything. She finished her letter, expressing how much she missed me and telling me to be careful. She told me to write to her as often as I could and to send my letters to the Hotel de Crillon.

I opened Raul's letter next and began to read it.

My adventurous nephew, Konrad,

I hope all is well on the wild frontier of Texas, and I hope you're finding the adventure you seek. I'm sure you know that four thousand troops from Louisiana have been sent to Texas. In fact, as I'm writing this letter, I'm watching hundreds of young men march through the city on their way to guard the United States' newest acquired territory, soon to be, that is. I truly hope there is not a war. However, I feel it is inevitable. I know I've already expressed my opinions to you concerning this unjust cause, so I will say no more on the matter.

Miriam and Charles have left for France, as I'm sure she has written you. I'm sure they will have the most wonderful time. They plan to return this winter, but I told them it might be best to stay in France until the war is over. I said I would say no more on that matter, didn't I? I apologize. Moving on... there's not too much going on here. With you and Miriam gone, it is rather boring, but I keep busy by writing and painting. I was thinking about doing a little traveling. I'm not sure where, for there are so many places I would like to go. It seems you have inspired me to go out and explore in my old age. Maybe when you return we can go on one of your adventures together. Maybe not somewhere as wild as Texas or the Western frontier, but somewhere neither of us has been, somewhere outside of America, maybe somewhere in the Caribbean. Jean Lafitte used to sing praises of the beautiful islands amongst the bluest waters in the world. And, of course, relaxing on a tropical island surrounded by beautiful native women would not be the worst thing in the world. I hope you return to New Orleans soon, alive and healthy, and until you do, enjoy yourself as much as possible.

Your loving, crazy uncle,
Raul

I chuckled as I closed the letter. I missed Raul. However, I wished he had not put the idea of an adventure to the Caribbean in my head. Now, I would just grow even more restless, for I had just signed on with the Rangers for another four months. I remembered that Anastasia had told me she dreamed of going to Havana, Cuba one day. Maybe we could all go when I returned. That is, if Anastasia returned to New Orleans with Miriam and Charles. That would certainly be a grand adventure. I walked over to my desk and sat down. I began to scribble a couple of letters to Raul and to Miriam.

When I finished writing my letters, I walked over to the post office. I gave my letters to the man at the front desk and walked outside. As I crossed the street, I noticed the people of the city had grown excited. Many people walked out of the stores and businesses. I looked down the street and saw a great force of mounted soldiers of the United States Army. The troops Mason and Raul had spoken of had arrived.

I crossed to the other side of the street and watched the soldiers pass. A war was certainly brewing, and it seemed as if President James Polk was doing everything he could to provoke it. America was lusting for more land, and Polk knew we needed a war in order to take it. I got a nauseous feeling in my stomach as I watched the soldiers pass. The feeling was part excitement and part dread, for I knew there was something wrong with the way matters were being conducted in the government. The cause just did not feel right. America had enough land. They needed no more, especially not the land that had been Mexico's for centuries.

I turned away from the troops and walked back to the market square. I went into the saloon at the inn where the Rangers were enjoying a relaxing day of rest. I sat down at the table where Jack, Mason, Kyle, and Cole were sitting.

"The troops are here," I announced.

"Are they?" Kyle asked. "Guess this war is going to happen sooner than we thought."

* * *

Over the next few months, we were very busy. We patrolled the borders and searched for wild bands of Mexican marauders and Indian horse thieves. In August, a Comanche war party attacked San Antonio and made away with almost forty horses. They had entered the city and left with their loot in less than five minutes. Our detachment was sent after them. We tracked the war party for two weeks. Our pursuit of the Indians took us west to the eastern outskirts of the *Llano Estacado*, then north across the Red River, and nearly as far as the Canadian River. We followed the horse thieves' trail all the way to the Palo Duro Canyon. Despite the harsh, unforgivable, and practically unlivable state of the land, it was absolutely gorgeous in all of its glorious ruggedness. Millennia of erosion and weathering had turned this god-forsaken desert into a beautiful, giant plain of mesas, plateaus, escarpments, and colorful rocks in the most random formations. The Palo Duro Canyon was a magnificent sight to behold. Amongst its vast, deep gorges and towering hoodoos, I felt insignificant. However, this feeling of insignificance only lasted for a moment. I began to let the overwhelming beauty settle in, as I peered over the endless desert plain and began to realize that just as erosion and weathering had shaped this rugged land, this rugged land had shaped the rugged men and women who had traversed it, as it was shaping me now. Never in my life had I felt more in tune with the natural state of my being. Long ago, man had lived according to nature and had let nature shape him, for man had been created to live in accord with the land. Over time, man began to create civilizations and societies, and as generations were born into these civilizations, that which made man live in harmony with nature began to fade from our blood until it was hidden deep enough to be forgotten. My desire to find that harmony within myself was what made my restless heart beat. Seeing that rugged land of West Texas made me believe that harmony was still attainable for an evolved, civilized man.

We eventually stumbled upon the Indian horse thieves in

the depths of the Palo Duro Canyon. We engaged them in a brief skirmish where only two Indians were killed before the rest retreated, leaving the stolen horses behind. We sent a few scouts after the Indians, but they knew the canyon better than any White man and quickly eluded us, so we began to drive the recovered stolen horses southeast toward San Antonio.

Along the way, Jack shot a mountain lion, and Javi and Gavin each killed four rattlesnakes, which made for a wonderful feast that night. Food had been scarce on our chase, so the meal was more than welcomed and long overdue. I had never eaten rattlesnake or mountain lion. The rattlesnake was much better than I had expected, but the mountain lion was by far the best meat I had ever eaten.

We returned the stolen horses to San Antonio, and the citizens were very grateful. We stayed in the city for a little while, sending out scouts to gather intelligence about activity on the border. I went on a scouting excursion and spent two long days roaming the land between the Rio Grande and the Nueces River. On my third day of scouting, I stopped in Montilla for lunch. Felipa, Anita, and Gabriela cooked a fine, hearty meal and were very happy to see me. After lunch, they begged me to teach them more about the world, which I was more than happy to do. A few of Gabriela and Anita's friends came to listen to the history lesson as well. After seeing their desire to learn, I decided to make my lessons a regular occurrence and went to Montilla every chance I could. I requested many scouting excursions, which the rest of the men were more than willing to turn over to me, for they did not enjoy scouting. It was dangerous to be alone in such a wild land in such turbulent times. They much preferred drinking and gambling in San Antonio during their free time.

The number of students listening to my lessons in Montilla grew each time I made the trip to the knowledge-hungry village. I borrowed and took with me a few books from Jack's library and began to teach Anita and Gabriela how to read and speak English. They learned very quickly.

Eventually, the entire village would gather in the streets to listen to my history lessons. I was a very good teacher, which surprised me. I was very passionate and got very excited when I told the stories that had shaped the world in which we lived. The way I told the stories of the past made the people of Montilla excited to learn. I remembered how I had found many things boring when I was a student in school. I remembered how often I had slouched in my chair and day-dreamed, as my teachers monotonously rambled on about things in which I was not interested. As I looked at the excited and awed expressions of the children and adults of an uneducated village, I began to realize how much I had taken for granted.

* * *

In late September, a wagon train of supplies was attacked on its way to San Antonio from Santa Fe, and all but one of the traders had been killed. The trader who had gotten away made it to San Antonio and informed us of what had happened. Mexican bandits had slaughtered his men and stolen their supplies. When Lieutenant Smith asked him to describe any of the bandits he might remember, the trader described a man who sounded like Vicente Montes. We quickly got our outfit together, which had grown to a force of thirty-three due to new recruits pouring in to join our ranks with the hope of fighting in a war against Mexico.

We rode quickly out of town to the site of the massacre. When we arrived at the site, we found the eight traders brutally butchered in a manner that made it look more like a Comanche raid than Vicente and his bandits. Javi studied the tracks and was certain it had been Vicente Montes.

We tracked the infamous bandit and his marauders westward

across the *Llano Estacado*, across the Pecos River, and into the Guadalupe Mountains. We followed their trail all the way to the Rio Grande where we lost them. Frustrated and exhausted, we turned around and began our long, rough journey back to San Antonio. Along the way, we were attacked by a Comanche war party. Even in our exhausted, half-starved state, we managed to fight them off and send them into a retreat. We killed four of our attackers, and one of our new recruits was killed. We tied his young, lifeless body to his horse and continued on.

We finally made it back to San Antonio in miserable condition. We nourished our bodies with a large, quick meal and drank all the water we could keep down. Once our stomachs were full, we went to bed. Almost everyone slept for a solid twelve hours. The next day, most of the men lounged around in the saloon, played cards, and drank whiskey.

I went to the post office to see if I had any letters. I did not. I went to my room and finished Book Seven of Paradise Lost. I would have read more, but I could not bear the stench of myself, so I headed to the bathhouse, where a kind, beautiful young woman drew me a bath. I smoked a *cigaritta* and drank a glass of wine as I relaxed in the bathtub. I could not have felt better at that moment. The kind, beautiful young woman came into the bathroom to refresh my tub with hot water, reminding me that I could, in fact, feel better. I thanked her and asked her to stay and talk with me. She smiled bashfully and sat down next to the tub. She asked me if I needed her to scrub me down, but I told her to just relax and even offered her some wine. She accepted and we chatted for a while. I was quite charming, and I could tell that she was not used to being charmed and wooed by a man. I imagined that most of the rough, uncivilized men in the city did not take the time to speak kindly to her and dig deeply into her soul to find out who she really was. I could also tell that she was not used to drinking wine. She opened up to me quickly and told me all about herself, her passions, and her desires. I charmed her, wooed her, and seduced her, and soon had her joining me in my bath.

Our stay in San Antonio was brief. In mid-November, Captain Hays ordered us on another excursion to patrol and roam the border. We did not see any action or receive any intelligence on our trip. After a little over a month, we returned to San Antonio in time for Christmas. I went to the post office where a letter from my parents awaited me. I took the letter back to my room and read it. They did not have much to say other than the usual parental clichés. They told me all that was going on in New York, explained how they were doing, and told me they missed me very much. They wished me a happy birthday and a merry Christmas and told me to write to them soon. I immediately wrote them a letter, while my fellow Rangers celebrated Christmas Eve with the rest of the town.

A few days after Christmas, Texas was officially integrated into the United States. Jack, Mason, Kyle, Cole, and I, along with most of our outfit, headed to Austin for a very lively New Year's Eve celebration. That evening, we stood with hundreds of citizens on Congress Avenue and watched a large parade of United States soldiers march down the wide street. Everyone clapped and cheered for their heroes. That night, we attended a grand ball and celebrated the arrival of the year 1846, although it seemed more like everyone was celebrating a war that was approaching all too quickly.

XI

General Zachary Taylor moved his army from Corpus Christi toward the Rio Grande. After crossing the Nueces River, the United States Army entered into what Mexico considered its own territory. According to the Mexican government, the United States had invaded Mexico, so Mexican troops were sent to the Rio Grande. At the end of April, United States troops walked into an ambush, and American blood was spilled upon American soil. Soon after, the Mexican Army attacked Fort Texas. By May 13, the United States had officially declared war on Mexico.

That was the news my fellow Rangers and I received when we returned to San Antonio in mid-May after a month-long excursion along the border. While Captain Hays recruited as many men as he could muster and moved his regiment to American Army camps at points south, our detachment was ordered to continue scouting and patrolling the border. Not only was it our duty to keep our eyes open for the Mexican Army, but the Texans were worried that bandits such as Vicente Montes would take advantage of the concentration of our forces on the war effort. Some believed that the Mexican government had even employed bandits to do just that. A lack of Rangers on the frontier would also make the citizens even more vulnerable to Indian raids. Therefore, our duty was to police the area and to essentially do what we had been doing before the war.

It was all happening so quickly, and I found it hard to comprehend that just over a year earlier I had left the United States of America and had arrived in the foreign country of the Republic of Texas. With a simple vote and a simple signature on a simple piece of paper by a simple man, I was no longer in a foreign country but back in America once again. And with another simple vote followed by the same simple signature from the same simple man, a dubious war between two countries had been declared. That simple piece of paper could be lost or destroyed, or time could turn it into nothing, and the same could happen to the simple man whose signature made the world turn. This man was nothing special. He was only flesh and blood — probably no smarter or better suited to make such great decisions than any other man of his upbringing, yet all he had to do was dip his pen in ink, write his name on a piece of paper, and let the puppets dangle from his fingers. God didn't have it that easy.

For the next couple of months, our detachment roamed the frontier and saw very little action. Aside from two skirmishes with a Comanche war party and a chase to push a small outfit of bandits back across the border, it was quiet on the frontier. All of the action was happening at the southern tip of Texas. We heard news about the battles at Palo Alto and Resaca de la Palma, which led to the United States Army's occupation of Matamoros. My fellow Rangers were not pleased with our assignment to patrol the frontier. They wanted to fight gloriously in battle and defend their country. Many of them wanted revenge against Mexico for the Alamo, for the Mier Expedition, and especially for the Goliad and Dawson Massacres where many of these men had lost friends and comrades.

In late July, we rode into Montilla to see if the villagers had seen or heard of any bandits or Mexican soldiers being in the area and to have a filling, tasty meal. As we rode through the village, everyone came out to see us. They greeted me by name with big smiles on their faces. The young children of the village, Gabriela among them, ran over to me excitedly and walked alongside my horse. Javi, who was riding next to me, looked at me in confusion.

"You're very popular here," Javi commented.

"When I go out on a scout, I always come here for a meal," I explained. "I've gotten to know the people quite well."

"Don Conrado de Montilla!" Javi jested. I rolled my eyes and shook my head.

Jack, Mason, Kyle, Cole, and I went to Felipa's home, where she greeted us each with a big hug. I kissed her on the cheek and told her I was glad to see her. Gabriela and the rest of the children stood outside the house, peering in through the doorway and windows, giggling as they stared at me. I smiled and waved to them. Jack, Mason, Kyle, and Cole looked at the children and then at me with confused smiles.

"What is this all about?" Mason asked.

"Has Konrad not told you?" Felipa asked.

"Told us what?" Mason asked.

"He is our teacher."

Jack looked at me and smiled. "Really? Is that why you volunteer to go scouting all the time?"

"It is," I replied honestly.

I heard Anita's voice outside and turned to see her trying to make her way through the crowd of children in front of the doorway. I told the children to clear a path, and they did. I took the two platters of food Anita was carrying and set them down. Now that her hands were free, Anita greeted me with a hug. Felipa and Anita began making lunch, and we all helped any way we could. After about an hour, we were eating.

"Will you be teaching a lesson today, Konrad?" Anita asked as we enjoyed our meal.

"I'm not sure that I will have time," I responded.

"Please, Konrad!" Gabriela begged.

"Please!" the children begged in unison.

"Your students are pleading," Anita teased with a smile.

I acquiesced, "All right, but just a short one today."

I handed my half-eaten meal to Gabriela and told her to share it with the others, and then I stood up and walked outside. After taking a book out of my saddlebag, the children walked next to me, and we headed to the center of the village where I usually gave my lessons. As the people of the village gathered around, I began to read a passage from the last volume of Edward Gibbon's *The History of the Decline and Fall of the Roman Empire.* My lesson was mostly about the fall of Constantinople and the end of the Eastern Roman Empire, as well as the last couple of years of the One Hundred Years War. Mason, Kyle, and Cole smiled in disbelief as they watched me give my lesson. I don't think they really understood why I was educating this small village. However, I could tell that Jack understood. I saw him walking around, looking at the children's faces, their eyes wide and their mouths agape. He smiled and nodded as he listened to my lesson. Some of the Rangers had walked over to see what was going on. Gavin looked at me in confusion, shook his head, and walked away. A few moments later, Gavin returned with Lieutenant Smith. Smith watched me for a few moments, stone-faced and squinty-eyed. I could tell that he was not pleased. I certainly saw no harm in what I was doing, but I knew the way Lieutenant Smith's mind worked. As far as he was concerned, I was educating the enemy. I continued my lesson, ignoring the lieutenant's and Gavin's cold stares.

As I was getting into the last part of my lesson, Dalton rode quickly into town. He had been scouting for the past two days. He climbed off his horse and walked over to Lieutenant Smith as the rest of the Rangers gathered around. I stopped my lesson but could not hear what Dalton was saying.

"We're moving out!" Lieutenant Smith ordered.

I apologized to the children and told them I would have to finish my lesson next time. Anita came over to me as the children began to disperse.

"Do you want to walk with me to my horse?" I asked Anita. "I have a gift for you."

"You do?" she asked, surprised.

"Yes, come with me."

I led her to Renegado who was tied off in front of Felipa's

house. The Rangers were getting on their horses and riding out of the village. I walked into Felipa's house, thanked her for the meal, and gave her a hug and a kiss on the cheek. Gabriela came running into the house, so I picked her up and hugged her. I promised them all that I would be back soon and then walked outside to my horse where Anita was waiting for me.

"Are you going to fight in the war?" Anita asked.

"No, we weren't invited. We're just chasing bandits and Indians," I explained.

Anita smiled. "Good."

"Your gift," I said, suddenly remembering, after finding myself lost in her eyes. I reached into my saddlebag and handed her a history book that covered the sixteenth century through the eighteenth century.

"What is this?" Anita asked.

"It's the book that covers the time periods of our next few lessons," I explained.

"Why are you giving it to me? Aren't you coming back?" Anita asked worriedly.

"Yes, I'll be back. I just think there's too much time between each lesson. I've been teaching you English and how to read, so I thought maybe you could give the lessons until I return again. They should be learning every day."

"You want me to teach?" Anita asked in confusion.

"Yes, and I know you can," I said confidently.

"You do?"

"Of course. You're very smart, and you're a very quick learner. All of the children look up to you, and the elders respect you. I think you would be a great teacher."

Anita smiled and nodded her head in acceptance. "All right. I will try my best. But only when you're not here. You're still the teacher. You're still my teacher."

"Very well," I agreed.

We stared at one another for a moment, lost in each other's

eyes. I leaned in and gently kissed Anita on the cheek, then pulled away from her slowly and stared into her eyes a moment longer. I told her goodbye and promised I would return soon, climbed onto Renegado's back, and rode out of the village. I quickly caught up with the rest of the Rangers.

"What's going on?" I asked Jack.

"Some bandits attacked La Grange," Jack said. "They looted a few stores and made off with some horses. Doesn't sound like too much damage was done, but we've got nothing better to do."

It took us a little over two days to reach La Grange. It was almost nightfall when we arrived. Lieutenant Smith asked a few of the citizens what had happened. They said six men had ridden into town, firing off their guns. Everyone quickly ran into their homes to hide, thinking it was a large group of bandits or, even worse, the Mexican Army. By the time they realized that it was only six drunken men, it was too late, and the bandits had already made off with six horses and what little loot they could carry.

"Sounds like some reckless bastards trying to take advantage of the war," Lieutenant Smith commented.

"Sounds like the worst goddamn bandits I've ever heard of," Gavin said.

Lieutenant Smith promised the citizens that we would find the bandits and return the stolen goods, and we rode out of town. After riding away from La Grange for only a few minutes, Lieutenant Smith stopped us.

"It's just a waste of time for all us to go after six stupid kids. Hell, they're probably still in the area talking about how clever they are. Jack, why don't you lead a small team to find these bastards," Lieutenant Smith ordered.

"Sure, lieutenant," Jack said. "Who do you want me to take?"

"I don't give a damn. Pick your own team," Lieutenant Smith told him.

Jack chose Mason, Kyle, Cole, Joe, Javi, and me to go after

the bandits. Lieutenant Smith approved and told us to rejoin the rest of the outfit in San Antonio after we caught the bandits and had returned the stolen goods. Then, Lieutenant Smith and the rest started out on the ride back to San Antonio.

"All right; let's get going, boys," Jack said.

We rode south as darkness began to blanket the sky. After about four hours, as midnight was approaching, we decided that it might be best to bed down for the night. We rode a little further to find a good spot to camp, and just as we were about to stop, we saw a campfire through the trees of a sparse forest.

"Do you think that's them?" Kyle asked.

"I don't know," Jack replied. "Could be."

"Well, if they're as stupid as everyone says, then I think it might be," Mason commented.

"Let's go have a look," Jack suggested.

We quietly climbed off our horses, entered the sparse woods, and crept toward the campfire. We didn't make a great effort to hide ourselves, for we knew that after staring at a campfire all night they would only be able to see blackness past the first few trees. When we were close enough to see the men, we stopped and observed six of them sitting around the fire. They each had their own bottle of whiskey and were taking very liberal swigs. They seemed quite drunk, and it was very hard to make out what they were saying. I looked around their camp for the loot and saw a pile of whiskey bottles and a few other things of little value. I didn't see the stolen horses, but I imagined they were nearby. These six men certainly seemed to be the bandits who had robbed La Grange for whiskey only to drink it in some woods a few hours away. They seemed pretty stupid to me.

Jack signaled for us to turn around. We went back to our horses, trying hard not to laugh while we were still within hearing distance. When we got back to our horses, we all started laughing hysterically.

"Is this a joke?" Kyle asked.

"If we just wait a couple of hours, we can haul them back to La Grange when they're unconscious," Mason said. "When they wake up in jail, they won't know what the hell happened!"

"I'll tell you what we're going to do," Jack said. "We'll round up their horses and the stolen horses tonight, and in the morning we'll scare the shit out of them."

We quietly rounded up the horses and took them back to our camp about a quarter of a mile away, and then we laid out our bedrolls and went to sleep at about two in the morning.

After we woke with the sun and began making our way toward the bandits' camp, we were able to surround them and move in, hiding in the grass and behind the trees. The six bandits were still fast asleep and snoring loudly. I noticed one of the bandits had fallen asleep with his foot so close to the fire that the flames had melted the toe of his boot. It was a pathetic sight. I looked over at Jack who was counting down with his fingers. He smiled when he got to one and fired a shot into the air. The rest of us each fired a shot into the air at different times. The bandits woke up and jumped to their feet in a confused, frightened, half-drunken daze. They ran to where they had left their horses, only to find that they were no longer there. We moved in on them and fired another round into the air. The bandits raised their hands in the air and surrendered. We couldn't help but laugh as we approached them, tied their hands, and led them back to the horses.

We arrived in La Grange at about noon and delivered the bandits to the local jail to let the town deal with them. We returned the horses to the owners and apologized that we had not caught the bandits before they had drunk all their stolen loot. The citizens thanked us for our efforts by cooking us a wonderful barbeque. After a hearty lunch, we told them we had to be going, and by two o'clock, we were on our way back to San Antonio.

XII

WE ARRIVED IN SAN Antonio early in the morning after camping only an hour outside the city. I headed straight to the post office, while the rest of the men headed to the saloon to meet up with the other Rangers. I walked up to the clerk at the front desk and asked if there was any mail for me. He handed me one letter. I thanked the clerk, walked outside, and stared at the letter curiously. It was from James Morrison. I sat down on the walkway next to the post where I had tied Renegado, opened the letter, and began to read it.

> *Dear Konrad,*
>
> *I know it is strange to be getting a letter from me of all people. I wanted to apologize and beg forgiveness for the wrongs I have committed against you and anyone else you hold dear. The things I said about Anastasia were cruel, uncalled for, and were said only out of my own insecurities and embarrassment. I have never been a kind man, but that is something I am trying to change. It took being wounded in a duel with you for me to realize how precious life is and how useless it is to treat people the way I have in the past. I would also like to thank you for not killing me. I know you could have if you had very well pleased.*
>
> *Unfortunately, apologies are not the reason I am writing to you now, though what I have written above is meant with complete sincerity. I'm afraid I have some grim news. Your dear Uncle Raul has passed away due to liver failure. It doesn't seem right that you're hearing this from me, but I do not know who else would tell you this awful news. I have written Miriam in Paris as well. I'm very sorry, Konrad, and I offer you my deepest condolences. I have made all the burial arrangements and covered all of the costs in that matter. Please let me know if you can return, and I will arrange to have the funeral*

as soon as you can get to New Orleans. Again, I apologize that you must hear this terrible news from me, but I thought it was important that you know. Please let me know if there is anything I can do.
   Your friend,
   James Morrison

I closed the letter and let the news sink in, as I exhaled a deep, shaky breath. My stomach tied itself up in knots as I clenched my jaw and swallowed the lump in my throat. Raul had wanted to go on an adventure to the Caribbean with me. My eyes filled with tears as I thought of the last time I saw him. He was seeing me off as I headed for Texas and had begged me not to go. I remembered looking back as he watched me ride away, that sad look on his face reminiscent of my parents' expressions the day I had left New York. A tear streamed down my face. Renegado lowered his head and brushed his face against mine. I petted his nose and thanked him for his sympathy.

The rapid thumping of hooves snapped me out of sulking daze. I looked up to see Jack, Mason, Kyle, Cole, Joe, and Javi riding swiftly up the street. They abruptly stopped in front of me as I wiped my eyes.

"What's wrong with you?" Mason asked.

"Nothing."

"Lieutenant Smith and our boys are headed to Montilla," Jack announced.

I stood up quickly. "Why? What's going on?" I asked.

"Lieutenant Smith received intelligence that the people of Montilla have been giving aid to Vicente Montes and his bandits. They think he's there now," Jack said.

"How long ago did they leave?" I asked worriedly.

"A couple of hours ago," Javi replied.

I jumped onto Renegado's back, and, without a word, I began riding quickly out of town, yelling for people in the street to move out of my way. I rode out of San Antonio and headed south for Montilla. I begged Renegado to run like never before and to endure as long as possible. I knew that if Lieutenant Smith and Gavin found Vicente Montes and his men at the village, the people of Montilla would be the ones who would suffer most.

Renegado rode as hard as he could for me. Jack, Mason, Kyle, Cole, Javi, and Joe tried to keep up with us but were soon lost behind me. I prayed that I would see Lieutenant Smith and the Rangers upon the horizon before they reached Montilla, but as the hours passed into the afternoon, I saw only the trail of their horses, and from the looks of it, they were moving fast.

As the afternoon passed into the evening, I brought Renegado to a fast walk, for he was quite tired from me pushing him so hard, and I could tell that he did not have much stamina left. I petted his neck and thanked him for working so hard for me. I looked back, and I could see Jack and the rest of the men about a half a mile behind me, and then I looked ahead and squinted as something caught my vision. There was smoke upon the horizon, right where Montilla was. I gave Renegado a kick to send him into a dead sprint once again and told him that this was the last stretch and that I really needed him to push hard for me. He gave me everything he had, and soon we arrived at the flaming village of Montilla. I stared in horror as my worst fears were realized. I saw Lieutenant Smith leading the Rangers out of the village. I quickly approached them.

"What have you done?" I asked, as I jumped off Renegado's back and ran into the village.

"What had to be done!" Lieutenant Smith called after me.

I walked through the streets of the village. Some of the homes were on fire, and as I peered through the smoke, I could see bodies lying in the street. As I walked past the bodies, I noticed that they were bandits. I walked deeper into the village where there were a few people walking around looking at the bodies, while others tried to put out the fires. I saw the dead bodies of a few men who

I knew were innocent villagers. A woman cried as she held the dead body of her husband. Then, my heart stopped for a moment as I came upon the body of a dead woman. I looked at her face. I had seen her before. When I saw innocent men and women had been killed, I began to worry.

"Anita!" I called over and over as I ran to Felipa's house. I looked inside, but nobody was there. "Felipa! Anita! Gabriela!"

I called their names as I choked on the smoke. I tried to wave the smoke out of my face as I passed a flaming house and turned the corner. My eyes, nose, and throat burned. I called their names again. Seeing the dead body of a young girl on the ground made my heart stop again. She was one of my students. I screamed louder.

And then I heard a woman crying. I ran toward the awful, sorrowful sound and saw Felipa on her knees. She was kneeling next to two dead bodies. I could see that one was a young girl and the other was a woman. My heart sank, for I knew the horrific sight I was about to see. I ran over to Felipa and dropped to my knees next to the bodies. I looked at their faces. It was Anita and Gabriela. My breaths shortened as I picked up Gabriela and held her in my arms. I knew they were dead, but my heart would not accept it. I tried to wake them up. I screamed for them to come back to life as I held them in my arms. As my heart began to accept their deaths, I began to cry with Felipa. I laid Gabriela and Anita down, kissed their cheeks, and cried on their chests. After a few moments, I regained my composure and put my arms around Felipa. She was crying uncontrollably.

"I'm so sorry!" I said. "I'm so sorry!"

Felipa cried in my arms but then suddenly pushed me away. "No! This is your fault! You did this!" Felipa yelled as she weakly pounded her fists on my chest.

"I'm sorry," I repeated over and over. I did not know what else to say.

Felipa finally stopped fighting me and buried her face in my chest. I let her cry in my arms for a few minutes before I told her that I needed to go deal with the man who was responsible. Felipa, disillusioned and in a dreamy daze, turned back to Gabriela and Anita and cried as she leaned over them. I closed Anita's open eyes with my fingers and stood up, wiped the tears from my eyes, and began walking out of the village.

As I walked to the entrance of the village where the Rangers waited, I began to turn my sadness and devastation into anger and rage. My heart pounded with fury. Hate and vengeance consumed me. Through the smoke, I saw the Rangers sitting upon their horses at the entrance of the village. I walked out of the smoke and out of the village and looked right at Lieutenant Smith.

"Draw your sword," I said coldly.

"What did you say?" Lieutenant Smith asked.

"Draw your sword!" I yelled as loudly as I could as I drew my saber.

"Listen to me, you mutinous, little shit; those people you think were innocent were harboring the most violent criminal in Texas!"

"Draw your sword," I demanded once more.

Gavin reached for his pistol. Jack, Mason, Kyle, Cole, Javi, and Joe quickly drew their pistols and pointed them at Lieutenant Smith and Gavin. The rest of the Rangers backed away.

"You've been challenged to a duel, lieutenant," Jack said. "I suggest you draw your sword."

"All of you mutinous bastards will be executed for your insubordination!" Lieutenant Smith yelled.

"Get off your horse and draw your goddamn sword!" I yelled. "I won't tell you again."

Lieutenant Smith gave me that cold stare, but this time there was a hint of fear in his eyes. He climbed off his horse and drew his sword.

"The second you swing that sword at me, you're a dead man.

Do you know the penalty for striking an officer?" Lieutenant Smith asked.

I immediately attacked with great ferocity. I purposefully struck his sword as hard as I could three times and kicked him to the ground. I stepped back as he stared up at me angrily. I could have killed him with a single cut, but I wanted to make the duel last so I could watch Smith sweat. I lowered my sword into a fool's guard. The tip of my saber was pointed at the ground, inviting an attack. Lieutenant Smith rose to his feet and charged. He swung at me with a wrath-cut, which came diagonally from his right shoulder toward my neck. I defended myself easily as he attacked with all his strength and anger. He swung his saber at me over and over with both hands on the handle, while I defended myself, holding my saber with only one hand. I did my very best to make him look like a fool in front of his men. Smith sliced at me with a middle-cut. I met his sword with great strength, knocking him off balance. I followed up with a quick jab, which landed the bell guard of my sword right on Smith's nose. He fell back a few steps, and his nose began to bleed. His eyes widened with anger, and he attacked again with even less coordination. His mind was growing angrier, and his body was tiring. I was growing a little angry myself, for this was just too easy and not as satisfying as I had hoped. I countered his attack by slapping him in the face with the side of my sword, the edge just barely nicking his cheek enough to make a cut. Smith stepped back and felt his cheek. He looked at the blood on his hand and then looked at me.

"Come on!" I yelled.

Smith charged at me, and I quickly stepped into his attack and put him on the defensive. I went at him with a series of master-cuts, which he could barely defend. I stabbed my sword through the flesh of his side, pulled it out, and stepped back as he screamed in pain. I attacked again, making a deep cut into his arm, followed by another deep cut into his thigh, which put him on his knees. He swung at me, but I knocked his sword away. He looked around at the Rangers, but they just sat their horses and watched.

"Someone give me a gun!" Lieutenant Smith ordered. None of the men budged. "That's an order, damn it! Give me a gun!"

I drew my pistol and cocked it as I pointed it at Lieutenant Smith's head. He looked at me with defiance. I lowered my pistol and dropped it on the ground in front of him. He looked down at the gun and then at me. I rested the bloody blade of my sword on my right shoulder. Smith took a moment to think about his options. He looked around at the men and then back to me. I saw his eyes glance at my sword and the way it was positioned on my shoulder. He looked back at me, and without looking down, he grabbed my pistol off the ground. Before he could point it at me, I brought my sword down over his shoulder and into his back. I pushed the sword through his heart and out his chest. He fell dead on his face. I took my sword out of his back, kneeled down, and took my pistol out of his hand. I looked at all of the Rangers.

"The people of this village were innocent," I said. "Do you think Montes gave them a choice? Do you give them a choice when you come here to eat their food? If Vicente Montes was here, then you should have waited to ambush him when he left! You don't go into a village to start a fight and put innocent people in harm's way!" I looked at Dan Sanders. He had fear and sadness in his eyes. "Dan, come here."

Dan sighed and reluctantly climbed down from his horse. I looked into his eyes sternly.

"Honest, Konrad, I didn't kill any innocent people. I only got one shot off in the whole mess of things. I shot one of Vicente's men and saw him fall, I swear!" Dan explained.

"Did you see any of these men kill an innocent person?" I asked him.

Dan looked around worriedly. "I saw Vicente's men kill two or three."

"Did you see any Rangers kill an innocent person?" I repeated.

"I saw Lieutenant Smith kill a couple of 'em," Dan answered.

"Anyone else?" I pressed. I looked into Dan's eyes as he looked up at Gavin. I looked at Gavin who was shaking his head. "Did you see Gavin kill an innocent person?"

Dan nodded and closed his eyes as if he was trying to block out the horror of what he had seen.

"Who did he kill?"

"He killed that poor little girl you liked so much!"

"You son of a bitch!" Gavin yelled.

I quickly turned around while raising my pistol, and as he reached for his pistol, I shot Gavin in the head. I turned back to face Dan. I heard Gavin's lifeless body fall to the ground with a loud thump.

"Did you see anyone else kill an innocent person," I asked once more. Dan shook his head. I looked at the village and noticed that a few of the villagers had gathered at the entrance. I turned to the remaining Rangers. "The rest of you will have to live with the memory of what you have done. Now, who burned the houses? Answer me!"

Four of the new recruits raised their hands and lowered their heads in shame.

"The lieutenant ordered us to do it," one of the new recruits said.

"That is the most pathetic statement I've ever heard," I said. "The four of you will stay here and rebuild this village night and day until it looks better than it did before." The recruits nodded in acceptance of their punishment. "The rest of you will bury the dead in the cemetery to the east of the village. Understood?" The men agreed. "Get to work!"

The Rangers climbed down from their horses and walked into

the village to gather the dead. Javi walked over to me and patted me on the back.

"You did the right thing, Don Conrado," Javi said. I nodded, and he walked into the village to help the others.

Mason, Kyle, and Cole went into the village to help. Jack walked over to me and looked me in the eyes, his face only a couple of inches from mine.

"I'm sorry, Konrad. I'm very sorry," he said with deep sincerity.

"Has anything like this ever happened before?" I asked.

Jack sighed and shook his head. "Lieutenant Smith has always been questionable in his methods. When Gavin joined us, it got worse. But we've never done anything like this, not with innocent people. I've been ashamed for a while for riding with Smith as long as I did. Most of these guys feel the same way. By killing those two, you just did what needed to be done and what none of us had been brave enough to do." I nodded. Jack patted me on the back and went into the village to help.

I stood alone for a moment with the dead bodies of Lieutenant Walter Smith and Gavin Callaghan on either side of me. I took a deep breath and went into the village to help the rest of the men.

XIII

We worked all night and into the next day. We carried the dead bodies of the innocent out of the village to the cemetery. We dug the graves and buried four innocent men, two women, and two children. The village held a funeral service that morning while the Rangers cleared the dead bodies of Vicente's men out of Montilla. I watched the funeral service from afar. Felipa cried as the village priest prayed for the souls of the dead.

I heard a commotion in the village and went to see what was the matter. I came upon the Rangers standing around a dead body.

"What's going on?" I asked.

"This here is Domingo Montes," Dan said, "Vicente's little brother."

I looked at the young bandit's face. He could not have been more than sixteen years old.

"Well, put him with the rest of them," I said.

"What do you want us to do with the bodies?" Ned Riley asked.

"Throw them in the Nueces," I said. "And throw them downstream."

Dan and Ned picked up Domingo's lifeless body and carried it out of the village to the rest of the bodies. Jack walked over to me as the rest of the Rangers went over to the dead bandits to take their bodies to the river.

"Vicente won't be too happy about his brother," Jack said.

"I imagine he won't be."

"He'll come back."

"Then we'll be ready."

"I think we should send Javi out to watch for them," Jack suggested.

313

"All right. Send him out," I agreed.

Jack nodded and ran over to Javi. Moments later, Javi was on his horse and riding quickly to the southwest toward the border. I looked around the village and made sure there were no more dead bodies. There were none. I walked out of Montilla to help the Rangers throw the dead bandits into the river.

After we had gotten rid of the bodies, we began to clean up the village and rebuild what had been destroyed. The sun beamed down as we worked into the hottest hours of the afternoon. I had asked the villagers to stay in their homes and let us do all of the work, but they insisted on helping. I sent Jack and Mason out to hunt for food for the villagers, and they returned with a good-sized hog, which they gutted, skinned, and cut up into hunks of meat. Felipa and a few other women took the meat and began preparing it for dinner.

By the late afternoon, the village was beginning to look more like it had before the attack. As I sat and wiped the sweat off my face, I looked toward the entrance of the village to see Javi quickly riding toward me. I walked over to meet him, and he pulled his horse to a quick stop in front of me.

"Vicente and his men are on their way back," Javi said, out of breath. The Rangers stopped what they were doing and moved in to listen to Javi.

"How far?" I asked.

"They're about three miles away, and they're moving fast," Javi reported.

"All right. Let's get ready for them," I said.

"Don Conrado, wait," Javi said.

"What?"

Javi looked at me with a concerned expression. "There are nearly two hundred of them."

I thought for a moment. I looked at the fearful expressions

on the faces of the villagers and then back to Javi. "We will take Vicente Montes today. Prepare for battle."

The Rangers quickly put on their gun belts and loaded their pistols and rifles. We stuffed extra ammunition wherever we could. Soon, we were climbing onto our horses and riding west to meet Vicente's army. I led the Rangers at a quick pace to keep the battle as far away from Montilla as possible.

We rode for about a mile and a half before we saw Vicente's army appear on the horizon nearly a mile away. His force looked to be the same size as it had been the first time I had met them in battle with Captain Hays. However, this time I was among half as many men. Our Ranger outfit numbered just thirty men.

As we neared firing distance, I commanded the men to spread out. The first shots exploded from Vicente's army. I commanded the men to speed up and hold their fire. I wanted to close the distance to make sure we did not waste a single bullet. Vicente's army fired again. I waited a few moments more before ordering the Rangers to fire at will. Our shots rang out incessantly as we emptied our rifles and pistols into the dense army. Vicente's men began dropping in great numbers. We reloaded as they fired upon us. We emptied our pistols into Vicente's army again as we closed in on them. We were only a hundred yards away. Vicente's men stopped and prepared for hand-to-hand combat.

"Now, Konrad?" Mason asked as he rode next to me.

"Wait!" I commanded. I drew my sword as we closed in on the bandits. "Now!"

The Rangers quickly pulled in from our spread-out line and slowed down to pull back. Mason, Jack, and I kept our speed as the Rangers fell in behind us. Soon we were in a wedge formation, closely compacted, and in the shape of a triangle, with Jack, Mason, and myself at the tip. We charged into Vicente's army. Our wedge formation stabbed through their lines like butter. The idea was to penetrate deeply into the center of their dense formation and fight our way out, and it was working superbly. Not only did the strategy work, but it had surprised the bandits and forced them to fight in a way to which they were not accustomed.

We ripped through them quickly and efficiently as they fell dead around us in massive numbers. The plan was working better than I had imagined. As we worked our way from the inside out, I did not see a single Ranger fall.

Blood sprayed onto my face as I cut through the ranks. My speed and skill could not be defended against. It only took me one or two strokes to kill a man and move on to the next.

The bandits on the outer ranks began to jump off their horses and charge into the center to fight us, since they could not get through their own lines. I jumped from Renegado's back and began fighting on the ground where I had more maneuverability. I killed much more efficiently on my feet. Many of the Rangers had jumped to the ground as well. The bandits were falling quickly and their numbers began to dwindle. The pace of the battle began to slow as we reached the point where we had to seek out bandits to fight. The time between engaging one man and moving on to the next became greater and greater, and soon the battle was over. I walked among the dead bodies as the Rangers cheered in amazement of their great victory. We had expected to send them into a retreat. Instead, we had cut their numbers down from over a hundred and fifty men to a mere seventeen, and not a single Ranger had been killed.

The remaining seventeen bandits were on their knees in the center of the battlefield, their weapons thrown away and their hands on their heads. Among them was Vicente Montes.

XIV

We rode into San Antonio two days after the battle with Vicente and his bandits. The citizens stood along the streets and watched as we led Vicente Montes and the other sixteen prisoners through the city. The citizens quickly recognized the infamous bandit who had terrorized the area for so many years, and they began to clap and cheer in excitement for his long awaited capture.

A large group of United States Army soldiers who were part of the force protecting Texas' interior walked into the street to stop us. A man in an officer's uniform walked out of the Rangers' Headquarters office and approached us.

"What do we have here?" the officer asked.

"Vicente Montes and sixteen of his bandits," I replied.

"You're Rangers, I presume," the officer asked.

"We are," I replied.

The officer looked us over and studied the bandits. "I can barely tell you apart from your prisoners," he said. "I'm Lieutenant Colonel William Harney of the Second Dragoons."

"I'm Konrad Quintero de Leon," I said.

"Are you the commander of this detachment?" Harney asked.

"No, sir."

"Well, where is he?"

"He was killed in the fight against these bandits, sir," Jack lied.

"I see. Who was he?" Harney asked.

"Lieutenant Walter Smith," Jack responded. "We had only one other casualty in the battle—Gavin Callaghan."

"I'm sorry to hear that," Harney sympathized. "Who is your ranking officer now?"

"He is," I said, gesturing to Jack. Jack looked at me in confusion.

"Good! And you are?"

"I'm Jack Burton, sir."

"Well, Lieutenant Burton, take your prisoners to the jail and then come brief me on what happened."

"Yes, sir," Jack said.

We followed the soldiers to the jail and put our prisoners in their custody. While the rest of the Rangers headed to the saloon at the inn, Jack and I rode over to the Rangers' Headquarters to brief Harney.

"Why am *I* the ranking officer?" Jack asked as we rode to the office.

"You are, aren't you?" I asked.

"I suppose, but you took command after you killed Smith. *You* led us into battle. We followed *your* strategy. I think you need to take command of our detachment."

"I'm not a leader, Jack; you are. I got lucky with my strategy. I don't know the first thing about commanding an army, nor do I want the responsibility," I admitted.

"Well, thanks," Jack said sarcastically as we walked into the Rangers' office.

"Have a seat, gentlemen," Harney ordered. We sat down in front of his desk. "Now, tell me what happened."

Jack explained every detail of the battle, including the fabricated detail of how Lieutenant Smith and Gavin were killed by the bandits. Harney was amazed by Jack's account of the battle.

"You charged an army of one hundred and eighty men with a force of twenty-nine Rangers?" Harney asked in surprise.

"One hundred and eighty-three to be exact," Jack said.

"And you killed all but the seventeen who surrendered?"

"Yes, sir," Jack said.

"That is a remarkable feat," Harney said.

"Thank you, sir. What are our orders now, sir?" Jack asked. "Should we go back out to guard the frontier?"

"We've just organized five companies of your mounted Rangers to protect the frontier. We've got more than enough men to guard Texas' interior," Harney explained.

"Then what would you have us do?" Jack asked.

"I'm sending you to Camargo," Harney said.

"Camargo?" I asked. "You want us to join General Taylor's campaign in Mexico?"

"Yes, I do. General Taylor is preparing his forces for an attack on the city of Monterrey. I need you in Camargo as soon as possible. They're going to need Ranger forces like yours," Harney said. Jack and I looked at one another questionably. "Is that a problem?" Harney asked.

"No, sir," Jack said.

"No, sir," I repeated.

"Good! Then I will need you to equip your outfit today and move out at dawn. It should take you about three days to get there. Go inform your men."

"Yes, sir," Jack said. Jack and I stood up and walked to the door.

"Good work, boys," Harney complimented.

We nodded and walked out of the office and through the market square to the inn where we found the Rangers wetting their dry throats with whiskey. Jack and I walked up to the bar and ordered a drink.

"What's the plan?" Mason asked.

"Listen up, fellas!" Jack announced. "Turns out the army doesn't need us to protect the frontier anymore."

The Rangers moved in closer to hear what their next assignment would be.

"So, what're we going to do?" Dan asked.

"They want us to go down to Camargo and join General

Taylor's army," Jack said. About half of the men cheered at the news. The other half didn't seem to care either way.

"When do we leave?" Kyle asked.

"Tomorrow — at dawn," Jack replied.

"Shit," Joe cursed. "Don't we ever get a break?"

"No, we don't," Jack said.

"To the war!" one of the new recruits toasted.

"And to Don Conrado!" Javi added. "For leading us in the capture of Vicente Montes and the destruction of his band of marauders!"

"To Don Conrado!" the Rangers cheered.

I shook my head irritably. Jack smiled at me and raised his eyebrows. "Cheers, Don Conrado," Jack said, raising his glass.

I raised my glass and drank to the toast.

The next morning, we awoke an hour before dawn and prepared to leave. We were freshly equipped and ready for what lay ahead. As we saddled our horses and rode into the street, the citizens of San Antonio came to see us off. They thanked us for our service and stuffed gifts of food, whiskey, and tobacco in our saddlebags. Lieutenant Colonel Harney came to see us off and wish us luck. We rode south out of town and rode at a medium pace toward Camargo.

* * *

After riding for three and a half uneventful days, we crossed the Rio Grande and soon found ourselves at General Taylor's camp in Camargo. As we approached the camp, a few soldiers raised their guns at us, thinking we were Mexicans. After quickly recognizing us as Rangers, Captain Hays rode over to the soldiers and told them to lower their weapons. He came to greet us, and we explained our situation. We told him we were Lieutenant Smith's outfit and that he had died in battle during the capture of

Vicente Montes. Hays led us over to the other Ranger companies, where we found ourselves in the presence of famed leaders such as Ben McCulloch and Archibald Gillespie. We had the pleasure of informing the company of our capture of Vicente Montes, whom all of the Rangers had wished to have the pleasure of catching. They teased us and said we got lucky.

Captain Hays took us to meet General William Worth, whose command we would be under. He welcomed us to the Second Division and told us he appreciated us coming to help. He didn't say much else. His mind seemed to be elsewhere. He seemed like a very sharp man and looked like a very competent leader.

We had only a day to become acquainted with the Second Division before General Taylor began to move us out to Cerralvo on the road to Monterrey. I had not realized how large our force was until we were on the march. Our army of six thousand troops stretched as far as I could see. It was an incredible sight.

It was a very difficult march. The heat was nearly unbearable, the road was in poor condition, and the water was bad. It was even worse for many other soldiers who were in poor health after their detainment in Camargo, which had been a terribly unhealthy town. As the days passed, the weather grew cooler, and the health of the soldiers improved, thus improving their morale.

After a six-day march, we arrived in Cerralvo, which was a pleasant, little town nestled in the foothills. The citizens welcomed us and provided us with good food and water.

Over the next few days, we set up camp and waited for directions from General Taylor. It did not seem like we would be leaving anytime soon, and McCulloch's scouts had seen no Mexican soldiers during their patrols of the area. The soldiers got comfortable and did not seem too worried about what lay ahead, especially our company of Rangers.

On our eighth day in Cerralvo, I began to grow impatient for many reasons. I knew a great battle was upon us, as the

Mexican general, Pedro de Ampudia, and his troops waited for us in Monterrey. I imagined that they must have sent for reinforcements, and I wondered why we did not attack as soon as possible.

General Zachary Taylor seemed like the worst candidate to lead an army. I would often wander around camp, making my way toward his tent, only to find the General staring off into the sky or burying his face in his hands in a fit of self-pity. I asked some of Hays' Rangers about our leader, and they said he was very incompetent and indecisive as well as militarily unintelligent.

"Well, that's not very comforting," I said.

The Rangers assured me that the other leaders, especially General Worth, more than made up for General Taylor's incompetence.

I was also growing impatient, or, rather, restless, as my obligation to the Rangers was about to expire in a month and a half. I had not decided whether I would stay on with the Rangers, and the fact that we were at war made the decision all the more difficult.

"I read that the Mexicans fight with old muskets and can barely reload them in a minute," Dan said one night as we sat around a campfire. "And their soldiers are peasants dragged from their villages in chains and forced to fight."

"That's a foolish lie," I said. "I imagine their newspapers say the same thing about us."

"I'm just sayin', Konrad," Dan responded.

"And I'm saying that if you believe nonsense like that, then you're going to be in for a very rude awakening."

"So you're sayin' they're good fighters?" Dan asked.

"They're probably very competent, yes," I said.

"How do you know?" Dan asked.

"I don't know. What I do know is that when two armies face each other with guns, people are going to die. And it doesn't take much skill to thrust a bayonet into a man's gut."

322

"Our enlistment expires in the beginning of October," Mason commented, changing the subject. "Y'all planning on reenlisting?"

"I know I am," Dan said.

"If we're going to be marching through Mexico for the next few months, then I sure as hell won't reenlist," Joe said.

"I don't think I will either," Cole said. "I'm tired of fighting. I'd like to go back to Texas — maybe work on a cattle ranch."

"What the hell is wrong with you boys?" Mason asked. "We're at war! We've got to fight! Kyle, you're reenlisting, aren't you?"

"Yeah, I was planning on it," Kyle answered.

Jack looked over at me. "What about you, Konrad?" he asked.

"I'm not sure," I admitted. "I'm with Cole. I'm just tired of fighting."

"Come on, Konrad!" Mason urged. "I thought you wanted an adventure!"

I smiled at Mason sadly. "War is not an adventure," I said. "And if it is, I will not have my adventure at the expense of other people's lives."

"Goddamn, you sound like a Whig, Konrad!" Mason said.

I looked at Jack, hoping he would chime in and agree with me, for I knew we had similar ideas about such things, but he remained quiet, staring sadly at the ground. I sat up and leaned forward, resting my arms on my knees.

"I also just found out that my uncle in New Orleans died," I said. "So there are some things I probably need to take care of back there."

"Raul?" Mason asked. "How?"

"Liver failure. I believe it was a long, drawn out affair."

"Damn! I'm sorry, Konrad," Cole said sympathetically. I managed a smile and nodded.

"When did you find out?" Kyle asked.

"When we got back to San Antonio after taking those thieves to La Grange," I said.

"I'm sorry, partner," Mason said.

"Thank you. I am, too." We were silent for a moment. I tossed my cigar into the fire and stood up. "I'm going to bed. Goodnight, boys."

They said, "Goodnight," and gave me their condolences for my loss. As I walked away, I felt my stomach coiling into knots, and a lump formed in my throat. Since I had received the news of Raul's death, I had not had much time to think about it or to really comprehend it. Talking about it out loud made it real and even more painful. I walked through the camp until I was finally alone, sat down next to a palm tree, and began to cry. I cried for Raul, for Anita, and for Gabriela. I cried until I fell asleep in the cold desert.

XV

ON SEPTEMBER 18TH, GENERAL Taylor's army of six thousand men left Cerralvo and began heading down the valley of the San Juan with Captain Hays and our Ranger companies leading the way.

In the evening, the city of Monterrey came into view as we came over a hill. My stomach jumped at the sight of the green and white city, for now the battle was in view and no longer a destination toward which we marched. It was tangible. It was a reality. I calmed my nerves by taking in the beauty of the area. Lying in the foothills, Monterrey rested humbly before the rugged, green peaks of the Sierra Madre Mountains. The land around us as we marched toward the mountains was wonderfully rugged and rocky with occasional shrubs and tall, thin trees. My admiration of the land was suddenly cut short by the sound of cannon fire. Smoke exploded from the city walls, and I watched as the black balls flew through the air, whistling their way to an exploding crash into the ground not far from our army. We were within cannon range now. The officers called for the troops to pull back.

Once we were out of range, we began to set up camp for the night. As darkness fell, General Taylor sent out a team of engineers to reconnoiter the city and assess its defenses and weaknesses.

Jack and I sat on a hill overlooking the city and smoked cigars while we waited for the reconnaissance team to return. The city was dimly lit by flickering flames and the moonlight, which was softened by the clouds moving in from the mountains. We could see the outline of the peaks of the Sierra Madres to the south.

"What do you think?" I asked Jack in the quiet of the night.

"What do I think about what?"

"The battle we're about to fight," I said.

"Well…" He paused for a moment. "There are fifteen thousand

people living in that city and nine thousand troops waiting for us to attack. I think a lot of people are going to die."

I nodded in agreement. "You don't want to fight in this war, do you?"

Jack chuckled and shook his head. "Naïve eighteen-year-old boys want to fight in wars. Guys like you and me, guys who think too much — we're not cut out for war. We just don't have the heart for it. I joined the Rangers for adventure and excitement, but I was a kid. I loved roaming around and seeing the land, but once we had our first little skirmish with the Indians, I knew I wasn't cut out to be a fighter."

"But you're a great fighter," I commented.

"Yeah, I am, and so are you. You get good at something if you do it long enough. But just because you're good at something doesn't mean that it's right for you. Fighting is just a bad habit for me — the worst habit. I've just gotten too damn comfortable with that life, you know?"

"Yeah, I do." I puffed on my cigar and exhaled the smoke. "Do you think you'll quit when your enlistment expires?"

Jack shook his head, puckering his lips. "No, I'm going to ride this war out."

"Why?" I asked. "If you don't want to fight anymore, then stop fighting."

"I can't, Konrad," Jack explained. "I'm the leader of our detachment now. I'm their lieutenant. I have to stay with my men."

His words struck me hard in the gut as I realized the burden I had placed on him without thinking. After killing Lieutenant Smith, I had put Jack in charge.

"Jesus, Jack, that's my fault!" I said. "I told Harney that you were in command of our detachment."

"It's not your fault," Jack said. "After Gavin, I was next in line in the chain of command."

"I thought you were best suited to lead the men. I didn't even think of the obligation I was putting on you."

"You're right; I *am* the best suited. But it's not my obligation; it's my duty," Jack said.

I thought for a few moments as we sat in silence. Finally, I said, "*Officium Per Pectus pectoris.*"

"What's that?" Jack asked, looking at me in confusion.

"It's Latin. It's the inscription on my sword. It means, 'Duty by Heart'," I explained.

Jack nodded as he thought about the phrase. "Duty by Heart," Jack repeated. "If we all lived that way, nothing would get done. There would be chaos."

I chuckled and shook my head. "Sometimes you disagree with me on things I would think you and I would see eye to eye on. You contradict yourself a lot."

"If we didn't contradict ourselves, we wouldn't grow," Jack said. "Besides, someone's got to play devil's advocate."

"*Touché,*" I said.

"I was talking with Lieutenant Meade the other day, and I asked him his thoughts on the war. He said he's never considered himself a soldier, but he knows he's an efficient leader. He said he doesn't believe in the war and doesn't like the way General Taylor has executed his campaign. However, he believes that if there must be a war, then it should be conducted efficiently, and that is his contribution to the war effort. He does what he can to do it right."

"I see," I said, still not convinced.

Jack sighed and looked down at Monterrey. "My heart is with these men, and my duty is with my heart," Jack said. "Fair enough?"

"Fair enough."

The next day, sinister storm clouds rested in the sky above the city, as the generals spent all morning planning our attack on

Monterrey based on the information provided by the engineers the night before. In the late afternoon, we received our orders. General Worth informed us that our Second Division was to march west of the town and take the road to Saltillo, thus blocking supplies and retreat. We quickly prepared for battle and formed our lines for the march. By five o'clock, Hays and our Ranger companies were leading General Worth's Second Division to Saltillo Road, unfortunately, without our horses.

Thunder began to crackle in the sky as we marched southwest. Flashes of lightning began to illuminate the clouds as they grew darker. We were a little over a mile away from Saltillo Road when the rain began to fall painfully hard. We were forced to stop where we were and bivouac in a terrible thunderstorm.

I don't think any of us got any sleep that night, partly because of the miserable conditions in which we had to camp, but the rain stopped by about three o'clock in the morning, and even then we did not sleep. I believe we were all too anxious to sleep and too afraid to let our guard down.

In the morning, the sun shined brightly from a nearly cloudless sky, save a few receding storm clouds. We began our march once again. We marched by the small, straw-roofed houses nestled amongst the hills on the outskirts of the city. I could see the inhabitants peeking through the windows as we marched to attack their city.

As we came upon the road to Saltillo, a heavy cavalry of Mexican lancers charged toward us from Bishop's Palace. We fired upon them with our weak artillery, and it was enough to break up the charging lancers. General Worth ordered our companies of Rangers to turn them back. We broke away from the Second Division and marched at double time toward the scattered lancers. They began to charge at us.

"Here they come, boys!" Captain Hays yelled wildly, looking even wilder with a red bandana tied around his head. "Give them hell!"

We fired on the lancers, and they tumbled from their horses. We charged at them as we fired our pistols and engaged them in a brief fit of hand-to-hand combat before the lancers turned and retreated to Bishop's Palace. General Worth sent another company to join our Rangers as we marched to attack Bishop's Palace. The general then took the rest of the Second Division and marched to Saltillo Road.

Bishop's Palace was a Mexican stronghold at the top of a tall, steep hill just west of the city. As we neared the stronghold, we saw that the retreating lancers had regrouped at the base of a hill with a small group of infantrymen. When we were about a hundred yards away, they began to fire. Soldiers inside Bishop's Palace fired down upon us as well. We returned fire as we charged toward them, roaring loudly over the explosions of our guns. I drew my sword as we prepared to collide with the Mexican forces. The rest of the soldiers fixed their bayonets. We collided with our enemy and engaged in intense hand-to-hand combat. They were sorely outnumbered and were quickly annihilated.

We immediately began to climb the hill as the soldiers in the stronghold fired at us. Our casualties were minimal as we moved quickly up the grueling hill, climbing on all fours like animals. I was among the first to make it to the top and was immediately confronted by a Mexican soldier who attacked me with his bayonet. With my left arm, I knocked his rifle away from my body, and with my right hand, I drew my sword and swiftly stabbed the soldier through the gut. I kicked the dying man to the ground and charged the palace as the rest of the Rangers began pouring over the hill.

We fought our way to the palace in close combat with scattered, unorganized resistance from the Mexican soldiers. We stormed through the doors of Bishop's Palace and were greeted by an explosion of gunfire. We fired back as we charged inside. Smoke from our weapons began to fill the palace, making it difficult to see. I fired my pistol with one hand and fought with my sword in the other, as we made our way through the palace and eliminated the Mexican forces trying to protect it.

The company of regular infantrymen charged into the palace just in time to fire off one round before the capture of the stronghold was complete and all of the Mexican soldiers were dead. One of the infantrymen rushed through the palace and went outside to replace the Mexican flag with an American flag. He cheered excitedly as threw the Mexican flag over the hill, raised our flag in the air, and stuck it in the ground. The rest of the soldiers cheered victoriously. I took a rifle off a dead soldier and walked over to the infantryman who had replaced the flag.

"Good work," I said. "You can carry a flag. Try a gun next time." I tossed the rifle to him and walked over to rejoin my Ranger platoon.

I walked to the back of the palace where many of the men had congregated outside. I joined them and took in the magnificent view, which overlooked the city of Monterrey. The soldiers around me were cheering enthusiastically as General Taylor's army engaged the Mexican soldiers to the east of the city. I looked to the south toward Saltillo Road. General Worth had taken the road and sent a regiment of infantrymen and cavalry to cross the river and attack the forts to the south of the city.

Captain Hays did not give us much time to rest. He ordered our Ranger companies out of the palace, leaving the United States Army troops to hold it. We descended down the hill and marched quickly to catch up with the regiment of infantrymen, which General Worth had sent across the river to the rear of the city. We crossed the river and joined the regiment just in time to help them take the next fort. The fort rested at the top of a hill nearly a thousand feet high. As we ascended the hillside, we were under heavy artillery and rifle fire. We made it to the top of the hill with few losses and charged the bastion. We took the fort with little resistance and turned the cannons on the Mexican Army.

Leaving a company of infantrymen to hold down the fort

and man the cannons, we descended back down the hillside and marched to attack the next hill. By the late afternoon, we had taken the entire ridge to the southeast of the city. We took the captured cannons and began to fire on the next fort, which was closer to the city. Our Ranger companies were sent out as skirmishers to attack the redoubt, but as we made our way to the fort, night fell upon us and another thunderstorm stopped us in our tracks. We spent the night in the cold rain with no blankets or food, and we had not eaten in two days. Artillery fire blasted sporadically throughout the night, keeping us awake and alert at our bivouac three hundred yards from the fort.

The next morning, we continued our march to the next fort, which was the last remaining hill to be conquered west of the city. We took on heavy fire from the Mexicans, but by noon the fort was ours.

In the mid-afternoon, Mexican reinforcements arrived and made a vigorous attack on our troops. I watched from the fort with my fellow Rangers as General Worth attacked the Mexican troops on their flank and drove them into the city while we fired the captured artillery upon them. The Mexican Army was now concentrated within the walls of Monterrey. We fired shell after shell into the city all night long.

The next day, we impatiently waited for our orders from General Worth, who was in turn waiting for orders from General Taylor. Captain Hays ordered our Ranger companies to rejoin General Worth and the Second Division, for it looked like they were reorganizing in preparation for an attack. When reunited with the Second Division, General Worth had formed two columns of soldiers, ready to march into the city and end the battle. General Worth, pleased to see Captain Hays and our Ranger companies, put us at the front of the lines to lead the assault. We stood there on the road as the troops in the forts fired heavy artillery into the city. We waited patiently for our orders.

It was just after noon when we heard the commotion of

General Taylor's army entering the city from the east. General Worth wasted no time and sent our two columns of soldiers marching down the road toward the city. I watched the white walls of the city as they drew closer and closer. As we came into shooting range, we began to take on some musket fire, but we pressed on even faster, our heads lowered and our rifles ready. The Mexicans continued to fire upon us, and I could hear the bullets zip by my head. I wished I had Renegado under me. It didn't feel right going into battle without him.

The barricade was getting closer. We were almost there. My heart raced with adrenaline and fear. My breaths became short and quick as many questions began to cloud my thoughts.

What if I die here today? I asked myself. *What if this is the last thing I ever do? Has my time come so soon? Could it be? Is it possible that my fate is to die here in the walls of this Mexican city? If it is my fate to die now, will I be happy with the life I leave behind? No! There is so much more I must do! So much I don't know!*

My mind raced with these questions, and I began to make myself anxious. I closed my eyes to stop my thoughts, but it did not work. And then Anastasia came into my mind. My God, Anastasia! I loved her, yet, I had not had the chance to be in love with her. I could not leave this world without knowing what it was like to lay for hours in her arms or without knowing everything there was to know about her. I had forgotten the taste of her lips! I could not die without the taste of her lips still lingering on mine!

I will not die here today! I told myself. *Not today! I will not die today!*

My thoughts were scattered when the Rangers around me began to let out the most frightening and unnerving sound I had ever heard. It was a battle cry of sorts, but it was something much more sinister and intimidating. The sound barreled from deep inside their chests and rose through their throats in a loud, screeching falsetto. It was a sound reminiscent of the Comanche war cry but somehow more fearsome and raw. This strange, animalistic battle cry persisted among the Texans all the way to the barricade as we prepared to fire.

"I will not die here today!" I yelled amongst the terrifying battle cries.

The Mexican forces at the barricade fired, and we fired back. We swiftly broke through the barricade and entered the city. Chaos ensued. Our Rangers led the Second Division through the city as we took on heavy gunfire from the houses and rooftops. Sharpshooters were placed throughout the city on the balconies and walkways high above us. We ran from block to block and house to house, slowly slaughtering the Mexican troops. The Rangers threw grenades into the homes and blew the Mexican soldiers out of the windows. I watched as Jack led our men bravely through the streets, barking out orders and sending our own sharpshooters to the balconies and walkways throughout the city to remove the Mexican sharpshooters and take their positions. Our Rangers followed Jack obediently and looked to him for leadership. Under the pressure of battle, Jack's ability to lead and command shined, more so than any other leader among us.

As we progressed through the streets, we were met by a large force of Mexican troops. The others charged them with bayonets, and I with my saber, and we engaged in the most intense hand-to-hand combat we had yet seen. My sword and I glided with the rhythm of the battle like a maestro and his baton, smooth and deliberate, yet fierce and unpredictable.

We pushed the Mexican force eastward toward the grand plaza of the city, while the soldiers continued to storm the houses one by one. Smoke filled the city as gunfire blasted incessantly from all angles. The slowly diminishing Mexican forces began to fall back down a street to the south. Hays ordered the Rangers to follow them. I stopped and took a deep breath while observing the madness around me, watching as the Rangers ran wildly through the streets and into residential homes, killing everyone they came across. I looked up to the walkways and balconies above the streets as American soldiers took out the Mexican sharpshooters, one by one. I saw Mason stab a sharpshooter in the back with his bayonet and throw him over the edge. The sharpshooter hit the ground with a bone shattering thump. I looked to the rooftops as a Mexican soldier leaned over the side and aimed his rifle. It looked as if he was aiming at me. I quickly raised my pistol, but he fired first. I fired back. His shot missed. Mine did not.

I looked ahead as the Rangers chased the Mexicans down the street, and I saw Cole stumbling around twenty yards away. I called to him, and he turned, reaching out to me with a bloody hand. I looked at his body and noticed blood coming out of a hole in his belly. He fell to the ground, and I began running toward him. I heard the deafening whistle of a cannon ball and looked up to see it coming toward me. I ran out of its path as quickly as I could. The cannon ball hit the wall next to me and exploded with a force that knocked me halfway across the street. I landed on the ground hard and rolled onto my stomach. I slowly opened my eyes as dust, debris, and bodies fell all around me. For a few moments, all I could hear was a ringing in my ears and the quiet, muffled explosion of gunshots. I pushed myself onto my knees and slowly stood up, checking my body for wounds and missing limbs. It seemed that I was still intact and uninjured.

My hearing slowly came back to me. The ringing left my ears and the gunshots became less muffled, until once again I was hearing them at their full force. And then I heard my name. I looked around and saw Cole lying in the middle of the street, alone and reaching out with his bloody hand. I quickly ran over to him and knelt down at his side.

"How are you, Cole?" I asked. A stupid question, but I did not know what else to say.

"Not good, Don Conrado," Cole choked. "Not good. I got shot in the gut!" Cole coughed up some blood, and I wiped it from his cheeks and lips. I looked down at the hole in his gut. Blood was oozing out rapidly. "It really hurts. They weren't lying when they said being gut shot hurt the worst."

"You're going to be all right, my friend," I lied. It looked like the bullet had gone through his stomach. "I'm just going to put some pressure on it to stop the bleeding." I put my hand over the hole in his belly and pushed. Cole screamed as the blood oozed out between my fingers.

"Stop! It hurts!" Cole cried. I took my hand off the wound, knowing that stopping the blood would not save him anyway. "It hurts enough as it is, Konrad."

"All right," I said. "What do you want me to do?"

"Nothing. Just hold my hand." I did as he requested and took his bloody hand in mine. "Are they still fighting?" he asked after a few moments. The chaos continued all around us.

"Yes, they are," I replied.

"I don't understand it," Cole said, wincing as he took short, shallow breaths.

"I don't either," I agreed.

"Now that I know what dying is like, I wish I hadn't killed all those people. Do you think they'll be mad at me in Heaven?"

I swallowed deeply and shook my head. "No, I think love is the only feeling that exists in Heaven," I told him.

Cole stared off into the sky and barely managed a smile. "Love — that sounds nice."

I watched the life slowly fade from his eyes as his grip loosened around my hand. And then he was gone.

"Goodbye, my friend," I said, closing his eyes with my fingers. I stood up and reluctantly rejoined the battle.

* * *

The next day, Jack, Mason, Kyle, and I, along with the rest of our Ranger detachment, walked down the streets of Monterrey, assessing the damage, while General Ampudia surrendered to

General Taylor. We walked into a residential area where a company of Rangers ran roughshod through the streets, from house to house, burning the homes and killing the inhabitants. Of all the horrific sights I had seen in the three days of this awful battle, that was the most disturbing and most spirit breaking. They screamed wildly as they committed acts of violence and cruelty against the residents and destroyed the city even more than it already had been. Three days of death and destruction, and these men had not yet had enough. I'd had enough. I'd had more than enough. I cringed as I listened to the screams of the innocent citizens and the crackling fires.

I turned to Jack, Mason, and Kyle and shook my head. "That will be all for me," I said. I turned and walked through our detachment of Rangers. I stepped over the dead bodies as I walked out of the city. That was all for me.

XVI

AFTER A LONG, SLOW-PACED journey, I arrived in New Orleans two weeks after the battle in Monterrey. I rode down busy Bourbon Street past Miriam's apartment, for I knew she was not there but was still in Paris. I had stopped in San Antonio on my way back from Monterrey to check my mail. I had a letter from Miriam in which she gave me her deepest apologies and condolences concerning the death of Raul. She expressed how heartbroken she was and how she had cried for days when she got the letter from James. She also explained that she was going to stay in Paris until the United States' war with Mexico was over. She and Charles did not think it was safe to return in such turbulent times. However, she did have some good news. Charles had proposed to her in Paris, and they were engaged to be married. The news was somewhat of a shock. Miriam had always been so much against marriage, but, on the other hand, she and Charles were a wonderful couple. I knew they would be happy together.

I rode on to Raul's apartment and tied off Renegado at the bottom of the stairs. I walked up to the door and it was locked. It was never locked. I took out my key, unlocked it, and slowly stepped inside. I stood in the doorway for a few moments as I looked around. It felt empty, lifeless. All of the furniture and decorations were covered with sheets. The curtains were closed and it was very dark. It *felt* very dark. I dropped my saddlebags just inside the door, took the sword off my hip, and leaned it against the wall. I did not have my Colt pistols or my rifle anymore, for I had thrown them into the Mississippi River when I had crossed on the ferry. I stepped back outside and closed the door.

I rode over to James' apartment on Royal Street about a block west of the Saint Louis Cathedral. I knocked on the door and

James answered. He looked at me with surprise and then smiled pleasantly. I had never seen him smile before.

"My God! Konrad, I can't believe you're here!" James exclaimed. I felt as if I was meeting a completely different person. "Do come in!"

I walked inside, and he offered me a seat and a drink. I accepted both and sat down while he poured our drinks. He handed me my drink and sat down across from me.

"It's wonderful to see you, Konrad," James said. "How are you?"

"I'm well, and you? You seem like you're doing great."

"Oh, I am. I'm a different man," James said.

"I can see that."

"You're a different man as well," James observed. The comment made my stomach jump for some reason. "I don't know how I recognized you so quickly with that beard and long hair."

I laughed and felt my beard. I had not shaved in about a month, and I hadn't cut my hair since I had left New Orleans for Texas. While riding with the Texas Rangers, I had lost the habit of grooming.

"Yes, I know. I could certainly use a shave. There wasn't much time for it where I was," I said.

"I don't imagine there would be. How was Texas?" James asked.

"It was a whole other world, wilder than any place I've ever been, but beautiful beyond description. The landscapes were just magnificent to the point where I'd find myself just staring for hours in disbelief," I explained, a bit surprised at my own excitement.

"It sounds wonderful. I presume you're not fighting in the war," James said.

"I fought in Monterrey. After that, my enlistment with the Rangers was up and I decided to return."

"Monterrey — I heard that was a terrible battle, with many casualties on both sides."

"It *was* terrible."

"I'm sorry you had to experience that," James said with empathy. "I'm also very sorry about Raul. He was a splendid man." I nodded and smiled. "I hope you don't mind, but since I didn't hear from you, I went ahead and had him buried. We held a service in his honor. Hundreds of people came. All of New Orleans' finest. So many people adored him."

"Thank you for doing that. I'm sure it was a beautiful service."

"I laid him in the Saint Louis Cemetery next to his father. Would you like me to take you to his tomb?" James asked.

"Sure."

James and I rode to the cemetery, which was just outside the French Quarter. We tied off our horses at the entrance, and James led me toward Raul's grave. We walked down the narrow walkway surrounded by extravagant society tombs and sarcophagus tombs to simple step tombs and markers. Despite the typical eerie and haunting feeling one might experience when at a cemetery, the Saint Louis Cemetery was actually quite beautiful and peaceful.

James suddenly stopped and pointed down a narrow walkway. "He's right down there about twenty yards further in a platform tomb next to his father," James said. "I'll let you go alone."

"Thank you, James," I said, placing my hand on his shoulder.

As I slowly paced down the narrow walkway toward the tomb, I felt something unexplainable fill the hollow feeling I had in my stomach. My whole body suddenly felt full, as if something was inside of me. I exhaled a deep breath as Raul's platform tomb came into view. I walked past the tomb of Rosendo Quintero de Leon, my grandfather. Next to it was Raul's tomb. Both their platform tombs were simple yet elegant and beautiful. I ran my hand over the top of Raul's tomb. I just stood there for a while. I didn't say anything. I had no flowers to lie at the foot of his tomb. I just stood there, staring.

After a few minutes, I walked back over to James and thanked him for what he had done. We walked out of the cemetery to our horses. As I untied Renegado, he brushed his nose against my cheek. I petted him and thanked him for his sympathy. He was such an intuitive companion. I climbed onto his back, and we rode back to the French Quarter.

We went back to James' apartment, where he apologized again for the way he had treated Anastasia and me and thanked me for merely wounding him at our duel. I told him all was forgiven on my part. As for Anastasia, I could not speak for her. We shook hands and promised we'd see each other soon.

I rode to the local stables and put Renegado in the care of the stableman. I walked back to Raul's apartment, which was now my apartment according to the wishes he expressed in his will. He had left everything to me. I went inside the grim apartment, opened the curtains, and removed the sheets from the furniture. I moved all of my belongings into Raul's bedroom. Most people would have probably left everything as it had been before their loved one had passed, and that was my first thought. But I knew I could not live peacefully in this home if I did not make it my own. When Raul's father had passed, he had done the same thing. I remembered Raul telling me that sleeping in his father's bed had made it easier for him to accept that he was gone. Maybe it would work for me.

When I finished, I poured myself a glass of Raul's favorite whiskey. Then I sat down at the table by the liquor cabinet where I would often find Raul in the morning, scribbling away on a piece of paper. With much difficulty, I wrote my parents a letter, informing them of Raul's death. I really didn't know what words to use to tell my father that his brother had died. I did the best I could and hoped it came out all right — and then I got drunk.

The next morning, I went to see a barber. I asked for a shave and a trim. He cut my hair first, trimming off about an inch and making it look nice. He then covered my face in shaving cream and sharpened his razor on a leather strap. He began to move the razor down my face. I could tell that it was going to be a very slow process.

"I can see that you haven't been around a city in a while," the barber commented. "Have you been out West?"

"Texas," I replied.

"I hear it's pretty wild over there."

"It can be," I responded.

"Were you fighting in the war?" the barber asked.

"For a little while. I was a Texas Ranger before the war," I said.

"I see… You're not a deserter, are you?" he asked bluntly.

I squinted at him angrily. "My enlistment ended on October 2nd."

"I see — just asking. What was the war like?"

"Just give me a shave," I commanded irritably.

"Yes, sir," the barber said. "I'll keep my mouth shut."

XVII

THE NEXT FEW MONTHS felt like a slow progression into madness. I found myself drinking quite frequently, which did not help my state of mind. I just could not find anything better to do. With Raul gone and Miriam and Charles in Paris with Anastasia, whom I could not get out of my mind, there was no one to drag me to any social events or anything of that nature. I was very bored and spent most of my time reading and drinking in Raul's apartment. I went out occasionally to walk around and get some exercise or to go downstairs to Leon's for a few drinks. At least once a week, I would take Renegado from the stables, ride him far away from the city, and spend a night or two in what little wilderness the area provided.

I felt an increasing amount of guilt. Part of it came from leaving my friends to fight the war without me, but most of it came from the things I had done. My dreams and waking thoughts were haunted by images of the violence in which I had participated, and these images could only be diluted by alcohol. My execution of Mateo Cabrera, the awful massacre in Montilla where I stared upon the lifeless, innocent bodies of Gabriela and Anita, and the horrific images of what I had seen and done in Monterrey, such as watching Cole die and watching the Rangers terrorize the city after the battle, all consumed me. I felt bad after leaving my friends, but I knew that I could not participate in that war any longer. It was a political war, and I knew it from the beginning. Raul had warned me. It was a war initiated by the United States Government in order to acquire more land and more slave territory, and I had been a part of it. I knew better, yet I had participated in it, and I could not take it back. It was not a war of freedom or justice. Why had I willingly gone with the Rangers to join Taylor's army? I'd had a choice, and I had chosen poorly.

* * *

On Mardi Gras, I sat out on my balcony and watched the masked, costumed people celebrating below me on Bourbon Street. I was nursing a bottle of red wine (my second that day) and remembering the last time I had celebrated Mardi Gras. It had been four years earlier. I had gone to the masquerade ball and had searched desperately for Anastasia all night. When I had finally found her, we danced and shared a passionate kiss, and that was the last time I had spoken to her. Soon after, she and James had announced their wedding plans, and I had run off to join John Fremont's outfit with Mason, Kyle, and Cole — God rest his soul. Had it really been four years since I had last seen Anastasia? What hold did she have on me that made her occupy my mind for so long? The simple fact that I longed to know more about her could not be enough to keep my interest for four years. I had longed to know many women before, but my interest in them had never stood the test of time. What was it about Anastasia that captivated me?

I finished my wine and refilled my glass. Bourbon Street was filling up as more and more people joined in the celebration.

After finishing my second bottle of wine, I had still not achieved the desired effect of drunkenness that I had been trying to obtain. I went to Raul's liquor cabinet, which had enough alcohol to keep a man drunk for a year or so. As I looked over the different wines, whiskies, and rums, I came upon a bottle of distinct characteristics. In the dark depths of the liquor cabinet, the bottle looked sinister, yet sophisticated. I took it out, and under the light of a candle I could see that the liquid inside the bottle was green. It was Maison Pernod Fils absinthe. I thought long and hard about uncorking the bottle and dancing with evil. I had vowed never to drink that green liquid again, but it was too tempting and I gave into its temptation. I uncorked the bottle, poured myself a glass, and splashed a bit of water into it to ease

343

the burn. Then I walked back out onto the balcony and peered over the railing at the revelers below. I raised my glass in the air, toasting the people below (though I doubt anyone saw me), and I took a sip. The absinthe stung my taste buds, glided down my throat, and filled my chest with a warm, euphoric feeling. I exhaled a deep breath and sat down. My eyes grew heavy as I let the green liquor take effect.

By the time I finished my glass of absinthe, I was in an intoxicated daze with no sense of time. There were no minutes, hours, or days. I just was. I was lost in a single moment.

The tired, lethargic effects began to wear off, and I felt a burst of energy. I stood up slowly, making sure I had my balance, and walked back inside. I danced around the apartment for a bit, acting like a fool. I made my way to the door and walked down the stairs to Bourbon Street where all the fun was being had. I joined in the celebration and danced and mingled in the street. I was the only person not wearing a mask and costume.

"What a beautiful mask," one drunk woman said to me. "Who were you before tonight?"

I smiled stupidly, having no clever response to give. She laughed, grabbed my face, and gave me a sloppy kiss. Just as quickly as she had kissed me, she was gone. I stood still and alone, watching as the heathens danced wildly around me. Who was I before tonight? The strange woman's question lingered in my jumbled thoughts. And then I saw her — Anastasia. She was dressed as she had been on Mardi Gras four years earlier. She wore the same unmistakable mask and carried herself with that same unmistakable confidence and ease. She looked at me, smiled, and then disappeared into the crowd. I immediately began to chase after her. I pushed through the crowd, desperate to find my love, which was the only thing that could save me from myself. I moved slowly through the dense crowd, but I was determined to find her.

I came to an opening in the crowd at St. Louis Street. I looked around and saw her heading down a narrow alley. I quickly ran after her. As I ran through the alley, I passed a masked couple kissing against the wall and then another couple doing a bit more than kissing. A man dressed as a court jester hopped toward me, laughing wildly. He stopped and stood before me, smiling from ear to ear. He bowed to me, and I walked on past him.

When I came to the end of the alley, I found myself amongst another great crowd of people. I looked around but saw Anastasia nowhere. With the depressing aspects of the alcohol taking its course, I stumbled back home, alone and miserable.

*   *   *

As time passed, the detachment I felt from civilized life began to weigh me down. I would see people in the streets and at stores, and I would feel absolutely no relation or connection to them, which led me to believe that I had no connection with humanity. I felt like an outcast, although I could make myself blend in at any given moment. That was the advantage of my sophisticated upbringing. I would take Renegado to the woods on the outskirts of town, where I would camp for a few days or a week and live off the land to rid myself of civilized life and to find my most natural and primitive self. But a short trip into the wilderness did not satisfy my restless heart or progress my journey of self-discovery; it simply gave me some balance. Had it not been for my regular trips into the wild, I might have gone completely mad from spending all of my time in the city.

At the beginning of March, I received a newspaper on my doorstep and took it out to the balcony to read it. I opened the paper and gazed upon the headline, 'BUENA VISTA: A BLOODY BATTLE IN NORTHERN MEXICO'. I read the article, which described the battle as the greatest the war had yet seen. I only got through half of it before I put it down. I could read no more. I headed to the liquor cabinet, took out a bottle of whiskey, and began to drink.

By four in the afternoon, I had made it halfway through the bottle of whiskey and decided to go for a walk. Feeling quite drunk, but not too drunk, I stumbled toward the docks. When I arrived at the docks, I gazed upon the activities taking place. Fishermen were preparing to go out again for the evening, while steamboats arrived with tourists and prospective residents.

Then, I gazed upon the slave trade in progress. A line of Africans stood to the side of a platform to be auctioned off to a large crowd of White plantation owners. As I watched the men bid on these Africans, my blood began to boil.

I watched the slaves step onto the platform, one by one. One African man would not move. As the line progressed forward, he remained still and defiant. The White slave trader yelled at him to move, but the African ignored him. The man pushed the African, who allowed the force to carry him forward a couple of steps, but quickly stopped dead in his tracks. The slave trader yelled a slur of obscenities and pulled the African out of line. I watched as the slave trader tied the African man's hands to a post while the auction continued as if nothing was happening. The slave trader stepped back and started whipping the African.

I quickly walked down onto the docks and made my way toward the slave auction. The crack of the whip made me move faster. When I came upon the scene, I grabbed the slave trader's arm as he was about to whip the African again. The slave trader looked at me in confusion and tried to jerk his arm free, but I was stronger than him. I punched him hard on the nose, and he fell to the ground. The rest of the slave traders quickly noticed and attacked me. I was able to fight off the first two, but I was quickly overwhelmed and pinned on the ground.

The slave trader I had initially attacked rose to his feet and told his companions to tie me to the post. I struggled to get free, but I was in the grip of four men, and there was nothing I could do. They untied the African who had been whipped and tied me in his place. I swore at the slave traders and begged them to do their worst as they ripped my shirt off of my back. The man who had been whipping the African took his whip and gave me a hard blow. I arched my back and winced in pain as the leather took off my first layer of skin. I did not cry out. In fact, I begged my torturer to hit me harder, so he did. I clenched my jaw and stared straight ahead as the whip came hard over my back, again and again. My flesh burned as it was ripped from my back. However, I did not give the slave trader the satisfaction of my pain. I remained quiet and took the blows without complaint, though I was enduring more pain than my body had ever endured or my mind had ever imagined.

As I neared my tenth lash, I heard a familiar voice screaming for the slave trader to stop. The lashings ceased, and I looked over to see James Morrison taking the whip from the slave trader's hand. I was barely conscious and could hardly comprehend what was going on. James quickly untied me and threw my arm over his shoulder. He dragged me from the docks, and I passed out.

XVIII

When I awoke, my back felt numb with a bit of a fiery tingling. I felt weak and sick. It took me a few moments to find the strength to open my eyes. When I finally did, I had no idea where I was. I was lying on my stomach on a bed. I sat up as much as my strength would allow and looked around. I was in a room with no windows, lit by dozens of candles. Incense burned, and strange-smelling concoctions cooked. My mind went wild as my nose took in the great array of smells.

The room was decorated with a contradictory variety of ornamentations. There were crucifixes, Virgin Mary statues, prayer beads, and other Roman Catholic and Christian-influenced ornaments and trinkets. There were also a few Muslim influenced effects. All of these ornaments were amongst even more ornaments, which looked to be of African influence. My mind worked slowly to make the connection, and I finally realized that I was in some kind of voodoo lair. I suddenly heard a strange hissing sound. I looked across the room where a large, four-foot snake was curled around the back of a chair. I gasped and scooted back on the bed.

Suddenly, the door opened, and a strangely-dressed, full-figured woman walked into the room, quickly shutting the door behind her. She was carrying a black cat.

"That is Zombi," she said, as she walked over to me. "Don't worry; he won't harm you."

"Where am I?" I asked.

"You're at my home," the woman said, setting down her black cat.

"Who are you?" I asked.

"I am Marie Laveau," she replied, pulling a chair next to the bed and sitting down. As she lowered herself below the shadows, I could see her face in the candlelight. She had pale, brown skin with very distinct facial features. Her lips were full, with the middle of her top lip coming down to a point to form a heart shape. Her cheekbones were high and angled, and her dark, brown eyes were slightly sunken in, making the bones that formed the sockets around them very distinct. Her nose was wide and prominent. She looked Creole with some strong African features. There was something about her, maybe her eyes, that was just mesmerizing. She wore a simple black dress with a red and yellow silk scarf draped over her shoulders. She wore many rings on her fingers and bracelets on her wrists, as well as a crucifix around her neck. A gold hoop dangled from each ear.

"What am I doing here?" I asked.

"Your friend, James, brought you here after you were whipped," Marie explained.

"You're taking care of me?" I asked.

"My medicine is taking care of you," she said. "Lay back down on your stomach. I need to clean your wounds and reapply the medicine."

I did as she instructed. I was skeptical but slowly rested my head on the pillow, not sure what to make of the situation. I looked down at the floor and watched as the black cat hissed at the snake crawling on the back of the chair across the room.

"Do they get along?" I asked, as Marie removed the wet piece of cloth from my back.

"Most of the time," Marie said. "But sometimes Peter likes to provoke Zombi."

"Peter is the cat?"

"Yes."

Marie observed my wounds for a moment. As the air began to get into my wounds, they began to burn as if my back was on fire. I winced, breathed deeply through my teeth, and exhaled quickly.

"I know it hurts. It's going to hurt more in a moment," Marie warned me.

She began to clean my wounds with alcohol. It was excruciating. She cleaned them quickly and began to apply a thick paste.

"What is that?" I asked, my heart racing from the searing pain.

"It is a special recipe. It will keep you from getting an infection, and it will heal the wounds twice as quickly. That is all you need to know," she explained. She was silent for a few moments. "Why did you attack that slave trader?" she finally asked.

"Because he was whipping that man," I answered.

"That man is a slave."

"Yes."

"Why did you protect him?" she pressed.

"Because it's wrong," I said, confused by her persistence.

"He is a slave. That's the way it is," she said.

"Just because that's the way it is, then I should not defend what is wrong?" I asked.

"You should stay out of matters that don't concern you," Marie said. "That's the way it is. Getting yourself whipped won't make it how it should be."

"Freedom by God — not by government," I said. "It's as simple as that."

"No, it's not."

I sighed, squinting in confusion about her attitude toward the subject. I closed my eyes as the paste began to make my back tingle.

"Marie Laveau," I said. "You're the famous voodoo queen. My uncle has talked about you before."

"Yes, I knew Raul very well," Marie said. "I was very sorry to hear of his death."

"How did you know him?" I asked.

"He came to me for help. He wanted to forget his love for a woman who had left him. I gave him some things to ease the pain and bring him luck, but I told him I couldn't make anything strong enough to get rid of her memory. He became very involved in our community's practices and rituals. He became quite spiritual. He believed that this woman had left an evil demon inside of him, and he tried for years to get rid of it. When the evil spirit continued to consume him, he stopped coming to see me and stopped coming to our ceremonies." Marie sighed and paused for a moment. "When I heard he was dying, I went to his home and sat by his bed for three days. I begged him to let me heal him and cure him of his illness. He would not let me. Then I begged him to at least let me try and rid him of his evil spirits so he could be at peace when he traveled into the next life, but he would not let me."

"Why didn't it work when you tried to rid him of his demons before?" I asked.

"Some people need their demons to survive," Marie said. "The evil spirits can give one power and a thoughtful mind. There are certainly sacrifices which one must make in allowing these demons to live inside them, but to some, it is worth the sacrifice."

I thought about what she had said as my back began to tingle into numbness. I pictured Raul, lying there in his deathbed, denying Marie Laveau her wish to give him peace. He was a stubborn man.

"Why did James bring me to you?" I asked.

"Do my methods make you skeptical?" she asked.

"No, not at all. I was just wondering if you knew each other," I explained.

"His slave, Pierre, brought him to me after you shot him," Marie said. "I took care of his wound, and he returned a few weeks later, asking me to rid him of the evil spirits that tormented him and those around him."

"Well, I see it worked for him," I said.

"Mmm, hmm," Marie groaned lamely. "There, that should do

you for now." Marie stood up, grabbed her black cat, Peter, and walked to the door.

"Thank you," I said.

"Don't mention it, dear," Marie said. She walked out of the room and closed the door behind her.

I looked at the snake, Zombi, on the chair across the room. "Nice lady," I said. The python flicked his tongue and titled his head to the ceiling.

* * *

The next afternoon, I awakened from a long sleep and watched as Zombi slithered to the back wall and curled up next to a hole in the corner. I watched him inattentively for about an hour. A mouse stepped cautiously out of the hole, sniffing the floor and scanning the room with its beady eyes. My attention was caught. I looked at Zombi as his head slowly lowered. The mouse had no idea he was there. Almost too quickly for me to see, Zombi struck and took the mouse into his jaws. With only its head in Zombi's mouth, the mouse squirmed and flicked its tail around rapidly. Zombi slowly took the mouse into his mouth a centimeter at a time. After about a minute, the mouse ceased to squirm. I was a little sickened by the sight, but I couldn't look away. I watched until the mouse was completely devoured and began making its way down Zombi's long body.

Marie walked into the room with a plate of food for me. She looked down at Zombi and instantly noticed that he was digesting.

"I see Zombi has had lunch," Marie said. "Your turn."

"I think I'll wait for my appetite to return," I told her.

"You need to eat," Marie insisted. "When you're done, drink this," Marie said, handing me a cup. I smelled the liquid inside and cringed.

"It smells awful. What is it?" I asked.

"It will help you heal. That's all you need to know."

Marie sat the plate of food on the table next to the bed and walked out of the room. I shoveled the food into my mouth, trying hard not to think about Zombi and his mouse. When I finished eating, I took a sip of the strange concoction Marie had given me. It did not taste as bad as it smelled, but it did not taste great. It just tasted strange. I gulped it down and went back to sleep.

Later that night, I awoke to the echoing thump of multiple drums. Feeling much better and in only a slight amount of pain, I hung my legs over the side of the bed and slowly stood up. I looked around the room but did not see Zombi, the python. I put on my pants and grabbed my shirt as I walked to the door. When I opened the door, the drumming became louder and I could hear people chanting. I walked through Marie's house, following the noise to the back door. I put my arms through my shirt and slowly lowered it over my back.

I opened the door and beheld a strange, intriguing sight. About two dozen Africans chanted as they danced around a fire, while a small group of percussionists tapped away to a strange beat. The dancing was different than anything I had ever before seen. There was rhythm to it, yet it was unpredictable and somewhat chaotic. Nobody moved in the same way. Everyone seemed to be in their own world as they went through their random, jerking movements. It was quite beautiful.

I continued to watch in amazement as the voodoo ceremony became more and more intense. One woman became completely possessed by a spirit and moved around wildly with a disturbing expression on her face. Three men had to restrain her as she screamed, cried, and convulsed.

Marie Laveau knelt down on the ground in front of her snake, Zombi. On her knees, she looked to be bowing to the snake. From where I was standing, it looked as if she was kissing him. She picked Zombi up, rose to her feet, and draped the snake over her shoulders from hand to hand. She danced around with the snake, her eyes closed and her head tilted back as she chanted prayers.

Marie took Zombi off her shoulders and laid him down on the ground. She walked over to the possessed woman, put her hand over the woman's face, and began to chant. Marie convulsed with the possessed woman as she chanted. After a few moments, Marie screamed, arched her back violently, and began to fall. A man quickly caught her. The possessed woman rose to her feet, seeming to be free of the spirit that had possessed her. Sweat poured down her face, and she smiled with relief. She began to chant and dance with the others. Marie joined them once she regained her strength.

I stood and watched until the end of the ceremony, completely captivated by the practice. I had no idea what was going on, but it seemed very spiritual and very positive despite its strange characteristics. However, it was only strange because I had never seen it before. For the voodoo practitioners, it was a way of life, a way of obtaining a full and happy existence. I found the ceremony and the rituals quite moving.

The next morning, just after I awakened, Marie came into the room. I was sitting up and feeling a great deal better.

"I think I'm ready to go home now. There's no need for me to be a burden any longer," I said.

"Yes, you're healthy enough now," Marie said, leaning over my shoulder and observing my back. "You'll need to come by once a day so I can reapply the ointment."

"Sure," I said. I pulled my shirt over my back slowly. "I saw the ceremony last night," I said. "It was beautiful."

"Well, you can come by anytime and participate. We'll either be here or behind the church," Marie said.

"Would you rid me of my evil spirits?" I asked, half sarcastic, half serious.

Marie looked deep into my eyes for a few moments. "No."

"No? What does that mean?" I asked.

"When you were first brought to me, I put my hand on your head and said a prayer," Marie explained. "I felt much power from the good spirits inside of you. And then I felt the power of the evil spirits. The good spirits and the evil spirits feed off each other and make each other strong. To rid you of the evil would be to rid you of the good, and you would live in emptiness forever."

"Then I'm like Raul," I said. "I need my demons to survive."

Marie looked at me sadly for a moment, and then she smiled. "Don't forget to come back once a day."

"Yes, madam," I said.

Marie led me out of the room to the front door. She pointed me toward Bourbon Street and told me that St. Louis Street was four blocks west. I thanked her for her help and told her I would see her tomorrow. I left her cottage on St. Ann Street and slowly made my way home through the French Quarter.

XIX

I HEALED QUICKLY OVER the next few weeks, and my scars were not as severe as I had feared they would be, but they were scars nonetheless, and I would carry them with me for the rest of my life.

I had sunk into the depths of apathy and depression, and for a few months, I felt like a lonesome, lifeless soul floating about aimlessly. My trips to the woods on the outskirts of the city ceased to bring me any feeling of relief, for the city no longer drove me into anxiety. My heart had gone quiet, or, rather, my ears had gone deaf. I still longed to travel all the way to the Pacific Ocean, but it was no longer a pressing matter. I drank more and more just to feel, for only alcohol could access my true feelings.

I read about the war with Mexico every day and ran my eyes carefully over the names of soldiers who had been killed in battle. I never knew any of the names. I thought of William Mason, Kyle Ripley, Jack Burton, and the others, and I wondered how they were doing.

One evening, after finishing a bottle of wine, I headed to the liquor cabinet for another. I took out the first bottle I saw, not concerned with the brand, and set it on the table. The drawer on the cabinet caught my attention for some reason. I remembered how I would often see Raul writing madly at the table, and when he finished whatever he was writing, he would put it in the drawer. I placed my hand on the knob and slowly began to pull the drawer out. It was stuck. I pulled hard, eventually forcing the drawer open. It was full of papers covered in Raul's artistically sloppy handwriting. I took all of the papers out and put them on the table. I sat down and began to look through them. They were all poems — hundreds of them. I selected one randomly and began to read the verses.

My wings have broken the clouds.
The harps of the angels echo loud,
As I soar toward the majestic heavens.
The smile on my lips like the moon, crescent.

Stay on my wing and do not let go, my love!
Let me take you to the heavens high above,
For only with the angels do you belong.
Join them, my angel, and sing their song!

But soft! We have flown too high.
To the heavens, we have come too nigh.
Like Babel, we have been struck down.
My wings are broken; we fall to the ground.

You call to me, but our tongues are tied.
My ears are deaf to your fearful cries.
You drift from my wings to fall alone.
My pride is a sin for which I cannot atone.

I poured a glass of wine and lit a cigar, and then I went on to the next poem. I spent hours reading Raul's melancholy verses of sorrow, all similar in tone to the first poem I read. They all seemed to be inspired by one woman who he had obviously loved deeply, only to have his heart broken. It seemed that his heart never mended, as I read the poem that had been at the top of the stack of papers, leading me to believe that it was the last one he had written.

Let me drown in my tears,
For I shall not reach the shore.
I have been swimming for ten years;
I can endure it no more.

357

My arms are weak.
My breaths are growing shallow.
The future looks bleak,
To a heart that is hollow.

Are her nights sleepless like mine?
Does she share my sorrow?
Does her heart stand still in time
Or does she live in tomorrow?

Does she weep for me?
Does she dream of our past?
Does she wonder what we could be?
Or have I faded from her thoughts so fast?

No. I am but a distant memory to her,
If that at all.
I am no more than the leaves beneath her feet,
In the fall.

Let me drown in my tears.
I am not afraid of dying.
Living without her is all I fear.
Hopeless and weak, I am done trying.

I let the sorrowful words linger. How awful for a man to die alone with a broken heart. But I suppose that is what he wanted. He wanted to be free of his pain and free of the hold this woman had on his heart, and now he was. I stacked the poems neatly and placed them back in their drawer.

* * *

On a warm afternoon in April, I sat out on the balcony reading *Zadig* by Voltaire, when the postman climbed the stairs and handed me a letter over the railing. I thanked him and set down my book as I looked at the letter. It was from Miriam in Paris. I opened it and began to read.

Dear Konrad,
By the time you get this letter, Anastasia, Charles, and I will be on a ship bound for New Orleans.

I read that first line of the letter over again, and then once more. Did I really see Anastasia's name? Was she really returning to New Orleans with Charles and Miriam? I couldn't believe it. I read the rest of the letter quickly. Miriam and Charles had decided that it was safe to return to America, for it seemed that the war was going to stay in Mexico and the West, and it seemed highly unlikely that it would spread to New Orleans. Charles also had his business to tend to. The letter went on with Miriam's usual excited rants and ended saying that if all went according to schedule, they would arrive in the early afternoon on the third of May and that it would be wonderful if I was at the docks to greet them. She did not mention Anastasia in the letter other than the opening line. Miriam wanted to make me sweat.

I closed the letter and took in the information. The third of May was only a week away. I refilled my glass of wine and took a sip. My heart raced as I thought about what it would be like to see Anastasia again. There was nothing I desired more than to taste her lips, to hold her in my arms, to feel her heart beat against mine, and to allow myself to be completely vulnerable to her. I was fully willing to embark on another adventure, the greatest of adventures, the adventure of love.

After months of sadness, loneliness, depression, self-loathing, and apathy, I finally felt something good again. Being reunited with Miriam would be a great comfort to my soul, for she was, no doubt, my soul's counterpart. Anastasia produced a different emotion inside of me, one I had not felt in months — curiosity. She had not left my thoughts since the moment I had seen her in the lobby of the Theatre d'Orleans. I had taken her with me across the Great Plains and had spent many sleepless nights thinking about her at Bent's Fort. I had taken her with me to Texas. She had kept me alive during that bloody battle in Monterrey. Our time together had been brief, but I always felt as if she was with me. My heart ached for her every day. Was it love or infatuation? Was it simply that we had not had the opportunity to see what could develop between us had our circumstances been different? With Anastasia returning to New Orleans, we could now let our scenario play out and see where it would lead. But did Anastasia feel the same way? Would she want to see if there was something special between us? Had she been thinking of me the way I had been thinking of her? Had she taken me with her to Paris? Had I haunted her dreams and given her sleepless nights? Oh! Miriam! Why did she not mention Anastasia but once in her letter?

It mattered not. In a week I would find out if Anastasia felt the same way about me as I did about her. I would open my heart to her and allow myself to be completely vulnerable. I had nothing to lose.

XX

ON THE MORNING OF the third of May, I went to the barber and got a close shave and a haircut. Afterward, I returned to my apartment and took a quick bath. By noon, I was pulling on the jacket of the suit, which Raul had bought me. As I adjusted the tie and looked myself over in the mirror, there came a knock on the door. Confused as to who it might be, I stepped quickly across the room and opened the door. Standing before me was Miriam and Charles. My eyes widened with surprise, but before I could speak, Miriam nearly tackled me to the ground with a powerful embrace that seemed all too strong for her size.

"Well, hello!" I said, feeling my face turn red as Miriam squeezed my neck.

"I've missed you so much!" Miriam said.

"I've missed you, too, darling," I said. With Miriam still squeezing my neck, I extended my hand to shake with Charles. "Good to see you, Charles."

"It's been far too long, my friend," Charles said with a pleasant, sincere smile.

Miriam finally released her grip around my neck. She grabbed my face and kissed me on the lips. As she stepped back to look me over, tears of joy were forming in her eyes while staring happily into mine.

"It's so wonderful to see you, Konrad," Miriam said, as a tear streamed down her cheek. I smiled happily and wiped the tear away with my thumb.

"Come inside," I invited. I stepped back and gestured for them to enter. Miriam stroked my cheek as she walked past me. I patted Charles on the back and closed the door behind him. "Have a seat. I'm sure you could use a drink after your long trip,"

I suggested, making my way to the liquor cabinet as Charles and Miriam sat down.

"A brandy would be wonderful, Konrad. Thank you," Charles said.

"Chardonnay for me, please," Miriam requested.

I poured their drinks, as well as a brandy for myself. Then I handed them their drinks and sat down across from them.

"To our long-awaited reunion," Charles toasted, raising his glass. We all touched glasses and drank.

"You're back early. I was just on my way to meet you at the docks."

"We arrived a little ahead of schedule," Charles explained.

"I see... and where is Anastasia?"

"She's staying at the Saint Charles," Miriam informed me.

"Why is she staying at a hotel?" I asked.

"She insisted. She didn't want to be a burden on anyone," Miriam explained.

"Why didn't she come here with you?"

"She wasn't sure how you would react," Miriam said. "I assured her that you would be more than happy to see her, but since you didn't write to her, she wasn't sure if you were still upset with her. I *told* you to write her, Konrad."

"I know I should have," I said regretfully. I paused for a moment. "How was your trip?" I asked, quickly changing the subject. "You're engaged to be married!"

"I know! I can't believe it," Miriam said excitedly.

"Neither can I," I said, giving Miriam a sly look.

"Yes, I know that I said I never wanted to marry, but this feels right," Miriam said, while looking lovingly into Charles' eyes. "It feels natural — like it's meant to be."

Charles kissed Miriam, and I smiled. They seemed very happy.

"Well, that's wonderful to hear," I said. "Congratulations on pinning this one down, Charles."

Charles laughed. "I'm a very lucky man. Thank you. You know, Konrad, when I decided to ask Miriam to marry me, I felt more inclined to ask you for your blessing rather than her father's."

I laughed. "Well, you certainly have it. When is the wedding?"

"We were thinking of Friday the twenty-eighth," Miriam announced.

"Of May?" I asked. Miriam nodded with her eyebrows raised. "That's only three and a half weeks from now."

"We've been engaged for so long, we don't want to wait anymore," Miriam said.

"Will you marry at the Saint Louis Cathedral?" I asked.

"That is our hope," Charles replied. "We will go by there tomorrow to see if we can make the arrangements."

"Good! It will be a beautiful ceremony, I'm sure," I said.

Miriam smiled at me and then looked around the apartment sadly.

"I sure miss Raul," Miriam said. "It's strange being here without him."

I nodded. "Yes, it is." I thought for a moment, not sure of what to say. "He's buried at the Saint Louis Cemetery," I finally said. "I could take you to his grave later if you want."

"I would like that," Miriam said. "I would like that very much."

"To Raul," Charles said, raising his glass.

"To Raul," Miriam repeated, raising her glass.

I smiled and raised my glass. "To Raul."

We touched glasses and drank. Miriam talked for half an hour about their time in France and told all of the funny stories. Charles chimed in now and then, and they laughed as they reminisced. I smiled and watched the happy couple enjoying themselves.

After a couple hours of conversation and catching up, Charles and Miriam went home to unpack. We had agreed to meet for lunch at Leon's the next day, after they had made the arrangements for their wedding at the Saint Louis Cathedral. After lunch I would take them to Raul's grave.

After Charles and Miriam left, I sat out on the balcony, contemplating. I sat there for hours, until night fell over the city. I didn't move a muscle. I was thinking hard about how I would pursue Anastasia. Should I be conservative and see how things develop, or should I be bold and tell her how I feel? After many hours of playing out the possible scenarios in my head, I decided it was best not to rush things. However, it wouldn't be too forward of me to go say "Hello" to her at her hotel. Once I decided to go see her, I stood up too quickly and got a bit dizzy. When I began to walk inside from the balcony, I realized that my left leg was asleep and I nearly fell over. Once my body adjusted to movement, I headed to the bathroom and looked myself over. I fixed my hair and adjusted my jacket and tie. Then I took a deep breath and walked out the door.

As I walked toward the Saint Charles Hotel, I told myself over and over to be conservative and friendly. *Show a little vulnerability, but not too much,* I thought to myself. *You haven't seen this woman in four years. You don't want to scare her off by being too forward. Be conservative. Be conservative. Stop thinking about kissing her. Conservative. Conservative.*

I arrived at the Saint Charles Hotel shortly after nine o'clock. I hoped she was not asleep already. It would be awful if I woke her. I asked the hotel clerk what room Anastasia was staying in and told him that I was a friend whom she would be quite pleased to see. The clerk flipped through the register, found her name, and told me her room number. I thanked him and walked nervously up the stairs.

As I paced down the hallway, my heart began to race like never before. I hadn't been this nervous when I charged into battle at the city of Monterrey. I was starting to sweat. I felt like an immature schoolboy. I took out my handkerchief and dabbed the sweat off my forehead. The door to her room came into view, and I feared I might have a heart attack. I stopped in front of her door and closed my eyes.

"Conservative," I whispered to myself. "Calm down."

I took a deep breath and exhaled it slowly. I opened my eyes. My heart slowed and I stopped sweating. I felt confident. I knocked on the door, stepped back, and waited. I heard her moving around inside. Her footsteps got closer and closer to the door. The knob turned. The door opened. Standing before me in the doorway was the most beautiful woman I had ever seen.

Anastasia's hazel eyes were sparkling as she stared into mine. Her lips parted as if she was going to speak, but she did not. We said nothing as we stood before one another. And then my heart took control and my body moved on its own. I stepped into the doorway and kissed her passionately. She kissed me back with just as much passion. She grabbed the back of my head and gripped my hair as she pulled me into the room. I kicked the door shut as she pulled me close to her. So much for being conservative.

My heart was beating fast, but my nerves were calm, as our natural chemistry forged together in that special connection when two hearts truly open up to one another and allow themselves to be completely vulnerable. And I was completely vulnerable in her arms, as she was in mine.

Anastasia pulled her lips away from mine and stared deeply into my eyes as she pushed my jacket off my shoulders. I took off my tie, and then she unbuttoned my shirt and removed it from my torso. I gently grabbed her face and kissed her as we moved to the bedroom. She pulled away again, stared into my eyes for a moment, and turned around. She moved her hair off the back of her neck and held it over her shoulder. I kissed her neck sensually as I untied the back of her gown. I noticed that she was wearing the necklace I had made for her from the pearls of oysters. She pushed her petticoats to the floor and stepped out of them. I unlaced her corset and pulled it from her torso. She turned and faced me in her thin, white, knee-length chemise and took a deep breath while pulling the chemise from her shoulders and letting it fall to the ground. She breathed short, shallow breaths as she stood naked before me. She was absolutely gorgeous in her natural form. Her figure was simply perfect. I moved in close to her. I touched her cheeks with my thumbs and slowly ran my hands down her slender neck, over her shoulders, and down her sides. She shivered and closed her eyes. I held her waist and kissed her softly. She returned my soft kiss with much passion, gently biting my lip as she began to take off my trousers.

I laid Anastasia on the bed and slowly lowered myself on top of her. I kissed and caressed every inch of her body, studying it carefully as if it were a famous sculpture. I didn't want to miss a single detail. I watched her closely and studied her response to my touch. Our bodies grew hot as we melted into one soul and one flesh. Everything felt right and natural. I was a different man. In her arms, I was not the man I saw looking back at me in the mirror. I was not the flawed human I believed I was. I was the man she saw me as, and she was the woman I saw her as. We were both perfect in each other's eyes. Together, we became the best of ourselves. We were two perfect beings making a perfect love. It was an extraordinary and beautiful experience.

After we made love, Anastasia and I lay on our sides in each other's arms. I stroked her cheek as she stared lovingly into my eyes. The sun was just beginning to rise, but we hadn't slept. We just stared at one another in a euphoric trance for what felt like hours before we could summon the energy to speak.

"How have you been for the last four years?" I finally asked with a smirk.

Anastasia laughed and rolled onto her back. "I can't believe this just happened like it did!" she commented.

"I'm glad it happened this way," I said.

"I am, too. I haven't seen you, spoken to you, or heard from you in four years, and as soon as I see you again, I just fall into bed with you." She rolled back onto her side to face me again. "But it feels like we were never apart. Don't you think so?"

"You've been with me every day. No matter where I was or how far away you were, you were with me. I longed for you and I missed you, but you were with me — if that makes any sense at all."

"It does. I know exactly what you mean," she said. She paused and ran her delicate fingers over my chest. "I've always had feelings for you. Something just drew me to you. And the more I saw you, the more powerful and strong those feelings became, and it scared me. I didn't really understand it. I didn't know what it was. I had been in love before, or at least I thought I had, and the feelings I had for you were foreign to me, and I didn't know what to make of it all. So, I ran away from you, and I'm so very sorry, Konrad. I wish I hadn't. I really do."

"Don't be sorry, my dear. I ran away, too. Remember? I was just as scared as you were."

"But you always seemed so confident," Anastasia said.

"I'd say it was more childish arrogance rather than confidence," I admitted. "I wanted you so badly that it hurt. I had to have you. I pursued you like a king out to conquer a nation. But I was scared, because I knew my feelings were deeper than that, and I didn't understand it either."

"It just wasn't the right time for us, was it?"

"No, but we're here together now, and this is how it's supposed to be."

Anastasia smiled and kissed me softly as she stroked my cheek.

I took her hand in mine and kissed it adoringly. "Now, we have to get you out of this hotel room and get you moved into my apartment," I said.

Anastasia gave me a playful smile. "Are you asking me to come live in sin with you?"

"No, I'm asking you to live in love with me."

"Well, in that case... yes, I would love to live in love with you — and in sin."

"Good! Now, let's get you packed," I suggested, but when I started to get up, Anastasia pushed me back down.

"Not so fast! I want to have you once more before we go," Anastasia demanded, as she got on top of me.

"Well, I guess I'd better give you what you want," I said.

"Don't you forget it."

She kissed me playfully, and we rolled around in bed and made love again. I had never felt so happy in my life.

XXI

I MOVED ANASTASIA'S BELONGINGS from the hotel to my apartment by carriage. It was mostly suitcases full of clothes and accessories. She had stored the bulk of her belongings in a warehouse just outside the French Quarter when she'd left for Paris.

As Anastasia and I were walking downstairs from my apartment to go get her things from the warehouse, we saw Miriam and Charles coming down the street. I instantly remembered that we were to have lunch at Leon's together and then we were to go to the cemetery.

"Fancy seeing you two together," Miriam said with a mischievous smile. Anastasia and I looked at each other awkwardly, not sure what to say. "Oh, don't be coy. Anastasia is absolutely glowing, and, Konrad, you look like you haven't slept in days. It's no mystery what you two were up to last night. I'm a woman. I can sense these things."

"Well, you're quite the detective, Miriam," I said. "Shall we have lunch now?"

"Sure — I imagine you're both quite hungry," Miriam said, still flashing her mischievous smile.

We walked into Leon's and sat down at a table for four. Miriam would not stop smiling as we looked over our menus. Claire, who was still working as a waitress, brought us coffee. We gave her our orders, and she took our menus and promised that our food would arrive promptly.

"When do the two of you plan on marrying?" Miriam teased as soon as Claire walked away.

"Oh, stop it, Miriam," I said.

"We're just enjoying ourselves right now," Anastasia said. "Right, Konrad?"

"Yes, precisely," I agreed. I loved this woman! "We're just taking it a day at a time."

Anastasia smiled and took my hand.

"That's what all young lovers say before they become engaged," Miriam said. "You two are such a wonderful couple! You look so handsome together, don't you think so, Charles?"

"I think you should leave them alone," Charles said with a smirk.

"I agree with Charles," I said.

Miriam slapped Charles on the shoulder playfully. "Charles doesn't know anything."

"Speaking of marriage," Anastasia said quickly. "Did you make arrangements this morning for your wedding at the Saint Louis Cathedral?"

"Oh, yes!" I remembered. "How did that go?"

"Oh! It went perfectly," Miriam said. "We're all set to marry on the twenty-eighth. We just have to send out invitations to make sure everyone comes to the biggest wedding of the year."

Miriam began to rant about how she wanted her wedding to be just like Queen Victoria's, with a white, satin gown and a Honiton lace veil fixed to a wreath of orange blossoms. Charles and I looked at each other with raised eyebrows. He rolled his eyes. I shrugged and shook my head as Miriam and Anastasia planned out the entire wedding.

After lunch, we all took a carriage over to the Saint Louis Cemetery, and I showed them Raul's tomb. Miriam was quite emotional. She and Raul had become very close during the time I was away. I knew she took it hard when I left on the expedition and then to Texas, and I imagined she relied on Raul to comfort her while I was gone.

Miriam cried, as she set a bouquet of flowers at the foot of Raul's tomb. I put my arm around her to comfort her as she placed her hand on the tomb and said goodbye. She cried all the way back to the carriage.

"That sure was nice of James to take care of all that," Miriam said through her tears as we rode away from the cemetery.

"Yes, it was," I said. "He seems like a changed man." I looked at Anastasia and she smiled.

From the cemetery, we rode to the warehouse where Anastasia had stored her belongings. The warehouse owner helped Charles and I load all her things onto the carriage. There wasn't much, and we were able to take it all in one load.

When we arrived at my apartment, Charles and I carried Anastasia's belongings upstairs and into the master bedroom. When everything was unloaded, Charles and Miriam left to get the invitations made for the wedding.

While Anastasia and I were unpacking her suitcases and trunks, she began to laugh as she went through the contents of one of her trunks.

"What's so funny?" I asked.

"I'm just realizing that I don't need hardly any of these things," she admitted.

"I could have told you that," I said.

"Most of these clothes are out of style, and I've brought plenty back with me from Paris. And that's all I really have, clothes, perfumes, jewelry. It's quite pathetic, isn't it?"

"There are books in here," I said as I opened one of the chests. "You can never have enough of those." I opened another chest. "And there are decorations and things of that nature in here. This apartment could certainly use a woman's touch."

"True," Anastasia agreed. "Then two chests out of five are useful. The rest is rubbish."

"I'll tell you what is most certainly not rubbish," I said, as I unwrapped the portrait that Raul had painted of her lying nude across the bed like the *Maja*. "This is your most prized possession."

"It really is," Anastasia agreed. She walked over and stood next to me. She held one side of the painting as I held the other. "I really missed this painting while I was away. Raul was so talented. On days when I felt sad or worthless, I'd just look at this painting and I would feel beautiful again."

I smiled and kissed her on the cheek. "Then we should hang it up immediately. I know just the spot."

I walked into the living room and pulled a chair up to the fireplace. I stepped up onto the chair and took down the obscure painting that hung there. I set it down gently, and Anastasia handed me her painting. I carefully hung it in the place of the previous painting.

"Is it straight?" I asked.

"Up a little on the left," Anastasia commanded. I did as she said. "A little more — perfect."

I stepped down from the chair and walked back to Anastasia to see how the painting looked. It fit perfectly above the fireplace and looked wonderful.

"Do you feel beautiful now?" I asked.

She smiled and kissed me passionately. "Thank you," she said.

"Let's get you unpacked," I said.

"Later," Anastasia insisted, as she stared seductively into my eyes. She kissed me again even more passionately. We lay down on the floor in front of the fireplace and kissed fervently with her portrait hanging over us.

By the time we finally finished unpacking, the sun was just beginning to set. I took a bottle of champagne out of the liquor cabinet and grabbed two glasses, and Anastasia and I went out onto the balcony to enjoy our first sunset together in her new home. I uncorked the bottle and poured us each a glass as the bubbles fizzed over.

"Here's to living in sin together," I said, raising my glass.

"To living in love," Anastasia corrected.

We touched glasses and drank. Anastasia drank her entire

glass of champagne down in a couple of big gulps. She held her glass up with a proud smile on her face and gestured for another pour. I obliged her.

"Are you nervous around me?" I asked.

Anastasia laughed. "No, I just think it would be fun to get a little drunk with you."

"Fair enough."

I finished my glass and poured myself another. We watched the sun slowly set behind the French Quarter as we sat across from each other and sipped our champagne.

"Are you excited about Miriam's wedding?" I asked.

"Heavens, no!" Anastasia said. "I was excited at first, but now I'm finding out that I have to help Miriam shop for everything and help her plan the whole thing. I have a feeling that it's going to be a big headache. I just want to relax and enjoy myself."

"There will be plenty of time for that," I pointed out. "The wedding will be over before you know it."

"You're probably right."

"How would you feel about James being at the wedding?" I asked.

"Why do you ask?"

"It's an issue that will come up at some point. I just want to know how you feel about it," I said.

"Well, I'm not sure how I feel about it. I got his letter in Paris, begging for my forgiveness. He said he was a changed man. Is it real?"

"I think it is," I said. "He really has no reason to lie about it unless he is trying to win you back, which I really don't think he is."

"Me neither," Anastasia agreed.

"What he did to you was awful and distasteful, but not unforgivable, especially four years after it all happened. I may be out of line in assuming that, but I just think there's no use holding a grudge over someone. That burden falls on you and not them."

"You're right, and I don't hold a grudge against him. I don't really even think about it. I just don't care anymore," she admitted.

"Besides, I made him pay for what he did to you," I said with a smirk.

Anastasia laughed. "My knight, defending my honor!"

"But I really do think he is a changed man, and I think it might do you good to go see him and let him apologize to you in person," I suggested.

"Really? I think it would be so awkward to see him, given our history and all."

"I think you're both far enough removed from the situation to see that it was a relationship built more on convenience than on love," I said. "I apologize if I'm out of line in saying that."

"Don't apologize. We both knew we were wrong for each other. Do you really think I should go see him?"

"I think it would be good for the both of you. Yes."

"All right, tomorrow then," Anastasia agreed. "Now, enough serious talk. Let's drink."

"Cheers to that," I said. We finished our glasses and I refilled them, emptying the bottle into my glass. "Looks like we need another bottle. Any suggestions?"

Anastasia thought carefully for a moment. "How about a good chardonnay?"

"A fine choice, madam," I said.

"Thank you, monsieur."

I went to the liquor cabinet, grabbed a bottle of chardonnay, and went back out to the balcony. I was a beautiful night. It was not too hot or too humid. There was a light, cool breeze. It was pleasant. Anastasia and I sat out on the balcony for hours, drinking wine and talking about life. She was wonderful to talk to, and we felt completely comfortable with one another. Just around midnight, we finished our last glass of wine and went to bed together. I wanted every day to be like that.

XXII

OVER THE NEXT FEW weeks, Anastasia and I spent almost every waking moment together. The only time we were not together was when Miriam would drag her away to help get everything together for the wedding.

When she was not helping Miriam, Anastasia and I would go for long walks through the French Quarter. She loved walking through the market to watch the butchers chop cuts of meat, to see the displays of fresh seafood, and to smell the wonderful aroma of the assorted spices. She loved the chaos of people, the clash of cultures, and the multiple languages being spoken. Every now and then I'd let her pick out a few things that looked good, and I'd cook us a nice dinner.

I introduced her to Renegado, and he took a great liking to her as she did to him. We'd sit upon his back, her arms wrapped around my chest, and we'd go for long rides through the countryside or down to the banks of the Mississippi River for a picnic.

Some days, we would just spend the entire day in bed, talking, playing, sleeping, making love, or just staring into each other's eyes for hours. Every evening, we'd sit out on the balcony and drink a glass or two of wine as we watched the sunset. We'd talk into the late hours of the night, learning every little detail about one another or sharing our views on life and different issues. I enjoyed every moment with her, no matter what we were doing, but what I loved most was listening to her talk and learning what made her who she was. Her thoughts and ideas were profound and interesting, and they challenged my own ideas and opinions. Every day was exciting with her. Every day was an adventure.

* * *

In my dreamy love daze, Miriam and Charles' wedding arrived seemingly out of the blue. I stood in Charles' dressing room with James and Jeffery, the short, talkative young man whom I had met at the opera when Miriam and I had first arrived in New Orleans. The three of us watched as Charles nervously fixed his tie in front of the mirror.

"How do I look?" Charles asked.

"You look dashing," James commented.

"Yes, despite the sweating," Jeffery added.

Charles laughed. "I'm a little nervous, I suppose."

"What have you to be nervous about?" James asked. "You're marrying a beautiful woman who loves you dearly."

"I know," Charles said. "I just want everything to be perfect."

"It will be," Jeffery assured him. "After all, Miriam planned the whole thing."

"Very true," Charles admitted.

There was a knock on the door. I walked over to the door and opened it. Charles' mother was standing there with a big smile on her face. She was a lovely, elegant woman and very energetic.

"May I come in to see the handsome groom?" Mrs. Devereux asked.

"Of course," I said.

Mrs. Devereux gently touched my cheek and walked over to Charles. "Oh! You look absolutely marvelous. You're such a handsome man."

"Thank you, Mother," Charles said, adjusting his jacket.

"You look just like your father the day we were married. I wish he could be here to see you now."

Charles smiled and kissed his mother on the cheek. "Me, too, Mother."

"I'm going to see if the bride is almost ready," I said.

I walked out of Charles' dressing room and across the lobby. I stopped at the sanctuary and peered inside. It looked like all of the guests had arrived. They sat in the pews, talking quietly with one another. A small chamber orchestra played Antonio Vivaldi's "Spring" from *The Four Seasons* concerti.

I continued across the hallway to Miriam's dressing room and knocked on the door. Anastasia opened the door and let me in. Miriam was standing in front of the mirror, looking herself over in her white Queen Victoria gown. Miriam's two friends, Sarah and Isabelle, were helping her adjust the dress.

"Is she almost ready?" I asked Anastasia.

"Almost," she said.

"I'm nearly ready, Konrad. Don't rush me," Miriam said.

"I'm not. I just wanted to come see how you look," I said.

"And?" Miriam asked.

"You look beautiful," I said.

"Thank you."

There was another knock on the door. Anastasia answered it, and Archbishop Antoine Blanc stepped into the room.

"We're ready to begin, Miss Monroe," the Archbishop announced. "The groom has taken his position at the altar."

"All right. I'm ready," Miriam said.

Archbishop Blanc nodded and walked out of the room. Anastasia peeked out the door and stepped back into the room.

"Jeffery and James are standing outside the sanctuary, ladies," Anastasia said.

Sarah and Isabelle walked out of Miriam's dressing room. Anastasia smiled at me and raised her eyebrows, and then she followed the other women out. I walked over to Miriam and stood behind her as she stared at herself in the mirror.

"You look absolutely gorgeous," I said. "You put Queen Victoria to shame."

Miriam smiled and looked at me in the mirror. "Thank you." She paused for a moment. "I wish Raul were here," she said. I smiled and kissed her cheek.

"Let's get you married," I said.

Miriam took my arm, and we walked out of the dressing room. I nodded to the doormen, and they opened the doors to the sanctuary. The chamber orchestra began to play Bach's *Arioso*. Anastasia was the first to walk down the aisle. She was followed by Sarah who was escorted by James, and following them was Isabelle who was escorted by Jeffery. They made their way down the aisle and took their positions at the altar.

Miriam and I stepped into the doorway of the sanctuary. The chamber orchestra began to play Bach's *Orchestral Suite No. 3* as I escorted Miriam down the aisle. Miriam loved her Baroque music. She was all smiles as everyone stood and watched her make her way to the altar. Her eyes were locked with Charles' eyes. It meant a lot to me that she had asked me to walk her down the aisle to give her away. Raul had been like a father to her, and had he been alive, I was sure he'd be doing the honors. I was honored to take his place.

When we reached the steps of the altar, I kissed Miriam's hand and gestured for her to go to her future husband. She smiled thankfully and walked up to the altar next to Charles, and I took my position behind Charles and in front of James.

Archbishop Blanc began the ceremony. Throughout the ceremony, I could not take my eyes off of Anastasia. She looked beautiful in her white satin dress. She flashed me an occasional smile while trying to remain attentive to the Archbishop's words.

When the ceremony ended and Miriam and Charles were officially man and wife, we went to the Orleans Ballroom for food, cake, drink, and dancing. It was a wonderful celebration, and Miriam was as happy as I had ever seen her.

* * *

The day after the wedding, Anastasia and I stayed in bed all through the morning and into the afternoon. Before we knew it, it was nearly four o'clock. I lay on my stomach, and Anastasia rested her head on my shoulder, softly humming a lullaby, as she ran her fingers over the scars on my back. Her stomach suddenly made a low, rolling, rumbling sound. She looked up at me with wide eyes.

"Sounds like you're hungry," I said.

"We should probably eat at some point. It would be a shame if we died of starvation while lying naked in bed because we were too lazy to get up."

"I could think of worse ways to go," I said.

Anastasia smiled and kissed my neck. "You know what we should do?"

"What's that?" I asked.

"We should get a string, put it through a hole in the floor, through the ceiling of Leon's, and attach a bell on the end. Then we could tug on the string and ring the bell every time we got hungry, after which, Emilio could make us food and Claire could deliver it here."

"That's a wonderful idea. I'm sure they would be happy to do that down at Leon's."

"It *is* a wonderful idea," Anastasia said proudly. "But for now, you'll just have to go down and get it."

"Me? I believe it's your turn," I said.

"You know it's your turn, Konrad. Besides, it takes me half an hour to get dressed. It takes you less than a minute."

I groaned and threw my legs over the side of the bed.

"Come on," she taunted. "Get some trousers on that adorable little bum and get some food for your hungry mistress!"

I pulled on my trousers, buttoned my shirt, and stumbled into my boots. Anastasia lay on her side, resting her head upon her hand. Her hair was messy and her makeup was off, but she looked absolutely stunning. Her hazel eyes were gleaming as she watched me dress.

"You see? Less than a minute," she said with a playful smirk. I picked a pillow off the floor and tossed it at her as I walked out of the room. "Thank you, my love!" she called after me as I walked out the door.

I walked downstairs to Leon's and sat down at the bar where Claire came over to greet me with a hug. We talked for a bit, and then I ordered boudin, *maque choux*, and a plate of assorted fruit. Anastasia loved fruit. Claire called out my order to Emilio and said that it was for me. Emilio came out of the kitchen to say "Hello" and said my food would be ready shortly. I thanked him and Claire.

I drank a cup of coffee while waiting at the bar. As I looked around the room, I noticed the many familiar faces of people who had frequented Leon's when I had worked here four years earlier. I looked down the bar at the man sitting a couple of seats away from me. Out of the corner of my eye, I had noticed him looking at me. I recognized him. His long, white hair, his droopy eyes, and his dark, wrinkled, leathery skin. I believed his name was Ben. I had served him quite often when I would work behind the bar. He would always come in at around four and drink until Leon's closed. It seemed that he was just getting started for the night.

He looked at me again. "You used to work here, didn't you?" he asked.

"I did — a few years ago," I replied.

"I thought so. What's your name?"

"Konrad. You're Ben, right?"

"You remember me! Where the hell have you been?" Ben asked.

"Well, I was out West for a while. Then I spent some time in Texas," I explained.

"You're a traveler!"

"I guess you could say that," I answered.

"I've always wanted to travel," Ben said. "I've always wanted to see the Rocky Mountains. Heard all kinds of interesting stories about the mountain men. Thought I might be one. Too old now."

"Where are you from?" I asked.

"Here — born and raised in New Orleans. My father was a fisherman his whole life. I've been a fisherman my whole life. Yep! The farthest I've been from New Orleans is a hundred miles off the coast. I tell you what, boy; you keep traveling. Travel as much as you can while you're young. Lord knows, I'd go with you if these old bones would let me."

I smiled, not sure what to say as Ben stared sadly down at his drink. Claire brought over a bag with the food I had ordered.

"There you are, dear," Claire said, as she refilled my coffee and poured a cup for me to take up to Anastasia.

"Thank you, Claire."

"You're welcome, sweetheart. Enjoy." Claire looked at Ben. "Another whiskey for you, Ben?"

"Yes, ma'am!" Ben said, finishing his glass and pushing it forward.

I grabbed my bag of food and the two coffees.

"Safe travels, Konrad," Ben said.

"Thanks, Ben."

I turned and walked out the door. I looked at Ben through the window as he took a sip of his whiskey, and then I walked up the stairs. Anastasia was sitting on the balcony with the bed sheet wrapped around her naked body.

"It's about time," she teased.

"My apologies, Your Highness," I quipped.

I walked into the apartment and back outside onto the balcony. I set our coffees down and then carefully set down the bag of food.

"It smells wonderful," Anastasia said. "What do you have for me?"

I took the dishes out of the bag and removed the lids. Anastasia smiled excitedly as she looked over the meal. I sat down across from her as she began to cut into the boudin. I smiled as I watched her eat. Anastasia was an elegant woman, but she was not shy about stuffing her mouth when she was hungry. It was quite amusing. I sipped my coffee as I thought about what Ben had said just moments before.

"Aren't you going to eat? You know that I hate to be the only one eating," Anastasia said.

"I'm thinking," I said.

"You shouldn't think on an empty stomach. You'd better have some before I eat it all."

"I'm not hungry," I said. Anastasia studied my eyes for a moment and put down her fork.

"All right — what are you thinking about?" she asked.

"I was thinking that we should go somewhere," I said. Anastasia leaned forward, rested her chin on her hand, and looked at me with great interest.

"Really? Where do you think we should go?"

"Somewhere peaceful. Somewhere outside of America. Somewhere neither of us has been. I was thinking Havana."

Anastasia's eyes lit up with excitement. "Havana? Really? I've always wanted to go there!"

"That's why I suggested it," I said, smiling at her reaction.

She jumped up from her chair, while holding the bed sheet around her body, and sat in my lap. "Do you really want to go to Havana? Don't tease me!" she said.

"I'm not teasing you. I mean it! Let's go!"

"When?"

"As soon as possible, on the next ship that leaves," I said.

"How will we pay for it?" Anastasia asked.

"Well, when Raul died, he left everything to me, and he wasn't a poor man," I replied. "In the last letter he wrote me, he said he wanted to go to the Caribbean. I'm sure this is how he'd want me to spend his money."

Anastasia smiled excitedly as she imagined the beautiful, clear-blue waters of the Caribbean Sea.

"Havana," she said dreamily.

"*La Habana*," I said.

"*La Habana*," Anastasia repeated. She took a grape and held it over my mouth but quickly pulled it away. "Wait… I like the way you think on an empty stomach."

"The thinking is done. The decision is made. Now, I need to eat," I said. Anastasia dropped the grape into my mouth.

"*La Habana!*" she said excitedly.

"*La Habana*," I said as I chewed the grape.

Anastasia kissed me softly, her lips still curled up in an ecstatic smile. I tickled her sides, and she let out a screaming laugh. I stood up, holding her over my shoulder as I carried her inside.

"Wait! Bring the fruit!" Anastasia commanded through her laughter. I turned around, grabbed the plate of fruit, and walked back inside. "I hope the birds don't eat the boudin," she said.

"There will be plenty of food in *La Habana!*" I said.

"*La Habana!*" Anastasia yelled, loud enough for the whole city to hear.

XXIII

Anastasia and I arrived in Havana in the middle of June. She held my arm with excitement as we stood at the bow of our ship. We sailed past *Castillo de Morro*, which was a beautiful fortress protecting the city. We sailed up the canal and past another great fortress called *La Cabaña*.

When our ship docked, Anastasia was in a great hurry to see the city. She pulled me alongside of her as we walked through the *Tacon* Market and found ourselves in the *Plaza de la Catedral*. She was all smiles as we gazed upon the *Catedral de San Cristobal*. I suggested we eat lunch and have a drink, but Anastasia was dying to explore. We walked through the narrow streets of the beautiful city, which was made up of buildings designed in the baroque and neoclassic style. I instantly fell in love with Havana, and it seemed as if Anastasia had as well.

We walked through the *Plaza de Armas* and made our way across town to the *Gran Teatro Tacon*, Havana's magnificent theatre. I told Anastasia that we could not possibly take in the whole city in one day and that we needed to save some excitement for the next day. She reluctantly agreed, so we walked back toward the *Plaza de Armas* to find a place to stay.

We came upon a small, quaint building nestled in a dense block along a narrow road one block west of the *Plaza de Armas* and adjacent to *Catedral de San Cristobal*. On the outside there were balconies just big enough for two people to stand. Many of the balconies were decorated with clothes hanging over the railings to dry or a thick display of plants. Anastasia thought it looked lovely.

We went inside the building and I inquired in Spanish about a room to the short, plump woman smoking a cigar at the front desk. With a big smile, the woman told us to follow her. She led us up the stairs to the third floor, which was the top floor. She opened a door and gestured for us to enter. We walked into a small, furnished room, which consisted of a cozy-looking bed with its headboard against the back wall and stretching perpendicular to the center of the room. Against the opposite wall was a dresser. To the right of the bed were narrow double doors leading out to the balcony and a small, circular table with two chairs. Anastasia walked over to the doors, which looked more like a window, and stepped out onto the balcony.

I continued to take in the room. On the wall opposite the balcony was a closet and the bathroom. I walked into the bathroom, which had a sheet for a door. It was a decent-sized bathroom and had a nice, simple bathtub, a small table next to it, and two cabinets on the wall.

"Konrad! Come look!" Anastasia called from the balcony. I walked across the room and stepped out onto the small, iron balcony. I stood behind her and wrapped my arms around her waist, for it was the only way that both of us could stand out there. "Isn't it lovely?" she asked, looking down to the narrow, cobblestone street below, full of lively pedestrians making their way to and from the plazas. In the distance, we could see the *Catedral de San Cristobal*, and looking down the street to our right, we could see the beginnings of the *Plaza de Armas*.

"I think it's perfect," I said.

"Oh, me, too!" Anastasia agreed.

"Shall we stay here then?" I asked.

"Yes!" Anastasia said, with certainty. "Let's stay here."

I turned to the short, plump woman and told her we would take it. She smiled gratefully and told me we could pay her at the end of every week, but I paid her a month's worth in advance, and she was quite happy about that.

Anastasia and I fetched a carriage back to the harbor to retrieve our belongings, which we had left with the station manager who had been more than happy to oblige us. We loaded our suitcases onto the carriage and rode back to our small, perfect apartment. The carriage driver helped me carry the suitcases up the stairs to our room on the third floor. I thanked him and gave him a handsome tip. As soon as the carriage driver left, Anastasia jumped into my arms and began to kiss me passionately.

"I guess you're happy?" I asked between her excited kisses.

"Very happy," she said.

"Good."

"Shall we have some dinner and see what Havana is like at night?" Anastasia suggested.

"That sounds perfect," I said.

We walked downstairs, and I asked the short, plump woman at the front desk where we might find a good place to eat. She suggested a restaurant called *Los Arcos* in the Cathedral Square.

Anastasia and I strolled down the lively streets, arm in arm, making our way toward the restaurant and taking in the nightlife of the city. Everyone we saw seemed very friendly and happy. We walked past bars where people were singing, dancing, and enjoying life. As we neared the Cathedral Square, we began to hear music playing. When we arrived in the square, the music played loudly and people danced in the plaza. They were dancing a dance I had never seen and to music I had never heard. I found the music to be soothing and beautiful as well as exciting and moving. Anastasia and I smiled at the dancers as we made our way to the restaurant called *Los Arcos*.

It was a medium-sized restaurant with tables outside in the square. There were six columns with five arches, hence, the name. Above the arches was a large balcony where restaurant patrons could sit and enjoy their meals while watching the activities below. We walked through the center arch, under the overhang of the balcony, and into the restaurant. There was a small band on a stage playing the beautiful music to which everyone was dancing. The man playing the guitar sang with a wonderful and unique voice.

A well-dressed, nicely groomed man met us at the entrance

and asked us where we would like to sit. Anastasia wanted to sit outside in the square where we could watch the dancers. In Spanish, I told the host our preference, and he guided us to our table. We sat down, and with a big smile the host told us to enjoy ourselves. As the host walked away, Anastasia smiled at me with excited eyes and took my hand in hers, and then she turned to watch the dancers.

"We haven't been here a day and I've absolutely fallen in love with this culture," Anastasia remarked.

"It's wonderful, isn't it? I've never seen anything like it."

Our waiter walked over to our table. He was a young man with a big smile.

"How are you two doing this evening?" the waiter asked in Spanish.

"Fantastic, my friend," I returned in Spanish. "How are you?"

"Very good, sir. Welcome to Los Arcos. What can I get for you?" he asked.

"Well, it's our first night here in Havana, and I think we'd like to try a Cuban cocktail to start," I said.

"Of course, and to eat?"

"Your favorite Cuban dish. Surprise us," I said.

"Very good," the waiter said. "I'll have your drinks out right away. My name is Esteban. Anything you need, just ask for me."

"Thank you, Esteban," I said.

"You are welcome, sir."

Esteban quickly headed back into the restaurant.

"What did you order?" Anastasia asked.

"I'm not sure. Something Cuban," I said.

Anastasia and I watched the dancers in the square as they moved gracefully to the slow, rhythmic music. Anastasia moved her shoulders to the beat. I found myself doing the same. It was hard not to. Esteban brought us our drinks in tall glasses. The liquid inside the glasses was clear with green mint leaves crushed at the bottom of the glass. A lime rested on the top of the glass.

"What is this concoction?" I asked as I smelled the drink.

"It's called a *Mojito*," Esteban said. "It's made with rum, lime, mint, and sugar cane. It's the best drink you will ever drink."

"I'll drink to that," I said. Anastasia and I touched glasses.

"To *La Habana*," Anastasia toasted.

"To *La Habana*," I repeated.

We took a sip, and it was delightful.

Anastasia's eyes lit up with pleasure. "This is fantastic!" she said.

"You like?" Esteban said.

"*Mucho! Muy bueno!*" Anastasia said.

"Good!" Esteban said with a chuckle, probably laughing at Anastasia's French-accented Spanish. I thought it sounded adorable.

"By the way," I said. "What is this music and dance?"

"It's called *habanera*," Esteban explained. "It comes from right here in Havana."

"It's beautiful," I observed.

"Yes, it is. I'll have your dinner out very soon. Enjoy the *Mojitos*."

"Thank you, Esteban," I said graciously. Anastasia and I took another sip of our *Mojitos*.

"I think I could drink this every day for the rest of my life," Anastasia said. "I know Miriam would love it. We should learn how to make it, so we can fix it for her when we return. If we ever do return, that is. I just love it here."

"We haven't been here a day, and already you never want to leave," I commented.

"Don't *you* want to stay forever?" she asked.

"I want to stay with you," I said, avoiding the question. Anastasia smiled and leaned over to kiss me.

The next morning, I awoke to the slow, peaceful, steady breathing of a sleeping Anastasia. I watched her as she dreamed whatever it was she was dreaming. It must have been something happy, for there was the slightest smile on her lips that told me she was content. She lay on her back with her right arm resting on her pillow above her head and her left arm extended straight out from her body and hanging off the side of the bed. Her right leg was intertwined with my left leg. As I watched her sleep, I began to ponder my feelings for her. There was no doubt in my mind that I was completely and utterly in love with her to the point of absolute vulnerability and intoxication. I knew that I had never felt about a woman the way I felt about her. I had been in love before, sure, but never to this extent. Never before had I felt this connected to another human being to the point where I could feel her moving through my veins to my heart as if she was all that made my body function. There were certainly the familiar feelings of love, which I had felt before many times — the lightheadedness, the vulnerability, the weakness in the knees, the obliviousness to the realities of the world around me, and the feeling that everything in the world was right and perfect. I had felt all of those feelings before with the women I had loved in the past, but never had those feelings been as strong as they were with Anastasia. I began to wonder why that was and why it had not been enough with my past loves.

There had been Katherine, my first love. I had met her in December of my first year at Oxford at a restaurant where many of the students frequented in order to meet young ladies. Katherine had been there with three other girls, but she was by far the most beautiful. I had been there with three of my new schoolmates, and we instantly felt that we were a perfect match for the young women sitting across the room. The problem was, we all wanted Katherine. Once we finished our dinner, we had a drink while we waited for the four ladies to finish theirs. When they did, we walked over to their table. Michael, the boldest and most experienced with women in our group of friends, offered to pay for their dinner and asked if they would like to join us for a walk. The ladies accepted his proposal, and we went for a walk along the River Thames. We all had a good time together, and Katherine and I hit it off quite well. I ended up walking her home that night, and I kissed her at the door. It was a wonderful kiss. It felt very special to me. It was like nothing I had ever felt before. Our relationship quickly blossomed as we spent almost every day together. By February, we were deeply in love with one another. However, we were both young, immature, and quite insecure with ourselves. She was jealous of every girl I talked to, as I was jealous of any man who looked at her. We were very dependent on one another, but, in our naivety, we thought that it was all right. We thought that was how love was supposed to be. After my first year at Oxford, Uncle Friedrich and I went to Spain for the summer. I became very independent that summer in my time abroad and away from Katherine, but she was still very dependent on me. A month after I returned from Spain, I ended our relationship.

Then, there had been Elizabeth, whom I had met at the Sheldonian Theatre for a performance of Shakespeare's *Romeo and Juliet* just two months after I had ended it with Katherine. Elizabeth was the sweetest girl I had ever met. She was also very exciting and enjoyed an active life. We had much in common, and we went to many plays and operas together, as well as to many balls. She made me feel like the most wonderful man on Earth, and we had much fun together. Then, when my second year ended, I went to Paris for the summer and returned to find that we had drifted apart. I had changed quite a bit and grown even more independent during my time in Paris. She was heartbroken when I ended it, and I felt horrible, for she was such a sweet girl.

At the beginning of my third year, I saw a beautiful, young woman walking alone in the Botanic Garden. Her glowing beauty had rivaled any woman I had ever seen before. I approached her boldly, but she gave me little more than her name, which was

Mary. She had been promised to another man, but that did not stop me. I became a bit of a troubadour, writing her songs and poetry that promised undying love. She entertained my love for her, and we had a brief affair. I quickly realized that she could not call off her engagement, so I ended our affair.

After Mary, I rushed into a relationship with a lovely, young woman named Annabelle. She had been sweet and kind, but her love for me was far deeper than my love for her. After only a month together, she began talking about marriage and our settling down in the countryside. She talked about having children and how she wanted three boys and one girl. I became overwhelmed and ended our relationship after only a month and a half. She was completely devastated, and I felt awful for breaking her heart. She had such a kind and pure heart, and I hated hurting her the way I did.

However, I quickly forgot Mary and Annabelle when my heart was stolen by an older French woman whom I had met at the Ashmolean Museum when she had come to Oxford to visit her younger brother, a student at the university. Her name was Sofia. I had just turned twenty when I met her, and she was twenty-eight. She was mature, very independent, and completely different than the young women I had loved before. I was instantly attracted to her maturity and her independent spirit. She opened my eyes spiritually and sexually, and I fell deeply in love with her. She came with Uncle Friedrich and me to Italy the summer after my third year at Oxford. She lived with us in Rome for a month before returning home to Paris to spend the rest of the summer with her parents. When I returned to Oxford at the end of the summer, I received a letter from Sofia saying that she had met another man in Paris and was going to stay there with him. She was the first woman to truly break my heart, and I finally felt what it must have been like for the women who I had left heartbroken.

After Sofia, I decided to take a break from love, but then there was Anastasia. As I watched her sleep, it was clear to me that there was something special about her. It was more than the timing, more than the connection we shared, and more than the feelings I felt for her. It was something indescribable, something I couldn't place, something that just *was*.

XXIV

T<small>IME PASSES QUICKLY IN</small> the intoxicating kiss of two lovers. Over the next four months, Anastasia and I lived a busy life of luxury together. We saw many operas and plays at the *Gran Teatro Tacon*. We learned to dance to the native *habanera* music. Once we learned to dance, we found ourselves out at the restaurants and bars almost every other night, dancing with the many new friends we made. We spent our days either exploring the city or relaxing on the beautiful beaches under the shade of a palm tree, while we stared out at the clear, turquoise waters of the Havana Gulf. We would swim in the ocean when the sun became too hot in the afternoons. On many occasions, we stayed out on the beach all night long, staring at the moon and the stars over the dark waters, until the soothing sound of the waves crashing lightly on the shore made us drift off to sleep in each other's arms.

On a dark, cloudy afternoon in October, I walked toward the beach from the post office, carrying a letter from Miriam. I met Anastasia at a favorite beachside restaurant of ours. I sat down across from her at a table on the patio. We were the only ones sitting outside.

"You didn't want to sit inside?" I asked her. "It's probably going to rain soon."

"I know," Anastasia said, staring off at the ocean. "But I love this calm before the storm. We can run inside when it starts to rain." She turned to me and smiled. She looked down at my hand and noticed the letter. "Is that from Miriam?" she asked.

I nodded. "Would you like to read it?"

"Sure," she answered, so I handed the letter to Anastasia. She opened it and began to read it aloud. *"My dearest and most missed friends, thank you for making me jealous with your last letter.*

Havana sounds like paradise. Charles and I would love to come join you, but unfortunately we have already taken our great vacation and Charles is now quite busy. However, if you decide to stay there for good, please let us know so we can come and live there with you. Charles and I have been taking Renegado riding almost every day like you asked, Kon. He seems to like us now, though it took him a couple of weeks to warm up to us. He is getting plenty of exercise, and he seems quite happy, though I'm sure he misses you very much. So, if not for me, come back soon for Renegado.

"I don't know if they have been reporting the news of the war between the United States and Mexico down there on your Caribbean island, but I thought I should inform you that Winfield Scott's army has captured Mexico City after a series of bloody engagements that lasted for a week in early to middle September. I have been checking your mail, Konrad, and you have received no letters from your friends in the Rangers, but the mail system is terrible at this time. However, I have checked the lists of names of fallen soldiers many times very carefully, and your friends' names have not been among them. I have every confidence that they are safe and in good health. The good news is that the United States has defeated Santa Anna and has captured Mexico City, which essentially means that the war is over. I pray for peace every day and that when it comes it will stay for a very long time.

"I hope the two of you continue to have a wonderful time in Havana, but I also hope you return to New Orleans soon. Charles and I miss you so very much, more than you know. We eagerly await your return, but we wish you the most wonderful time while you are away. With all our love, Charles and Miriam." Anastasia smiled and folded the letter. "She's so sweet. I do miss her."

"Me, too," I said, looking up at the clouds and then at the large crashing waves. I did miss Miriam, but my mind was on Jack Burton, William Mason, and Kyle Ripley. I missed them and worried about them greatly. Anastasia immediately sensed what I was thinking.

"Are you all right?" she asked.

I looked away from the ocean and turned to her. "Yes, but I just..." I paused, trying to find the words to complete my sentence.

"You worry about them, don't you — your friends fighting in the war?" she asked.

"Sure, I worry," I admitted.

"Well, Miriam said their names were not on the list of fallen soldiers, and with Mexico City captured, they probably won't fight another battle," she said. Her words were comforting.

"I know, but sometimes I just feel like I should be there with them," I explained.

"That's understandable," she empathized. "But since you feel so strongly against this war, don't you think that it would be even more painful to fight alongside your friends for a cause you know is wrong?" I remained silent. "They're your friends, Konrad, and they understand that you can not fight for something in which you do not believe, and they respect you for that, as I do, just as you respect Jack for doing what he believes is his duty."

"I know you are right," I said after a moment of silence. "I guess it's just one of those situations where no matter what choice I were to make, I would feel like it's the wrong one, even if I know in my heart that it was the right choice."

Anastasia looked at me sympathetically. She reached across the table and took my hand. Her touch eased my sorrow. I kissed her hand. The waiter walked over to our table and set our food down before us. Anastasia had ordered our favorite Cuban dish, *Ropa vieja*. We thanked the waiter, and he walked back inside the restaurant. Just as we took our first bite, a loud thunder clap exploded across the sky. Anastasia jumped, made a worried face, and then laughed at herself. Suddenly, the rain began to pour down with great ferocity and density. We quickly grabbed our plates and ran inside the restaurant. We laughed as we wiped the water off of our bodies as best we could. We sat down and ate our meals as we watched the violent storm attack the city.

* * *

On a warm, clear evening near the end of October, Anastasia and I went to our favorite restaurant, *Los Arcos*, in the Cathedral Square. It was the restaurant we had gone to on our first night in Havana. It was a lively night, and we danced to the *habanera* music until we could barely move our legs. Sweaty and exhausted, we sat down at our table beneath the arches and ordered two *Mojitos* from our waiter, Esteban. He brought our drinks promptly, along with a couple of handkerchiefs to wipe the sweat from our faces. We thanked him and I gave him a nice tip. Sitting side by side, Anastasia and I sipped our drinks as we watched the dancers move fluidly to the beautiful music.

"We've really had a wonderful time here, haven't we, Konrad?" Anastasia asked.

"Yes, we have, my dear, a wonderful time," I agreed.

"Are you ready to go back to New Orleans?" Anastasia asked.

"I'm ready when you are," I replied.

"I absolutely love it here, and I know I've said it before, but I can't tell you enough how much you bringing me here means to me. I never imagined I would get to see Havana. It's truly a dream come true."

"Being here with you has been a dream come true for me," I said. "Is it time we go back?"

Anastasia smiled. "I think it is. I really miss Miriam and Charles."

"I do, too. I'll book us passage back to New Orleans first thing in the morning," I promised.

Anastasia kissed me and slipped her hand around my arm. She laid her head on my shoulder and raised her glass.

"To *La Habana*," she said.

"To *La Habana*," I repeated. We touched glasses, took a sip of our drinks, and watched the dancers move fluidly to the beautiful music.

BOOK III
Truth by Will

I

ANASTASIA AND I ARRIVED in New Orleans on the fourteenth of November. We decided to go see Miriam immediately, otherwise she would be offended. We walked three blocks east to their home on *Rue Orleans* between Bourbon and Royal streets. Anastasia knocked on the door, and we were greeted by Miriam's warming excitement. After Charles and Miriam invited us inside, we all sat together and had a drink, while Anastasia told them all about our time in Havana.

Once Anastasia had told Miriam about our trip, I excused myself to go see Renegado. I told them I would meet them for dinner at the Saint Charles Hotel at seven.

When I arrived at the stables, Renegado immediately caught my eye. While the rest of the horses walked in circles around the corral, Renegado stood still, staring off into the open country. My poor friend. A few rides a week into the country was not nearly enough to satisfy him. He needed adventure. He needed an excursion. I went to the stableman and he fetched me my saddle and brought Renegado to me. I petted Renegado's neck and cheeks, and he nuzzled me with his nose. He stomped his feet excitedly, ready for a good ride. I saddled him and we rode out of town. I had to keep pulling on the reins to stop him from running before we got out of town, but once we got to the countryside, I let him go. I held onto the reins and clenched my legs into his sides as he stretched his legs in a dead sprint. Renegado ran as hard as he could for a good half mile before slowing down to a trot to catch his breath. It felt good to be sitting on his back again.

After a good, long ride, I took Renegado back to the stables and walked over to the Saint Charles Hotel for dinner. Charles, Miriam, and Anastasia were already sitting at a table in the hotel restaurant.

"How was your ride?" Miriam asked as I sat down.

"It was good. I've missed that horse." I helped myself to the champagne, which was icing in a bucket in the center of our table.

"Konrad, I've been reading this book by Samuel Reid," Charles stated. "He rode with your Rangers for a bit and covered the beginning of the war. Have you heard of him?"

"He rode with McCulloch's Rangers. I've heard of him but never met him."

"Yes, McCulloch's Rangers. The book is called *The Scouting Expeditions of McCulloch's Texas Rangers.*"

"What do you think of it?" I asked.

"It's quite fascinating. I'd be interested in your take on the book. You could tell me if it's all true or embellished or just rubbish."

"I'm sure it's a mixture of the three. That's usually how such books are," I said.

"What do you mean?" Charles asked. "Is Reid not a reliable source?"

"Most of what he says will be true. Much of the truth will be embellished. Him being in a foreign atmosphere and situation will cause him to see things as much bigger and greater than they actually were. And there will certainly be some rubbish to boost the sales."

"Why don't you read it and tell me what you think," Charles suggested.

"I've lived it, Charles. I don't wish to relive it. Besides, I've just told you what I think."

"Fair enough. I don't imagine you would want to relive it. My apologies for pressing the matter."

I held up my hand and shook my head, gesturing that it was nothing for which to apologize. I did not know why I reacted the way I had. I felt a bit of angst. For what reason, I did not know. It had begun upon the back of Renegado. Riding him that day at full speed through the countryside had caused me to recollect adventures of the past. I remembered the freedom of the open plains, the wildness of the frontier, and that feeling of my heart beating in concert with my soul. Havana had been a wonderful trip. It had been exciting and new, and I had experienced it with the woman I loved. Now, I was back in New Orleans with Anastasia, of whose love I could never tire, and we were happy together. We lived in harmony with one another and had beautiful conversations and made the most extraordinary love. What more could a man ask for? A sane man, an ignorant man, would view my situation as ideal. However, I did not feel sane or ignorant; I felt trapped. I felt as if I was missing out on something. Anastasia and I had gone to Cuba on a wonderful adventure together, and that would be enough for her. That excitement would keep her satisfied for a long time to come. Now, she would be content to enjoy the relaxed yet exciting lifestyle of New Orleans. I, on the other hand, cringed at the thought of lying in bed all day, strolling through the streets, or relaxing at a café. I thought of all the operas, plays, dinners, parties, and senseless conversations I would have to endure. I loved Anastasia with all my heart, and just being with her almost made the boring prison that was city life bearable. I had hoped that love would calm the restless beat of my heart, but it had not. It merely hindered my ability to hear it.

When my steak came, I took one bite and ate no more. It was a terrible cut with too much fat. When the waiter asked if I would like another, I declined. Instead, I just had another glass of champagne. Charles, Miriam, and Anastasia knew something was wrong. I assured them that I was only worried about my friends fighting in the war. They nodded empathetically and accepted my explanation.

* * *

On the twenty-first of December, Anastasia, Miriam, and

Charles celebrated my birthday with me. I, of course, had not wanted any celebration or party of any sort, but Miriam would not allow it. We went to the Theatre d'Orleans for a performance of *La Juive*, a grand opera by Fromental Halevy. I put on a smile and pretended to enjoy myself. I used to love the arts. I did still, but they had lost their flavor. I had been around the arts for too long; the excitement was gone. As I sat in the balcony, watching the fifth act of the opera when Eleazar and Rachel were preparing to jump into the boiling water, all I could think about was the fact that I was now twenty-seven years old. It hadn't really hit me until that moment in the fifth act. I had been only twenty-two years old when I'd first arrived in New Orleans. Had it really been five years? It certainly did not feel like it had been that long. I thought back to the day I left for Oxford. I had not yet turned eighteen. That had been ten years ago! Oh! How time flies by! If decades pass in blinks, then how quickly do moments pass? My heart began to race with anxiety. I was twenty-seven years old! I knew I was still quite young, but there was something about that number that made me shiver with fear and angst. I felt death creeping around the corner. I had not yet seen the Pacific Ocean. I left New York five years ago with only one goal placed in my open mind, that I would see the Pacific Ocean. That was five years ago. Why had I not yet seen it? I had done many great things and had enjoyed many great adventures, but the Pacific Ocean still held a firm place in my heart as one of my greatest desires and curiosities. Would seeing the Pacific Ocean calm the beat of my restless heart?

"Are you all right?" Anastasia suddenly asked, interrupting my thoughts. I looked at her in confusion. "You're sweating profusely and your breaths are short. What's wrong?"

I wiped the sweat from my forehead and upper lip and looked at my shaking hand. I did not feel hot. I slowed my breathing by taking a long, deep breath.

"I'm fine," I said, but my heart was racing. *Be quiet, damn it!* I told my heart. It began to beat faster.

"Maybe you should go get some fresh air," Anastasia suggested.

"Yes, I think you're right," I agreed. I stood up, and Anastasia began to stand with me, but I put my hand on her shoulder and insisted she stayed.

I quickly made my way down the stairs, through the lobby, and out the doors of the theatre. I took in a deep breath of humid air and began to cough. I put my hands on my knees and bent over as I coughed violently. Without warning I vomited, just as a finely dressed couple walked by. They quickly stepped away from me.

"Damned drunk!" the man said.

I wiped my mouth. The coughing ceased. My heart slowed. I took a deep breath and exhaled slowly. My breathing was normal again. I took out my handkerchief and wiped the sweat off my face. The theatre attendants began to walk out the doors. I waited in the street for Anastasia, Miriam, and Charles. They came out shortly with concerned expressions on their faces. They asked me if I was all right, and I said I felt a little sick. I told them I should probably call it a night and go to bed. We said our goodbyes, and Anastasia and I walked back to our apartment. I quickly undressed and lay down in bed. Anastasia brought me a glass of water, and I drank it down quickly. She undressed and lay in bed next to me, looking at me with concern as she asked me questions about how I felt. I lied and told her I felt weak and mildly feverish. I didn't tell her my real sickness was extreme anxiety.

Anastasia soon fell asleep, but I lay awake in bed for hours. I looked at her and watched her sleep. I loved her so much. I really did. Why was that not enough for me? Was love not a great adventure? What will satisfy my restless heart? Will my heart ever be satisfied, or will it always desire more? I pushed the covers off my body and climbed out of bed. I walked outside onto the balcony and smoked a cigar as I stared up at the moon and the stars. I looked at the time on my father's gold pocket watch. It was almost three-thirty in the morning. It was a beautiful, peaceful hour. I enjoyed the cool, damp wind and admired the clear, dark-blue sky, as I listened carefully to the arrhythmic beats of my heart and tried to decipher what it was telling me.

With the next day came even more confusion when I received a package in the mail from Uncle Friedrich. I had not heard from him since I left England. I opened the package, which contained a book and a letter. The letter was brief and written in Latin:

My Dear Nephew,
Happy Birthday, Konrad. It's hard to believe you are twenty-seven years old now. You were just becoming a man the last time I saw you. Time is a clever and sneaky thief. Time is also a teacher, and I hope you have been learning much. You have always had a great thirst for knowledge. I hope you have retained that. To make sure that you have, I have sent you a book by a young Danish philosopher whom I met in Berlin just after you returned to America. His name is Soren Kierkegaard, and he is a brilliant young man. I feel you will relate to his ideas quite well. Good luck to you, my nephew and friend.
Justice by God, Truth by Will, Duty by Heart,
Friedrich

I folded the letter and looked at the book entitled, *Either/Or*. It was written in German. I read the preface and found myself entranced as I came to the first section called "Diapsalmata". It opened with a French poem, which read:

Greatness, knowledge, renown,
Friendship, pleasure, and possessions
All is only wind, all is smoke:
To say it better, all is nothing.

I read the words of the poem over again, then twice more, and then I heard Anastasia's footsteps coming up the stairs. I closed the book and smiled as Anastasia and Miriam appeared at the top of the stairs.

"Hello, ladies," I greeted. "How was tea?"

"It was hot," Anastasia said. "How do you feel?"

"I feel fine," I said.

"Good. We're going to lunch with Isabelle and Sarah," Anastasia said.

"Would you like to join us?" Miriam teased.

"As tempting as that sounds, I think I'll just stay here," I replied.

"Would you like us to bring back any food from the restaurant?" Anastasia asked.

"No, thank you."

"All right. See you soon."

The ladies left, and I went back to reading the book by the Danish philosopher. I had only gotten a few profound pages into the book when I was struck by a line, which I had to read over twice and ponder:

I feel as a chessman must feel when the opponent says of it: that piece cannot be moved.

I do not know why that line struck me the way it did, but I it resonated deeply with my thoughts. I continued to read the poetic epigrams and anecdotes, often rereading the verses and stopping to ponder their meaning. Despite my constant rereading, I quickly finished the first section of the book before the ladies returned from lunch, so I began reading the next section.

Anastasia ended up staying out with the ladies until the late hours of the evening when darkness had long begun to fall but had not yet reached its peak. She offered me no apologies or explanations for staying out for so long without informing me of her activities, for she knew I did not require an apology or explanation. That was the beauty of our relationship. We were not one of those couples that needed to know where the other was at all times and what they were doing when they were away. When we were together, we enjoyed a beautiful dependence on one another. When we were apart, we enjoyed our own independence outside of one another. I was never jealous or untrusting of her, nor was she of me. We were confident in our love, and we knew that no one else could compare. But how long would all of that last? Our relationship was young and built quite loosely upon hedonistic values and an innocent love that saw no further than the day in which we were living. And maybe that was how love should be, but how long could we hold on to that? How long could we live our lives *our* way? How long could we love each other our way before the pressures of society turned us into the couple it wanted — no — the couple it needed us to be in order for it to function properly. Were we really so special that we could escape that inevitability? Was our love really strong enough to fight against the doom that was destined to befall us?

Anastasia had long since gone to bed as I asked myself these questions. I had just finished reading the section of *Either/Or* called "Silhouettes" and was more than halfway done with the book. Why had these questions come to mind? What had inspired them? Our relationship was only seven months old. I suppose it's natural for a man to ask such questions when he feels that the seriousness of a relationship with a special woman is increasing quickly and is getting out of his control. At this point in a relationship, the woman is usually thinking about marriage and is practically in the first stages of wedding planning, while their counterparts are asking the questions I was asking myself. It's humorous, the difference in the minds of a man and a woman. However, almost more than humorous, it is tragic. But even more than tragic, it is beautiful.

I had done enough pondering for the evening. The Danish philosopher, Soren Kierkegaard, had provoked me greatly, more so than most philosophers whom I had read. I blew out the candle by which I had been reading and went inside. I undressed and crawled into bed with my lovely Anastasia. She didn't open her eyes, but she rolled over to cuddle with me. She put her arm over my chest and laid her head on my shoulder. I kissed her head and thought how beautiful she looked with the blue moonlight pouring in through the window. Then I wondered, as I looked at her head resting on my shoulder, how long it would be before my arm went numb.

II

THE NEXT MORNING, ANASTASIA went out for coffee with Miriam. I once again picked up *Either/Or*. I read quickly but often stopped to think about what I had just read. As I read the section called "Rotation of Crops", I felt as if the author had written it specifically to me. The essay focused on the topic of boredom and man's infinite struggle to overcome it. The answer: rotation of crops, changing the method of cultivation to keep life interesting. It was a beautiful metaphor, and one I instantly understood.

After finishing the essay on boredom, I closed the book and looked around. I looked at my giant apartment full of riches and luxuries. From my balcony, I gazed upon the city, knowing that anything I could ever want was at the tip of my fingers. All I had to do was reach for it. This was discomforting. It always had been, but a line from Kierkegaard's "Rotation of Crops" hit me hard in the gut and opened my eyes to what I already knew.

The more a person limits himself, the more resourceful he becomes.

What a wise and profound and true statement. A man cannot grow with the world at his fingertips. He must step away from the world so that it is just out of reach, forcing him to evolve in order to take what he desires and needs. What did I desire? In my head I was confused, but my heart ached for adventure.

I leaned back in my chair and closed my eyes. I began to daydream. It was a dream I had dreamed before. It was a dream of a settled life, a dream of what my life could be. In this dream, I have a permanent job as a history teacher at a New Orleans school. Anastasia and I are happily married with two children, a boy and a girl, and we live in a beautiful home in the countryside just outside the city and not far from the river. Charles and Miriam are our neighbors. They have three children of their own. All of our children are about the same age and play well together. On the weekends, Charles and Miriam come over to our house, or we go to theirs. The children play in the yard, while Charles, Miriam, Anastasia, and I drink tea on the porch. Charles and I talk about work and money and politics while Anastasia and Miriam talk about the children. On the weekdays, I wake up early in the morning, before the sun begins to rise, and I get dressed for work. Anastasia is already awake and preparing breakfast. I eat quickly, kiss her goodbye, and then walk out to the stables and saddle Renegado. We ride into town on the same simple, straight path we ride every day. I go to work. I come home on the simple, straight path. Anastasia is making dinner. I kiss her and play with the children. We eat dinner and have a nice family conversation. Very soon afterward, Anastasia and I put the children to bed. Later, I read the newspaper and smoke a pipe. Then I go to bed. Anastasia is already there, fast asleep. I undress and lie down next to her. I lie on my back, staring at the ceiling. Tomorrow I will do it all again, and I am happy.

* * *

The New Year arrived, and New Orleans welcomed 1848 with the usual lively celebration. Miriam, Charles, Anastasia, and I spent the evening at the Orleans Ballroom, dancing and socializing. Just before midnight, we all returned to my apartment and watched the fireworks from the balcony. We drank and talked into the early hours of the morning.

For the next month, I read the newspaper religiously, as it seemed that the war with Mexico was reaching an end. In mid-February, I finally received a newspaper with the headline I had been waiting for: 'WAR WITH MEXICO ENDS WITH THE TREATY OF GUADALUPE HIDALGO'. I quickly skimmed over the details of the treaty. It did not say much about the return of the soldiers. The important thing was — the war was over.

Beneath the article was a map, which showed the territory that would be ceded to the United States as a condition of the treaty. It was basically most of the land that Mexico had claimed west of Texas to the Pacific Ocean. Mexico would relinquish all claims to Texas and recognize the Rio Grande as the southern boundary with the United States. The United States would soon stretch from the Atlantic Ocean to the Pacific. James Polk had done exactly what he said he would do. He was certainly a man of his word; however, he wasn't much of a man of conscience. I set down the paper and breathed a sigh of relief as I turned my focus from my disagreements with the war to the fact that it was over and that my friends would soon be returning safely home.

I quickly scribbled a letter to Mason, telling him that I was in New Orleans and to let me know what his plans were now that the war was over. I told him that he, Jack, and Kyle should come to New Orleans if possible. I put the letter in an envelope and quickly took it over to the post office to have it delivered to San Antonio.

As I walked back to my apartment, I began to feel guilty for the restlessness and boredom I was feeling. I thought of Miriam and Charles and how much they enjoyed my company and friendship. I thought about how much Miriam loved me and how upset she got every time I left. I thought about Anastasia and how unfair my restless feelings were to her. I loved her — I truly did and always would. I had never felt about a woman the way I felt about Anastasia. The love we shared was a rare and remarkable love. Our relationship was passionate and honest. We talked about everything together and were not afraid to speak our minds. We shared a special connection and understanding for one another, and I knew that there was no woman more perfect for me.

Then why did my heart still beat that restless beat? I had ignored it for the first eighteen years of my life. Why could I not ignore it now? This restless beat, this inconsistent drum, this lost rhythm that only a few ever hear, was beginning to feel more like a burden than a blessing. Had I not fallen in love with Anastasia and Miriam and Charles, or, rather, had they not fallen in love with me, then it would be easy to follow my heart. It seemed that following my heart had become like any other addiction. The more I gave in, the more I needed it. I was at the point where I could not tell if it was more painful to leave or more painful to stay. I loved Anastasia and I loved Miriam, dearly and fully. Was love not enough to satisfy my heart? What kind of man was I to require more than love to find happiness?

When I got back to my apartment, I hid my questions and my frustrations behind a smile as I kissed Anastasia passionately. I made love to her, hoping that it would make me forget all that had been on my mind earlier.

As we lay in bed after making love, I could still feel that restless beat pounding in my chest.

III

Spring brought with it life and color but gave way all too quickly to the hot temperatures of summer. The heat made me tired and lazy, which kept me from showing my restlessness on the outside. During winter and spring, my knee would bounce uncontrollably when I sat, or I'd constantly be tapping my fingers on the table. I often found myself pacing across my apartment. I'd go on long rides through the countryside and camp in the woods for a few nights. By summer, my anxiety had worn me down into a bored, lazy, exhausted shell of a man. At least that was how I felt inside. On the outside, I did a good job of hiding my boredom and my desperation from Anastasia and Miriam.

I still loved Anastasia with all my heart, and I showed my love for her every day and at every opportunity. We still went for long walks and picnics by the river. We still spent entire days in bed together and entire nights making love. My feelings for her were just as strong as they had been — stronger. And they grew stronger every day I was with her. However, my desire for adventure and the beat of my restless heart grew stronger every day as well. My desires battled one another for dominance. I tried to keep my mind neutral while my heart was torn. I was growing weary.

* * *

I sat on my apartment's balcony, sweating in the wet heat of early July. It was only eight o'clock in the morning, but it was already miserably hot. I was slowly drinking a glass of white wine to ease into sobriety after a night of heavy drinking. Miriam, Charles, Anastasia, and I had gone to the theatre the night before. I couldn't even remember what play we had seen. We had a few drinks before the play, and after the play we went to a few parties. I barely remembered returning home to my apartment.

Anastasia was still fast asleep as I sat out on the balcony and enjoyed the morning. It was quiet in the French Quarter except for a few chirping birds. I read the newspaper as I snacked on some black olives, which I had dipped in oil and seasoned with pepper and garlic. The olives tasted good, however, I wished I had chosen a robust red wine. The pepper and garlic made the sweet, white wine taste bitter.

I turned the page of the newspaper and began reading an article about the discovery of gold in California. As I read, I noticed something floating in my peripheral vision. I turned to see a spider descending slowly from a single string of silk. He kicked his front two legs rapidly, searching for a foothold. As I watched the spider lower itself slowly, I was reminded of something Kierkegaard had written:

When a spider flings itself from a fixed point down into its consequences, it continually sees before it an empty space in which it can find no foothold, however much it stretches. So it is with me; before me is continually an empty space, and I am propelled by a consequence that lies behind me.

The spider finally landed on the iron railing of the balcony. I rested my chin on my hand as I watched him crawl along the railing.

"Good morning."

Startled, I quickly turned to see Miriam walking out onto the balcony. I had forgotten that she and Charles had slept in the spare bedroom the night before.

"Sorry, I didn't mean to startle you," Miriam apologized.

"Oh, it's quite all right. I forgot you were here."

"So did I," Miriam said with a chuckle as she sat down across from me. She ate an olive. "These are good. Don't you love that feeling of waking up and not being sure where you are?"

"Sometimes, sure."

"I think it's nice to forget where you are every now and then. You know your life is boring when you wake up every morning and immediately know exactly where you are."

"Indeed," I agreed.

Miriam glanced down at the newspaper I had been reading. I saw her eyes skimming over the headlines. She looked up at me and studied my eyes for a moment.

"Gold in California," Miriam said. "Are you thinking about being a prospector?"

"I have no interest in gold."

"You have an interest in California."

"I was just reading the newspaper, Miriam," I said.

Miriam smiled and ate another olive. She poured herself a glass of water from the pitcher. It was probably quite warm.

"I can't have children, Konrad," Miriam said suddenly. She did not look at me when she said this. I looked at her in confusion and disbelief. I quickly pulled my chair next to hers as I could see that she was holding back her tears.

"What are you talking about? How can you be sure?" I asked.

"Charles and I have been trying for over a year now, ever since the wedding. When nothing happened after six months, I went to see a doctor. He told us to try for another six months. We tried for six more months — nothing. We went back to the doctor, and he said I was infertile. He said we could keep trying, but he doesn't think I will ever be able to conceive." Miriam began to cry.

I put my arm around her and comforted her, "You *will* keep trying. You never know what could happen. Maybe it didn't work last year. Maybe it will this year, or the next."

"No, Konrad, it will never happen for me. I'm just not fit to

416

be a mother." Miriam sniffled and wiped her tears. "I just want to be one so badly, Konrad!"

I held her as she cried in my arms. I didn't know what to say. What could I say?

"And I know that Charles wants to be a father more than anything. He's always wanted a little boy. I wanted a girl. I think a little girl would be so wonderful, but I've let Charles down. I'm no good to him."

"No, Miriam, you haven't let anyone down," I argued. "Listen to me, Miriam. Look at me." I grabbed her face, and she looked at me with her tear-filled eyes. "It's not your fault. It's nobody's fault. You can't blame yourself. Do you understand me?" Miriam nodded. "Don't ever think you're no good. Anastasia, me, and especially Charles will always love you no matter what. You are an amazing, beautiful, powerful, strong woman, the strongest woman I've ever known. You are an angel and a warrior. You are extraordinary."

Miriam managed a smile. I wiped the tears from her face and kissed her on the cheek and forehead. She told me she loved me, and I held her close until she stopped crying.

IV

I AWOKE IN THE middle of the night from one of the strangest dreams I had ever dreamt. In a confused, lost daze, I climbed out of bed and walked out onto the balcony. I stared at the full moon as I tried to comprehend the images my mind had produced in my state of unconsciousness. Anastasia came out onto the balcony. She stood behind me, put her hands on my shoulders, and kissed the back of my neck.

"Is everything all right?" she asked.

"I had a strange dream," I told her, still staring off into the sky with some lingering confusion.

"What happened in your dream?"

I squinted as I tried to remember the details. "It started in Egypt on the Nile River, outside of Cairo. I found myself standing before the Sphinx amongst the Pyramids. The Sphinx told me to go to India, so I sailed down the Red Sea and across the Arabian Sea to Bombay. From there I began walking northward. I wasn't sure where I was going, but I knew I had to travel north. After a long journey, I found myself at the base of the Himalaya Mountains. I began to climb them. At the highest peak, I stood before Gautama Buddha, who preached to me the Four Noble Truths. When he finished his teachings, he parted the clouds below us and showed me the entire world. It was a world full of suffering, pain, and ignorance. Then he parted the heavens above us and showed me a different world. It was a world of happiness, enlightenment, and Nirvana. He then asked me which world I would like to live in."

"Which world did you choose?" Anastasia asked.

"I told him I would need to think about it, so he left me there on the mountain top alone, between both worlds, meditating to decide which to live in. I woke up before I made my decision."

"Which one would you pick now?"

"Neither," I said. "I like this world where we are, and we can be either happy or we can suffer. It all depends on the day and what we experience each day."

"You don't think we can just be happy all the time?" Anastasia asked.

"Who would want to be? It's boring. I enjoy feeling different emotions. Besides, happiness and suffering go hand in hand. You can't know one without knowing the other."

"You don't think people should strive for happiness?"

"I think people can spend their whole lives trying to live in a constant state of happiness, but in the end, they'll find themselves exhausted and unsuccessful."

"So you don't think happiness is the meaning of life?"

"If it is, I'll be very disappointed."

Anastasia and I went back to bed. She fell right back to sleep, but my dream kept me awake.

* * *

It was a swelteringly hot Saturday, and the city was particularly busy when I returned from a ride in the countryside. I dropped Renegado off at the stables and walked through town. I walked past the chaotic docks and through the crowded streets of the French Quarter. Everyone seemed to be moving quickly. It was awfully hot and unbearably humid. I loosened my tie, unbuttoned the top of my shirt, and briefly removed my hat to push back the wet hairs sticking to my forehead.

I walked over to the market to meander about and observe the fresh foods on display. I entertained the idea of buying a few things and making dinner for Charles, Miriam, and Anastasia. However, what was meant to be a relaxing walk suddenly became overwhelming and stressful. There were so many people in the market, and the heat was incredible. I wiped the sweat from my face and tried to take a deep breath, but it felt as if the swarms of busy people around me were stealing my air.

I rushed out of the market and into the streets. The transition was no better. Why was the city so busy on this particular day? And this heat! The heat had never bothered me before this summer.

I pushed my way through the crowded streets. Deep down, I knew it was no busier than usual. I was having one of my anxiety attacks. I was long overdue. I quickly made my way through the French Quarter and ran up the stairs to my apartment. I slammed the door shut and quickly poured myself a glass of water. It helped, but it was not enough. I refilled my glass with whiskey.

"Konrad!" Anastasia yelled, as I was about to sip my drink. I jumped, a bit startled. I turned in the direction of her voice. It sounded like she was in the bath.

"Yes?"

"A letter came for you today. It's on the table. It looks like it came from Texas."

I quickly turned around and looked down at the table. The letter sat right in the middle of it. I slowly stepped over to the table and set down my drink. I grabbed the letter and opened it quickly. It was from Mason.

Dear Konrad,

You know I'm not much for writing letters, so I'll make this brief. Jack and Kyle and I are here in San Antonio, finishing out the remaining days of our commitment to the Rangers. We did not see much action after you left. We were sent back to San Antonio to protect the frontier. Had a few scrapes with the Comanche. Got sent back to Mexico with Hays after General Scott took Mexico City. We fought some guerrillas and then the war ended. Now we're back in San Antonio, bored out of our minds. From your letter, it sounds like you are too. We've been talking with a few of the boys about plans now that the war is over. Apparently there's gold in California. I'm sure you read all about it in the paper. Me, Jack, Kyle, and a few of the other boys figured now that California is ours, we might as well try and get rich off our new land before everyone else does. Hell, we've got nothing better to do. I know how bad you've been wanting to see the Pacific Ocean, and I know you're always up for a new adventure, so get to San Antonio as soon as you can. We're waiting, partner.

    Will Mason

I folded the letter. My heart was racing with excitement as I thought about an adventure to California.

"Was it from your friend Jack Burton?" Anastasia called from the bath.

"Will Mason."

"What did he say?"

I walked into the bathroom. Anastasia was relaxing in the tub amongst the bubbles, drinking a glass of wine.

"He was just telling me about the war. He said they didn't see much action after I left."

"That's good. Would you like to join me?" Anastasia asked.

"Is it a cold bath?"

"Sort of."

I felt the water. It was warm, and I was still sweating profusely. "It's way too warm. I'll have a heat stroke."

"It's not as warm as it feels. Once you're in, it's quite cool."

"It doesn't feel quite cool."

"It is — trust me."

"I'll take a bath later," I said.

"Fine. Will you give me a kiss?" Anastasia asked. I smiled and leaned down. I kissed her, and she grabbed my waist and pulled me into the tub with her.

"You're right; it is quite cool," I said.

"I told you to trust me."

I undressed in the tub and put my wet clothes on the floor. Anastasia poured me a glass of wine. We toasted and relaxed, as we enjoyed the coolness of the water.

* * *

As Anastasia slept soundly next to me, I lay in bed, wide awake, as I thought about Mason's letter. It had been the only thing on my mind since I had read it. There was no question as to whether I wanted to go; I desperately wanted to go. It was my dream to see the Pacific Ocean, and my heart was yearning for another adventure. A year ago, I would have left for Texas the moment I read the letter, but things were different now. Now, there was Anastasia. I loved her, and a very large part of me did not want to leave her. The very thought of leaving her pushed my heart into my throat. However, the thought of staying in New Orleans while my friends went to California drove me insane. My heart was torn, or was it? No, my heart was certain, and my mind was trying to fight it.

All night long I lay awake as my mind tried to make sense of my heart's desires. As the sun began to rise, I was filled with guilt as I realized that I would rather embark on another adventure than stay with the woman I loved; at least that was how I saw it. My heart was calling me to go to California. That did not mean I did not love Anastasia. I knew that, but I could not help but feel guilty. She loved me so much. She had devoted herself to me, faithfully, and would do anything for me. She had come back from Paris to be with me, and now I was going to leave her. It was not right. She did not deserve that.

Frustrated and half-crazed, I climbed out of bed and got dressed. I rushed out of my apartment and quickly began striding westward down Bourbon Street. Four blocks later, I turned onto St. Ann Street and promptly arrived at my destination. I knocked on the door of the small cottage. I waited impatiently for a few moments. There was no answer. I knocked again. The door opened, and Marie Laveau stood before me.

"Konrad. It has been a long time," she said lamely. "Come in."

"Thank you," I said as I walked into her cottage. "Did I wake you?"

"No."

"Good. Am I intruding?"

"Why have you come to me, Konrad?" Marie asked.

"I need you to cure me," I said.

"Cure you of what?"

"My restlessness. It has become a burden. I'm in love with a woman, a woman I don't want to leave, but my heart tells me to go! It is always telling me to go! I'm always leaving. I'm always looking for something new. I'm always restless. I want to settle down and be with the woman I love."

"Do you really *want* to settle down?" Marie asked.

"No, and that's why I need you to cure me or do what you must. I need you to make me *want* to settle down," I explained.

"What you are asking for does not exist."

"You can exorcize evil spirits and demons, but you can't still a man's heart?" I inquired, agitated.

"No, I can not. And even if I could, I would not perform such an exorcism."

"You won't even try? I'll pay you."

"It is not a question of money."

"Then what? Why won't you help me?" I pressed.

"I can't help you, young man. I told you this before when you asked me to rid you of your demons," Marie explained calmly. Even with my frustrated, agitated, assaultive tone, she remained calm and relaxed. "This restlessness of which you speak is who you are. It is a blessing and a curse. First, you listened to your heart and embraced it. Now, you try to ignore it. You are trying to be everything you despise. It has become harder for you to listen to your heart and even harder to follow it. To follow it means to sacrifice, and sacrifice can be painful, but it is necessary. To ignore your heart and to choose not to follow it would not just be painful; it would be deadly. It would be suicide to your soul. You must follow your heart. You must. I know you love this woman, but you must leave her. Her love alone will not fulfill you."

"I thought that love conquers all," I stated.

"Love conquers sight. Ignorance conquers all."

Hopeless, I was nearly in tears. I fell to my knees. "I have to leave her — I must."

"Yes — you must."

I closed my eyes and cringed as I began to accept what my heart was telling me to do. I had to listen to it. I had to follow it — I must.

V

I LEFT THE COTTAGE of Marie Laveau just after the sun had risen. I walked slowly down Bourbon Street toward my apartment, filled with both relief and dread.

I walked up the stairs and quietly opened the door to my apartment. I gently shut it and crept into the bedroom. Anastasia was still asleep. I undressed and climbed into bed with her. Without opening her eyes, she rolled over to cuddle with me. She put her leg over mine and put her arm around my stomach. We quickly fell back to sleep in each other's arms.

We slept for a few hours. When we awoke, I went downstairs to Leon's to bring breakfast up to the apartment. Anastasia and I ate breakfast in bed. I snacked on the fruit and drank coffee, while Anastasia filled up on sausage, eggs, and bread. She had a wonderful appetite, and I enjoyed watching her eat. Somehow, she managed to never put on weight. I, on the other hand, had a horrible appetite. I was spoiled when it came to food. I required much variety in my diet and much flavor, otherwise I would get bored with food. Anastasia would always tell me that being around me made her hungry because I ate so little.

"Where did you go this morning?" Anastasia asked, cutting a piece of sausage.

"I woke up and couldn't fall back to sleep, so I went for a walk. I was feeling a bit antsy."

Anastasia did not ask me why I had been feeling antsy. The look on her face told me that she already knew. When we finished breakfast, I picked up all the plates and utensils and put them on the dinner table. As I walked back into the bedroom, Anastasia was staring at me sadly with her penetrating eyes. I stopped in the doorway and stared back at her. I sighed and leaned against the wall.

"You're leaving, aren't you?" she said.

"Yes."

"When?"

I shrugged and shook my head. "Soon — quite soon."

Anastasia closed her eyes sadly and lowered her head. When she opened her eyes, they were filling with tears. I walked over to the bed and sat down next to her.

"I've seen it in your eyes for a while now," Anastasia admitted. "It's as if you're always looking past everything into some world I can't see. And ever since you got that letter from you friends, you've just been… I don't know… elsewhere. Where will you go?"

"California," I said.

"For how long?"

I shook my head. I had no answer.

She sighed and looked into my eyes with her intense, piercing stare. "Is it me?"

"No."

"I know it's not, but I suppose I just had to ask."

"I don't want to leave you—"

"Then don't."

"I have to. I need to see the Pacific. I need to see more. I'll come back to you, I promise. This is just something I need to do right now."

"You promise you'll come back to me?"

"I promise. I love you, Anastasia. Nothing will keep me from coming back to you."

She took a deep breath and sighed. She swallowed the lump in her throat and held back her tears with great strength. We held each other in silence while we sat on the bed.

* * *

When I told Miriam the news about my leaving, she reacted

quite dramatically. She yelled at me for a bit, and then she cried for a bit. She asked me what Anastasia thought about my plans, and I told her that she understood.

"Well, I don't know how she does it," Miriam said. "I don't think I'll ever understand you."

After spending an hour trying to explain to Miriam why I needed to leave (as I had many times before), I walked home and began to pack. Anastasia helped me. We did not say much to one another. It was a very melancholy evening.

When we finished packing what little there was to pack, I set my things by the door. Anastasia slowly walked toward me with her head lowered, staring at the floor. She stopped when her toes were touching mine and finally looked up into my eyes. Her eyes were filled with tears, and her lips quivered. A tear fell from her right eye and slowly moved down her cheek, so I wiped it away with my thumb. She took my hand in hers and kissed it as a tear fell from her left eye. I slowly leaned in to her and let our lips touch softly. She pulled away and looked into my eyes for a moment. She then wrapped her arms around my neck and kissed me passionately. I stroked her cheek with my left hand, and, grabbing her waist with my right hand, I pulled her body against mine.

We had made love many times, but nothing compared to the love we made that night. It was beautiful and perfect in every way. Every moment was powerful and magical. It was like nothing I had ever experienced before.

In the morning, I awoke before Anastasia and walked down to the stables. I rode Renegado back to my apartment and tied him off at the bottom of the stairs. When I entered the apartment, Anastasia was freshening up in the bathroom. When she came out, she was beautiful and glowing, despite the sadness in her eyes. I kissed her and grabbed my things. We walked downstairs, and she petted Renegado's neck as she watched me load my belongings onto the saddle. I put my saber on its belt and fastened it to my hip. It was the only weapon I carried.

Just as I finished loading what little I was bringing with me, Miriam and Charles came strolling down the street to say goodbye.

"Looks like we're just in time," Charles observed.

"You weren't trying to leave without saying goodbye, were you, Kon?" Miriam accused, only half joking.

"I wouldn't dream of it."

Miriam hugged me and kissed me on the cheek. "Are you all packed and ready to go?" she asked.

"Yes, I am. I should get going."

"Well, good luck to you, my friend," Charles said. "Bring a gold nugget back for us, all right?"

"I'll try my best."

Charles and I shook hands firmly, and he patted me on the back, squeezing my shoulder as he released his grip on my hand. I patted Charles on the shoulder and stepped over to Miriam. Her eyes were a little glossy.

"I'm really getting tired of doing this, Kon," Miriam said. "I really am."

"I know. I'm sorry."

We embraced, and she held me tight and didn't let go for a while. I heard her sniffling as she kissed my neck and pulled me closer. She finally let me go and stepped back. She lightly stroked my cheek and then suddenly looked away as she began to cry. She buried her face in Charles' chest as he comforted her.

I turned to Anastasia. She was being strong. Her eyes were clear and showed no sign of tears. They were sober and intense.

She stepped up to me and stared into my eyes. "You come back to me, all right?" she said. "Do what you must do for as long as it takes, and then come back to me. Don't let anything stop you."

"I will come back to you."

"I'll be waiting for you."

I smiled and kissed her softly and then passionately. Then we held each other for a few moments. She pulled away from me and looked into my eyes.

"I love you," I said.

"I love you."

She continued to stare into my eyes with her intense, penetrating stare as if she was looking into my soul. I loved it when she looked at me that way.

"Be careful," she finally said.

I nodded, kissed her once more, and then climbed onto Renegado's back. Anastasia walked over to Miriam and put her arm around her. I turned Renegado around and faced the three of them. I smiled and said goodbye, taking one last look at Anastasia. She stared into my soul and smiled. She kissed her hand and blew the kiss to me. As she blew on her hand, a light breeze came to bring the sweet morning air. The wind blew Anastasia's hair across her face as she continued to smile at me and stare into my soul. I smiled back at her as I let that image imprint itself in my mind. If she was perfect every day, then there was no word to describe the way she looked at that moment. She was the metaphor to which all beautiful things were compared.

I waved and turned Renegado around. We rode away down Bourbon Street. I wanted to look back, but I knew that if I did I would not be able to hold back the tears, for it was taking every bit of my strength to keep from crying. I exhaled a few shaky breaths and clenched my jaw. Miraculously, my eyes did not produce any water.

That image of Anastasia stayed in my mind as I rode out of town, and it stayed with me throughout the entire day as I rode west across Louisiana. I had to be crazy to leave a woman like that. However, I would have gone crazy had I not left. Either way, it seemed as if I was doomed to insanity.

VI

I arrived in San Antonio six days after I left New Orleans and left Renegado at the stables. I had made good time, for Renegado had been anxious to stretch his legs on a long journey. After walking through town, I entered the *Plaza de Armas* and slowly moved through the market past all the vendors and their stands of various goods, supplies, and food. I loved the smell of the market, and all of the different foods being cooked teased my senses. I didn't realize how hungry I was until I was in the middle of the market square, so I bought a bowl of chili and ate it as I continued walking through the market toward the inn where the Rangers stayed. I eventually made it through the busy market and arrived at the inn. I finished my chili, set the empty bowl on the window sill, and walked inside.

The saloon was not busy, aside from two card games where I recognized a few of the men at the card tables. They were Rangers from another detachment. I had not known them well enough to greet them. They stared at me as I walked toward the bar, so I nodded to them and they nodded back. I stepped up to the bar and ordered a whiskey.

"Jack Burton or Will Mason around?" I asked the bartender as he poured my drink.

"Jack Burton is working out at Fred Van Patten's ranch. Will Mason is still around. Should be in his room."

I paid for my drink and quickly gulped it down.

"Thank you," I said.

I walked upstairs to Mason's room and knocked on the door. I heard him stomping around, and then the door swung open. He stood before me, sporting a thick mustache with a triangular patch under his lower lip to complete the ensemble. He smiled at me excitedly.

"I knew you'd make it," Mason said. He opened his arms, and we embraced and patted each other on the back.

"Wouldn't miss it for the world," I said.

"Come in, partner."

I walked into the room. Mason banged on the wall.

"Kyle! Wake up! You'll never guess who's here!"

"I ain't asleep!" Kyle's voice bellowed from the other side of the wall. "And if it's that ugly son of a bitch Konrad, tell him I don't want to see his smelly, sorry ass!"

"Good to hear he hasn't changed," I said to Mason. He smiled and shrugged.

I heard the door to the next room open and slam shut, and then Kyle rushed into Mason's room with a big smile on his bearded face. His hair had grown down to his shoulders.

"There he is!" Kyle said excitedly. He gave me a big bear hug and looked me over. "Damn! You look clean and pale — and bored. We're going to have to fix that."

"You look anything but clean, and you smell even worse," I teased, although it was true.

"Why, thank you."

"I do like the beard. I'm glad to see that you can finally grow facial hair," I commented. I looked over at Mason. "You, on the other hand…" I said, grabbing his mustache. "What the hell is this?"

"It's fashionable, is what it is," Mason said, pushing my hand away.

"You're many things, Mason, but fashionable is not one of them."

"All right! Let's go have a drink," Mason invited.

We walked downstairs to the bar and ordered a round, which Mason bought. We toasted to California and ordered another round.

"What's this I hear about Jack working at some ranch?" I asked.

"Fred Van Patten's ranch," Mason said. "Yeah, he cowboys up there from time to time, branding cattle, moving herds, trading horses."

"Is he not coming to California with us?" I asked.

"Yes, he is. We'll get him on our way out."

"Hell, it was his idea," Kyle commented.

"When are we leaving?" I asked.

"I don't know," Mason admitted, his eyebrows pressed together as he looked at Kyle with squinting eyes. "Want to leave tomorrow?"

"Sounds good to me," Kyle said. "You all right with that, Konrad?"

"The sooner the better."

We drank a few more rounds while I told them about Havana and Anastasia. I described her well and quite thoroughly. They told me I was crazy for leaving a woman like her. They filled me in on what had happened during the war, which for them had mostly been patrolling the frontier after the battle in Monterrey. After the war, their Ranger detachment had disbanded. About half of the men joined Hays' detachment, while the rest went their separate ways. Mason and Kyle, along with Joe McLeod, Ned Riley, and Javi, had stayed in San Antonio and had been "living the good life", as Mason put it, ever since.

As Kyle refilled our glasses, Joe, Javi, and Ned walked into the saloon with big smiles on their faces when they saw me. I shook their hands, and they pushed me around a little and roughly patted my shoulders and back. I had forgotten what it was like to be in the company of informal men. It was refreshing. The bartender gave them each a glass and Mason filled them. We toasted and drank, except for Javi, who did not drink.

"How do y'all feel about leaving tomorrow?" Mason asked Joe, Javi, and Ned.

"Tomorrow's fine with me," Joe said as he sat down.

"You're all coming, too?" I asked, surprised and excited.

"Is that all right with you, Don Conrado?" Javi asked.

"I suppose so."

We drank and shared stories until late in the evening. It was good to be back with my old friends. It felt as if we had never been apart. There was no getting reacquainted or long moments of awkward silence. We naturally picked up right where we had left off.

* * *

In the morning, we awoke groggy and dehydrated, but our spirits were quickly lifted as we imagined the journey ahead. We soon gathered what little we had and went down to the stables. The sun was just presenting an orange sliver of itself as it began to cut into the dwindling night sky. We saddled our horses and loaded up our belongings, packing as much food as our saddlebags could hold.

As I finished loading my saddle, I noticed that Mason had a different horse than the beautiful Appaloosa he used to ride. Now, he was saddling a dark-brown stallion with a white diamond on his nose and four white socks.

"What happened to your mare?" I asked.

"Poor Athena got shot out from under me in the war," Mason answered.

"I'm sorry to hear that."

"This here is Perseus. He's a good horse."

"Do you name all your horses after Greek mythology?" I asked.

"Yeah, my father was obsessed with Greek mythology. I think it was the only thing he knew a lot about, and he was proud of that. I've also always found it interesting."

It saddened me that Athena had died. I was with Mason when he got her for the Fremont Expedition, and she had been a good, reliable horse. It was a shame she was gone.

Mason looked down at my hip and smiled. "I see you're still carrying that saber." He observed the opposite hip where my Bowie knife hung, then grabbed my shoulder and turned me around. "No pistol?" He looked at my saddle. "And no rifle? Where the hell are your firearms?"

"I threw them in the Mississippi on my way back from Monterrey," I said.

"Well, that's a very touching statement you've made to... ah... *me*, but you can't ride to California with nothing but a saber and a Bowie knife."

"Why not? There are plenty of firearms between the lot of you," I responded.

"It's not just for *your* safety, Konrad; it's also for ours. If we get attacked by Indians or bandits, I'd be much more comfortable knowing that you were properly armed."

When everyone was saddled and loaded up, we climbed onto our horses and began riding northward out of town. I stopped at the post office and scribbled a quick letter to Anastasia to let her know I had arrived in San Antonio and was on my way to California. We also stopped at the gun shop where I bought a rifle and a good Colt pistol. By sunrise, we were riding out of town.

At noon, we arrived at the Van Patten ranch. It was a good-sized ranch nestled in the picturesque Hill Country just north of New Braunfels on the north bank of the Guadalupe River.

We rode up to the large yet modest house. Jack walked out of the house and onto the porch. He looked about the same and smiled as we approached. His hair was an inch or two longer and he was clean-shaven, which was rare.

"Thought you backed down," Jack said. "I was expecting you three days ago."

"We had to wait on Konrad's lazy ass," Kyle said.

Jack nodded. "How are you, Konrad? It's been a long time."

"It has, and I'm well. How are you?"

"Good, just dandy. Tie off your horses and come around back. We're just sitting down for lunch."

We sat at a long, crudely-crafted dining table outside under the shade of an overhang that extended about thirty feet out from the house. Fred Van Patten, the owner of the ranch and patriarch of the family, sat at one end of the long table, while his wife Helen sat at the other end of the table. They had two young children, a boy and a girl, who were very pleasant and entertaining. The rest of the table was filled with ranch hands like Jack. There were eight men employed at the Van Patten ranch, and they were all quite lively at lunch and very friendly.

Mrs. Van Patten had made a glorious traditional German meal, which consisted of thick pork-based sausages, Spatzle noodles, and dumplings, along with onions, cabbage, and tomatoes. It seemed as if we had come on the right day.

"So, you boys are headed off to California to pan for gold, huh?" Mr. Van Patten asked. He was a tall, big-boned man, with sharp, blue eyes and fine, blond hair.

"We are indeed," Mason replied.

"You think you'll strike it rich?" Mr. Van Patten's son, Jeremy, asked. He was only twelve years old, and it was obvious that he was going to grow up to look just like his father.

"We might," Mason speculated. "But we ain't too worried about the gold, you see. It's about the journey — the adventure. When you're traveling through the Rocky Mountains, looking up at the peaks towering over you like gods, or when you're riding across the painted sands of the desert where you'll see colors you didn't know existed — that's worth more than gold."

"Wow!" Jeremy said with his eyes wide open.

There was a brief silence as everyone imagined what Mason had described.

"Well, I'll take your gold then," one of the ranch hands finally said. Everyone laughed.

That night, we sat around a big fire down by the river. Two of the ranch hands played their fiddles, and one played the banjo, while everyone danced and sang around the fire. Mason accompanied the other instruments with an empty jug by blowing into the top.

As the night progressed, the Van Patten family went back to the house to go to bed. We stayed out at the fire with the ranch hands for a while longer. One by one, the men began to retire to the bunkhouse until it was just Jack, Mason, and me. We smoked cigars as we stared at the dying flames of the fire. Mason only smoked half of his cigar before tossing it into the fire and going to bed. Jack and I stayed and talked by the fire for a while longer.

"How did you manage to get this job?" I asked.

"My first mission with the Rangers was going after a few rustlers who had stolen a bunch of Fred's horses. We caught the rustlers and returned the horses. Fred was grateful, of course, and said if we ever needed work that we could come to his ranch. I took him up on the offer a year later and absolutely loved it. Now, anytime I need a break from the Rangers, I just come work for him."

"Cowboying is good work then?"

"It's the best kind of work. Perfect for men like you and me. I love being a cowboy. How about you? Have you been in New Orleans this whole time?"

"Most of it. I went to Havana, Cuba for a while."

"How was that?"

"It was great. It's a beautiful city."

"Did you go by yourself?"

"No, I went with Anastasia."

"Anastasia?"

"Have I not told you about her?"

"No, who is she?"

"She's the woman I've been living with for the last year."

"Really? You in love with her?"

436

"Completely."

"But you're not married?"

"No."

"And she's not pressuring you to marry her?"

"No."

"And she let you leave to pan for gold in California?"

"I wouldn't say… 'let'."

Jack smiled and shook his head. "She a whore?"

"Jesus, Jack, no!"

"Well, she sounds too good to be true. Either she's a whore, or she's the perfect woman."

"She's the perfect woman. No question about that."

"Well, good for you. I could never find a woman who understood my need to go from place to place. God, I haven't had a steady woman in years."

"Do you miss having a woman?"

"Sometimes, sure. Love is a wonderful thing. But I'm in love with adventure. I'm in love with the mountains and the plains and the deserts. The frontier is my lover."

Jack and I talked until the fire had died down to glowing embers, and then we went to bed.

We woke up a couple of hours before dawn. Helen made us a hearty breakfast, which we made sure to cherish, for it would be awhile before we ate that well again. We then saddled our horses and thanked the Van Patten's for their generosity.

Darkness still blanketed the sky thoroughly by the time we began riding northwest. To the east, the sun showed no sign of rising, not for a while anyway. The moon and the stars lit our way, as we began our long journey westward to California.

VII

ON THE MORNING OF our seventh day of travel, I awoke to the ringing of the alarm on the gold pocket watch my father had given me. It was three-thirty in the morning.

We awoke at three-thirty every morning in order to eat breakfast, drink coffee, saddle the horses, and leave camp by four-thirty. We needed to move quickly in order to make it through the mountains before the weather turned unfavorable in the early fall. We had left on the fourteenth of July, and by Jack's estimate, it would take us just under two weeks to get to the mountains and about a month to get through them. If all went according to plan, we would be riding out of the Rockies at the beginning of September.

We were making good time. We were a week into our journey and had already entered the Caprock Escarpment, a beautiful stretch of land between the High Plains and the Llano Estacado.

For breakfast, we ate broiled deer meat and hard biscuits, all washed down with coffee. Once the coffee took effect and removed the cobwebs of sleep, we saddled our horses and continued northwest toward the Rockies.

We rode for three hours through the peaceful, dim light of dawn before the sun finally claimed the sky and illuminated the beauty of the Palo Duro Canyon. Mesquite and juniper trees were scattered over the colorful rock and sand of the canyon, bringing out the different shades of red, brown, and yellow. The sky was as blue as I had ever seen and was full of beautiful, white clouds, thick and distended.

In the late afternoon, the beautiful, white clouds turned grey and connected to form a large blanket over the sky. Thunder rolled in the heavens, and rain soon followed. We quickly rode to the highest ground, for flashfloods in the canyon were a great possibility. In the distance lightning flashed, but it never struck near us. We rode through the rain, and after about an hour it stopped. The grey clouds lingered above us, and to the west a rainbow formed.

"The Norse believe that the rainbow is the bridge between Heaven and Earth and that only the gods and those who are killed in battle can use it," Jack explained.

"The Greeks say that it's Iris delivering messages to the gods," Mason added.

"No, no, no!" Kyle disagreed. "It's where the leprechaun keeps his pot of gold!"

We rode for a couple more hours before we stopped and set up camp. Our clothes were soaked, so we hung them up to dry and sat naked around the campfire while we ate dinner. It would have been a humorous sight for someone passing by to behold.

In the morning, my alarm rang at three-thirty as usual. After our morning activities, we left camp and rode slowly through the dark. Soon, the sun rose and shot its glorious rays over the canyon, revealing one of the most beautiful spectacles I had ever witnessed. The depths of the canyon below us was filled with a thick, resting fog. It was eerie and mystical. As we rode along, it felt as if we were riding on top of the world through the heavens. It was completely surreal and beautiful, like nothing I had ever experienced, even in my dreams. However, our ride through the heavens was short-lived. The fog soon dispersed, and we rode on the Earth once again.

* * *

Soon, we were crossing the Canadian River, and by day ten we were well into the Great Plains. I had seen the Great Plains before, but not the southern end. Riding across the wide expanse of tan grasses and gentle hills, with only blue skies upon the horizon, was calming, yet somehow unsettling. Maybe it was the enormous, eccentric white clouds bellowing loudly in their size, as they sat like gods perched in the blue heavens to watch the immortals below.

We encountered two herds of buffalo, which we watched from afar as they grazed. We did not hunt them. Even a small buffalo would have provided too much meat for us. Besides — where there were buffalo, there were Indians, who we wished to avoid.

On one particular day, we rode down into a valley to refill our canteens in the stream. We climbed off our horses to let them drink, while we walked out into the water and refreshed. We almost didn't even notice the drove of wild horses standing in the water downstream. They did not look at us or run away. They ignored us and drank, knowing that we were no threat. They were a magnificent sight and were beautiful in their wild freedom, a freedom, which seemed to ooze from their glistening bodies. They were some of the most beautiful creatures I had ever seen.

Later that day, we watched them run across the plains. Their glistening coats, their bulging muscles, their flowing manes, and their elegant stride struck my heart in the most delicate way and brought tears to my eyes. I watched them run free, and I felt my heart pounding like their hooves on the high plains. I wanted to join them — to run free with the mustangs, and so did Renegado. He knew he belonged with them, and I had to hold him back. The herd ran westward, into the late afternoon sun, and turned into a silhouette before disappearing on the horizon.

Our ride westward was serene and relaxing, despite the fact that we were traveling for about fifteen hours out of every day. Our companions between our knees took on the burden of travel. However, I knew that Renegado was enjoying the journey as much as I.

The landscape transformed from graceful, gentle plains to a more rugged plain with sparser grass, harder ground, and scattered rock formations. In the distance, slicing across the sky like a purple, serrated blade, stood the Rocky Mountains. I was as close as I had ever been to them, and we were quickly moving closer.

That evening, we stopped about an hour before sunset and set up camp. Javi cooked a delicious deer and rabbit stew, which we ate as we watched the sun fall behind the peaks of the Rockies.

After some light conversation, I lay down on my buffalo robe and pulled my Mexican blanket over me. I set the alarm on my watch for three-thirty as usual, and using my saddle as a pillow, I stared up at the stars for a while. I thought about Anastasia as I lay there and realized that this journey to California would not be my last journey. It would not cure my desire for adventure. When it was over and I returned to New Orleans, I would not be able to settle down with Anastasia and give her the love and attention she deserved, for I would already be planning my next journey. I realized that I needed travel and adventure, not to just *feel* alive, but to *be* alive. I needed nature. I needed the wild. I needed the unknown. I needed these things in order to be the being I was intended to be. In the cities, in society, I was a product of my environment. The person I was in regular society was determined by the people around me, by my fellow prisoners and by the lawmen in the government. In nature, I was free. When I was traveling, I was free. I belonged to nothing. I was not an American. I was not an Oxford graduate. I was not an aristocrat. I was not a cook, or a physicist, or a philosopher, or a teacher, or a scholar, or a Texas Ranger, or a soldier, or a linguist, or an elitist, or a Democratic-Republican, a Whig, a Federalist, or any other label that was applied to me so that society could have me properly identified. In nature, I just *was*. I was simply "Man". I was pure, and that was beautiful to me.

My eyes grew heavy. I rolled over onto my side and watched the flames of the fire slowly die down. Finally, I fell asleep.

I awoke from a light sleep more abruptly than I had ever awakened before. I was not sure what the sound was that woke me. Then I heard the sound again. It was a scream. I looked across the glowing embers of the fire, and I could see a nearly naked, painted figure standing over Joe. As my eyes adjusted to the scene, I could see that the figure was an Indian and that he was scalping Joe.

I fumbled around for my pistol. I heard a gunshot. I looked up to see Jack firing his pistol at the dozens of Indians storming our camp, yelling their horrific battle cries as they attacked. Mason got to his feet and began to fire at the Indians. I finally grabbed my pistol and sprang to my feet. Just as I began to take aim, I was tackled to the ground from behind. I squirmed and fought as five more bodies piled on top of me and held me down. My pistol was pried from my fingers. I saw Jack and Mason fall to the ground. The Indians quickly jumped on top of them as they had done me.

I fought and tried to break free, but I could barely move. There were too many of them. I could feel them binding my feet with stout thongs of buffalo hide. My hands quickly followed.

"Don't let them take you alive, Kyle!" I heard Mason yell.

I could not see Kyle, or anything for that matter. My vision was blocked by the painted bodies holding me down. I heard a gunshot, and then, "Come on, you bastards!" It sounded like Kyle's voice. Suddenly, I felt a profound impact on the side of my head. My eyes immediately went blurry, and I felt my consciousness leaving me as if I was falling asleep. I tried to keep my eyes open, but it was beyond my control, and my world went black.

When I awoke from my unconscious state, I felt as if no time had elapsed, but I knew it had, and probably a significant amount. It was still dark, and the moon did not suggest that it would be giving way to the sun anytime soon. I could not have been unconscious for too long. However, I was now securely tied to the back of a horse and was being led by one of the Indians. I could see nothing past the Indian who led me, and I could just barely make out the outlines of the figures riding behind me, but nobody was riding next to me. I had no idea what had been the fate of my friends, and my heart raced as I imagined the fate that awaited me. I had heard many stories about the rituals of the Comanche, which is who I assumed these Indians were, for we had been traveling through Comancheria, the land of the Comanche. The stories I had heard were horrific, morbid, and gruesome. I feared the worst. I imagined that a slow death of unbearable pain awaited me, either that or a miracle.

I bounced uncomfortably on my abdomen as the horse to which I was tied was led through the darkness. After about three hours of traveling, I could see the outlines of teepees in the distance. One of the Indians galloped past me and the Indian who was leading me and rode into the village.

When we finally rode into the center of the village, a large crowd awaited us. I was taken off the back of my horse and forced to stand before the crowd. Mason, Kyle, and Jack were taken off their horses and placed next to me. I was quite relieved to see them. I could see that Kyle and Mason were just as scared as I, but Jack's face was made of stone, a defiant stone at that.

"Where are the others?" I asked, referring to Joe, Javi, and Ned. Mason just shook his head and did not look at me.

The Indians quickly approached us and began to violently strip off our clothes. Once we were all naked, we were then clothed in the Comanche fashion, which consisted of buckskin leggings and a buckskin shirt fringed at the bottom and at the cuffs. They did not give us moccasins. I imagined it was to make it more difficult for us to run.

Once we were dressed in the buckskins, the Indians began looking through our clothes for plunder. The Indian searching my clothes came upon my gold pocket watch. He looked it over curiously. He managed to get it open and held it to his ear. Suddenly, the alarm on the watch went off. It must have been three-thirty. The Indian quickly held the watch as far away from his body as he could, staring at it in fear and awe. The rest of the Indians stepped closer to the watch but kept their distance. They talked quickly to one another. Mason looked at me in confusion. I shrugged and shook my head.

The Indian holding the watch pointed at me. After a minute the alarm ceased, and the Indians stepped closer to observe the watch. It seemed that the Indian holding my watch was explaining to the chief that it belonged to me, for he kept pointing at the watch and at me while talking quickly. The chief nodded, said something to one Indian, and pointed at me. The Indian quickly rushed over to me and untied my hands. I was then handed the watch. Holding the watch gently in my hands, I looked at all of the Indians as they gestured for me to make the alarm go off again. I had just been given a great opportunity.

I closed my eyes and began to move my lips as if I was saying a silent prayer. Slowly, I began to raise the watch toward the sky as I wound it to set the alarm. I opened my eyes for a moment and saw that the Indians were watching me in awe and wonder.

With the alarm set, I continued to hold the watch to the sky as I recited silent gibberish. After about a minute, the alarm went off again, and the Indians reacted with bewilderment, fear, and excitement. I was asked to perform this task twice more before the chief took the watch from me, placed it in a deerskin pouch, and tucked it away in his bosom. He gestured to me, and the young warrior who had discovered the watch along with another Indian grabbed me by the arms and began to lead me away. I looked back at Mason, Kyle, and Jack. They were soon approached by Indians and led away as well.

I was taken inside one of the teepees. Four stakes were driven into the ground, to which I was securely tied in a way that spread my limbs as far apart as possible in the manner of Leonardo Da Vinci's *Vitruvian Man*. It was most uncomfortable. The two Indians left me alone in the teepee. I tried to free myself by pulling the rope from the stake. When that did not work, I tried to jerk the stakes out of the earth, but they were driven firmly and deeply into the hard ground. When I finally gave up, my wrists and ankles were bleeding. It was no use. The Comanche were thorough. There would be no escape for me. I was a prisoner. All I could do was wait for death and imagine what it would be like. That was torture in itself.

VIII

For two weeks, I was confined to the teepee. For two weeks, all I saw were wooden poles wrapped in buffalo skins. For two weeks, my only view of the outside world was through the small smoke hole at the top of the teepee or during the brief moment when the flap was pulled back and my captors would enter to give me food and water.

The only times I was untied from the stakes was to eat, and, from time to time, to perform my "watch trick". I was not even untied to relieve my bowels. I was forced to relieve them where I lay. They poured water on me every now and again to clean me, but it helped very little. It was a humiliating and grotesque experience.

After two weeks, just as my mind was beginning to lose a sane grasp on the situation, I was untied, stripped naked, and dragged out of the teepee. The light of the sun burned my eyes and sent a jolt through my brain. I squinted as my eyes slowly became used to the light of day.

When my eyes finally adjusted, I saw the village for the first time. It was not as large a village as I had expected. There were about fifty teepees, and it seemed as if the settlement was less than temporary.

I was brought to the capacious square in the center of the village. To my horror, I saw Mason and Kyle, naked as I was, bound and hung to large, thick posts stuck in the ground, three feet apart. Their hands were tied above them, and their feet were tied to the post just above the ground. Across from Mason and Kyle was Jack, who was bound to a post in the same fashion. I had not seen any of them since the night we were brought to the village.

My Indian escorts led me into the square to the post next to

Jack, facing Mason and Kyle fifteen yards away. My hands were pulled high above my head and stretched until my feet were off the ground, and then my hands and feet were tied to the post. It was extremely painful. Any movement to ease the pain only made it worse. I looked across the way at Mason and Kyle. Their faces were understandably distraught. Kyle was crying, and Mason was breathing heavily and quickly. I looked over at Jack whose eyes were closed. His head was back against the post, tilted up toward the sky. His face was calm.

"Jack!" I said in a harsh whisper. "What the hell is going on?"

"I don't know, Konrad. Just keep your mouth shut and don't fight it. There's nothing we can do."

"Nothing we can do about what? What are they going to do to us?"

Jack shook his head and did not answer the question. The people of the village had gathered in the square and were seated east of us. West of us, the chief and his war party of about fifty warriors approached the square slowly, shuffling their feet and taking small steps, their bodies jerking as strangely as the sounds coming out of their mouths. It was a dance of some sort. They were obviously performing some kind of ritual. As they entered the square, I saw that each warrior was carrying a flint spearhead and a tomahawk. They danced in a circle around us.

"Let us go, goddamn it! Please! Let us go!" Mason yelled. His pleas were ignored as the war party continued to dance around us.

"What the hell are they going to do to us, Jack?" I asked quietly.

"I don't know, Konrad. Be quiet and close your eyes. We can't fight it. Close your eyes and go somewhere else. No matter what happens, don't open your eyes and don't scream. Go to Anastasia. Lay in her arms. Forget where you are right now. Go somewhere else."

"What are you talking about?"

Jack kept his eyes closed. He was somewhere else. I closed my eyes and tried to go elsewhere. I tried to go to Anastasia, but I could not. I had to know what was happening here. I watched as the Indians continued to circle us. They did not even look at us.

All of a sudden, one of the warriors jumped out of line and charged at Kyle with his tomahawk raised. Kyle screamed in fear and closed his eyes. The warrior brought the tomahawk down over Kyle's head and stopped just an inch from his skull. He pulled the tomahawk away and went back in line with the rest of the warriors. Kyle slowly opened his eyes, trembling in fear as he cried. He began to urinate. I had never seen a man so scared. I could not blame him. I felt the way he looked. I was just too overwhelmed to convey my emotions.

The warriors continued to break out of line randomly and charge at us with their tomahawks raised, only to pull back at the last second. That was their idea of torture, making us wonder when the real strike would come.

The two youngest warriors broke out of line, one charging at Mason and the other charging at Kyle. They grabbed them by the hair, swiftly scalped them, and then quickly fell back into line.

Mason and Kyle screamed out in agony as blood poured over their faces and dripped from their beards onto their chests. I turned away in disgust and sadness for my dear friends. I awaited my turn. The war party passed by Jack and me, but they left us alone.

The war party went around once more and then stopped to let out a loud war yelp. They then continued their march. As they passed Mason and Kyle, each warrior scraped his flint spearhead across their skin, cutting just deep enough to draw blood and uncomfortable pain. The entire war party passed them, each warrior cutting them just a little bit. Mason and Kyle screamed hysterically. When the war party finally moved beyond them, their bodies looked hellish, almost completely covered in blood.

The war party came to Jack and me and passed us without doing us any harm. I did not understand why, but I was certain that my torturous, slow death was soon to come. The warriors continued on their path and went back around toward Mason and Kyle. Once again, each warrior cut their flesh with his spearhead and left Jack and me unmolested. This pattern continued for what seemed like an eternity. They circled us more times than I could count.

Kyle eventually lost the strength to scream. He just cried and groaned as the warriors cut him over and over. Mason continued to plead with the warriors to leave them alone and show them mercy. His cries were ignored.

When the warriors grew tired, they stopped in the center of the square and sat down to rest. Some lit a pipe and passed it around, while others shouted and laughed at Mason and Kyle, who had not stopped crying in pain. Their flesh was torn and mangled, and in some places it was just dangling from their bodies. Their torsos were completely covered in blood. It was the most horrific sight I had ever seen. While Jack kept his eyes closed and blocked everything out, I could not take my eyes off my dear, suffering friends.

"Please, end it! Show mercy, for Christ sake! Please! Just kill us already!" Mason yelled with a trembling voice. "Lord, put me out of my misery!"

The war party stood up, got back in line, and began marching around us once again. They continued to cut and mutilate Mason and Kyle. They had to be cutting muscle at this point, for there was no skin left on their bodies. Jack and I were left alone. I could bear it no more. Kyle had grown too weak to cry and looked to have passed out. In his semi-unconscious state, he began to convulse and then finally vomited. Mason yelled at the Indians and screamed to God, begging for mercy.

I closed my eyes and lowered my head. I tried to go elsewhere in my mind. I saw my apartment in New Orleans. I walked through it toward the bedroom. Anastasia was lying in bed with an inviting smile. She gestured for me to join her. Mason's screams interrupted my dream, and I almost lost my vision. I squinted and brought it back. I walked toward the bed. Anastasia held her hand out to me. I reached for it. Our fingers were almost touching.

Suddenly, my head was grabbed by a pair of strong hands. Another pair of hands drove its fingers into my eye sockets and forced my eyes open. They were doing the same to Jack. They were forcing us watch the torture of our friends. That was *our* torture. Jack's mind had been somewhere else for the duration of the ritual, and for the first time, he was seeing what was happening to his beloved friends. The horror was unbearable for him, and he began to fight and scream and yell obscenities at the warriors.

"Make them stop, Jack!" Mason yelled.

"It's almost over, Mason! Be strong! It's almost over!" Jack yelled to Mason.

"I don't want to die now, Jack! I don't want to die!" Mason confessed.

Jack's eyes filled with tears. The tears streamed down his face and onto the fingers of the Indian who was forcing his eyes open.

"I'm sorry," Jack barely managed.

The marching suddenly ceased, and the warriors broke into a war dance in front of Mason and Kyle. Kyle's eyes were almost completely drained of life. While barely retaining consciousness, his mouth was agape as he struggled for breath. Mason cried in fear and pain. At this point, however, I think it was mostly fear.

Two of the warriors stepped forward out of the war dance and approached Mason and Kyle. They raised their tomahawks and let out an ugly war cry. They swiftly brought their tomahawks down into the skulls of Mason and Kyle and ended their suffering. I was both relieved and saddened. The Indians then untied Mason and Kyle and carelessly tossed their lifeless bodies aside.

Jack and I waited for the same gruesome death as the warriors marched over to us, but to our surprise we were untied and escorted away from the square in opposite directions. It seemed that they were taking me back to my tent. As the warriors escorted me away from the square, I looked back to take one last look at my friends. The dogs were already licking the blood off their bodies.

IX

I WAS CONFINED TO my teepee for a week after Mason and Kyle were so brutally slaughtered, and then the women of the tribe began to tear down the village. Their teepees were deconstructed and packed onto the backs of mules and horses. It took only half a day to pack up the village. The women had done all the work, while the lazy men sat around, ate, and smoked their pipes.

By early afternoon, the tribe of about two hundred men, women, and children began to move northwest, leaving behind no evidence that they had ever been there. My hands were bound by a long rope, the other end of which was tied around the neck of a big, black horse ridden by one of the warriors. As I was pulled along behind the big, black horse, I looked around for Jack. I did not see him. I had not seen Jack since the day Mason and Kyle were killed. I looked around for Renegado as well, but I did not see him either. I felt alone and scared. Why were they keeping me alive? Why had they spared Jack and I on that awful day? Where were they taking me? Wherever we were going, I was sure that my death awaited me there.

* * *

For a week we moved slowly northward along the foothills of the Rocky Mountains. We probably traveled no more than fifteen miles each day, so on the seventh day, I guessed we had traveled about one hundred miles.

At about noon on the seventh day, Jack was brought over by his escort to walk next to me. He was bound in the same way as I, being led behind a horse. I was glad to see that he was still alive.

"Where have they been keeping you?" I asked him.

"In a teepee, tied to the ground," Jack said.

"Me, too," I said. "Do you have any idea what's going on?"

"They're moving the village, following the buffalo."

My warrior escort turned around on his horse and yelled something brief in Comanche.

"What do you think they're going to do with us?" I asked.

My warrior escort turned around and yelled, angrier this time.

"I don't think they want us to talk," Jack said.

"I don't give a damn what they want," I said defiantly.

My escort turned around and said something to the man behind me. I turned around to see who he was talking to and was promptly met by a hard fist landing a powerful blow upon my cheek. I fell to my knees but quickly got back to my feet as the horse continued to drag me. I moved my jaw around and winced in pain. I shook my head. I could feel the blood trickling down from the open gash where the Indian's knuckles had landed squarely on my sharp cheekbone. I got the message.

Shortly after my cheek began to swell, I gazed upon an extraordinary sight. We had arrived at another Comanche village. However, this village looked to be four times the size of the last one. The teepees stretched on for as far as I could see. I guessed that the entire village took up a space of about seven acres. The village was nestled snuggly in a beautiful valley surrounded by towering mountains. It was like a fortress.

We approached from the east, and to the north I could see what looked to be a large river valley. I listened carefully and could just barely hear the sound of rushing water.

"What river is that?" I whispered to Jack.

Jack looked to the north and thought carefully.

"I think it's the Arkansas."

Now that we had an idea of where we were, we could plan an escape. Bent's Fort couldn't have been more than one hundred miles to the east. If we could somehow sneak away and steal a couple of horses, we could make it to Bent's Fort in a day or two.

From the look on Jack's face, I could see that he was thinking the same thing.

The inhabitants of the village gathered to welcome their fellow tribesmen. There had to be close to a thousand people living in the village. As we were dragged into the village, the people stepped aside and formed a path. They stared at Jack and me intensely. Some stared with curiosity and some with hatred. Some of the children laughed at us.

We were taken to the center of the village, where we came to a square of about one acre in size. In the center of the square was a large lodge, which looked to be the place where meetings were held. We stopped before the lodge and waited. I observed the village carefully. It was structured much like any town. All of the tents were set up in blocks, and the blocks were divided by roads or pathways. The largest tents were near the square, and they got smaller the further back they were.

Suddenly, a man who I instantly assumed was the chief, given his manner of dress and his manner in general, stepped out of the lodge with six elders. The chief of the village I had come from walked over to the other chief and paid his respects to the man who was obviously his superior. I listened carefully to them speak. I gathered that the name of the war chief of the village I had come from was Shabbakasha, and the civil chief of the large village was Tabbaquena.

As they spoke, Shabbakasha pointed to me numerous times. Tabbaquena nodded and gestured for a demonstration. Shabbakasha said a few words to my warrior escort, who jumped off his horse and quickly untied me. He pushed me to the center of the square and presented me to the great chief. Shabbakasha handed me my watch and gestured to the sky. The people of the village gathered around and watched me closely. I looked at their curious faces. I nodded to the chief and closed my eyes. I began my prayer of gibberish and slowly raised the watch to the sky as I wound up the hands to set the alarm. A minute later, the alarm rang. Everyone jumped back in fear and awe. I had to try hard to hold back my laughter.

The alarm sounded for a minute and then ceased. Tabbaquena stepped toward me and said something, which I could not understand. I pointed to myself, to my watch, and then to the heavens, indicating that I used the watch to communicate with their gods or spirits — or whatever it was they worshipped.

Tabbaquena and Shabbakasha took the watch back from me and spoke briefly. Then they ordered two warriors to take me away. I looked back at Jack, who nodded simply and looked away. The two warriors took me into one of the larger tents near the square. My ankles were bound, and my hands were bound in front of me, which was nice. They left me alone in the tent, free to roll around as much as I wanted. It may sound funny, but after being tied to stakes in the ground with my limbs spread apart and unable to move in any way, rolling around with bound feet and hands was a wonderful luxury.

After a week in the tent, I began to grow impatient. They had been treating me better by allowing me to go outside of the tent to relieve my bowels, and they fed me just enough to keep me alive, but the waiting and the not knowing was beginning to drive me insane. I was filled with anger. Bound in a dark tent all day, all I could think about was what these Indians had done to my dear friends, Mason and Kyle. My imagination ran wild with ideas of what fate awaited me. I began to plot my escape, revenge, or suicide. Escape was practically impossible, and I never had an opportunity for revenge or suicide, so I sat quietly, alone in my tent with nothing but my thoughts to comfort me. However, my thoughts were beginning to make me uncomfortable.

One night, I finally reached my breaking point and decided to try and escape. My plan was good — I thought. I would scoot on my belly, my feet and hands bound, quietly through the village. I would scoot all the way to the Arkansas River, which was not far, and I would go into the water. I would float down the river all the way to Bent's Fort. Either that or I would drown. I welcomed either possibility at this point.

In the middle of the night, when the village was quiet and everyone was asleep, I rolled onto my belly and scooted to the edge of the teepee. With my bound hands, I lifted the flap and looked around. I saw no one. I scooted out of the tent, using my knees to push and my elbows to pull. I did this as quietly as possible, moving very slowly through the village. I moved steadily along. I had gotten maybe a quarter of a mile before one of the filthy, ugly Indian dogs began barking incessantly as he ran toward me. I rolled onto my back as the dog charged at me. I raised my legs and kicked at him as he jumped on me. I hammered my bound hands down onto his nose and head, but he continued to attack me. Eventually, one of the Comanche warriors ran out of his tent and pulled the dog off of me. Another warrior came over to me and stomped on that tender spot between my chest and abdomen. I rolled onto my side, coughing for air. The two warriors dragged me back to my tent and tied me to one of the poles. No more rolling around for me.

* * *

Over the next month, I was asked on a few occasions to perform my "watch trick", which I refused to do. I'd had enough. I was tired of awaiting my fate. I was ready for them to end it. I tried to provoke them from day to day by yelling obscenities at them and other nonsense, which they could not understand. They just laughed at me.

I refused to eat, hoping I could starve myself to death, but eventually they just force-fed me, which was much more successful than I would have imagined. Why were they keeping me alive? I did not understand what was happening or why I was there. The questions were driving me mad.

Finally, after refusing to do my "watch trick" every time I was asked, two warriors came to my tent, untied me, and escorted me to the square. Tabbaquena came out of the lodge with the elders. He was holding my watch and held it out to me. I shook my head and began to weep. I could hold it back no longer. I dropped to my knees at Tabbaquena's feet.

"What do you want from me?" I asked. "What? I have nothing to give you! Why have you kept me alive? What do you want? Tell me or kill me!" They looked at me in confusion. They had no idea what I was saying. I fell forward in desperation with my face in the dirt, grasping the back of my head. "Please, let me go! Just let me go!" I rose to my knees and looked up into Tabbaquena's eyes. "I'm in love with a woman. Do you understand love? I love her, and I never should have left her. I never should have left. Please, let me go back to her. I promised her I would return. You have to let me go. Please, let me go back to her. I never should have left her. Let me go back, please!"

Tabbaquena looked at me in confusion and held out the watch once again. I shook my head in frustration and began to cry even harder. It was no use. It was hopeless. Tabbaquena gestured for my escorts to take me away. They grabbed my arms and lifted me, but I would not stand on my feet. As they dragged me away from the square, I cried and begged for them to let me go, but my cries were ignored.

X

I WASN'T SURE HOW long it had been since my emotional scene in the square, but one random day, to my surprise, Jack was brought into my tent. I had not seen him since we had arrived at the village of Tabbaquena. His escorts sat him down across from me and left us alone.

"What is going on?" I asked. "Why have they brought you here?"

"I believe Shabbakasha and his tribe are leaving again, and I am to go with them," Jack said.

"And I will go with you?"

Jack shook his head. "I believe they mean to keep you here. That is why they have allowed me to come to your tent. They're giving us a chance to say goodbye."

"Why would they take you and leave me?" I asked.

"I don't know."

"What do they plan to do with us, Jack?"

"I don't know, Konrad. I just don't know. But I believe your chances are better than mine."

"What do you mean? We must escape together before you leave! Now!"

"Be quiet and listen carefully to me, Konrad. You have to forget about me. There is no doubt in my mind that I will die in the same way Mason and Kyle were killed. It's only a matter of time. I may be able to escape, but the chances of that are almost completely impossible. There is a chance for you, Konrad. That watch, for some reason, has hypnotized these people. They believe it holds a sacred spirit and that only you can communicate with that spirit. If you act with great intelligence, patience, and prudence, then you can use that watch to your advantage and survive long enough to escape."

"But, Jack, I—"

"Just listen to me, Konrad. I don't have much time. If you want to live, do exactly what I tell you. Become one of them. You start by obeying their every command, by being completely submissive. It will be degrading, but you must do this. After a while, you will earn their trust. They will be more lenient with you, but not too lenient, not lenient enough for you to escape, but lenient enough for you to study them. You're a linguist. You can pick up languages fairly easily with enough dedication. Learn their language. Learn it fluently. Speak to them in their tongue. Forget your mother tongue. Study their culture carefully and adopt it as your own. Adopt their customs and their religion. Become completely enveloped in their way of life. Make them believe that you would rather be with them than with your own people. Then they will believe that you are one of their own. And that is when you will escape."

"That could take years," I pointed out.

"You must be patient. If you want to live, that is what you must do. Do you understand me?"

"Yes, I do. But you must do the same."

"I will if I can," Jack said with a look of hopelessness in his eyes. He had already accepted his death. "We've had some great adventures, haven't we, Konrad?"

"We have."

"I don't regret this one. I don't regret any of them. I've traveled all over this continent. We just got unlucky this time around. I suppose it was bound to happen. Everyone's luck runs out at some point. Men like us, the wanderers, the travelers, we were never meant to live to be old men. We go out and take a life that doesn't belong to us. We broke all the rules of society, the rules of man. We challenged man and God; therefore, we're doomed. But we knew that when we chose this life. And we did *choose* it. Sometimes, we like to say that it chose us, but it didn't. We chose to be the way we are. We chose to see the world the way we do.

We chose to break the hearts of everyone who ever loved us. And now it's time for me to pay for it. I guess I just thought I'd get to see a lot more of the world first."

Jack sighed and smiled at me. I had never seen a sadder pair of eyes. The warriors came into the tent and grabbed Jack.

"Wait! Just a little longer!" I yelled.

"Do what I said, Konrad," Jack instructed, as they pulled him out of the tent. "When you get out of here, go to St. Louis. There's a woman there named Josephine Bissette. Find her and tell her my fate. Tell her I love her. Tell her I've always loved her."

"Jack—"

Jack just smiled and shook his head. "Goodbye, my friend," he said. And then he was gone.

I leaned back against the pole to which I was tied and sighed sadly. "Goodbye, Jack," I said quietly to myself. "Goodbye, my friend."

XI

I DID EXACTLY AS Jack had told me to do. For the next month, I was obedient and cooperative in every way. I performed my "watch trick" every time I was called upon. I was calm and somewhat cheerful, and by the end of the month, I was allowed to spend my days in the square with Tabbaquena.

I treated Tabbaquena like he was my highly respected professor and I was his devoted pupil. I spent all of my time with him, his wives, and the elders. I was not permitted to leave the square, and there were eyes upon me at all times, but the square was large and I was grateful — and I was making progress.

I obeyed every command and carried out every chore I was given. I went to the river to fill Tabbaquena's buffalo horn with water throughout the day, and I cooked for him at every opportunity. I spread his mattress, cleaned his tent, and lit his pipe. It was demeaning, but the thought of escaping and returning to Anastasia got me through each day.

While I carried out my chores and waited on the chief hand and foot, I studied the tribe's customs and language, and I made it obvious. I asked many questions using body language, and we communicated quite well. I learned that Tabbaquena's name meant Sun Eagle, and Shabbakasha meant Roving Wolf. However, learning their language was a difficult process, more difficult than any other language I had learned. I was not receiving proper lessons but was deciphering a code by simply listening carefully and observing. I watched their body language, their lips, and their reactions. I progressed slowly, learning just a couple of new words each day.

The Indians were quite impressed by my desire to learn their culture and did not seem at all skeptical of my intentions. It seemed as if they were beginning to like me. By spring, I was allowed to leave the square and roam the village. The warriors kept a close watch on me. It had taken a season to acquire, but I seemed to have gained a little of their trust. However, I knew it was not enough. I had to have their complete trust, and I had to make them believe, without a doubt, that I was one of them. I was not sure how long it would take, but I hoped I could remain patient.

*   *   *

By the end of the summer, which marked a year of being a captive amongst the Comanche, I had essentially assumed the role of the female Indian. I performed all of the duties that the females of the tribe performed, and I was not invited to participate on the hunts, which was the only thing the men of the tribe did. If the men were not such lazy creatures and did half the work the women did, the Comanche village would be a wonderful society. However, the behavior of the men was quite pathetic. If the task was not hunting or fighting, they took no interest in it. They were even too lazy to deal with their own kills. If they killed an animal on a hunt, they would leave it and return to the village. They would then tell a squaw where their kill lay, and she would ride out to tend to it alone. But the women seemed happy to perform all their duties and did not seem to think it unfair.

As time went on, I became a friend of the Comanche. They treated me as one of their own and not as a prisoner. They pierced my ears and hung brass loop earrings from them. They also tattooed my chest and arms with signs I did not understand.

I played games with the young warriors, some of which were quite physical, and I received a good beating. Even though I made a point of making myself seem physically inadequate, harmless, and not aggressive in the slightest, I do not think I would have been a match for these young warriors, for they were some of the most tremendous athletes I had ever seen. Their agility, strength, and speed were somewhere between that of a man and a lion.

I was also free to walk around the village without a warrior escort following close behind. I was free to go down to the river alone to fetch water for myself and for Tabbaquena. There were very few points of downtime when I could really explore the village and the area surrounding it, but each day I ventured further and further away from the square and took leisurely walks during which I would carefully observe everything going on around me. I found the corral where they kept the horses and was relieved to see that Renegado was among them. The Comanche loved to eat horseflesh, and I had feared the worst for Renegado.

* * *

On a cold day shortly after the first snowfall of winter, I strolled through the outskirts of the village where people lived in smaller tents. I held my buffalo robe closed with one hand, as I wiped away the snow on my beard. I walked down a narrow path between two blocks of teepees I had not been past before. The women were outside, tending to their usual duties. They paid little attention to me.

As I came to the end of the village, I saw a woman who immediately grabbed my attention. Her face was painted, and she wore a buffalo robe. Her head was wrapped in beaver fur; however, I could see a lock of golden hair hanging from under her hat. I couldn't believe it; she was a White woman. I looked around and saw that she was alone, so I approached her slowly and curiously. Soon, I was close enough to see the White features in her face. She looked up at me cautiously with her beaming, blue eyes.

"Hello," I said in English. She looked at me in confusion for a moment and then went back to dressing a buffalo hide. "I'm Konrad." She looked up at me and smiled and then went back to work. "How are you?" She continued working. "Do you understand me?" No response. "How are you?" I asked in the Comanche language. She looked up at me and smiled.

"I am fine. How are you?" she responded in Comanche.

"I am fine. Do you speak English?" I asked in Comanche. She looked at me in confusion. "Do you speak the 'White tongue'?"

She shook her head. She didn't understand English, yet she was White. I didn't understand.

"What is your name?" I asked, continuing in Comanche.

"Haiwee," she said. It meant 'The Dove'.

"I am Konrad." She chuckled at my strange name. "Are you a captive here?" I asked, still confused by this young girl who was probably no older than sixteen.

"Captive? No!" she said. She seemed offended.

"How long have you been here?" I asked.

"What do you mean?"

A young warrior stepped out of Haiwee's tent and looked at me angrily.

"What are you doing over here?" the warrior asked. "Go tan hides with the women!"

I lowered my head submissively and nodded to the warrior. I took one last look at Haiwee and walked back to the square.

That night, lying next to a warm fire in my teepee, I could not stop thinking about the young, White girl, Haiwee. Who was she? How did she get here? Why could she not speak English? The only explanation I could think of was that she had been captured when she was just a child, maybe before she could even speak. She was more than likely raised as a Comanche and only knew their language and their customs, and she had been living as one of them for so long that she had no recollection of any other life. How many young White girls scattered amongst the numerous Indian tribes were suffering the same fate as Haiwee? Was that the fate that awaited me — life as a Comanche?

I had spent over a year with this tribe and had long ago

abandoned the fear of being put to death at some random, unknown moment. I had realized that they intended to keep me alive. If I tried to escape and was caught, then surely I would be killed in a horrific fashion similar to that of Mason and Kyle, whose images haunted my thoughts in my waking and slumbering hours. If I was going to live, I had only two options — escape or complete submission into the Comanche life forever. I had no intention of doing the latter; therefore, escape was my only option.

I had done everything Jack had said. I had immersed myself completely into the Comanche life and lived as one of them. I had earned their trust and made them believe I preferred the Comanche people over my own. I spoke their language, I knew their customs, and I had become their devoted, respectful friend. I had bided my time. Now, I was ready to make my escape.

XII

I WAITED UNTIL SPRING to make my escape, for tracking me down would be too easy in the snowy winter. For the first three weeks of the season, I ventured down to the river every other day or so and gathered berries, checked the beaver traps, tried to spot bears and other game, and gathered wood. I did this until it seemed natural, until it had become a daily ritual. I did it until it would seem abnormal for me not to do it.

On a warm day in late March, I walked down to the river. As I walked out of the village, I looked back. Nobody seemed to notice that I had left.

When I got down to the banks of the river, I began to gather berries and walk around aimlessly, all the while carefully checking my surroundings and looking back toward the village to see if anybody was watching. Slowly, I made my way downriver. I got further and further away from the village. Nobody was watching. I was doing well.

As soon as the village was out of sight, I dropped the berries and began to sprint as fast as I could downriver. I ran faster than I ever had before. My heart was racing and pumping adrenaline into my legs to give me seemingly superhuman speed. The adrenaline carried me. I ran and ran, and I did not tire. I held my speed. My legs moved on their own. I was not in control of my body. In my head, I felt like I was flying. I did not look back. I don't know if I was afraid to, if I thought it would slow me down, or if I just didn't care. I just kept running as hard as I could. I ran until I forgot why I was running. I ran until running was the only thing my mind knew. And then I stopped. The adrenaline had done all it could. My body needed to rest. My lungs needed air. I walked with my hands on my head for twenty yards, sucking in short, shallow mouthfuls of oxygen. I stopped at a tree and leaned against it. I began to take deeper breaths, and soon the dizziness in my head began to go away. I looked back toward the village. Nothing.

Once I had caught my breath, I began running at half speed down the banks of the river. I needed to make it to the mountains. If I could just make it to the mountains, then I could get lost in them and hide from my pursuers. But I was in a valley with very little vegetation or hills to hide me. The safety of the mountains was about half a mile away. If I could just give everything I had to get there, I would be free.

Just as I was about burst into a dead sprint, I heard the familiar yelps and calls of the war party behind me. Struck with fear by the awful noise, I dropped to the ground and onto my stomach. A group of warriors were on horseback searching for me. I would not be able to outrun them, and I only had a few minutes before they spotted me in the valley. I crawled down the banks of the river and searched desperately for something hollow to breath through. There was nothing. Seeing no other option, I crawled into the freezing water, which was running high and fast with the melting snow from the mountains. I immediately regretted my decision to try and swim away from them while hoping they wouldn't spot me in the river. The water was so cold that I could not move my hands or legs to swim. Instead, I floated through the icy rapids, desperately trying to breathe, but I was so cold that even a task as simple and as natural as breathing was nearly impossible. My breaths were shallow and few. I choked on water and hit my legs and arms on rocks, though I could barely feel them since my limbs were practically numb.

Swim! I told myself. *Swim, damn you!* With all my strength, I threw my right arm forward, pulling the rushing water past me, and did the same with my left arm. I began to kick my legs. I was swimming. I couldn't feel my body, but I was swimming and moving quickly. I pushed the cold out of my head and let my body grow used to the water.

As I swam, I saw a big rock hanging over the river about two inches above the water. If I could get under it, I would be hidden and able to breathe. I swam hard toward the rock. The current grew strong as I approached it. I grabbed the rock with my numb, brittle fingers and held on as if my life depended on it as the water tried to push me down the river. With all my strength, I pulled myself under the rock. I dug my feet into the smooth, slippery rocks beneath me and searched desperately for finger holds on the underside of the rock so that my hands would not be exposed on the outside. I found the perfect hold. It was basically a handle that I could close my fist around. However, it was the only hold I could find. I would have to hold on with one hand.

I drove my fingers into the rock and got a solid grip, while I continued to hold my head out of the water on the outside of the rock. I listened carefully. I could hear the Indians coming. I took a deep breath, closed my eyes, and pushed myself under the rock. There were two inches between the surface of the water and the bottom face of the giant boulder. My lips kissed the rock as I tried to keep as much of my head out of the water as possible, which was basically just my forehead. I immediately began to feel the cold set in once again. The water lapped over my face, occasionally getting into my mouth and causing me to choke. I tried to choke as silently as possible as the Indians searched for me in the river.

The seconds passed like hours. My right hand, which was holding my body under the rock, began to burn fiercely. It seemed that the pressure had caused it to warm up too quickly, and now it felt as if dozens of knives were slowly slicing across my hand. It didn't help that the sharp, hard rock was grinding into my palm. I was losing my grip. I switched to my left hand, almost losing my hold in the process. My left hand began to experience the same slicing, fierce burn even more quickly than my right had. I was losing the hold. I winced in agony as I tried to hold on with all my strength. I endured the pain as long as my body would allow, and then my mind lost control of it. My hand slipped from its hold, and the water pushed me out from under the rock.

When I came out from under the rock, I immediately saw one of the warriors standing at the top of the bank. He quickly saw me and called out to the others. I tried to swim away as he rode down to the water with a lasso in hand. He threw the rope out with expert accuracy, and the lasso fell over my head and left arm. The warrior pulled it tight around my neck and armpit. I stopped dead in the water. I fumbled my feet around and somehow managed to get a sturdy foothold as the warrior tried to pull me out of the water. With my feet firmly in place, I grabbed the rope with both hands and pulled as hard as I could, jerking the unsuspecting warrior and causing him to fall from his horse.

I quickly took the rope off of my body and began to swim. I looked back to see the warrior chasing after me. He jumped into the water. I turned to face him. He leapt and landed on me. I caught his face on my hand. With my fingers, I gouged at his eyes and nose as I tried to strangle him with my other hand. He pushed my hand from his face and punched me twice, knocking my head into the water. I tried to punch him back, but I could get no leverage. He wrapped one arm around my neck and left arm, and then he grabbed my right arm with the other and began to pull me out of the water. I managed to get my right hand free, while he continued to pull me to the bank. I dropped my hand into the water and fumbled around until I grabbed a rock. When the warrior pulled me out of the water, I brought the rock down hard onto his testicles, causing him to let go of me. I quickly rolled over to face him and promptly slammed the rock into his skull. I struck him once more with the rock and he lost consciousness.

I stood up and looked around. I saw no Indians. A hundred feet upriver was the warrior's horse. I began running toward it. As I ran, I removed my heavy, soaked buckskin shirt. I rubbed my chest briskly to regain some warmth and feeling in my body. I jumped onto the back of the horse and rode up to the top of the bank just as the other warriors were approaching. I quickly turned the horse around and rode down into the river and across to the other side. The warriors followed. I kicked my horse's sides and yelled at him to get him running faster. He was a fast horse, a war horse. He sprinted gracefully across the valley toward the mountains.

My pursuers were close behind, and they were catching up to me. My horse was fast, but the warriors' horses were just as fast, and they knew how to ride them. One of the warriors finally caught up and rode next to me. He leapt from the back of his horse and tackled me off the back of mine. We fell hard to the ground, with the warrior landing on top of me. The fall knocked the air out of my lungs. I fought for breath as the warrior held me down. The rest of the warriors quickly climbed down from their horses and helped him hold me down.

I was quickly bound, thrown over the back of one of the horses, and taken back to camp. The warriors laughed at my attempt to escape, and they laughed at the warrior I had hit with a rock. They laughed at the gash on his head, which was gushing blood. He laughed at his own wound as well. He seemed unaffected by it.

When we arrived at the square, Tabbaquena looked at me with much disappointment and gestured for the warriors to take me to my tent. In my tent, four stakes were driven into the ground to which I was once again securely tied in the spread position of the *Vitruvian Man*. Now I was sure I was going to be put to death. Never before had I felt closer to death than at that moment. And I knew that I would have to wait until their next war dance, which could be a long time. I wondered which would be more painful, the torment of waiting or the torment of torture.

An hour after I had been bound to the stakes, Tabbaquena entered my teepee, brandishing a sinister, black, stone knife. He approached me with a blank stare. My heart raced with fear. He knelt down at my feet and ran his cold fingers up the calf of my left leg. Then he fluidly moved the knife behind my knee and sliced through the outer ligament. I screamed out in searing agony as Tabbaquena walked out of my tent without saying a word or even looking into my eyes.

The pain was unbearable, and I couldn't move to do anything about it. Bound to the ground, I cried and screamed as my left leg shook violently and uncontrollably. Looking down, I could not see the wound, but I could see the puddle of blood forming beneath it.

Tabbaquena had severed one of the ligaments behind my knee to keep me from running. He had not severed it completely, but enough to keep me off my feet for a long time. And, if that was not enough, for the next month he came into my tent every few days and bent my knee to keep the wound and the ligament from healing, which was even more painful than the initial cutting of the ligament. The pain was constant and excruciating, and I feared that my leg would be rendered unusable.

XIII

Every day I waited for death. I even wished for it. By the summer of 1851, after three years as a prisoner of the Comanche, I had sunk into a deep depression. I lived inside myself, in the darkest depths of hopelessness. I did as I was told and put up no fight. I emotionlessly did my "watch trick" when called upon.

My beard had grown long and scraggly, extending to the center of my chest. My hair, oily and unkempt, hung about six inches past my shoulders. I was fed just enough for me to survive, and I had therefore grown skinny and malnourished. My cheeks were sunken in, as well as my dark, exhausted eyes.

The ligament Tabbaquena had severed behind my knee had healed, though my leg was always stiff, and I was stuck with a limp that I would have to bear for the rest of my life. I made no more attempts to escape. Crippled and malnourished, it was useless.

Tabbaquena kept me at his side at all times. I even had to sleep in his tent. I waited on him hand and foot and emotionlessly did everything he asked me to do. I was his slave.

* * *

On a bitter afternoon in the beginning of fall, a great ruckus began to spread through the camp. Tabbaquena and I stepped out of his tent where I had been preparing his pipe. As we walked to the lodge to join the elders, a group of sixty or so warriors rode into the square with four White prisoners. I was suddenly struck motionless and wide-eyed, with my heart racing, as I stared at their frightened, dirty faces.

The White prisoners looked to be a family. There was a middle-aged man and woman and their two children, a young man and a young woman. The young man looked to be about seventeen years old, and the young woman looked to be about fifteen or sixteen. The mother and daughter were crying and looked as if they had been crying for a while. The young man was scared, but calm.

"Please, let my family go! Take me!" the father said bravely.

"Be quiet!" one of the warriors said. He struck the father across the face with the back of his hand. The mother and daughter cried harder.

Tabbaquena told them to take the prisoners to separate tents while he held a council to decide what to do. The prisoners were taken away, and I was bound to a pole inside Tabbaquena's teepee while he and the elders held a council in the lodge.

Tabbaquena returned to his teepee after two hours of deliberating with the elders. He untied my hands and gave me a piece of buffalo jerky.

"What was the decision of the council?" I asked.

"We will have a war dance today," Tabbaquena said.

"You will torture and kill them?"

"Only the men," Tabbaquena said emotionlessly.

"And what of the women?"

"They will join our tribe."

I shook my head angrily. For the first time in nearly two years, I was feeling something.

"You are barbarians," I said. "Merciless barbarians."

Tabbaquena ignored my insult. He ate his jerky and laid down on his buffalo robe.

In the late afternoon, the people of the village gathered in the square. I stood with Tabbaquena and watched as eight warriors escorted the White prisoners to the center of the square. The prisoners were stripped naked and tied to posts, just as Mason, Kyle, Jack, and I had been. The father and son were on one side, and the mother and daughter faced them on the other side. They were all crying. The father tried his best to comfort his family, but it was useless. They were all assuming the worst, which was nowhere near as bad as what they were about to experience.

The war party of two hundred warriors shuffled into the square, doing their strange, ritualistic dance. They danced around the prisoners for a few minutes. Two warriors finally started the torture by running out of line and scalping the father and son. Their cries were painful, but not as painful as the cries of the women who were being forced to watch while the warriors held their eyes open.

The torture was exactly as it had been with my comrades. The father and son were sliced with flint spearheads by each warrior in the line as they circled around and around. I felt like I was reliving that terrible experience all over again. Tears filled my eyes as Mason and Kyle's cries echoed in my head. Instead of the father and son tied to the posts, I saw Mason and Kyle.

The sun began to set behind the mountains, and the warriors took a break from their war dance to make a fire and smoke their pipes, while the father and son hung bleeding from the posts, their flesh almost completely gone. The son was unconscious but breathing. The father was grimacing in excruciating pain.

Once the war party had their fill of tobacco, they reformed their line and continued the dance as they circled the prisoners.

After another hour, the warriors gathered between the prisoners. They continued to dance as they prepared for the execution of the men. Tabbaquena pushed me forward and began leading me to the center of the square where the warriors danced. He took me before the father and handed me his tomahawk. He pointed to the father and nodded.

"Kill," Tabbaquena said.

"Kill?" I asked. "You want me to *kill* this man?"

"Yes, kill him now."

"Why me?"

"Because it is my will."

I looked down at the tomahawk in my hand and then looked to the poor man tied to the post before me.

"Please," the father begged. "Finish it."

I gripped the tomahawk hard, but I could not will myself to raise it and drive it into the man's skull. I just couldn't do it. I looked at Tabbaquena who was waiting patiently. I wanted to kill him right where he stood. I had a weapon. In one swift, fluid motion, I could plant his own tomahawk in his skull. However, I could not bring myself to kill him either. I looked at the women hanging on the posts across the square, their eyes being held open by the dirty, bloody hands of the executioners. I didn't want to see anymore.

I limped over to Tabbaquena. I grabbed his hand and placed his tomahawk in it. I raised his hand so that the tomahawk was over my own head.

"Kill me!" I demanded. "Kill me now! Please! Do it!"

Tabbaquena looked at me in confusion and jerked away from my grip, still holding the tomahawk over my head. I dropped to my knees and held my arms out invitingly.

"I beg you! Please! Do it! Kill me! Do it!"

Tabbaquena reared back and began to bring the tomahawk down. I closed my eyes and waited for death. A few moments passed, but death did not come. I opened my eyes and looked up to see that Tabbaquena had thrown the tomahawk into the skull of the father. I fell forward onto my hands and began to cry. I wanted to die. I could bear it no longer.

That night, I lay on my buffalo robe in Tabbaquena's tent, staring out of the smoke hole at the stars. Anger filled every ounce of my being, and I could not sleep. Since my last escape attempt nearly two years earlier, I had felt nothing. My heart was still. My thoughts were silent. I had accepted my fate of being a slave and a prisoner until I died. But the White prisoners had caused me to feel again. They had provoked my thoughts. They had made my heart beat again. They reminded me of what these

Comanche warriors had done to my friends. They reminded me that Tabbaquena had crippled me for life. They reminded me that these Comanche warriors had interrupted my adventure and had crushed my dream of seeing the Pacific Ocean. They had kept me from the woman I loved. They had ended my life. I would accept it no longer. I would not let Tabbaquena be the final chapter of my life.

I will not die here, I thought. *I will not die here.*

XIV

For two months I desperately plotted an escape, but to my frustration, I could not think of a plan I believed would work. However, I had begun to store dried meat in a hole I dug under my mattress, and I had managed to steal a knife from one of the teepees, which I also buried under my mattress.

I weighed my options, and there were few. There was not much I could plan. The village did not require or provide an elaborate escape plan. All I could do was leave at the right moment and escape into the mountains. I would need a good, fast horse. I would need Renegado. I could not escape on foot, nor did I have the heart to leave my dear friend behind.

* * *

On a cold morning in what I believed to be January, I was violently roused from my sleep by Tabbaquena. I awoke grumpily, and he told me that it was time for the hunt.

I put on my buffalo robe and followed Tabbaquena out of the teepee to the square, where about two hundred and fifty warriors had gathered for the hunt. It was not just any hunt. It was the biggest hunt of the year, and every warrior participated. It was the time of the year when the buffalo hides were the thickest. The warriors would ride out to find the herd. Sometimes they would ride for many days. When they found the herd, they would slaughter as many buffalo as possible. It was the only time they killed more than they needed.

One of the warriors brought me a mule to ride. Tabbaquena was presented with Renegado as his steed for the hunt. He knew it irritated me when he rode my horse. I also noticed my saber attached to the side of the saddle. I had not seen it since it was taken from me on the day of my capture. Why did Tabbaquena have it all of a sudden?

I climbed onto my mule as Tabbaquena climbed onto the back of Renegado. Tabbaquena gave the order to leave, and our large army of warrior hunters rode out of the village.

We rode southwest into the mountains. The snow was soft and fresh from a storm the night before. The air was crisp and dry but not too cold, and it smelled of pine. By the early afternoon, the white, melancholy clouds moved out of the sky and gave way to the sun, which beamed with glorious intensity, making for a fine day to ride deep into the mountains.

For three days we searched for the big herd. Early on the fourth day, our scout rode quickly into our camp to inform us that he had located the buffalo. He said there were about a thousand buffalo in a valley ten miles to the west. We immediately climbed onto our mounts and began riding hastily to the valley of the buffalo.

After riding for about five miles, we came to a large ravine. As we rode down into it, the warriors began to shout and panic. I could not hear what they were saying. And then, across the valley, I heard war cries echoing against the mountains. I realized that the warriors had been shouting "Apache!"

A dark cloud of men on horseback moved swiftly across the ravine. The Comanche warriors quickly drew their bows and knocked their arrows, while forming their lines in preparation for battle. The warriors let out a bloodcurdling war cry and charged down into the ravine to meet the Apache warriors in battle.

Both armies of warriors let out continuous battle cries as they drew closer to one another. Tabbaquena and I watched from the top of the ravine. We had a magnificent view of the battle that was about to take place.

The Apache fired their arrows first. A few Comanche fell. They returned fire with a storm of arrows. Arrows continued to fly from both sides until the two tribes collided and engaged in the fiercest hand-to-hand combat I had ever witnessed.

As I gazed upon the great battle, I suddenly realized that a wonderful opportunity had just presented itself to me. Fate had smiled upon me.

My mind raced with ideas. I looked at Tabbaquena, who was completely engaged in watching the battle. My eyes moved down his body to Renegado's side and stopped on the handle of my saber sticking out of its scabbard. My eyes wandered further down, all the way to the ground. I spotted a stick protruding from the snow. I could see that it was thick, but I could not see how long it was. It might have been six inches long for all I knew. I hoped for the best.

With my plan taking form, I looked down into the valley at the bloody engagement. I took my buffalo horn off my shoulder and took a sip of water. As I was about to put it back over my shoulder, I purposely dropped it. Tabbaquena looked down at my buffalo horn lying in the snow. I shrugged and climbed off of my mule to pick it up, and Tabbaquena turned his attention back to the battle. Instead of picking up the buffalo horn, I grabbed the thick stick protruding from the snow. As I slowly pulled it up, I could feel that it was indeed long.

Just as Tabbaquena looked down at me, I pulled the stick out of the snow, and in a swift, fluid motion, I swung the stick into his face, knocking him off of Renegado's back and onto the ground. I dropped the stick and quickly pulled my saber out of its scabbard on Renegado's saddle. I looked down at Tabbaquena and glared vengefully into his eyes as I drove my sword down into his chest. His bloody mouth opened wide as the cold steel tore through his heart. I reached down and pulled the pouch, which contained my pocket watch from his neck. I took his buffalo horn and his hunting knife as well.

I quickly pulled my saber from Tabbaquena's lifeless body and looked down at the battle, which seemed to be slowing down. It didn't look as if any of the warriors had seen what I had done to their chief. I needed to move quickly, so I climbed onto Renegado's back and instantly felt a warm sense of security fill my body.

"It's you and me again, my friend. Let's get away from these people," I said to Renegado, giving him a nudge and turning him around. I grabbed the reins of the mule I had been riding, and, leading the mule behind us, we began to ride back the way we had come. After about a mile, we turned northwest and rode into a dense coniferous forest. We were moving quickly. Renegado and I fell back into our old routine splendidly. He was just as determined as I to get away from the Comanche, and he showed great intuition in eluding our captors. I fully trusted him, allowing him to lead me rather than the other way around.

We traveled deeper and deeper into the mountains, heading west all the way, until darkness came upon us. The terrain, being as wild and unpredictable as it was, made night travel quite dangerous. I took Renegado and the mule into a densely wooded area and found a spot as good as any to rest. I tied the reins of both animals to either of my hands and curled up between them, pulling my buffalo robe closed over my chest and face.

I, of course, did not sleep. I stayed awake all night, listening for my pursuers. I had not seen or heard any sign of them following me, but I could feel them. I had killed their chief. They would most certainly come after me. However, I was heading west into a territory with which I knew their tribe was unfamiliar. They did not venture far into the mountains, for they were Indians of the plains.

In the twilight of morning, I was on Renegado's back again and riding westward. I was cold, never having warmed up from the well-below freezing temperatures of the night. I had been shivering since I had sat down to rest. I knew I was malnourished and did not have any fat on my body. I would be lucky to survive another night in my condition, especially as I ascended higher into the mountains. It was time for the mule to carry out his purpose.

As the sun began to rise, I climbed off of Renegado's back and went to the mule. I petted his nose and neck, and I thanked him for his help. I took Tabbaquena's hunting knife and cut the mule's throat. I pulled him to the ground as he squirmed in my arms, fighting for life. After a few moments, he stopped moving. I filled mine and Tabbaquena's buffalo horn with the warm blood spilling from the mule's neck. The blood was rich with nutrients that could keep me alive. I put my mouth to the mule's throat and drank his blood straight from his wound. It was salty, metallic, and awful. However, it instantly began to warm my body, and I felt my energy rise.

With the buffalo horns filled with blood, I began chopping off the mule's head with my saber. It took quite a few good whacks to sever the head, but it finally came off. I then went on to skin the mule using Tabbaquena's hunting knife. The skin would help keep me warm in the below freezing temperatures at night. I skinned the mule faster than I had ever skinned any animal of notable size.

The skin and the head were off, so I began cutting off the fattest hunks of meat. Once I had all I thought I could carry, I began to pack everything onto Renegado's back. I rolled up the skin and tied it onto the front of the saddle. I filled the saddlebags with meat and packed snow on top. And, lastly, I tied the head of the mule to the back of the saddle. Then I climbed onto Renegado's back and gave him a nudge. As we rode away, I saw the wolves coming down from the forest to feast on the carcass I had left behind.

XV

THE FURTHER WEST I rode, the higher I ascended into the unforgiving mountains. I had been riding for three days with no sleep and no fires. I not seen or heard my Comanche captors and had begun to think that they had given up on me — I hoped.

I was in fair condition. My health had improved thanks to the mule meat and blood. I stayed somewhat warm at night using the mule skin for cover. A fire would have been nice. The warmth it could provide would have been great, but I would have been even happier to have been able to cook the mule meat. Raw and frozen, it was extremely unpleasant.

As the days passed, I realized that I was either not being pursued or that I had lost my pursuers. Either way, I felt that it was safe to make a fire. I stopped two hours before dark and began gathering wood. I found dry moss on the bottoms of some of the tree trunks, which would make for good tinder. I built the base of my fire and began the grueling process of trying to get it lit. I started by trying to rub two sticks together but had no luck. I began searching for a stone that could make a spark, and it did not take me long to find a good-sized piece of flint. I brushed the snow off the flint and placed it next to the tinder. I drew my saber and cut down onto the flint — nothing. I hit it again — nothing. I hit it once more, and there was a spark. I hit it harder, and there was a bigger spark. I hit it over and over, and the sparks jumped into the dry moss and sticks.

Eventually, the moss began to smoke. I blew on it, and the tiny flames began to flicker. The fire grew quickly and enveloped the tinder. I added more wood and made the fire nice and big. I let the flames warm my blood and smiled happily as the cold stiffness began to leave my body.

I cooked some mule meat and enjoyed a hot dinner. Mule

meat was not too bad when it was cooked, but it could certainly have used a little seasoning.

As the sun began to set, I looked out to the west over the rugged, magnificent terrain. Despite my poor situation, I could not help but notice the extraordinary beauty of the mountainous wilderness that surrounded me. I looked out toward the setting sun, as it fell behind the snowcapped peaks resting in the clouds. They looked sinister and deadly, and soon I would have to cross them. They would be the highest and coldest part of my journey, and the terrain would be unsympathetic. I wondered if I would survive.

* * *

The sharp, freezing wind bit fiercely at my face, as I rode along an icy ridge, crossing the highest pass of the mountain range. The weather was worse than I had expected. The wind was incessant and powerful, and it whipped through the peaks with blinding ferocity, sometimes bringing snow with it. The temperature could not have been much higher than zero degrees Fahrenheit. The ground on which I rode was icy and unpredictable, and it seemed as if it could give out at any moment.

As I pressed on, I could not see how much further I would have to go while enduring the miserable conditions, for the clouds and the snow were constantly obstructing my view to little more than a few feet in front of me.

At night, I slept in tiny crevasses where I could hide from the wind, but after two nights in those mountains without food that wasn't frozen solid and without a fire, I began to grow weak and tired. I was also beginning to feel the initial effects of hypothermia.

Being desperate, I was forced to do something that pained me greatly. With Tabbaquena's hunting knife, I made a small incision in Renegado's flesh at the base of his neck. He did not flinch or seem to notice what I had done as the blood began to flow from the wound. I put my lips to the wound and drank the blood. I quickly felt a warm sensation move throughout my body. I only took a little blood and then rubbed snow on the wound. I thanked Renegado for his sacrifice. I took some grass from the saddlebags, which I had stored before we entered the lifeless, white wilderness. I held the grass to Renegado's lips, and he ate it.

Renegado was a warrior. He endured the situation with grace and strength. Human, horse, or otherwise, I have never encountered a creature with more character than that of my noble Renegado. In those mountains, he was my savior.

After four grueling days, Renegado and I rode out of the godforsaken, snowcapped mountains. We were lucky to be alive. As soon as the land provided, I made a great fire and sat by it for two days while Renegado grazed. During that time, I cooked the head of the mule, which I still had. I ate everything I possibly could off the skull — brains, eyeballs, and tongue included. It was absolutely horrid, but I needed all the nutrients I could get.

Once I was rejuvenated, Renegado and I began to press on westward through the mountains.

For the next three weeks, I survived on berries and plants, and occasionally rabbits and squirrels when I could trap them. Renegado and I traversed steadily through the mountains, and about six weeks after our escape from the Comanche, we found ourselves riding down the western foothills of the Rockies, gazing upon a tamer land stretching out before us. I looked back at the snowcapped mountains from which I had descended, and I felt a great sense of accomplishment. Taking a second glance back at the ferocious mountains, I felt extremely lucky.

* * *

I rode across the mesas and through the canyons, and I observed magnificent rock formations as I rode through a hard, red desert.

I rode through a colorful desert of great buttes, monoliths, and white sandstone domes and cliffs. The land just west of the Rocky Mountains consisted of some the most incredible rock formations I had ever seen, formations that widened my eyes, dropped my jaw, and left me in complete awe.

I continued to ride west. I rode west across the land that John Fremont had called the Great Basin. I continued to ride west. I did not know why. I did not think about it. I just rode and observed and allowed myself to become immersed in the beautiful land across which I traversed. I suppose that subconsciously I knew I was trying to reach the Pacific Ocean, but as I rode, I was simply in the moment. I was taking it one step at a time, and each step took me west. With each new place I saw, my mind was curious to see what was past it. So, I continued west.

I continued west into the Sierra Nevada Mountains, where I rode through lush, green meadows and dense, coniferous forests. I gazed upon lakes, rivers, and waterfalls. I rode beneath towering granite rock faces and across the wide, gaping valleys. I weaved through a grove of enormous Sequoia trees. I had never felt so small as I did at the base of those colossal trees.

I continued west.

* * *

I do not know for how long I traveled. It could have been a week. It could have been a year. It could have been an eternity. There was no measure of time or distance where I was. Measurement was useless. Each moment was measured by the way my environment made me feel. Time stands still when one becomes completely aware of the wonder of creation.

I rode along through a green, hilly country. The ground was soft and fertile. It was a particularly beautiful day, and the sky was clear and vibrantly blue. The sun was bright, but its rays were soft and not too hot. As I rode through the hills, I heard a strange sound, a sound I had not heard in a long time. It was not the wind blowing through the trees. It was not the wind whipping through a deep gorge. It was not the rushing water of a river.

My heart began to race as I ascended a gradual slope, which looked to drop off quite suddenly. When I came to the edge of the cliff, I stopped and gazed out upon the wonder before me.

The sound I had heard was the gentle waves of the Pacific Ocean, lapping onto the sandy shore. Tears filled my eyes as I stared out over the inviting blue waters, stretching as far as the eye could see and meeting the sky on the horizon. I had left home in New York on the Atlantic Coast in hopes of traveling across the Western frontier to the Pacific Ocean, and here I was. It had taken me ten years to reach the Pacific Coast, but I had finally made it.

I rode down onto the beach and held my hands high in the air, victoriously, as Renegado ran down the beach. I jumped from Renegado's back and fell to my knees in the sand. I held the sand in my hands and laughed as I watched it fall through my fingers. I threw the sand into the air, jumped to my feet, and began sprinting toward the ocean. I splashed into the water and yelled excitedly as I dove into the waves. I swam out into the ocean and let the waves crash down upon me. It felt like a dream. I couldn't believe that I had made it. The sense of accomplishment I felt was beyond any triumph I had ever felt before. I had conquered my Goliath. I had painted my Sistine Chapel. I had composed my *Don Giovanni*.

I walked out of the ocean and sat down in the sand next to where Renegado stood. I lay down and watched the sun plunge into the ocean on the horizon. Renegado lowered his head to mine and licked the salt off my face.

The last sliver of the sun disappeared, and the twilight lingered in the sky. The moon rested over the ocean and cast a strip of bluish-white light over the calm waters. I closed my eyes and fell asleep on the beach.

XVI

I ARRIVED IN SAN Francisco three days after I reached the coast. It was the first White civilization I had seen since leaving San Antonio four years earlier. I rode along the harbor where dozens of ships were docked. Looking out into the bay, it was so thick with ships that I could barely see the water.

The city was enormous and quite dense. It was extremely busy, and I found myself a bit overwhelmed. People stared at me strangely. I imagined that I looked strange to them in my Indian dress. I had not bathed, shaved, or cut my hair in four years. To them, I must have looked like a filthy beast.

I rode into an area called Portsmouth Square, where I found a barber's shop with a washroom. I tied Renegado out front and walked inside. The barber had only one client at the moment, and he was just starting his shave. The barber and the client both looked at me in confusion and disgust.

"I apologize for the smell and my appearance," I said. It was strange to hear myself speak. I could barely get out the words. "I've been a prisoner of the Comanche for the last four years. I don't have any money, but I'd be much obliged if you would allow me a warm bath and a razor to shave with."

Their expressions of confusion and disgust turned to expressions of awe and disbelief as they stared at me with wide eyes and mouths agape.

The barber's wife drew me a hot bath in the washroom. She gave me a bar of soap and bashfully walked toward the door.

"Excuse me, ma'am," I said as she opened the door. She stopped and turned to face me. "What is the date?"

"It's the fourteenth of April," she replied.

"What year, ma'am?"

"1852."

"Good. I thought so."

The barber's wife smiled and started to leave.

"Oh! And one more thing. I don't have any other clothes, and I'd rather not walk around looking like an Indian. I'd be very grateful if you could find me some civilized clothes, a gentleman's clothes."

The wife nodded and walked out of the washroom, closing the door behind her. I undressed and slowly lowered myself into the bathtub. The hot water felt amazing. I closed my eyes and let out a sigh of relief as my body became relaxed. I fell into a euphoric daze.

When I awoke from my brief nap, the water in the tub had lost much of its heat and was turning lukewarm. It had also turned brown with my floating filth. I scrubbed myself thoroughly with the soap and washed my hair.

Once I was clean, I stepped out of the tub and dried off. I noticed a proper outfit hanging on the door. The barber's wife must have brought it in while I was napping. I wrapped the towel around my waist and went to the mirror. I barely recognized myself, and not just because of the long beard and long hair. I was skinnier than I had ever been, skinnier than any man should ever be, and I had aged. I could not believe how much I had aged. My eyes were worn, and the skin around them was wrinkled. My skin looked leathery and rough. How old was I? I had not thought about my birthday in years. I quickly calculated my age. My God! I was thirty-one, and I would be turning thirty-two at the end of the year. How time had flown! All the while I thought it had been standing still.

I lathered my face with warm cream and began shaving off the hideous growth. It took nearly an hour to shave off my beard, and I cut myself half a dozen times. When I looked at my smooth face in the mirror again, I recognized myself a great deal more; however, I still thought I looked quite old.

I put on the fine clothes the barber's wife had provided for me. They were quite nice. They were made of good material and were expertly tailored. The cut was foreign to me, but I had not been keeping up with the times as far as fashion was concerned — or anything for that matter. As I looked myself over in the mirror, it felt good to be wearing civilized clothes again.

I ran a comb through my hair, which I had not cut. I tied my hair back into a tail with a black ribbon and walked downstairs. The barber was kind enough to give me some money for a meal and a place to stay for the night. I thanked him and his wife for their hospitality and promised that I would mail them what I owed them as soon as I got to New Orleans. They told me that it wasn't necessary, but I insisted. I walked to the door, and as I opened it, I turned around.

"Where is the post office?" I asked.

"It's across the street and about five buildings up," the barber answered.

I nodded, thanked him again, and walked outside. I climbed onto Renegado's back and rode up the street to the post office. I tied Renegado out front and walked inside. The clerk behind the desk smiled a big, goofy smile and looked at me with curious eyes from behind his glasses.

"What can I do for you, sir?" the clerk asked.

"Do you, by any chance, save letters that aren't picked up?" I asked.

"How long are we talking here?" the clerk asked curiously.

"Four years."

The clerk stared at me for a moment. "Let me check. What's the name of the person to whom the letter is addressed?"

"Konrad Quintero de Leon."

The clerk nodded and went into the backroom. I leaned up against the counter and waited patiently.

Ten minutes later, the clerk came out of the backroom with a letter in his hand.

"One letter for a Mr. Konrad Quintero de Leon," he said proudly.

"Really? You're joking!"

"I don't joke, sir. Here you are."

The clerk handed me the letter. I quickly opened it and stepped outside to read it. As I pulled the letter out of the envelope, a few dried, dead lilac petals fell out. I turned the envelope over, and dozens of dead lilac petals fell out and floated in the wind. I smiled as I opened Anastasia's letter. I smelled the paper; it still carried her scent. After four years, it still carried her scent! My heart raced as I began to read her words.

My dear and loving Konrad,

I have sent this letter just a week after you left. If you're reading this, then it means you have made it to San Francisco safely, and, hopefully, you have already sent me a letter to inform me of your safe arrival and to tell me how very much you miss me. I miss you greatly, but it fills me with much joy and inspiration to know that you are off following your heart on a grand adventure. You are a brave and intuitive man, Konrad. That is why I fell in love with you. I hope your journey and your experience is everything you hoped it would be, and I hope that your swim in the Pacific Ocean is nothing less than magical.

I have some (hopefully) good news for you. I certainly think it is good. However, before I tell you the news, I want you to know that I want you to stay in California for as long as you feel you need to stay. I want you to come back to me when you are ready to come back, no matter what. That being said, my good news for you is that I am pregnant with our child. I was a bit suspicious before you left, but I did not want to say anything. After you left, I went to the doctor and my suspicions were confirmed. In about eight months, I will be giving birth to our child. You are going to be a father, Konrad. I hope that you think this is good news. I think it is just wonderful. Now, I do not want you to rush back here. Miriam and Charles are here to take care of me. I want you to stay and do what you must. I just thought it was important that you know. I love you so very much, and I will be here waiting for you when you return. For now, enjoy the world as much as you possibly can!

Love, forever and always,

Your gorgeous mistress,

Anastasia

I love you.

I could not believe the words I had just read. Anastasia was pregnant with my child! No, she was pregnant four years ago. That meant I had a four-year-old child waiting for me back in New Orleans.

It took my mind a few moments to absorb the information. I was a father. I had a son or a daughter in New Orleans. I laughed excitedly. A strange, dreamlike feeling swept over me, and I felt as if I was floating. I rushed back into the post office.

"I'm a father!" I told the clerk. I had to tell somebody.

"Congratulations, sir!" the clerk said. "A boy or a girl?"

"I'm not sure, but I'm a father!"

"You better get home to him or her. I'm sure they'd like to meet their daddy."

"Of course." I thought for a moment, and my dreamlike state was suddenly awakened by reality. "However, home is in New Orleans."

"That's quite a ways away," the clerk pointed out.

"What do you recommend? I'd prefer not to ride alone."

"Well, there's always people coming and going. Lots of experienced guides get hired to bring people out here. I'm sure you can find some that are heading east and ride along with them."

"That would be great. Where might I find company like that?"

"The saloons are a good place to start," the clerk offered.

I thanked the clerk for his help and left the post office. I rode into a busier part of the city and went into the first saloon I came across. The saloon was busy in the middle of the afternoon. The patrons were quite lively and loud. I walked up to the bar and ordered a whiskey. The bartender poured my drink.

"Do you know where I might find some guides or a party heading east?" I asked.

The bartender looked around the saloon. His eyes stopped, and he pointed to a table at the back of the saloon.

"Those fellows back there are heading east pretty soon, I think. Talk to them."

"Do you know their names?" I asked.

"The one on the left, facing us, is Michael Fitzgerald."

"Thank you, sir."

I walked to the back of the saloon and approached the table where Michael Fitzgerald sat with three other men.

"Michael Fitzgerald?" I said.

"Who's asking?" Michael inquired, eyeing me carefully. He was a mean-looking man with squinting eyes, yellow, rotting teeth, and stringy black hair.

"I'm Konrad Quintero de Leon. It's a pleasure to make your acquaintance."

I held out my hand, and Michael shook it skeptically.

"Whatever you say, partner. I'm Michael. This here is Billy Anderson. That's John Taylor, and the big fellow is Jacob Wadsworth."

"It's a pleasure to meet you, gentlemen," I said. They nodded and grunted inaudible greetings.

"What can we do for you?" Michael asked.

"Well, I need to get to New Orleans, and I heard that you were heading east soon. I was wondering if I could ride along with you."

"Yeah, we're leaving for Independence, Missouri tomorrow morning. You're welcome to tag along, but it's going to cost you. Our services aren't free, you know."

I exhaled a deep breath and proceeded to explain calmly to the gentlemen the exact extremities of my situation. When I finished, Michael was very apologetic and offered to escort me to Independence free of charge. I thanked him and told the men I would see them in the morning.

I rented a hotel room for the night with the money the barber had given me and had a wonderful sleep in a comfortable bed. In the morning, I met my escorts outside the hotel. We loaded up with supplies and were riding out of San Francisco by sunrise.

XVII

WE HEADED EAST ALONG the California Trail with my four escorts leading the way. I was quiet and kept to myself while the four of them talked incessantly, touching on every possible topic one could dream up. They were an entertaining bunch. They could also be quite annoying. But they moved quickly along the trail, and they knew the land very well, which was all I really cared about.

We crossed the Great Basin, rode past the Great Salt Lake, and reached the Rocky Mountains in early May. Michael and the others knew the trail through them like the back of their hands. We traversed easily but slowly through the mountains.

After descending into the eastern foothills of the Rockies in early June, I instantly felt a sickening pain in my stomach, and my heart raced with fear. I was in a land all too familiar. We had ridden out of the mountains at least two hundred miles north of the Comanche village where I had been held captive for nearly four years, but it felt all too close. I did not share my fears with my traveling companions, but I think they could see that I was quite uncomfortable.

The Great Plains brought back the memory of my first adventure with Mason, Kyle, and Cole on the Fremont Expedition. We rode on across the Smokey Hills and across the Blue Stem Hills, arriving in Independence, Missouri on the eighteenth of June. I thanked Michael, Billy, John, and Jacob for escorting me halfway across the continent. They were kind enough to give me some money for a steamboat ticket and a hotel room in St. Louis, for which I was very grateful. I bade them a quick farewell and continued my journey alone to St. Louis.

* * *

Four days after leaving Independence, I arrived in St. Louis. It was much different than I remembered. A large portion of the city had burned in a fire in 1849, though it seemed bigger to me despite that fact. The population had more than tripled since the last time I was there.

I went down to the docks and bought a ticket for the steamboat leaving first thing the following morning. I asked the ticket man if he knew a woman by the name of Josephine Bissette. He did not.

With sunset a couple of hours away, I rode slowly through town to find a hotel. I had not forgotten my promise to Jack. He had asked me to find Josephine Bissette, to tell her of his fate and to tell her that he loved her. I meant to keep my promise. I rented a room at the first hotel I came to and began asking around, hoping that someone would know where I could find Josephine.

I asked everybody I saw but had no luck. As the sun began to set, hopeless, I walked into a saloon and ordered a whiskey. I asked the bartender if he knew of a Josephine Bissette. He shook his head.

"Did you say Josephine Bissette?" an old, drunk man sitting next to me asked.

"I did. Do you know her?"

"I know of her. I believe it's Josephine Peters now."

"She's married?"

"Yep. Poor kid," the old man mumbled.

"Who's poor?" I asked.

"The young man who used to work for me many, many years ago. He used to go on and on about Josephine Bissette. Guess he got beat to the punch."

"You wouldn't happen to be a carpenter by any chance?" I asked.

"Used to be," the old man admitted. He showed me his shaking, brittle hands that could no longer handle the work.

495

"That young man who worked for you, was his name Jack Burton?"

"Yes! Yes, it was! Do you know Jack?" the old man asked excitedly.

I sighed sadly. "He was a very good friend of mine."

The old man looked at me in confusion. "Was? Did he die?"

"He was killed by the Comanche," I said.

"I'm sorry to hear that."

"Do you know where I can find Josephine?"

The old man gave me directions to the Peters' house. I thanked him for his help and left the saloon quickly. I rode to the Peters' house on the outskirts of town, which was a nice, little home with a small yard and garden, all surrounded by a white picket fence. The sun had just set, and the evening stood still in the twilight.

I climbed off Renegado's back and tied him to the fence. I opened the gate and walked across the yard. I stepped up onto the porch and knocked on the door. A few moments later the door opened. A broad-shouldered man with a thick, blond mustache and kind eyes stood before me. He looked at me curiously.

"How can I help you?" Mr. Peters asked.

"I'm looking for Mrs. Josephine Peters," I replied.

"May I ask who's looking for her?" Mr. Peters asked skeptically.

"My name is Konrad Quintero de Leon. A friend of mine who used to know her asked me to come here on his behalf. I'm afraid I have some bad news."

Mr. Peters studied my eyes carefully for a moment and then opened the door all the way.

"Come in," he invited.

I stepped into the house and looked around. It was quite simple and seemed very typical of a small, country house.

"She's in the bedroom," Mr. Peters said. "Have a seat, and I'll go and get her."

I sat down at the table and waited. I thought about what I was going to say and how I was going to say it. The whole situation was a little strange to me. I was going to tell a married woman that her past lover had died tragically and that his last wish was for me to tell her that he loved her. But it had been his last wish, and I would honor it.

I was startled by the sound of footsteps walking toward me. A pretty, young-looking woman with curly, blond hair walked into the kitchen. I stood up politely as she walked over to me. She had the rosiest cheeks I had ever seen and an adorable button of a nose. Her smile was inviting and soothing. I instantly saw how Jack could have fallen in love with her.

"Hello, I'm Josephine," she said, extending her hand. I shook her hand gently.

"I'm—"

"Konrad. Yes, I know."

"Your husband told you."

"No, Jack did. I've been expecting you," Josephine said, staring deep into my eyes.

I squinted in confusion. "I'm sorry — you've been expecting me? What are you talking about?"

"Have a seat, Konrad," Josephine offered. I sat down and she sat next to me.

"Did Jack write to you and tell you about me or something? I don't understand," I said.

"No, he did not write. He came to see me in person two years ago and told me you would be coming to see me."

"Two years ago?"

"He's alive, Konrad," Josephine said with a joyful smile.

"He escaped?" I asked, as I absorbed the information.

"Yes, he's alive and well. He said he cut through his ropes with a knife that he had come across by chance. He snuck out of the village, stole a horse, and escaped in the middle of the night when everyone was asleep. He said he didn't think they even pursued him. He came straight here, knocked on the door, and the first thing he asked me was if Konrad Quintero had come to see me. I told him you hadn't, and he was very upset. He told me everything. He told me how he had made you promise to come and tell me what happened to him and that he loved me and always had. He said this right in front of my husband, too. The only thing Jack was ever afraid to say was I love you. Then he goes and says it right in front of my husband. I hadn't seen or heard from him in eleven years. Then he just shows up at my door. I guess that almost dying makes people want to say the things they never said before."

"Yes, indeed it does," I said. "Where is Jack now?"

"Well, he was certain that you would escape. He told me to tell you when you got here that he was in Texas working at the Van Patten ranch. He said you would know where that is."

"I do." I smiled and shook my head. I was eternally grateful that Jack was alive, but I wasn't surprised. The good news still filled my body with a much-needed wave of life.

"After he came to see me, he said that he was going to Texas to get the Rangers to go and free you from the Indians. I got a letter from him saying that the Rangers wouldn't go after you since it was out of their jurisdiction. He also wrote half a dozen letters to the U.S. Army asking for their help, but they never answered him. He seemed pretty upset."

"Well, I made it out without the help of the U.S. Army or the Rangers."

"Yes, you did. I know Jack will be very glad to see you."

"Well, I should be going. I have to catch a steamboat first thing in the morning," I said.

"Why don't you stay here? We have a guest bedroom," Josephine offered.

"That's very kind of you, but I've already paid for a hotel room in town."

"All right. I'll walk you to the door."

Josephine and I stood up and walked to the front door. She opened it and sighed.

"I'm glad you're safe. Ever since Jack told me about you, I haven't stopped praying for you."

"Well, your prayers worked," I said.

"And had the situation been different. If Jack had not been so fortunate, I would have been very grateful that you carried out his last wish."

I smiled and bowed respectfully.

"Good luck, Konrad," she said.

"Thank you, Josephine. Goodbye."

I walked across the yard and through the gate of the white picket fence. I climbed onto Renegado's back and waved to Josephine in the doorway as I rode back toward my hotel.

XVIII

I ARRIVED IN NEW Orleans in the early afternoon on the Fourth of July. The docks were as busy as I remembered as I led Renegado off the steamboat. We moved quickly through the chaos. My limp had been improved by the assistance of a cane I had bought in St. Louis. Once we were off the docks, I climbed onto Renegado's back and rode hastily through the streets to the French Quarter.

We promptly arrived at my apartment. I climbed down from Renegado's back and quickly raced up the stairs. I tried to open the door, but to my surprise it was locked. I knocked, but there was no answer. I climbed over the railing and onto the balcony. I tried to open the balcony doors, but they were locked as well. I looked through the window. The apartment looked as if no one had been living there for quite some time. Confused, I climbed back over the railing and went down the stairs. I climbed onto Renegado's back and rode quickly to Miriam and Charles' house on *Rue Orleans*.

I soon arrived at Miriam's house, tied off Renegado, and walked to the front door. I smiled excitedly as anxious butterflies flew around chaotically in my belly. I knocked on the door and tapped my fingers on my thighs as I waited. There was a click on the door, a brief pause, and then the door opened slowly. Miriam stood before me. Her eyes immediately widened and filled with tears. Her jaw dropped in disbelief.

"Oh, my God! It can't be!" Miriam said, as her bottom lip began to quiver.

"Hello, Miriam," I said.

"Konrad—" she choked.

She raised her right hand to cover her mouth and caught herself on the doorway with her left hand as she lost her balance. Her whole body shook, and she began to cry. I stepped toward her, and she fell into my arms. I held her tight in my arms as she cried. She cried loudly and hysterically.

"I thought you were dead," she barely managed.

"I'm alive, and I'm here."

As I held Miriam, Charles came rushing into the hallway to see what the commotion was all about. When he saw me, his jaw dropped in disbelief and he rushed toward me.

"My God! Konrad!" Charles yelled. Miriam stepped aside, keeping her arm around my neck as Charles and I embraced. "We thought you were dead! I can't believe you're alive!"

Charles stepped back and looked at me. He shook his head in disbelief. I held Miriam as she continued to cry hysterically.

"I went by my apartment, but it didn't look like anyone has been living there," I said. "Where is Anastasia? Is she here?"

Miriam looked at Charles with wide, water-filled eyes. Charles closed his eyes slowly and looked down at his feet. My stomach tightened for a moment as I noticed their reactions.

"Where is our child? Did she have a boy or a girl?"

"Oh, God," Miriam said. She grabbed her stomach as if she was going to be sick.

"What is it? Are you all right? Charles?"

"Konrad, there's something we need to tell you," Charles said.

I ignored the tight feeling in my stomach by smiling it away. I looked down and saw a little girl standing in the doorway, staring at me curiously. Her eyes stared straight into mine. The tight feeling in my stomach. I ignored it and smiled it away once again.

"Oh, my goodness! Miriam, Charles, you have a daughter?"

Miriam gasped and looked down at the little girl. Charles quickly picked her up and took her inside. I watched him in confusion as he disappeared with the little girl.

"Konrad, listen to me—"

The tight feeling in my stomach. "Where is Anastasia? Where is our child?"

"Konrad…" Miriam shook her head as she began to cry.

Charles walked back into the doorway without the little girl. Miriam turned to Charles and shook her head.

"I can't," Miriam said.

"You can't what? What is going on?" I asked.

Charles stepped toward me and looked deep into my eyes. "Anastasia had much difficulty giving birth to your child. She was in labor for a day and a half," Charles explained.

I nodded quickly as my stomach tightened.

"The doctor tried, but they could not get the baby out, so Anastasia had to make a choice. It was either her or the baby."

I put my hands over my mouth as my jaw dropped in terror. Water filled my eyes.

"She, of course, chose the baby," Charles said. "I'm sorry, Konrad. Anastasia died."

Every muscle in my body tightened as I denied my instincts to completely break down. I held my chest with one hand and my mouth with the other. My whole body was shaking. As the reality of Anastasia's death sank in, I became aware of another reality. I looked into the doorway and pointed down to where the little girl had been standing.

"That little girl… was my daughter?"

Miriam nodded as she cried with me. She put her arms around me and held me tight. I began to lose control. My muscles loosened, and I began to cry hysterically. I couldn't breath. I fell to my knees in sorrow, holding my pounding chest as my heart exploded and shattered. I should never have left Anastasia. Now she was gone.

I cried in Miriam's arms, there in her doorway, until I was drained of all emotion and fluid. Miriam and Charles took me inside their house, and we sat down in their living room.

"So you have been taking care of our daughter ever since she was born?" I asked.

"We've raised her as our own," Charles said.

"What is her name?" I asked.

"Anastasia," Charles replied. "We thought it was only right to name her after her mother who gave her life for her."

I clenched my jaw and swallowed the lump in my throat as I nodded in approval.

"May I see her? My daughter."

"Of course," Miriam said. "Follow me."

Charles and Miriam led me down a long hallway. We stopped at a closed door. Miriam started to open the door.

"Wait," I said. "May I go in alone?" I asked.

"Sure," Miriam said. She stepped back, and I stepped up to the door and knocked.

"Come in," young Anastasia invited.

I opened the door and walked into the room. Young Anastasia was sitting on the floor, playing with her dolls. She looked up at me and smiled.

"Hello," she said.

"Hello," I returned, smiling joyfully.

I stepped slowly toward her. She was beautiful. Just like her mother, she was impossible to look away from. She had her mother's eyes, lips, and hair, and she had my nose, cheeks, and chin. She was adorable. Her smile pushed every ounce of pain I was feeling out of my body. It mended my shattered heart.

"What's your name?" young Anastasia asked me.

"My name is Konrad," I said, sitting down in front of her.

"Hi, Konrad. My name is Anastasia." She couldn't say her name quite right. The second and third A sort of blended in with the S. However, she said her name with confidence, pride, and elegance beyond her years.

"It's a pleasure to meet you, Anastasia. Who is that you've got there?" I asked, pointing to her doll.

"This is… this is my baby. Her name is Sarah. Want to know how old I am?"

"How old are you?" I asked.

"I'm three years old," Anastasia said proudly.

"That's old!" I said excitedly. "Can you show me how many that is with your fingers?"

Anastasia looked down at her tiny, little hands and fiddled with her fingers. After a few moments, she held up two fingers.

"Hold on," I said. I took her little hand in mine and pulled up her ring finger to make it three. "There, you forgot this one. One, two, three."

Anastasia looked at her fingers, observing them closely. She looked at me and smiled her healing, adorable smile. I smiled back at her as tears filled my eyes and ran down my cheeks. Anastasia put her hand to my cheek and wiped away the tears.

"Why are you crying?" she asked. "Are you hurt?"

I shook my head and smiled. "No, I'm just happy."

I closed the door softly as I walked out of Anastasia's room. Miriam and Charles were waiting for me in the hall. I followed them down the hallway, and we walked back into the living room. I told them that I was going back to my apartment to get some rest. Charles gave me my key, and I hugged them goodbye.

I rode through the Quarter, emotionally drained. I dropped Renegado off at the stables and walked back to my apartment. I unlocked the door and went inside. It was hot and damp. I went into my bedroom and lay down on the bed. I pulled Anastasia's pillow to my face and smelled it. It still held her scent. I squeezed the pillow tightly and cried until I fell asleep.

I awoke in the middle of the night to the sound of fireworks. I climbed out of bed and went to the liquor cabinet. I picked up a random bottle of wine, uncorked it, and poured myself a glass as I walked out onto the balcony. Down in the streets, the New Orleanians were celebrating the Fourth of July.

I sat down and watched the fireworks explode in the sky. The people screamed and cheered and danced and sang. The city was full of joy and pride.

The explosions in the sky began to grow distant and quiet. The cheering voices were faint. I closed my eyes. All I could hear was the offbeat drumming of my heart. It pounded that strange, restless beat, that inconsistent, lost rhythm. I listened to my restless heart, and I saw the faces of all the people I left behind every time I went away, all the people who loved me so dearly. The expressions of sadness on their faces as I rode away on one journey after another were burned into my memory, as were their expressions of happiness and joy upon my return.

I remembered the sad yet proud expressions on my mother and father's faces the day I left for New Orleans on a spontaneous journey to explore the West. How would they look if I were running into their arms right now? What would their expressions be? I imagined my mother smiling, her mouth fully agape with surprise and happiness, her eyes wildly wide with excitement. My father would have a big, proud, happy smile on his face. He would try to hide his teeth, but his lips would eventually part, and he would begin to laugh joyfully.

I remembered looking back at Raul as I rode off to join the Rangers. He was smiling sadly as he looked down at the ground and walked back inside. That was the last time I ever saw him. I tried to imagine what his expression would have been had he been alive when I returned from the war. I pictured him looking at me with a confident smile and a knowing nod, as if he knew I was going to be walking through his door precisely when I did.

I remembered Miriam crying in my arms when I told her I was going to Texas. She thought I didn't care enough about her to stay with her. She thought that she had done something wrong. No matter how many times I explained to her my need to travel, she never really understood. And nobody acted as excited as Miriam when I would return from one of my journeys. I had broken her heart and put it back together too many times.

I remembered the last time I saw Anastasia. She was blowing a kiss to me as I sat upon Renegado's back. Instead of crying, she was smiling playfully and perceptively. She understood my heart. She would have let her heart break a million times watching me leave before she would ever ask me to go against mine. I didn't deserve her. I never should have left her.

And then I thought of young Anastasia, my daughter, my baby. I could never break her heart. I never wanted an image of her sad face to haunt my thoughts as I rode away from her. I couldn't do that to her as I had done to everyone else I loved. I couldn't leave and break her heart, only to return to repair it and break it when I left again. Her mother hadn't deserved it, and neither did she. I would not allow myself to do that to her.

I knew what I had to do to end it. I had to stop the vicious cycle. I had hurt the people I loved too many times. I would do it no more. I went inside, took a pen and paper, and began to write a letter.

My dear Miriam,

It seems that no matter how deeply I love the people who so deeply love me, it will never be enough to make me stay. My heart will always yearn for the distant lands of the unknown. I have hurt my loved ones too many times. I wish I could take it back, but I cannot. The only thing I can do is make sure that I do not do the same thing to my daughter, which is why I'm going to leave before I break her heart. I'm going to Texas to find Jack Burton. After that, I'm not sure.

You have never understood why I am always "running away", and neither have I. But I think we can both understand why it is in the best interests of Anastasia that I leave now. You and Charles are her parents. You always have been. Take good care of her. Take good care of my Anastasia.

I will always love you, and I will always be with you,
Konrad Quintero de Leon

I folded the letter, wrote Miriam's name on it, and left it on the edge of the table. I packed what little I intended to take and put it by the door. I walked around the apartment, studying every inch of it, as I reminisced about all of the wonderful times that had taken place between these walls.

I walked over to the liquor cabinet and refilled my glass of wine. I opened the drawer that contained Raul's poems. I took them over to the table and sat down as I fumbled through them. Feeling inspired, I put down Raul's poems and began to scribble a few verses of my own.

My poem slowly took form and grew. I thought carefully and cast my emotions to the pen. Tears streamed down my face as I wrote the last line. I put my poem on top of Raul's stack of poems. I put them back into the drawer and closed it.

I walked over to the piano and sat down slowly. I gently felt the ivory with my fingertips without playing a note. I closed my eyes and began to play Beethoven's *Pathetique*. As I played, I could hear Raul instructing me to play with more pain. More pain! There was certainly enough pain in it now.

When I finished playing the piece, I noticed that the sun was beginning to rise. I stood up and walked to the door, where I picked up the things I had packed. I fastened my saber to my hip and took one last look at the apartment. My eyes stopped on the painting of Anastasia hanging above the fireplace. She was smiling that playful, seductive smile. I smiled back at her. I blew her a kiss and walked out the door, closing it gently behind me.

XIX

I saddled Renegado and rode him out of the stables. He was happy to be moving again. It felt right to him, and it felt right to me, as well. We rode out of town, took a ferry across the Mississippi River, and headed west toward Texas to find Jack Burton. After that, I wasn't sure. It did not matter. I continued west.

I continued west with the golden, eastern sun rising behind me, and with the words of my poem echoing in my head:

Sitting still, I feel my spirit grow weak.
Broken hearted, I live amongst the meek.
But I shall not inherit the Earth.
I've taken it already, as if mine, from birth.

I've traveled near, far, and in-between,
Not for money, duty, man, or queen.
I have lived to love and loved to live,
With a childish heart I too freely give.

But a heart that gives too often takes.
It becomes a thief of the love it makes.
I'm haunted by the faces of those I've left.
To those who gave all, I'm forever in debt.

Saint Christopher, still this traveler's heart!
Give me silence and a steady beat!

Will there ever be rest in me
Or must this restlessness be my destiny?
Do hearts such as mine deserve peace
Or will happiness always be a distant reach?

We travelers, we wanderers,
We hopeless love squanderers,
We vagabonds, we vagrants,
We lonesome, nomadic pagans.

We who fly in the wind like dust,
We who for adventure lust,
We restless hearts with no end in sight,
We of endless starts, forever in strife.

We who drown with the masses in an unmoving pond,
And thrive only in lonely rivers moving far beyond.

The muscle in my chest dies if untested.
Damn my restless heart — and bless it.

5926169R0

Made in the USA
Lexington, KY
28 June 2010